Wishing Water

Wishing Water

Freda Lightfoot

W F HOWES LTD

This large print edition published in 2011 by
W F Howes Ltd
Unit 4, Rearsby Business Park, Gaddesby Lane,
Rearsby, Leicester LE7 4YH

1 3 5 7 9 10 8 6 4 2

First published in the United Kingdom in 1995
by Coronet Books

A CIP catalogue record for this book is available
from the British Library

ISBN 978 1 40747 778 7

Typeset by Palimpsest Book Production Limited,
Falkirk, Stirlingshire
Printed and bound in Great Britain
by MPG Books Ltd, Bodmin, Cornwall

Lissa Turner seems to have everything a girl could ever hope for: she's pretty and intelligent, has warm and devoted parents and a beautiful home in the Lake District. But despite her good fortune, Lissa is not happy. For her real mother abandoned Lissa while she was still a baby, and her feelings of confusion and vulnerability have persisted. As soon as she is old enough she takes up a job in Carreckwater, a lively village in the heart of Lakeland. She makes many friends but is wary of close relationships. Secretly Lissa wants nothing more than to be loved and cherished, but her lack of faith in herself launches her into a disastrous marriage with sinister consequences . . .

1951

CHAPTER 1

Lissa Turner kilted her thin cotton skirts and slid from the sheep-cropped turf into the icy waters of Allenbeck, squealing with delight as it foamed against her bare legs. She swivelled her head round to look up at the boy, still standing on dry land, very nearly over-toppling herself in the process.

'Come in, it's wonderful.'

She wriggled her toes, the stones grinding and slipping beneath her feet, and tried another step. Above her head a lapwing climbed on lazily beating wings, finishing in a dizzying display of joy in the May sky. Not always so blue in these Lakeland hills, it came as no surprise to Lissa to find it sun-filled and blue. For today was a special day.

Today she was to see her mother.

All around them grew alder and silver birch, pale slender stems crowding the edge of the small gushing stream, eager perhaps to cool their own feet in the exhilarating flow from the rocky depths of the high mountains. Over the low hump of Gimmer bridge, built a century or more ago with painstaking care and not a scrap of mortar, as was the way in this part of Westmorland, she could see right along the rough track to the stile where the road divided. If she took one twisting path she would come to Broombank, her home, and where Meg and Tam lived. The other climbed up over Larkrigg Fell to the place she should live, Larkrigg Hall. The place where her mother would be preparing a special tea this very afternoon for their first meeting in years. Four years to be exact, not since just after the war when Lissa had been only seven and too young to understand anything.

But she understood now. In Lissa's pansy eyes was more knowledge than she admitted to, certainly more than was considered good for her. Her stomach tightened into a knot of excitement. Lissa meant to enjoy this day, to wring from it every drop of pleasure she could.

'What if you fall in?' grumbled the boy, pausing in the act of unlacing one boot as he wondered if he would get the blame, if she did.

Lissa gave a gurgle of laughter. 'Then I'd get wet.' The idea at once took root and she wanted nothing more than to feel the icy water flowing and stinging over every part of her young flesh. Something tickled her toes and she wriggled them, seeing darting slivers of dark shadows race away.

'Oh, look, there are millions of minnows here,' she cried.

'Don't talk soft. Millions, my foot,' he scoffed.

'There are.'

'Catch some then, clever clogs. Bet you can't'

'I can.' Lissa lifted the jam jar that had been hanging on a string about her neck and, still holding her dress with one hand, dipped it with the other into the gushing waters. The tiny fish fled. Not one was to be seen. The water that gushed into the jar was quite empty of life. 'Oh.' She sighed her disappointment.

'You're ignorant, Lissa Turner. All girls are ignorant. Can't catch fish to save your life.'

She stopped caring about the sharp stones and swivelled about to splash him with a spray of the foaming water. 'Yes I can!'

'Here, give over,' he protested and taking up a flat stone, tossed it carelessly into the beck, missing her bare feet by inches. The water splashed in great wet globs over her clean print frock and up into her face, making her gasp at its coldness.

'Oh, you rat!' But the imp of mischief in her could not resist retaliation, so she dipped her hands in the cold water and scooped up great washes of it. Though she aimed at the boy, laughing on the shore, she soaked herself more than him.

'Nick, we could go for a swim. A real one. Why don't we?' She was breathless suddenly with the unexpectedness of her idea, eyes shining with excitement. Why hadn't she thought of it before? The perfect way to celebrate a special day.

'We can't go for a swim.' The boy sounded contemptuous, as if she was wrong in the head. 'You know we're not allowed to go alone up to the tarn.'

'Oh, phooey.'

'And our Daniel can't swim yet.'

'I can too,' came a piping voice from some yards away but neither of them took any notice of the smaller boy, knee-deep in water and mud, engrossed in his hunt for wild creatures.

'Anyroad, Miss Clever-Clogs is going out to tea.' The older boy spoke with lilting mockery in his tone. 'With the witch up at the big house.'

'She's not a witch,' Lissa hotly protested, uncertainty in her voice.' She's my grandmother so how can she be a witch?'

Nick put on his superior expression.' If she is, how come you've never been to see her before then?'

Lissa desperately searched her mind for a reason. Not for the world would she admit the truth, that her grandmother would have nothing to do with her. Any story was better than that. 'She's not been well.'

The boy grunted his disbelief and Lissa wished she could stamp her foot at him but the water hampered her.

'If you want to know, she's been waiting for my mother to come home. She couldn't get here for my birthday but she'll be here today.'

'Huh! Rather you than me. The old bat's a witch I tell you,' Nick insisted. 'And you'd best come out of that beck, before our Meg catches you.'

Lissa had been thinking exactly the same thing but she hated to be told so. 'I'll please myself what I do, Nick Turner.'

'You're just a girl, and as a boy and your cousin I'm responsible for you, like I am for our Daniel here. Anyway, your hopeless at fishing.'

Lissa was incensed. Though she'd gladly slipped down to the beck at Nick's suggestion, bringing her jam jar to catch a few minnows, that was only because she hated to be confined, even for a minute, while the adults chattered on about the Festival of Britain Tea Party in the village hall, how good Betty Hutton had been in 'Annie Get Your Gun' at the pictures last week, and other matters which were of no importance at all.

'I'm three months older than you so how can you be responsible for me? Nor are you *really* my cousin, so there.'

The boy's lip curled with superior mockery. 'Huh, no one believes that old tale Aunty Meg tells about her finding you in a Liverpool orphanage.'

'Believe what you like, it's true.' Lissa slapped more water at him. 'I *do* know who my mother is though, so there. She's flying all the way from Canada to see me. Today!' The joy of it sang in her heart.

'Meet your mother? Looking like that? Oh, aye, you will be popular.'

Lissa's heart gave a little jump of fear. Oh, no, she couldn't meet her looking a sight. Katherine was beautiful, everyone said so. For weeks Lissa had watched as the dress had been painstakingly stitched, anxiously waiting for the day when she could wear it. But, unable to resist Nick's challenge, she'd ruined everything.

'It's all your fault,' she cried, tears pricking the back of her eyes. 'I can catch fish just as well as any boy.'

But Nick only laughed, quite without sympathy for her plight. She turned, meaning to get out of the stream, her movements as liquid and graceful as the swirling waters that washed about her white slender limbs, hair ribbons slipping loose in the wild tumble of glossy black curls. For all she was still a child, it was abundantly clear to anyone that Lissa Turner would grow into a beauty, one very much with a mind of her own.

'Drat you.' Lissa slapped at him again with the flat of her hand, then laughed out loud as he lost his footing, arms flailing round and round like a windmill in the wind, and almost in slow motion fell backwards into the water. Fortunately it was more wide than deep at this point and he was as much winded as wet. But for Nick, surprisingly angry.

'Now you've done it,' he shouted.

He looked so funny sitting there on the pebbles with his bony knees poking up out of the frothing water that Lissa laughed till the tears rolled down her cheeks. Then Nick joined in too while Daniel rolled on the grass and waved his feet in the air with delight.

Too late now to argue. Too late to complain she was in her best dress and she really mustn't risk spoiling it. And Lissa desperately wanted to prove she was as good as him.

'Keep still,' she ordered. 'Don't frighten the fish away with your cackling. I'll show you.'

She carefully kilted her skirts between her legs, tucking the hem into her waist band at the front, stuffing the trailing bits up the lace-trimmed elastic of her best knickers.

Then she waded slowly out into the fast-flowing stream, close to the bridge where there were fewer stones and the water spread out wide and deep and dark beneath a tunnel of greenery. As it came above her knees she stopped. For what seemed an age Lissa waited until the tiny minnows had grown used to the pale trunks of her legs and brushed against them with casual ease. Very slowly she bent down, holding the jar in the flow of the river. At first there was nothing and her heart fluttered with despair.

Then she saw it, a great fat black cloud of darting fish. In seconds her jar was crowded and she swooped it out of the water with a cry of triumph.

'I've done it. See.'

Her delight was short lived, for the swift movement rocked a stone beneath her foot and the heavy water took instant advantage, pushing resolutely against her. Even as she struggled to find her balance Lissa knew herself lost. Holding the jar high in her hand to save her precious fish, she sat with infuriated dignity, almost up to her chin in the deep water.

Meg stared at Lissa with horror in her grey eyes. 'How could you?' She widened her gaze to

11

encompass the two muddy boys, unusually subdued. 'How could any of you behave so badly, today of all days?'

They all stared miserably at the pools they were making on the slate floor, deeming it prudent not to reply.

'Upstairs with you, madam.' Meg ordered, then jerked a thumb at her two nephews. 'You two had best go to the outhouse, clean that mud off and get out of those wet things. I'll find you something dry to wear, though I can't promise it'll fit, nor save you from trouble when you get home.'

She felt a jolt of pity for their sad faces as they trailed off to do her bidding. At any other time Meg would have laughed at their predicament. It was no more than childish fun after all. She could remember she and her brother Charlie being in exactly the same predicament on any number of occasions. But she was short on humour today. Kath's letters always seemed to put her in a temper, even now, after all these years. There was still the gnawing fear that she would come for Lissa and take her back with her, and Meg would never see her lovely girl again. Canada was the other side of the world, after all.

She could remember, as clearly as if it were yesterday, the time Kath had come for her daughter. Lissa had been seven years old by then. Seven years in Meg's care, and Kath had imagined she could simply collect her, like a parcel, and ship her away. But Meg had refused to allow it.

'Lissa stays here with me, at Broombank, where she belongs,' she'd said, and that had been that.

Surprisingly Kath had made no protest. She had merely smiled her beautiful smile, shrugged slender shoulders and walked out of Meg's life with that elegant swinging sway to her hips, to start life in Canada with her new husband.

She'd written once or twice a year since then, often claiming that she would visit soon, but nothing had ever come of these promises.

Until today.

A soft touch at her elbow brought her back to the present. 'Here,' said Tam, handing her a steaming bowl. 'Sponge her down quickly with some warm water and she'll be right enough. Did you never get mud in your own eye, Meg O'Cleary?'

Meg looked lovingly into her husband's face and her lips lifted into a smile. How could she resist when she loved him so much? Tam leaned over the bowl and dropped a kiss upon her nose.

'Tis a lovely woman you are, Meg, when you're thinking with your heart. I'll go and deal with them two tearaways and take them back meself. See if I can stop your father tanning their hides. He is staying at Ashlea again, is he not?'

'Yes,' Meg sighed. 'Poor Sally Ann.'

'She gets on with him better than you do. I'll see these lads don't suffer his wrath.' Taciturn and dour to a fault, the boys' grandfather Joe was supposed to be retired in Grange-Over-Sands but spent every moment he could at his old home, Ashlea, using the excuse that he was helping his daughter-in-law, Sally Ann, widowed by a stray bomb, and never remarried. Joe had remarried, at the end of the war, but the marriage hadn't prospered.

'Thanks.' Meg gave Tam a warm smile of gratitude, drew in a deep breath and started up the stairs. Lissa could be as troublesome to deal with in her own way as Joe. There were no arguments from her now as Meg stripped off the sodden dress. No tantrums or tears as the dripping, best white underwear with the lace trim was replaced by everyday interlock vest and knickers.

'You'll have to wear your yellow cotton frock,' Meg said, hiding a smile as she saw the pretty nose wrinkle in disgust. 'Don't like it.'

Meg sighed, biting back the retort that perhaps Lissa should have thought of that before she decided to go fishing for minnows, but managed, with difficulty, to hold her tongue. 'Which then?' thinking over Lissa's wardrobe which shrank daily as the child grew. Soon, all too soon in Meg's opinion, she would be a child no longer. Budding womanhood would take over. It was certainly long past time they had a talk about it.

'I shall wear my jersey skirt and blue embroidered blouse,' Lissa said, deciding on what she considered to be her most sophisticated items.

'Isn't it rather warm for jersey?'

'You're wearing a skirt and blouse.'

14

So the blue jersey it was. The tangled dark locks were brushed and fresh ribbons found to put them back into their tidy bunches, one at each side of the rosy, scrubbed cheeks. The sparkle was back in the arresting eyes, the tongue loosened once more into chatter. 'Oh do let's hurry, Meg. We mustn't be late. What will she be like? I don't remember her. Will she like me?'

The questions came thick and fast as they set off to walk the two miles up to Larkrigg Hall. Meg's heart went out to the child, for didn't her own anxiety match Lissa's?

'Of course you will recognise her, once you see her. She will be surprised how much you have grown.' Meg didn't like to talk about the love aspect. She couldn't. She found it impossible to credit Kath with the ability to love a daughter she'd abandoned so soon after her birth. Not even a war would have persuaded Meg to do such a thing. But then there had been other, more pressing reasons, best not remembered.

The slopes of Larkrigg Fell rose gently ahead of them, with the steep crag of Dundale Knott at their backs, its comical lop-sided appearance belying the very real dangers to be found on the crags and crevices that scarred its surface. As her beloved dog, Rust, had once discovered to his cost. He was at her heels now, as always. Battle-scarred and not so spry as he'd once been, yet fit enough to walk the fells with her every day tending the sheep, despite his thirteen years.

15

'Come on, old boy,' she urged, a softness to her voice whenever she addressed him. 'He's panting a bit more than he should, Lissa. Maybe I'd best retire him.'

Lissa rubbed the dog's ears, one brown, one black. 'You know he couldn't take to that. Where you are, so must he be.'

Funny thing, loyalty, Meg mused. It could cement a friendship or, misplaced, just as easily ruin one. Hadn't she learned so herself once?

To their left was Allenbeck. It began high on Larkrigg Fell where it gathered its strength to burst out as a waterfall, known locally as a force, and tumbled onwards through Whinstone Gill, a deep cleft cut into the rocks forming a wooded ravine, till it ran out of power and passed under Gimmer bridge at a more sedate pace.

Now they climbed the sheep trods through Brockbarrow wood which in its turn flanked the southern shores of the tarn. Brockbarrow wood. The place for a lover's tryst. And betrayal.

'What shall I say to her?' Lissa worried. 'What can we talk about? She doesn't know me or any of my friends.'

Anxious dark blue eyes gazed up at Meg. Jack's eyes. She swallowed. 'Tell her all about yourself. About how you like to help on the farm, how you're learning to play the harmonium. How you are changing schools this year and mean to go to the High School.'

'If I pass my certificate.'

'Of course you'll pass.'

'I'm so nervous. Isn't it silly?' A small hand crept into Meg's and she squeezed it encouragingly.

'I'm pretty nervous myself as a matter of fact.'

'Are you?' An odd relief in the voice.

Somewhere high above a curlew mewed its plaintive, lonely cry, but Meg was aware only of Lissa's deep thoughts. The worst part of Kath's letters were her promises to visit, the way they unsettled the child, made her think and ask endless questions.

'Tell me again how you came to Liverpool to find me,' Lissa asked, wriggling close, and Meg stifled a sigh.

'I've told you a dozen times. Kath couldn't keep you. She was going into the WAAFS' because of the war. She gave you to me to keep safe, at Broombank.'

'Did she come to see me a lot? Did she miss me?' Lissa frowned. 'I can't seem to remember.'

'It was difficult, with the war and everything,' Meg hedged.

'I suppose so.' More deep thoughts, Lissa wishing she could understand it all properly. She wished and wished so hard sometimes that it hurt, deep in her tummy. If only her mother would come, just once. Her child's faith in the goodness of life made her certain that Kath would be kind and beautiful and tell her that she loved her, and Lissa would learn all about that secret part of herself she couldn't quite discover.

She worried sometimes that perhaps it was her fault that Kath had left. Perhaps she'd been a disappointment and her mother had been glad to give her up.

Today, at last, all those fears could be swept away.

All Lissa had ever seen of the world was this dale, these familiar mountains. She ached to see the rest of it, live the life she felt was her due. She adored Meg and Tam, loved them as if they were her real parents, but what kind of life might she have had if she'd been Lissa Ellis instead of Lissa Turner? How would she have been different? It was hard to work it out.

A tall Scots pine stood like a sentinel on a small rise before her. Beyond that, Lissa knew, was the last sheep trod they needed to climb. This would join the long sweeping drive that led up to Larkrigg Hall through a pair of stone gate posts. It was a fine, nineteenth-century house, set high on a ridge as its name implied, surrounded on all sides by strangely shaped rocks and crags that poked out of the thin soil like old bones. A house that might have been her home, if things had been different.

Or she might, even now, have been in Canada, seeing other mountains, riding the ponies on her mother's ranch. These dreams had filled her head for years, keeping her awake at night. Now, she was sure they were about to be realised.

'Will she tell me who my father is, do you think?' Her voice was soft, robbed of breath by the wind and the intensity of her excitement.

Meg and Kath had both avoided this part of the story. How they had both loved the same man, Kath had borne his child and Meg had loved her and brought her up. It hurt and embarrassed them both still, to think of it.

Meg drew the child into the circle of her arms. 'One day we'll talk about it,' she said with a smile. 'When you are old enough to understand.'

'I'm old enough now. I'm eleven. Not a baby any more, Meg.'

No, more's the pity, she thought, and tightened the ribbons that were, as usual, slipping down the glossy curls. 'It isn't important, not really. You have me and Tam. Remember that we love you. You are our own darling child so far as we are concerned.'

'I know.' Lissa wished that it was enough. But somehow it wasn't.

Larkrigg Hall, a rectangular, solid house, bigger than it looked at first glance, with a plain, protestant look to it, stood at last before them. Only its tall trefoiled windows and great arched storm porch relieved the austerity of the grey stone walls. Meg pushed Lissa forward and politely rattled the knocker, for the inhabitants of Larkrigg Hall did not follow the more usual country custom of using the back door for callers. Meg could feel her heart start to thump uncomfortably at the thought of Kath waiting within.

The door creaked open and Amy Stanton,

19

Rosemary Ellis's housekeeper, stood four-square on the slate step. Solid and forbidding, taking her pleasures where she could find them in ill health and local disasters, she almost smiled upon them now.

'She hasn't come,' she bluntly informed them. 'Mrs Wadeson sent a telegram this morning. She says she's sorry but she won't be here after all.'

The door had almost closed before Meg came out of her shock. Slamming her hand against the polished panels she stopped it most effectively, but then she hadn't spent years lifting and managing sheep to be put off by an old door, solid oak or no. 'What did you say?'

Meg lifted her chin in that stubborn way she had and the high-cheekboned face took on a dignified beauty that had melted stouter hearts than Amy Stanton's. There was no sign of a thaw in this one.

Even to Lissa's miserable observation it was clear that Meg was wasting her time.

'Amy?' A stentorian voice from within settled the matter and the door shut fast with a solid clunk. Meg muttered something unpleasant under her breath that Lissa didn't quite catch then, taking her hand in a firm grasp, grey eyes sparkling with a rare anger, she set off at a cracking pace back down the long drive, dragging the child with her.

'Come along, sweetheart. Let's go home.'

It was Grandfather Joe, surprisingly, who offered a solution. Following that bitter disappointment,

Lissa had written again to her mother, asking if Kath had another date in mind. The letter had not been answered. Not that she cared, she told herself. What did it matter if Katherine Ellis, now Mrs Wadeson, did not love her?

Yet somehow it did. It mattered very much. Lissa felt full of curiosity, ached to meet her. Not because she felt herself unloved by Meg, far from it. Meg had been the best mother anyone could wish for. It was simply a need to fill in the whole picture, to know who, exactly, she was. She couldn't explain it any better than that, not even to herself. It made her feel all uncomfortable inside to know she'd been dumped.

'What's up with thee, moping about with a face like a wet fortnight? Stop fretting,' he said, shaking out his newspaper as if to remind her that the worries of the world, such as the progress of the Korean War which he followed with great interest, were far more important than any a young girl might have. 'It'll all be t'same in hundred years.'

'I suppose it will,' said Lissa sadly, though this was not a philosophy she could warm to. 'Do you believe in wishes, Grandfather?'

Joe pondered the question then chuckled. 'I remember doing some wishing as a child, by the water every spring. Eeh, what daft-heads we were.' Laughing softly at his own youthful foolishness, he returned to the paper. 'Will thee look at the price of wool? Might as well work for nowt.'

'Grandfather.' Lissa's voice was coaxing, her

smile bewitching. Aware he had a soft spot for her she knew she never got anything out of him by being miserable, for all he put on such a dour face himself. She leaned against the arm of Joe's chair and gazed up into his face. 'Tell me about the wishing.'

Joe regarded the child he'd come to think of as his granddaughter with a serious eye. 'It's not to be taken lightly,' he warned.

'Oh, no,' Lissa assured him. 'I wouldn't.'

He glanced around, as if he was about to impart a great secret, or preferred Meg not to know what he said. 'Water has special powers, tha knows. Whether it be beck or tarn, each has its own sprite or fairy and it don't do to cross them.'

Lissa solemnly shook her head, not daring to speak. Would this be the answer she so badly needed?

Satisfied he was not about to be mocked, Joe said, 'When we was no more'n bairns we'd go every Maytime to the well or some other special watering place and fill our hands with water. Sometimes we'd use a bottle and add a drop of sugar or a twist of liquorice to drink, then give the rest back to the water sprite. Or we'd drink from us hands and give a gift instead, like a flower or a penny. You ask Meg about Luckpennies. Carry the luck for you they do.'

'Why do they?'

'Why?' Joe looked confused. 'Nay, lass, how should I know?'

'But did you make a wish? And did it ever come true?'

Joe was anxious to return to the latest figures from the auction mart. 'Course we did. But I'm too old to remember what we wished for, let alone if it ever come true. It's all a lot of nonsense anyroad. You have to drink it up quick, afore it leaks out of your hand, and say your wish with your eyes closed.' Then thinking of Meg's possible reaction to these superstitions, he added for good measure, 'But you must believe in the Good Lord and say your prayers every night.' Nodding wisely and recklessly mixing Christian and pagan traditions. 'Then you'll get what's good for you and no more.'

Lissa felt excited. She said her prayers every night already, but she thought she'd try the wishing as well, just in case. It could do no harm to try.

Nick had one or two wishes of his own which he could do with having answered, concerning learning to play football and getting a new bicycle, so he was ready enough to share the experiment with Lissa. It seemed harmless enough.

The beck was considered too mundane and the water too gushing for any sprite to survive in it. There was nothing for it but to try the tarn. Strictly forbidden, tucked darkly behind Brockbarrow wood, they chose an afternoon when Daniel had been taken, protesting, to the dentist, since they didn't trust him to keep a secret. It was June, not

May, but Lissa hoped the fairies wouldn't mind, this being their first visit.

'We mustn't get wet or fall in this time,' she warned and Nick gravely agreed. The tarn might be small and round, a sheet of water innocently sparkling in the sun on a beautiful day like this, but it was bitterly cold, had been trapped in this cup of land since the Ice Age and nobody knew quite how deep it was. It was not a place to mess with. Both children gazed on the ruffled waters and shuddered. They could well believe that sprites lurked beneath its glittering surface, perhaps even devils.

The small ceremony took no more than moments to complete. There was no time to waste as they were fully aware they risked the wrath of their respective parents should their trip be discovered.

'I'll go first,' Lissa said, dipping the small Tizer bottle in the clear water.

As she drank the sweet liquorice water she closed her eyes and wished with all her might that one day soon her mother would come. She sent her thoughts winging far across water, mountains and sea to a distant, unknown mass of land painted red on her geography atlas and known as Canada.

Send my mother home, her inner voice begged.

Then it was Nick's turn. They glanced sideways at each other and giggled.

'It's a bit daft is this,' he said. 'Go on. Get on with it.'

When he had done they emptied the rest of the brown liquid into the tarn and watched the wind sweep the sunlight like a shower of diamonds across the small lake. It seemed, to Lissa's lively imagination, like an answer, and a great sense of peace and certainty came upon her. It would work out all right in the end, she felt sure somehow, deep in her heart.

CHAPTER 2

Time passed. Lissa tried not to think of her mother and was happy enough in the dale. Each spring she and Nick continued to make their wishes, though never revealed them or owned up to whether they ever came true. That was far too risky and might spoil their chances, though Nick did boast one day that he'd got picked for the school football team.

Lissa wrote regularly to Canada, and twice a year, on her birthday and at Christmas, received a reply. These were always a disappointment, telling her little, closing with the promise that one day Kath would come but never offering any definite date. Then on her thirteenth birthday a different sort of letter arrived.

Meg handed it to her, frowning. 'It's from Mrs Ellis. She's declared herself ready to receive us.'

'Oh.' Lissa was stunned. Was this good news or bad? She couldn't quite make out from Meg's attitude. 'Why now?'

'Perhaps a bout of conscience? Though I very much doubt it. Have you been writing to Canada?'

Lissa nodded, saying no more when she saw how

Meg's face tightened in that odd way she had whenever Kath or Canada were mentioned.

'We are to call next Wednesday, at three o'clock precisely. You must put on your best frock. Only I would prefer you not to fall in the beck this time. Let us try to present a civilised image, shall we?' Meg gave a wry smile and Lissa giggled with relief.

'I'll do my best.'

Lissa knew, the moment she stepped into the house, that she hated it, which was deeply disappointing. They passed through a dark hall where a glassy-eyed stag's head glared down at them, causing her to shiver. Then they were shown into a small, oak-panelled room of faded gentility, dark and depressing. Where was the pretty turquoise and gold drawing room Meg had spoken of? Lissa had imagined delicate, tasteful furniture. Instead, most of the house seemed dusty and shut up, judging by the number of forbiddingly closed doors.

At first sight everything in the room appeared to be draped in some sort of covering; filled with mats, runners, tablecloths, even the piano shrouded in an Indian rug. A single, rose-shaded lamp bloomed in the window embrasure. It should have given a cosy feel but it only cast gloomy shadows across the walls.

Lissa's small nose wrinkled with distaste at the stale smell that met her nostrils. The room was as unaccustomed to fresh air as it was to visitors.

A figure rose from the shadows by the empty

fireplace and Lissa started, stepping back in sudden fright as she recalled Nick's constant teasing about a witch, and felt glad suddenly of Meg's warm reassuring hand as it slipped over hers. But then she was almost grown up now, and didn't believe in witches.

'Miss Turner.' The voice sounded cold and disembodied. Glancing anxiously up at Meg, Lissa caught the ghost of a knowing smile and knew instinctively that these two were old adversaries.

'Mrs O'Cleary, if you recall. But you always used to call me Meg.'

A pause, during which Lissa received the decided impression that she was being scrutinised from head to foot, though since the room was so dim and the woman was in shadow, she couldn't be sure.

'I see you have brought the child.'

Meg smiled again. 'Of course. This is Lissa. My daughter.'

Lissa felt as if she should curtsey, the moment so crackled with tension. Instead, she screwed up her courage, took a step forward and held out her hand, remembering her manners. 'Good afternoon . . .' she began, smiling politely, and stopped. How to address this woman whom she knew to be her grandmother but had never been acknowledged as such? She bit on her lower lip and waited. The rose-coloured light flickered across the thin, unsmiling face, showing up the whiskers on her chin.

Ignoring the small outstretched hand, Rosemary Ellis turned away, leaving Lissa feeling foolish, forced to retreat to Meg's side.

'Pray be seated.' A regal gesture indicated a roomy sofa. It too was so swathed in paisley shawls, arm shields, antimacassars and cushions, so that Lissa dared hardly sit upon it for fear of disturbing the arrangement. 'Amy, tea, if you please. For our guests.'

'Very good, madam.' Amy quietly withdrew, closing the double mahogany doors as she went.

Meg whispered in her ear. 'Don't put your dirty shoes on the rug, it's Persian, and very valuable.'

Lissa sat gingerly next to Meg, trying to tuck them out of the way, which wasn't easy. She fixed her eyes upon a display of dried leaves in a copper bowl that sat incongruously upon an upturned seed box in the wide, marble hearth. A spider hung from a thread on one leaf and Lissa watched it, fascinated.

They sat in silence in the cold room for what seemed an eternity. Somewhere a clock chimed and she counted out three strokes. Lissa's back started to ache and her legs to fidget. Meg cast her a warning glance, then clearing her throat, turned to Mrs Ellis with a smile.

'I trust you are keeping well? I haven't seen Jeffrey . . . Mr Ellis for some time. How is he?'

'Much the same. Never goes out these days.'

'Might we see him?'

'I do not think that would be wise.'

It was a relief when the double doors opened again and Amy wheeled in the tea on a clattering tea trolley that had seen better days. Meg touched Lissa's hand. 'Go and help Mrs Stanton serve the tea, sweetheart.' But as Lissa rose to do so, a stern voice bade her remain where she was.

'I hope we have better manners here at Larkrigg than to permit guests to serve themselves.' Lissa sat down again, accepting the china cup and saucer with the first flutter of nervousness. Misery was sharp within her. This was not at all how she'd imagined her first meeting with her grandmother would be. She had so longed to see her, and the inside of the old house where her mother had lived as a girl.

It confused and intrigued her to think that a member of her own family, whom she didn't even know, lived behind these grey stone walls. Now here she was at last, and nothing was as she had hoped. Perhaps Lissa hadn't quite expected words of love. But a smile, a word of welcome would have warmed her. There was none.

The only consolation was that through the tall, trefoiled windows she could see the friendly mountains that she loved so much, their dark faces streaked with snow filled gullies for spring had been late this year. The house stood so grandly on its ridge that its face looked beyond Larkrigg Fell to the majesty of Kentmere Pike with the dark sentinel of Dundale Knot closer to hand.

Perversely Lissa wished herself out amongst

them, where she might find the peace and sanctuary they offered; instead of here, where she felt an outcast. Unwanted.

She realised with a startled jerk that Rosemary Ellis was addressing her with some question and she had missed it. In horror, Lissa glanced at Meg for help who, sensing her predicament, attempted to breach the gap.

'Lissa attends the High School. She goes into Kendal each day by bus.'

'The High School?' The words were spoken with contempt, as if the idea were unthinkable. 'How very utilitarian.'

'It's a very good school as a matter of fact.'

'Katherine was educated privately. Only the very best of everything, naturally. Still, a local establishment is probably more appropriate in the circumstances.' Rosemary Ellis fixed her cold gaze upon Lissa, who began to feel quite sick.

Lissa hated the increasing tension in the room and watched in dismay as Meg attempted to laugh away the implied criticism, though it seemed to be through gritted teeth.

'How is Katherine? She is well, I hope?'

'Perfectly. My daughter leads an exceedingly busy social life. Her husband, Ewan Maximillian Wadeson III, has quite a position to keep up. A property owner of some renown.'

'Then she shouldn't make promises that she intends to visit when she clearly hasn't time,' Meg daringly stated, making Lissa jump. Rosemary

stiffened and gazed down her long nose at Meg.'
She can't simply drop everything. On a whim.'

'It was always her idea to visit. We did not request it.'

'Well, I certainly did not, Mrs O'Cleary. For my part, I believe the past is best left buried.'

Lissa gazed perplexed at her grandmother. What did that mean? Best left buried. She couldn't be buried, could she? She was here, alive and well, a physical reality. Lissa felt a bit guilty suddenly, for though Meg might not have made any requests to see Kath, she certainly had. Constantly. She thought it best not to mention those, though perhaps this was an opportunity to get a few questions answered. She edged forward in her seat.

'What is she like, my mother? Does she look like me? Or like you?' Here, Lissa's young mind quailed at this dreadful possibility, and she hurried on without stopping. 'You still haven't told us, Grandmother, why she keeps letting me down. Is it my fault? Will she be coming soon? She did promise, really she did. "I'll come as soon as I can", she said. When do you think that will be?'

Rosemary stared as if shocked that the girl owned a tongue, let alone a mind churning with questions. 'I really couldn't say, and I am not your grandmother.' She turned away to sip her tea with patrician disdain, the subject closed so far as she was concerned. Not for Lissa.

'Why can't you say? Perhaps she would prefer it if I were to visit her in Canada?' Lissa strove to keep the eagerness from her voice. The thought of crossing half the world in a huge ship in search of this elusive, beautiful mother excited her, but she hated to show how much in front of Meg.

'That would be most unsuitable,' Rosemary said, shock evident in her voice. 'The very idea!'

'Why? Doesn't she want to see me?'

Cold, pale eyes raked Lissa from head to foot then turned chillingly to Meg. 'You have taught the child no manners. Which does not surprise me, brought up as she has been with farming stock.'

Lissa saw Meg flinch as if Rosemary Ellis had struck her. Her own head was starting to ache and disappointment made her reckless. She decided she might as well be hung for a sheep as a lamb.

'Is he my father then? This Ewan Maxi person? Or is it because I'm a bastard that you don't like me?'

'*Lissa*!' Meg cried.

The effect was astonishingly gratifying. For one terrible moment she thought her grandmother was about to faint. Lissa saw at once there would be no denial and felt a wicked surge of gladness that someone else could suffer hurt, as she had so many times. She watched, intrigued, as the whiskered chin and palid cheeks went stark white, grew wine red, then changed to brilliant purple.

'I must apologise for her behaviour,' Meg was hastily saying, frowning grimly at Lissa.

'The child is out of control. You clearly allow her to run wild. Spoil her, without doubt.'

'I don't think it possible to spoil a child. Where else would she find the love she needs, if not from me and from Tam?' Brave, reckless words, chillingly received.

'Enough. Do you take me for a fool?' Icicles dripped from the thin voice. 'I know why you persist in keeping up this contact with Katherine. Which is why I have called you here today, to inform you that it must stop. There will be no more contact between you. I am not too foolish to recognise a clever ruse when I see one.'

'Clever ruse?' Meg's eyes widened.

'Indeed. To get money out of me. Or my husband, as no doubt you have cleverly done in the past on many occasions, gullible fool that he is.'

'I beg your pardon?'

'Come, come, *Mrs O'Cleary*, do not pretend with me. He helped you get a mortgage once, I seem to remember. But you will not succeed. I do not acknowledge your illegitimate child as any responsibility of mine.' She turned away and pulled on a bell pull. 'Now we have the matter straight, I believe this interview is over.'

Meg looked as if someone had punched her in the face. Her voice shook. 'How dare you? How dare you suggest such things? And in front of the child.'

'It's all right,' Lissa said, anxious to calm Meg. 'I understand, and I really don't mind about being a bastard, only I would've liked to know why I wasn't wanted.'

The shock waves of this little speech almost knocked Lissa off her seat. Rosemary Ellis shot to her feet, clasping and unclasping her hands in agitation. 'If that child uses that word once more in my presence . . .' A tall, angular figure with good bone structure, but any beauty she might once have possessed had long since dissipated. A sour mouth thinned perceptibly, even as Lissa gazed wonderingly upon it.

'Stern discipline is what this little madam needs. Though I can think of no respectable establishment which would admit her, and you seem quite unable to provide it.'

It was a long moment before Meg answered, concerned as she was about Lissa, seeing the tears brim in the violet eyes, young ears taking in every nuance of the argument. Very quietly she got to her feet. 'We need no help to bring up our own daughter, Mrs Ellis, and you are the last person I would ask, if we did.' Meg was trembling with anger. 'Had I known you were going to attack us with your nasty insinuations, I would have left Lissa at home.'

Lissa was, in fact, paying less attention than Meg realised. The whole scene had made her feel distinctly odd. A pain started deep in her belly and she wanted, very suddenly, to be sick. She clamped her teeth tightly together in desperation as the room began to swim about her.

Meg was speaking from a long way off.

'If you had not been so hard hearted as to throw

your daughter out all those years ago, you might have found a bit more love in your own life. Which might have spared you this warped view of the world, Rosemary Ellis. And certainly would have benefited Kath, as well as your poor husband. Yes, Jeffrey was kind to me in the past, but I asked him for nothing and he gave me nothing but his advice and support. I *never* took any money from him. Ever. Although I greatly valued his friendship. I will not stay and bandy insults with you. I want nothing from you, not now, nor in the future. I agree with you about the letters. I too would prefer it if they stopped. Please ask Katherine to refrain from making promises to Lissa which she has no intention of keeping. It is thoughtless and unkind and causes nothing but hurt and upset for the child.'

Lissa groaned as the pain shot deeper, like a great weight between her legs. Neither woman heard her.

'You have clearly read too much into her words. Katherine responds as best she can only because the child insists on writing to her.' The older woman was almost spitting her contempt now as the two stood facing each other, determined adversaries. Meg held to her point.

'Kath encourages this fantasy of Lissa's that they might meet one day. It does enormous damage. Every time Kath lets her down the child feels rejected all over again.'

'Utter rubbish!' The whiskered chin shook.

'Rejected indeed. You cannot believe that Katherine or I owe any responsibility to a child who readily admits herself to – to be what she is. Ours is a respectable family. She is no fault of ours.'

Meg dropped her chin and drew in a long, shuddering breath, steadying herself, fighting the urge to tear this unfeeling, cruel woman to shreds. How dare she deny Lissa's parentage? So concerned was she with her efforts that she did not notice how the colour drained away from Lissa's cheeks. She only heard a stifled moan and then the air seemed to be filled with a piercing scream, bringing both women whirling.

'Look what you've done. Both of you,' Lissa screamed, terror in her voice. 'You've killed me. I'm dying. Meg, I'm dying.'

The blood of womanhood was running down the young girl's legs, soaking into the bright white ankle socks and on to the valuable Persian rug.

'Dear Lord,' cried Meg, horrified.

'As I said, Mrs O'Cleary. Discipline and control. Entirely lacking, you see.'

Meg sat on the edge of the big bed she shared with Tam, wringing her hands in anguish. 'I should have told her long since. I've failed her, leaving it so late. She was scared out of her wits, poor lamb. I should have explained all about Jack too, then she mightn't have felt the need to shock with that dreadful word.'

37

'You've told her now?'

'Yes, everything.'

Tam slipped an arm about her to pull her close. 'Don't worry over it. You wouldn't be the Meg we all know and love if you were mooning about the house fussing over us all the time.'

'Even so, it was a mistake. That dreadful woman. Discipline and control, my Aunt Fanny!' Meg's hands clenched tight, as if she would have punched Rosemary Ellis on the nose were she present. 'You wouldn't believe the things she said to me, what she accused me of.'

Tam stroked the golden curls away and tucked them behind her ears, kissing the lobes as he did so. 'Haven't you told me, sweetheart, a dozen times already? You mustn't let the woman get to you. She is a vicious, bad-mouthed old besom and not to be listened to. I forbid you to take Lissa to see her again.'

Meg turned to gaze into his moss green eyes, startled for a moment by the unusual vehemence in his lilting voice. 'Forbid?'

'Why should our little girl be subjected to such an attack? Tis not her fault if she was born on the wrong side of the blanket, now is it? So keep her away in future. We don't need any of them.'

For Lissa it was a turning point, of sorts, for the rejection cut deep. There were no more letters to Canada, no more wishing for her mother to come. She had Meg and Tam who she loved to bits. She told herself she needed no one else, certainly not a mother who didn't love her. But she still worried about whether she was really wanted, ached to know who she really was and where she truly belonged.

The following months and years weren't easy, and there came a particularly difficult period when Meg fell pregnant. To her shame, the thought of a baby in the house appalled her. It would take all Meg's time and attention. It seemed to prove how unimportant she was, for why should Meg want a baby at all when she'd always claimed Lissa was everything to her?

Her fears seemed to be justified as Meg withdrew into a world of her own, rarely hearing when Lissa spoke to her so that she had to say everything twice.

Mealtimes were changed to suit Meg's delicate stomach. She went to bed early instead of sitting chatting by the fire, leaving Lissa to make her own supper. Even iron her own clothes. It was quite incredible how life changed. To Lissa's increasing dismay Meg became perfectly obsessed with making plans for the baby, took to having weird food fancies, morning sickness and back ache. And Tam's loving preoccupation with her grated every bit as much.

There seemed nothing else for it but to play the martyr or how would they ever remember she lived here too? If they saw she was unhappy, Lissa decided, then they would pay her proper attention. So she refused to speak to either of them, took to spending hours alone in her room, hoping someone would notice she was missing and come and look for her. Yet if they did, she would sulk and say she wasn't hungry. They asked if she was sickening for something because she ate so little. Except at night when they were both asleep. Then she would secretly raid the larder for cuts of meat and slices of apple pie. It made her feel wickedly decadent.

'You don't care about me any more,' she said, sulking furiously. 'Nobody does. I must be a very unlovable person. No wonder my mother deserted me.'

Meg's look of horror brought a burst of sweet delight into Lissa's rebellious heart. 'What a thing to say. Of course I care. I love you dearly, Lissa. And so does Tam.' The kettle started gently to steam.

'You brought me up. That's not quite the same thing, is it?' The tone was cruelly mocking but Lissa didn't care. She wanted to hurt Meg as she was hurting, deep inside.

'Of course it's the same. You are very special to us and always will be.'

Hot tears pricked her eyelids and Lissa blinked them angrily away. 'That was only duty. You had no choice. You didn't even choose me. I was dumped on you.' With tremulous pleasure she watched the terrible effect of these words dawn on Meg's face. Instantly the feeling drained away and she was drenched in guilt. She wanted to run to Meg and smooth away the stricken look, to beg her forgiveness and say she hadn't meant it.

'Oh, Lissa,' was all Meg said, which made her feel worse than ever. Desperately, she tried to put it right.

'Come for a ride. Not to Brockbarrow wood but somewhere different. I'm bored with everywhere round here.'

Meg looked distressed. Tam had got Lissa a lovely little mare, but Meg never let her go too far alone, insisting she was always accompanied. 'I can't. Not today, love. Why don't you ask Tam to go with you?'

Lissa pouted. 'Tam says he has to do all *your* jobs as well as his own these days. He's too busy.'

'It's a difficult time.'

The kettle was rattling furiously on the stove and Meg quickly lifted it to pour the scalding water into the teapot. There was so much she wanted to explain, about life, about trust, about love, but she couldn't seem to find the right words, the right approach to get through to Lissa any more. The huge farm kitchen filled with the comforting aroma of hot tea but when she turned back to the table, loving words of caution on her lips, Lissa was already on her feet, knocking back her chair with a fierce hand.

'Don't bother. I knew it was a waste of time to talk to you. You aren't interested in me any more.' With that she stormed out of the house.

She rode defiantly right along the quarry road, forbidden territory. The triumph she felt at breaking Meg's strictest rule made her hum with pleasure. It promised to be a beautiful autumn day. The late afternoon sun was shining brilliantly by the time she'd ridden Goldie through Brockbarrow wood and onwards to the tarn. It glittered on the rippled surface wrinkled as an old man's bald head.

Lissa reined in the pony and let it take a drink at the water. A picture of herself and Nick, shaking their bottles of liquorice water, came to mind. What a childish thing to do. What innocent babes they had been. As if a stretch of water could answer their wishes. As if wishing could find a mother, or make Meg still love her. There was a tight feeling in her throat but she ignored it. It wasn't her fault if no one understood or cared for her? Or was it? A bleak thought.

'What will I do when I'm grown up, Goldie? Where will I go? I can't stay here where I don't really belong.' Lissa thought about this for a moment. What would it feel like to be a woman? What was she now? Not a child, surely.

'Perhaps I'm invisible. Perhaps that's why Meg doesn't notice me and Kath forgot all about me. I don't really exist.'

There was a sharpness to the air, filling her with a sudden rush of exhilaration. Energy flooded through her, as if she could reach out and touch the whole world spread out before her.

What did it matter if Meg and Tam didn't love her? She was young and they were old. This was her time. If she did not know exactly who she was or where she belonged she could at least be free to do as she pleased.

Forgetting the last of Meg's rules, Lissa pulled off her clothes and sank beneath the icy surface. She couldn't risk more than a minute in the water but it felt good.

Afterwards she lay on the bank to dry herself, and fell asleep.

Lissa woke to watch the morning mists lift like a bride's veil, revealing the purple mountain tops, making her give an involuntary gasp of pleasure. How beautiful they were. How magnificent. Again she swam in the tarn, unable to resist the sparkling water, and this time she splashed and even laughed, a natural youthful optimism starting to grow inside her. When she had done, she put on her clothes and set off for home.

Meg would be cross with her for staying away all night and make her feel worse than ever. Lissa tried to work out how best to explain. She supposed it had been wrong to break Meg's rules, but what would she care now that she had the baby to think of? Nor did it help her case that Goldie had disappeared. Which was a worry. Lissa could only hope the pony had trotted home.

Oh, but how she longed for some of Meg's loving comfort.

Lissa still hadn't decided how to explain staying out all night when she pushed open the heavy door and walked into a kitchen alive with activity.

'Where have you been?' These sharp words came from Sally Ann, who was dashing about in a frenetic sort of way quite unlike her usual placid self. 'Meg has been worried sick. Been out all night looking for you. We all have.'

Grabbing a towel she ran off into the living room. Lissa followed, frowning as she struggled to find an answer. She never did find one.

There was Tam who should have been out on the fells at this time of the day. Nick and Daniel in muddy boots not usually allowed in the kitchen, standing about looking helpless and goggle-eyed. And a strange man she didn't even recognise. In the midst of all of this pandemonium, Meg, quietly sobbing as her life blood spread out on the rush matting, rather as Lissa's had once done at Larkrigg. Only this was worse, far worse. This meant there was to be no baby and Lissa knew that was her fault too.

When Meg came back from hospital she was not the same. A light seemed to have been switched off behind her face and Lissa could not bear to look at her. Tam had warmed the bed with a stone hot water bottle and now she was installed in it, her hair scraped back like a child's, grey eyes translucent and sad.

Lissa knew she had to speak. 'Am I very wicked?'

'No, of course not. What a thing to say.'

'My mother was.'

Meg took a deep breath and plucked at the bedclothes, as if she was too tired to be bothered with all of this now but knew she must put Lissa's mind at rest. 'Kath is different from you. Besides, she wasn't wicked. You mustn't take any notice of your grandmother's warped view of things.'

But Lissa felt compelled to purge her soul. 'I didn't want that baby. I was jealous of it.'

Meg's eyes pricked with tears. 'I know. There was no need to be. Anyway, that was my last chance. I'm too old to try again.'

A terrible silence as Lissa shouldered the guilt of this bleak reality. 'Are you sad?'

'A little, but I have you.' Meg managed a smile. Her lips were trembling. Lissa wanted to ask if that would be enough but dare not, fearful of the answer. Meg turned her head away and did not notice her need. Was it possible to will a baby to die? She had never meant that to happen. Never. Lissa left the room, unable to witness Meg's distress.

Jeffrey Ellis died and Lissa attended the funeral with Meg as was only right and proper. Larkrigg Hall seemed even more gloomy than before and her grandmother's glare only marginally less frozen than the stag's head in the hall.

Meg informed her that her grandfather had not forgotten her, as she had imagined. 'When you were

45

small he gave me a sum of money to invest for you. Not great, Lissa, but it will provide a nest egg for you when you come of age.'

Lissa wasn't interested in nest eggs. She wanted life to happen. She wanted action, to lift the gloom that had grown to be a part of her. She hurried back to school where everyone was singing 'Cherry Pink and Apple Blossom White' and tried not to think of her witch of a grandmother who lived alone high on the fell.

When she turned sixteen she left without taking her exams, despite all advice to the contrary.

There was pressure from Meg to stay at Broombank, surprisingly enough, from Nick too.

No longer a boy, he was broad and strong now, a grown man with a shock of red-blond hair. She could tell by the glances he gave Lissa that he did not see her as a nuisance any longer. Nor did she miss the looks exchanged between Meg and Sally Ann. Lissa knew that if she stayed at Broombank, in no time at all they would have her married off and settled at Ashlea with Nick, her life decided for her. That wouldn't be right. Not for her, nor for Nick.

The trouble was, she didn't know what she wanted and that made her feel unsettled and inadequate. In the end Lissa decided she could only find whatever it was outside the dale. When she told Meg she was to leave, her face seemed to crumple.

'Leave? Why? Where would you go?'

'To find a job.'

'But you're too young to leave home. We could work together, at least until you decide what you really want to do. Wouldn't that be fun?' Meg's hands were red raw with the salt she'd been rubbing into some freshly killed pork and Lissa looked at them with distaste.

'There's no work for me here, Meg. You have your sheep, and Tam. I don't belong.'

'Of course you belong.' Meg again felt the grip of loss around her heart. She reached for a cloth and wiped her hands upon it, then rested them on Lissa's shoulders, drawing her close. 'How lucky I am to have you,' she said. 'No woman could have had a better daughter.'

'Nor I a better mother,' Lissa said, hugging her, knowing it was true and wishing it could be enough. The two exchanged tentative smiles.

'We've had our differences, our difficult times, but what mother and daughter doesn't? Broombank will always be your home.'

'Broombank is your home, not mine. Turner was your name before you married Tam, not mine. Who am I? Not Lissa Turner. Not Lissa Ellis. Who? Where do I belong? I have to build a new life and find my own place in it. Don't you see?'

A small silence then Meg blinked and gave a tiny nod. 'I suppose so.' She wanted to talk about the baby, to say that she didn't blame Lissa for what had happened, but couldn't trust herself to say the words without crying. Perhaps a part of

47

her still did blame Lissa for so thoughtlessly staying out that night, causing them so much worry and anguish. She could not offer the forgiveness Lissa so desperately needed so the breach between them was soothed, but not entirely healed.

It came as a great relief to Meg that Lissa decided not to go to Canada. She'd been almost sure that she would. But Lissa had been adamant.

'I won't go where I'm not wanted.' There was such bitterness in her firm young voice it cut Meg to the heart.

'Are you sure this is what you want?'

She had agreed to drive Lissa into central Lakeland to look for a summer job, with many provisos of course, and words of caution. Lissa had not spoken all the way through Staveley and Windermere, nor as they drove the long road that followed the lake as far as Waterhead at Ambleside.

Meg changed gear and eased her way out of the traffic and into Borrans Road, driving past the steamer pier, closed at this time of year, and on past the open field wherein lay the Roman Camp of Galava, her mind full of worries instead of the magnificent view.

As they turned left and headed out towards Clappersgate and Skelwith Bridge, the mountains of the Langdales rising ahead of them against an unusually blue sky, Lissa spoke.

'Yes, this is what I want.'

Birdsong filled the air, and the scent of new grass, but neither remarked upon it. Spears of pink and green were about to unfurl on the oak and horse chestnut and for a moment Lissa's heart lifted. Her life was not over. She could begin again. She was sixteen years old and could make of her life whatever she wished.

CHAPTER 3

Jan Colwith stood on a box behind the huge glass drapery counter and adopted the pleasant expression of polite enquiry necessary for a difficult customer.

'I'm sorry, madam, these are the only kid gloves we have in at present. Would you wish me to order a particular size or colour for you?'

Jan could hear the hiccuping sounds of her brother's deep voice trying to imitate Bill Haley issuing from the stockroom. The woman raised finely arched brows and Jan smiled apologetically, vowing to kick him the moment this dreadful woman had gone.

'I see little point,' the customer said tartly. 'I shall call again when you have more time to attend to me, or perhaps I should wait until I go into Kendal. I am sure they will have a much better selection there. Good day to you.'

'Good day, madam, and thank you for calling.'

Derek Colwith erupted through the curtain behind her, snorting with laughter. 'How can you be so polite to that dragon?'

'The hideous noise you were making didn't help

50

one bit.' Jan pushed back her straight brown hair, hooking it behind her ears with agitated fingers, brown eyes narrowing short-sightedly at her brother.' Are you quite mad, Derry? You shouldn't even be here Miss Stevens will have my scalp if she spots you.' She glanced nervously about the shop, expecting her employer to emerge from among the dusty mannequins which stood, arms raised in silent appeal, in the wide window.

'Stop fussing. If I can't call in at lunch time and talk to my own sister it's a poor do. Anyway, I might buy something, mightn't I?' He swaggered outrageously, making Jan giggle as he strolled into the centre of the floor, hands in pockets, to gaze about him with a fine display of urbane assurance. They both knew he didn't feel half so brave as he appeared but that was all part of the joke. If the last customer had been a dinosaur, Miss Stevens was a dragon.

'What a sight you do look, Derry. Where did you get those socks?'

'Don't you like them?' He hitched up his trouser legs an inch or two, which was no mean feat judging by their narrowness, to reveal bright, lime green socks. He grinned. 'Cool, eh? They're luminous. I've got some shocking pink ones too.' He pulled out a comb and started to slick back his already neat quiff which made Jan laugh all the more.

'No wonder Miss Stevens calls you a Teddy Boy.'

She looked again at the socks and the thick crepe

soles of his shoes. Her gaze slid over his long grey jacket, only an inch or two short of Teddy Boy length. Admittedly the lapels were not velvet but they tapered narrowly and hooked with a double link button at the waist. The most conventional garments he wore were a pristine white shirt and a slim grey tie. At weekends he was fond of a rather dashing silk waistcoat or a leather jacket and skin-tight jeans. But today was Friday, a work day.

'Sorry to disappoint you, sis, but I'm not really a Ted. Get as near to it as I dare but haven't quite got the nerve to go all the way. Besides, old Brandon would never permit any of his clerks to dress so outlandishly, even in their free time. Old fuddy-duddy, that's what he is.'

'What does he think of your socks?'

'Er, he hasn't seen them.'

'Make sure he doesn't then or you may be forced to apply to Miss Stevens for a job.'

Derry rolled his eyes heavenwards with exaggerated charm. 'I'd rather chew nails for a living.'

Jan started tidying away gloves. It had been a long morning, starting shortly after eight, and she was tired. Her legs were aching, she was hungry, and not really in the mood for her brother's jokiness so she spoke more sharply than she intended. 'What did you want anyway?'

'Ooh, sorry to bother you.' He fingered the net on a hat that dangled on a T-shaped counter stand and Jan slapped his hand away. 'Only to tell you I won't be home this evening. I'm going over to

Tony's.' His apparent nonchalance did not sit easily with the glance he slanted at her.

Jan pursed her lips then let them burst open in a tiny explosion. 'Oh, that's so unfair. So I'm to cope with things on my own again, am I?'

'You do it so well.'

'Dad will be hurt.'

'Let him be. He should have thought of us before he brought that-that creature home.'

'You didn't think she was a creature once.'

'I've learned different.'

Jan's eyes were pleading. 'I know you're hurting but don't make trouble, Derry. Please. We have to live with the situation whether we like it or not. There's nothing else we can do.'

'I don't have to sit there watching them bill and coo. Where my mother used to sit,' Derry said, a fierce brightness in his brown eyes.

Jan fell silent, unable to summon up the energy to argue, or the right words. After a moment she said, 'Mum's gone, Derry. Dead and buried. Life goes on.'

He started circling the shop again, running his hands over the glass counters, flicking the ribbons that hung in brightly coloured rows from their reels, spinning a stand of buttons round like a whirligig.

'Stop that, you'll do some damage.' Jan studiously gave her attention to smoothing out the gloves, slipping each one into its appointed place in the drawer, a sick feeling settling in her stomach at the prospect of a difficult evening ahead.

53

'Had any applicants for the vacancy yet?'

Jan shook her head. 'Most of Carreckwater are wary of Stevens Drapery.'

'Except you.' Derry raised enquiring eyebrows at her, but his smile was conciliatory.

'I don't have much choice, do I? I like to eat.'

'Where is she now, the old harridan?'

'At lunch.'

'It's nearly two. What about your lunch?'

'I get half an hour. When she comes back. Just time for a quick sandwich and to powder my nose.' Jan wrinkled it ruefully as she stowed the glove drawers back under the counter. 'Speaking of lunch, hadn't you better go and eat yours?' She glanced at him, anxious suddenly. 'You did remember to pick it up from the kitchen dresser, didn't you?'

He sighed and propped one elbow on the counter, cupping his chin in his hand while he grinned at her. 'Yes, sister dear, don't fuss over me. I'm a big boy now.'

'I sometimes wonder.'

'I've eaten my corned beef sandwiches and very good they were too, though a touch more pickle would be appreciated.' He didn't tell her that he'd also popped into the pub for a meat pie and half a pint of bitter.

'Cheek! Do them yourself in future. I'm not your servant.' She aimed a swipe at him and laughed as he ducked. Then, as wickedly spry as if he were still a boy of ten instead of seventeen, he leapt up into the window and positioned himself among the mannequins.

Jan squealed her dismay, running round the counter to make a grab for him. 'Derry, stop it. You mustn't play your silly games here, especially not in the window. You'll cause mayhem. Miss Stevens may be back at any moment. Do behave.' She'd grown quite breathless with anxiety as her words fell upon deaf ears. Her brother simply grinned, sticking his arms out in imitation of the mannequins.

'Why do they stand in this silly way?' he asked.

'Because they do.'

'Don't you think I add a touch of class? Perhaps people will like my socks and come in and buy them.' He glanced out through the window as if expecting a queue of people to have formed already and found himself looking down into a pale, oval face with wide, dark blue eyes.

He was startled, as, apparently, was she. Then a wide mouth broke into the prettiest smile he'd ever seen and he stared entranced for what might have been eternity.

'*Mr Colwith*. Have you quite taken leave of your senses? Get out of my window this instant.'

The dragon had returned, via the back door, which was most unsporting of her in Derry's opinion. The stentorian voice made him jump so violently he knocked his head on the low ceiling. Turning too quickly he sent one mannequin in a smart apple green two-piece flying. Instinctively he tried to catch it but that only made matters worse as he elbowed the stomach of the one behind him and his thick crepe soles got caught up with another. The mannequins came down like dominoes, arms and legs flying free in a kind of celebratory *danse macabre*. All he could do was helplessly watch them fall, a bright blonde wig dangling from the link button of his jacket.

He stepped down into the shop considerably chastened. 'I'll put them all back . . .'

Miss Stevens grasped his ear in a pincer-like grip and marched him to the door.

'Out!' she barked.

Derry cast an agonised glance at his sister but Jan was beyond words, her face as white as the sheets that were used to drape the precious models in the stockroom.

'Look, I'm sorry . . .'

'Hello!' The pansy-eyed girl stood in the doorway. 'The card in your window says that you need a new assistant. I don't mind hard work, and could start right away if you like, by fixing the accident you seem to have had.'

Lissa had fallen in love with Carreckwater the moment they drove into it. She thought it a delightful little village, situated as it was in a wooded valley in the heart of Lakeland with its very own small lake. To the north was Rydal and Grasmere, to the south Ambleside and Windermere. The jagged, snow-tipped peaks of the Langdales stood proudly to the west, and in the east Kentmere.

Beyond that came Broombank and her own beloved fells

She knew that it was her cheek that had got her this job, and best of all, the other girl shop assistant had quickly offered accommodation in her own home.

'If you don't mind sharing, that is?'

'Not at all.'

Lissa had raced off at once to collect her suitcase from the car and tell Meg she could go home without her. It had been hard, suddenly, saying goodbye to Meg, despite the friction that had grown between them recently but at the same time Lissa was excited, looking forward to a new beginning.

'You'll write regularly, and come home to see us from time to time?'

'Of course I will. I'm not a million miles away, am I?'

They stood facing each other, uncertain, awkward, then Meg put out her arms about Lissa and hugged her. It felt slightly awkward and Lissa knew Meg still felt some resentment over her desire to find Kath, as well as her more recent teenage rebellion. Now Lissa just wanted to lean her head on her foster mother's shoulder and beg her forgiveness, to try to explain all that was in her heart and somehow make her understand. But Meg was stepping away from her, moving to the car, smiling a distant smile as if she couldn't wait to get away.

Lissa didn't see Meg's tears as she drove away.

★ ★ ★

'It'll have to be a camp bed in my room,' Jan apologised as they walked home that evening.

Lissa assured her that would be fine. 'I'm so thrilled to have got the first job I've applied for. Did many people apply for it?'

'Er, well, as a matter of fact, you were the only one.'

Lissa looked startled for a moment then both girls burst out laughing.

What did it matter? She knew she would enjoy working with Jan. Lissa liked her friendly smile, her brisk, no nonsense way of doing things, and her petiteness. She already loved the rows of dark Lakeland stone cottages that seemed to huddle convivially along narrow streets or gossip together in ancient courtyards.

The two girls chatted freely as they made their way down a crooked flight of stone steps by the old stone church.

Lissa wanted to keep stopping to gaze in the shop windows, one selling jewellery, another clocks and ornaments made from slate. Here was a tiny gallery hung with lovely pictures to please the tourists while yet another sold more practical items of paraphernalia needed for climbing the beautiful mountains that surrounded the small village.

She was beginning to feel quite buoyant about the future. She might even come to think that Carreckwater was as exciting as Canada in the end. Carrec, Jan told her, was an old Celt word for rock, which rose precipitously all around the lake.

The small cottages gave way to larger Victorian villas strung out around the perimeter of the lake. The kind of houses, she guessed, that had been built by the rich cotton magnates in the last century.

'Sorry to disappoint you but we don't live in one of those.'

'So, no butler and maid-service to go with the camp bed then?' Lissa teased.

'Nope, you have to wait on yourself.' Jan grinned, then frowned, looking oddly uncomfortable as if suddenly regretting her hasty offer. Lissa, thinking she'd offended her new friend, hastened to reassure her.

'I'm not serious. I live in an old farmhouse. Big, admittedly, but draughty, freezing cold much of the time, and desperately quiet.' A vision of Meg and Tam seated within the warmth of the great inglenook rose in her mind's eye, and she caught her breath at the wave of homesickness that struck her right between the ribs. Jan didn't notice, she was too deep in her own thoughts. They turned left, away from the villas and entered a labyrinth of cobbled streets beyond.

'You can catch a glimpse of the lake from the attic window and that's about it. Not that anyone lives in the attic, it's full of junk.' Then rushing on in one breath, 'I'd best warn you that things aren't exactly what you might call normal, in our house at the moment.'

'Oh?'

Jan flicked a glance at her new friend, wondering how much she should divulge of the Colwith family problems.

Lissa must be about the same age as herself, Jan decided, a year younger than Derry who was just turned seventeen. But there was an odd stillness about the girl that troubled her. As if she had known great sadness or was afraid to reveal any part of her real self. Jan wondered what had brought her to Carreckwater. Only the retired and the holidaymakers came voluntarily as a rule. She didn't want to put her off or make things sound worse than they were. Life was tricky enough. Thanks to Derry as much as anyone. She came to a quick decision to take a leaf out of her brother's book. Whenever Derry didn't want anyone to probe too deeply into his feelings, he hid behind a shield of jokiness.

'Let's face it,' she said, laughing, 'no one would willingly come to live with my family. What a shower!'

'I'm sure they're not as bad as all that.'

'Don't you believe it.' Jan pushed back a swathe of dark hair and her small pointed face broke into one of her infectious grins. 'You'll probably be glad to leave after only a day, and who would blame you? Though I confess it'd be a great help to me if you did stay. Keep me sane. Oh dear, that sounds awful.'

Lissa found herself responding to the ready smile

even as her mind thought, no, it didn't sound awful at all. It sounded about right. People generally thought only of themselves in her experience, thrusting from her memory all Meg's selfless acts of generosity over the years. 'I don't care what your reasons for asking me are, I'm grateful for the offer.'

But she did care, she cared very much. How she would love someone to invite her into their life simply because they liked her and wanted her for herself.

Jan tucked her arm into Lissa's. 'I knew as soon as I saw you that you were kind. Clever too, I shouldn't wonder. Not like me, thick as a brush and half blind into the bargain.' She burst into a peal of merry laughter. 'Derry says I should carry a label: "Dangerous. Too vain to wear spectacles." Then everyone would know to keep out of my way. I hate doing the window for that reason, and you did it a real treat today.'

Lissa was laughing too, and could feel their friendship growing, minute by minute. It was a good feeling, so perhaps things wouldn't be so bad after all.

'Here it is. Colwith Castle. Well, Nab Cottage in point of fact.'

'What's wrong with it? It's lovely,' Lissa said, gazing approvingly at a stone cottage, the end one of a row, with winter jasmine growing up one corner of it. 'Delightful.'

'It's my dad,' Jan blurted out. 'Mam died just three months ago.'

'Oh, I'm so sorry.'

'It was expected. She'd been ill for a long time. But Dad, well, he took it into his head to marry again. Derry thinks it's too soon, too disrespectful, and to the wrong person.' Jan pulled a wry face. 'I dare say he's right.'

'I see. And what do you think of your new step-mother? Do you get on? Is she nice?'

Instead of answering, Jan pushed at a small, green-painted gate and held it open while Lissa squeezed through the resulting gap. They'd called at the grocer's on the way home and what with Lissa's suitcase and the shopping they were both heavily loaded. They walked up the short path and straight in through the green front door.

'You can decide that for yourself.'

The first thing that struck Lissa about the Colwith household was the overpowering heat. The windows and doors were all firmly closed against possible cool spring breezes and a young woman sat huddled close to two bars of an electric fire. It glowed bright orange against the brown tiles of the fireplace – the same colour, in fact, as her lipstick. Her frizzed, bleached hair was held up with combs on top of her head, revealing a pair of purple glass earrings that swayed and bobbed about her rouged cheeks. She wore a pink fluffy sweater and a tight black skirt which she had pulled up to her thighs to warm her bare legs, mottled with scorch marks from the heat.

A blue budgerigar chirped noisily from a cage that hung on a stand in the comer. During the ensuing conversation Lissa watched it, fascinated, as it alternately chattered to itself in a mirror or bashed the life out of a swinging bell. Perhaps the heat was meant for him.

'About time you got here,' the woman grumbled. 'I have to go soon, you know.' She didn't get up, or offer to help, as Jan marched straight through to the kitchen with the shopping. 'Put the kettle on, love. Your dad will be home in a minute and he'll not like being kept waiting for his tea.'

'Why didn't you do something about it yourself then?' said Jan from the kitchen. 'Surprise me for once.'

'I'm off to work soon. Don't I see enough food, waiting on at the hotel, without starting here? Anyroad, it's your house, as you're so fond of reminding me.' She leaned back in her seat with a smile of satisfaction as if she had won some sort of contest.

Embarrassed by the animosity in the atmosphere, Lissa set down her bag and stared at the rings of faded orange flowers on the worn brown carpet, wondering what to say, what best to do. Could this be a sister that Jan hadn't mentioned? Surely not the new Mrs Colwith? She was little older than herself. Twenty at most. How old would Jan's father be? She glanced at the woman and at Jan who was busily slamming things into kitchen cupboards. Too old.

'So who have we here?'

Lissa started, as if caught out in her thoughts. She stepped forward, one hand outstretched. 'Hello. I'm Lissa – er – Lissa Turner.'

Grey-blue eyes, heavily ringed with black mascara, gazed curiously up at her. 'You don't sound too sure. Mind you, I'm having trouble remembering me own at the moment.'

'Oh, so you are?'

'Old Mother Riley.'

'What?'

'Who the hell do you think I am?'

Jan came to her rescue. Hooking her hair behind her ears in a now familiar nervous gesture, she flickered a smile at Lissa. 'This is Renee. My new stepmother.'

Renee giggled and reached for a pack of cigarettes that were propped on the corner of the mantelpiece. 'Right laugh that, eh? We were in the same class at school, her and me. Now I'm her bloody mother.'

Lissa tried not to let it show that the information jolted her, readjusting the age of the teenage bride from twenty back down to sixteen, seemingly old beyond her years behind the mask of make-up. 'Oh,' she said, ineffectually. 'I see.'

Lissa watched with interest as the match flared and was applied to the cigarette, the bright tip glowing to an orange disc. It seemed to match the unidentifiable swirls on the wallpaper and the worn carpet. Come to think of it, the whole room was filled with strips, blobs and circles of orange and red, some bright and dazzling, others smudged and faded. It made her head spin. No, that must be the heat. Even the linen antimacassars on the brown moquette three-piece suite were embroidered with pretty ladies in orange crinolines and red poke bonnets.

It was a shabby, tired sort of room, rather untidy, with several mugs and cups and saucers scattered on every surface which Jan was now hastily gathering up. A pair of filthy fur-trimmed slippers sat on the tiled hearth looking rather like a dead cat, and an ash tray overflowed with cigarette ends.

'May I sit down?' Lissa considered the settee covered with discarded newspapers and old woollen cardigans and hesitated.

'Suit yourself.' Without moving from her chair Renee called to Jan who had scurried once more into the kitchen, 'What's for tea then?'

Jan appeared at the door, saw Lissa's dilemma and swooped the settee clear, making irritable clicking noises with her tongue. 'I've bought some smoked haddock. I thought I'd poach it with a bit of butter.'

'We haven't got none. Only a scraping of marg left.'

'I got paid today so I bought a packet.'

'Is it Friday already? Crikey, how the week does fly when you're having fun.' Renee drew deeply on the cigarette then threw back her head and blew smoke rings up at the yellowed ceiling. Lissa tried not to look impressed.

At that moment the door opened and Renee was out of her seat in a flash, flinging herself into the arms of a man who brought with him a smell of sawdust, the sharp tang of paint, and damp fresh air. From what Lissa could see of him he was small and stocky, wearing blue jeans and a dark navy sweater. Renee removed his peaked cap and started to run her fingers through his dark hair, instantly twining her pliant body against his so it was hard to tell them apart. Lissa quickly averted her gaze from the deep, passionate kiss which followed and threatened to continue indefinitely. Her heart went out to her new friend, and their eyes met for a moment in shared sympathy and understanding.. She could see exactly why Jan had been glad of some company.

'Ooh, you devil you!' gasped Renee, wiping orange lipstick from his lips and cheek. 'Have you brought it then?' She squealed when Jimmy Colwith grinned.

'It's coming on Monday. A Ferguson. Twelve inch. How about that? Next door's is only nine.'

'Oh my giddy aunt! A television of me own.' Renee screamed, flung her arms about Jimmy's neck and started to kiss him all over again.

When the celebrations were finally over she staggered back to her chair by the fire. 'My God, you do go at it once you start, don't you? Give a girl a break, will you?' She flopped down, legs sprawling, and again Lissa averted her gaze from the look of almost naked lust in the girl's translucent grey-blue eyes. It made her feel slightly sick.

'Who have we here?' Jimmy Colwith came and propped himself on the arm of his wife's chair, slipping his arm about her shoulders and letting his hand dangle, one finger gently circling her left breast. Lissa could tell by the amusement in his eyes that he guessed she found the gesture offensive. What had she let herself in for, coming here? Meg would be outraged.

Jan was explaining about her taking the job at the shop and needing a room.

'Only for a little while, till I find a place of my own,' Lissa quickly put in, making a silent vow to start looking this very weekend.

'In Carreckwater? You'll be lucky. Rents are sky high these days with all the trippers. It's more profitable to take in summer visitors than shop assistants as lodgers.'

'I suppose it is.' Her heart plummeted.

'We've not that much room here neither. Where did you intend sleeping? With our Jan? Or our Derek?'

Lissa blushed bright scarlet and Jan slammed her hand down so hard on the table, the little cruet set danced.

'Dad, how can you? Lissa is my friend, my guest, and only just walked in the door. She doesn't understand your weird sense of humour.'

'Then we might as well start as we mean to go on, eh?'

'It's all right,' said Lissa, manufacturing a laugh. 'I can take a joke with the rest.'

'Course you can,' said Jimmy, pleased with the small sensation he had created. 'Anyway, she could always bunk in with me, when Renee's on nights. I don't mind sharing.'

There was a small, tight silence.

Renee leaned forward, patting Lissa reassuringly on the knee. 'It's all right, lovey. He won't bother you. He has enough trouble keeping up with me.' And she smiled so warmly that to her surprise Lissa found herself smiling back.

They all sat at the small table, covered with an orange checked cloth, and Jan brought in the smoked haddock which smelled surprisingly tasty. Lissa felt herself start to relax.

Derry caused a slight stir by unexpectedly turning up to share the meal with them. A disagreement at once took place between brother and sister since he had assured her he would not be home this evening.

Lissa cast a covert glance in his direction as he took off the overlong jacket and slackened his tie, leaving it to hang loose over the white shirt. He was really quite attractive close to, she couldn't help but notice. She hadn't paid too much attention in the shop since Miss Stevens had chased him fairly smartly off the premises. Now Lissa caught him returning her scrutiny, grinning mischievously at her, and she bent her head quickly, trying to concentrate on her meal, acutely aware of him as he came to sit beside her.

'You could have warned me that you might change your mind, Jan was complaining, cutting her own piece of fish in half, preparatory to shovelling a portion on to a clean plate for him. Lissa felt instantly guilty since she was the extra person at dinner.

'Derry can have mine. I'm not really hungry.' She was starving. She had left home at eight to give herself ample time to conduct her search and had skipped lunch, despite Meg's protests, out of sheer nervousness.

Jan looked doubtful, as if she knew it would be polite to refuse but was sorely tempted all the same,

'Go on, take some,' Lissa urged.' We can at least share two portions into three, make it better all round.'

So Jan was persuaded, ignoring Derry's grins and winks at Lissa, which made it patently obvious the motivation for his change of plan. Nobody commented upon the fact that neither Jan's father nor Renee volunteered to share their portions. The pair silently got on with their meal, eyes never leaving their plates except to dwell lingeringly upon each other.

'You can come and listen to me practise afterwards, if you like?' Derry offered, as if bestowing a gift.

'Practise is what he needs,' Jimmy said, through a mouthful of fish. 'Spare her ear drums, laddie.'

'Practise what?' Lissa was intrigued despite herself.

'Guitar, what else?'

'Fancies himself as Elvis Presley, my son does.'

'No, I don't. We have a skiffle group, not a rock 'n' roll band. Not that you would know the difference for all you pretend to be young and with it.' Derry flung a glowering glance at Renee before returning his glare to his father. 'You're square, you know that? An old has-been. We can't go on listening to Perry Como for ever.'

'At least he sings in tune.'

Jan held up her hands as if conducting an orchestra with her knife and fork. 'That's enough you two. Eat, please. Remember we have a guest.'

There was silence as everyone finished off their meal.

Later, Derry and Lissa dried the dishes which Jan washed, Renee and Jimmy having vanished somewhere upstairs.

'So? How about it?' Derry persisted. 'We practise in the school hall. For the Saturday dance tomorrow. Will you come?'

Lissa glanced at him and in that brief instant longed, more than anything, to say yes, she would love to come. He looked so friendly and smiling, his brown eyes warmly inviting as if he really wanted her to go with him. She longed to live the life of a normal young person, a teenager as they were now called. Somehow Lissa felt she had missed out on so many things. Her clothes were out of date, her hair style flat and uninteresting. She never wore make up or listened to music. She didn't own a single record or record player, so how could she? Why, she hadn't even seen this great film everybody was raving about, 'Rock Around the Clock'. And had never, in all her life, been kissed by a boy.

Sweet sixteen and never been kissed. It was such a cliché it made her cringe. Going to a girls' school had of course given few opportunities but then Derry wasn't asking her for a date, was he? He was merely suggesting she come and watch him practise. Probably only wanted to show off. He would have a girl friend already. Someone pretty and 'with it'.

Best not to get involved.

'No, thanks,' she said airily, lifting her chin so he couldn't guess how shy and insecure she felt. 'I have to unpack and I'd like a quiet evening if you don't mind. It's been a long day.'

'Give her time to settle in, for heaven's sake,' Jan protested.

The expression on his face could have been taken for disappointment had Lissa not known better. 'What about the dance tomorrow then?' he asked. 'Will you come to that?'

She lifted her eyebrows and managed to shrug her shoulders with perfect disdain at the same time. 'I really don't think so.'

71

But the next day as she watched Jan try on various garments and agonise over what to wear Lissa felt sorely tempted to change her mind. She'd felt very strange inside when Derry smiled at her. A warm, tingly sort of feeling that had been most pleasant.

She pictured his face. It was really not at all bad looking with its long straight nose and curving lopsided smile. Brown eyes, thickly fringed with surprisingly long dark lashes, held an expression of permanent mischief, as if he knew some secret about life that had passed others by. Lissa guessed that he kept his brown hair slicked back with brilliantine in order to achieve that fashionable 'Tony Curtis' hair style he wore. It probably wasn't nearly so dark when just washed, she found herself thinking, and decided on the whole that whatever its colour, the style suited him. Deny Colwith seemed pleasant enough, if a bit full of himself, despite the rather odd clothes he wore.

So why hadn't she said yes?

Because she couldn't be sure he really wanted her to accept? Because he would have a circle of friends already and she wouldn't fit in.

'You don't want me hanging on your coat tails,' she said now.

'I hadn't thought of wearing any but it's not a bad idea. Bit different, eh?' Jan joked.

'You know what I mean.'

Jan twirled her circular cotton skirt, checking she showed just the right amount of petticoat and no stocking tops. 'Don't talk daft. You should come. The white blouse or the blue, do you think?'

Lissa considered. 'The blue. I'd rather not, if you don't mind.' She'd decided long since to have nothing at all to do with sex, or love either for that matter. She had no wish to make the same mistake as her mother and bring another unwanted child into the world. She would stay an unmarried virgin, like Queen Elizabeth I. So going to dances with young men was not a good idea. She did wonder though, if that were the case, why the idea of accepting was so very enticing.

Perhaps she really was wicked, just like Kath.

'You should hear our Derry play,' Jan was saying. 'He's not half bad. Even I, his ever non-loving sister, can tell that much.' She took out some green eye shadow and began applying it thickly to her lids.

Lissa watched with interest, deciding that although Jan wasn't pretty in the accepted sense of the word, there was an attractive, homely quality about her. A friendly girl, she was the sort of person you could rely on, or so Lissa hoped. However, the eye shadow would do little for her eyes while she screwed them up in that squinting way she had. Though not for the world would Lissa say as much.

'I'm sure he is,' she agreed, watching intrigued as Jan outlined her lips with coral pink lipstick. 'Does he have a girl friend?' Now why had she asked that?

'Oh lord, yes, millions. They hang about him like wasps round a jam pot. Sickening it is.'

She should have known.

'But there'll be loads of talent there. Male talent that is. It'll be fun.'

If Lissa had been about to change her mind the mention of all these unknown friends at once put paid to the idea. She was an outsider. Jan was only feeling sorry for her and she had no intention of joining the crowd round Derry Colwith.

'I've nothing to wear, and no money to buy anything,' Lissa said, settling the issue.

'You could borrow something of mine,' Jan offered, not disagreeing with this statement.

Nevertheless Lissa kept to her decision not to go to the dance and sat at home and felt sorry for herself instead.

CHAPTER 4

The following weekend Lissa spent searching the village for a flat or even a room of her own which she could afford, but to no avail. The week after, she met with no greater success. After a month or more of fruitless searching Lissa had almost given up hope of ever finding a place of her own. Everywhere was either too big or too expensive. A winter let would have been easy to find, but with summer coming, the landladies could make more money out of the growing numbers of holiday makers.

She paid the Colwith family a small sum each week in return for her bed and board and she and Jan got along famously. Lissa had even grown used to the eccentric behaviour of Jimmy and Renee.

But she avoided any contact with Derry.

Fortunately he was out most of the time, either at work, or with his skiffle group. He enjoyed boasting of their success, of the way the girls would scream whenever he made an appearance. The moment he swaggered in through the door each evening he would jauntily challenge them with his disarming grin and claim to be worn out by their ardent attentions. Lissa refused to listen and would find some excuse to go upstairs.

Every morning Jan and Lissa walked together to work, enjoying the softness of the air as spring gradually changed into summer and the streets of the small town grew busier. At lunchtime they often took their sandwiches down to the lake, sitting on the benches by the band stand, feeding crusts to the mallards and moorhens that crowded the shore line and laughing at the upturned wagging tails in the water.

Their friendship was now teetering on the confiding stage and one morning as they were happily unpacking a new delivery of lingerie, giggling together over old ladies' pink bloomers and corsets, Lissa felt able to risk a personal question.

'Does it bother you, your father marrying a girl your own age?'

Jan gave her an old fashioned look. 'What do you think? Anyway, she wasn't just any girl, she was Derry's girl friend. Hasn't he told you? He brought her home for tea and Derry never had a look in from the moment they set eyes on each other.'

'Goodness!' Lissa tried not to picture Derry with the voluptuous Renee. It disturbed her somehow. 'Doesn't Renee mind? About the age difference, I mean.'

Jan shrugged. 'She's sixteen. Dad is forty-five. Makes you want to throw up, doesn't it?'

Lissa agreed that it did. 'No wonder Derry won't

speak to her.' There had been several unpleasant scenes in the last few weeks when Derry had simply refused to acknowledge Renee's presence, even so far as not setting a place for her at the dinner table. Jimmy often flared up in fury at his son, accusing him of insolence. But Lissa's sympathies were now with Derry. She could recognise pain behind the jaunty insolence in his brown eyes. It was how she had felt every birthday when her mother had promised to come and never had.

'What about your family?' Jan casually asked. 'You must miss them. Will you be going to visit them soon?'

'I expect so. Meg will want to know how I'm getting on.'

'Why do you call your mother Meg?'

'She isn't really my mother.' Ever sensitive that people might be disapproving of her true status, Lissa had decided to be perfectly blunt about her illegitimacy. She had no intention of pretending to be what she was not. 'I was dumped on her as a baby.'

'Dumped?'

Jan forgot all about unwrapping corsets as she became absorbed in Lissa's swiftly told tale. 'Oh, how dreadful, to be abandoned.' Her brown eyes, so like Derry's, grew round and moist. 'And this Meg, she's loved you as her own daughter ever since? How wonderful.'

'Yes, I suppose it was. Not that she was given much choice in the matter.'

77

'Is that your real name then, Turner, or your adopted one?'

'I'm illegitimate. A bastard. I don't have a name?' Lissa shrugged her shoulders with a laugh to show that she didn't care one way or the other and met Jan's sympathetic gaze with belligerence in her own. 'I wasn't even adopted.'

Jan blinked, alarmed by the sharpness of the tone, then after a moment said, 'Not your fault though, was it? You didn't ask to be born. Why be so angry about it?'

'I'm not angry.'

'You sound it.'

'I don't need pity or advice, thanks very much.'

Jan flushed and paid excessive attention to opening a new package but couldn't resist asking, 'Have you ever met her then? Your real ma, I mean?'

Lissa shook her head and started to rip up the empty carton, stamping the cardboard flat. It made her feel a lot better. 'Once, I think, when I was a child. I don't remember her. She lives in Canada. I'm sorry, I didn't mean to be rude.'

'That's OK.' Jan smiled. 'I wouldn't want sympathy either. Anyway, no one need know if you don't tell them.'

The violet eyes sparkled with the light of battle. 'I'm not pretending. I am what I am. This is me. Take me or leave me.'

Jan looked startled for a minute and then grinned. 'I'll take two, ta very much.' Then they both burst into fits of girlish giggles, the prickly moment past.

'I wish this shop sold something more interesting than old fashioned corsets,' Lissa complained, happily changing the subject and holding up a satinette underskirt with straps two inches wide. These slips still have a 1930s look.'

'Some of our stock genuinely is that old, very nearly antique,' Jan giggled. 'Miss Stevens wouldn't hear of "going modern", as she calls it. She might get *teenagers* in her shop and that would never do. Anyone would think young people were a new invention, a disease, the way she carries on.'

They fell about giggling as they priced up the unpretentious underwear and stowed it away in the ranks of glass-fronted drawers that lined the walls of the draper's shop.

It was then that the idea popped into Lissa's head, quite out of the blue, and she wondered why she hadn't thought of it before. 'Hey, I know. We could find a place together.'

Jan's eyes opened wider than her myopic vision usually permitted as she gazed in astonished wonder at Lissa. 'Are you serious?'

'Never more so. Why not'

'It's quite the thing for young career girls to do nowadays, or so I read in Jimmy's newspaper.'

'Is that what we are, career girls?'

'Well, why not? I intend to make something of myself, don't you? Though I haven't quite decided how yet. Having a flat together would be a start in the right direction, wouldn't it? Good fun too, don't you think?'

'Oh,' breathed Jan, not able to believe her luck in finding such a friend.

'We could afford more rent between the two of us. Make it much more economic.' Lissa grew enthusiastic as she thought of a place she'd looked at just the other day. She tossed aside a pink corset she had been rolling up to grab her friend excitedly. 'I've seen a converted boathouse. Wooden, close to the lake so admittedly horribly damp, small of course, and with a minuscule kitchen, a spiral staircase and two tiny loft bedrooms above. But with the most fabulous views. Two pounds ten shillings a week. We could go and take a look this lunchtime if you like?'

'Ooh, yes. That would be lovely.' Jan's smile formed a perfect triangle of delight in her small face, and then almost as suddenly faded away. 'We'd have to get permission off our parents. They'd have to sign the lease or something.'

Lissa shrugged. 'So what? Meg trusts me, though no doubt she'd come over and check it all out.' She rolled her eyes in exaggerated style as if saying, Parents, how fussy they are.

Jan still looked anxious. 'Dad might not care for me going. He likes me at home, expects me to help with the cooking and cleaning since Renee works long hours at the hotel.'

Lissa laughed. 'Hang that for a life. Let the wonderful Renee look after him for a change.

She took him on, didn't she? For better, for worse, for washing and for cooking.' Lissa held up the long pink corset, suspenders dangling. 'She'll be needing one of these if she doesn't get out of that chair soon and start to do a bit more work. That would really please your dad.'

Then they were both giggling so much they didn't hear Miss Stevens come in, eyes slightly glazed from the small comforter she had been enjoying in the stock room. Her stentorian voice, however, had benefited from the stiff gin and soon put a stop to their hilarity.

Suitably chastened, but desperately trying to avoid each other's eyes in case they set off a second attack of giggles, they got back to unpacking corsets.

Philip Brandon stared through the glass panel of his office door, peering beneath the gold letters that read BRANDON AND BRANDON, SOLICITORS AND COMMISSIONERS FOR OATHS, and frowned. He could plainly see his young clerk, playing the fool, no doubt in pursuit of Christine, the new typist, when he had been specifically instructed to sort the morning post and stamp it with the date received. Worse, Miss Henshaw, Philip's personal secretary, sat smiling upon both of them, as if there were nothing untoward in such horse play during office hours.

He got up from behind his wide mahogany desk, tugged at his waistcoat, then took off his spectacles and polished them furiously. The glass in them was quite plain but they were useful as they gave dignity and an air of authority to his somewhat boyish face. He replaced them carefully, hooking the wire frames around each ear as he again peered through the gold lettering.

Christine was squealing, dropping papers all over the place as she put up her hands in weak defence, her breasts bouncing beneath her white blouse in delightful unison. Philip contemplated how they would feel pressed up against him. His hand twitched convulsively as if testing their softness in his hand. Perhaps as a pillow for his head. For a moment he envied Derry then felt guilt wash over him like a hot tide.

Blinking furiously, he straightened, stiffening his spine to a more proper posture. What was he thinking of? He thrust open the door and stepped into the outer office.

'Have you finished with the morning post, Colwith?' he asked in his quiet voice, and the occupants of the room froze, as if captured on camera.

Derry was the first to recover. 'Won't be a jiff.'

Philip winced. 'Can we use the English language within the precincts of the office? Bring them through when you are done. Five minutes, if you please.'

'Yes, sir,' said Derry, adopting a suitably sober expression. Christine had fled to her big black typewriter in the corner and was already pounding heavily upon it, bent on proving how hard she was really working.

Miss Henshaw was looking flustered as if it had been she who had been running about and squealing so outrageously. Philip glowered at her before returning to his desk, to let her know that he did hold her largely responsible. She flushed a dark red and bent her sensible, neatly cropped grey head more arduously to the conveyance she was laboriously typing. When the telephone shrilled at her elbow she almost snatched it up.

'Brandon Solicitors. Can I help you?' she trilled in her bright telephone voice, pencil. poised over her pad. 'Of course. One moment, please.' Miss Henshaw flicked switches and pulled plugs on the ancient switch board. 'Mr McArthur.'

'Thank you,' said Philip, in a tone meant to show she was not forgiven. Miss Henshaw took the point and got back to her typing. 'Behave, you two. You'll get us all the sack.'

Derry only had to look at her with that butter-wouldn't-melt-in-his-mouth smile and she was putty in his hands. It made her day just to watch him strut up and down the office. He certainly gave her a giggle and something to think about in her cold lonely bed at night. Vera Henshaw rather liked young men. She'd used to dream about Philip at one time, about what might have been between them had things been different and he not a man of affairs and she his simple secretary. Foolish even to have considered the possibility.

83

Didn't every secretary fall in love with their boss? And Vera knew she wasn't really his type. He preferred smart, attractive young women, not tired ones in floppy cardigans with the first signs of varicose veins.

Vera Henshaw sighed. It could have been so perfect, she a mere thirty-nine, or thereabouts, and he a mature thirty. But of course he would never marry, not now Felicity, his fiancée, had died. How that poor girl had suffered! But Philip had remained loyal. He'd not so much as glanced at another woman in all the three years since, the dear man. It was as if he was afraid to. As if by doing so, he would in some way blight her sweet memory. Though in Vera's considered opinion he sorely needed a good woman to shake him out of his mourning. Unfortunately, she was not that woman.

She mopped up a tear and on finding herself the object of scrutiny from her fellow workers, threw them a sour look. She put back her spectacles which hung from a cord about her neck and took out her frustration on the keys, her fingers hammering the words while her mind continued its deliberations.

There was a moody, brooding quality to his dark good looks, a sadness about him. The ears flat to the finely shaped head, full lips, and dark, unfathomable eyes that gave away none of their secrets. A real charmer he could be when he put his mind to it. No doubt about it, plenty would be glad to be the wife of Mr Philip Brandon.

Miss Henshaw sighed again. Realised she'd got her fingers accidentally on to all the wrong keys and had typed several lines of nonsense. She ripped out the paper with an exasperated click of her tongue. Really, she was becoming as irresponsible as the two youngsters.

'Have you finished that post, Derry?' she barked, venting her wrath on his hapless ears. 'Well, get it along to Mr Brandon or you'll find yourself at the labour exchange next week. And poke that fire. My feet are frozen.'

Her poor circulation was not helped by the hours she spent at this desk, she told herself morosely. A martyr to her work she was. Life had been so much easier when she was a junior with old Mr Brandon and they'd had all those clerks with scratchy pens for the paperwork. Miss Henshaw tucked her feet into a small knitted blanket she kept for the purpose and frowned at him so that he could see she meant what she said.

He blew her a kiss, wicked mischief on his grinning face.

'Impudent monkey. Get along with you.' But Miss Henshaw was smiling. Derry Colwith brought a bit of much needed sunshine into this gloomy office.

Derry sat most of each day at an old high sloping desk where he could gaze out of the window dreaming of fame and riches. And one day, he was sure, he would find it. Letting out a wistful sigh at the thought, he winked at Vera and, swaggering to the inner office door, tapped on the glass with one knuckle and marched right in to lay the stack of letters on the blotter before his employer.

'Thank you, Mr McArthur. I'm glad we are agreed. I think you will find it to be the wisest course. One moment, my clerk has entered.' Philip covered the mouthpiece with his hand while he pushed a pile of bank books across the desk to Derry. 'The McArthur probate. Take these books to the bank and inform the manager of Miss Amelia McArthur's death. Her nephew is the main beneficiary.'

'Right,' said Derry, picking them up and turning at once to the door. This was the part of the job he liked best, wandering about town on some errand or other. If the bank didn't take too long about it he could nip in to see Jan and Lissa, maybe have a quick coffee with them. He brightened at the prospect. He was getting nowhere with Lissa so far, but he still fancied his chances.

'Did you hear me?' Philip barked, with unusual impatience.

'Sir?'

'I said to call at the building society first, ask them to close the account and have the money transferred into the office account.'

'The office account?'

'Yes, you fool. In preparation for probate.'

'Right you are.'

When Derry had gone, whistling happily and

86

slamming the door too hard so that the ancient glass shook perilously, Philip removed his hand from the mouthpiece, carefully gathered his strained patience and continued with his conversation. He almost purred into the phone.

'Sorry to have kept you, Mr McArthur. Where were we? Ah, yes, death duties. No indeed, no one should be obliged to pay more than is absolutely necessary. Certainly your aunt would not have wished her money to go to the government.'

A pause while the caller on the end of the wire expressed his thanks and Philip Brandon's dark eyes took on a gleam as hard as the polished wood of his own desk.

'Such a gesture would of course be entirely at your own discretion. I shall be in touch.'

He rested the receiver back in its cradle and allowed himself a rare smile. Everything was progressing most satisfactorily, most satisfactorily indeed.

Happiness did not come easily to him. Life had been harder than he had bargained for since leaving Oxford. He'd been lucky, he supposed, missing the worst of the war and young enough to make something of his life afterwards. But Philip had resented the way he'd had to pinch and scrape, the way austerity had gone on for so long. As a member of the professional classes it didn't seem quite fair that he should suffer at all.

The initial pleasure he'd felt at finding himself in sole charge of the practice on the death of his father had soon dissipated when he'd learned the true state of its finances. It had given every appearance of a bustling, one-man practice, dealing with conveyancing, probate and estate work, inventories and valuations. Only a small amount of court work came his way, for which he was thankful. Litigation was rarely profitable and it gave a poor impression for a high class practice to be too involved with the nefarious goings on of the criminal classes.

He should have been a happy man. He loved his work, spent as many hours in his office as he possibly could, only reluctantly leaving it to return home in the evening to a plain meal served by his housekeeper. But he was not happy. Not at all.

The problem was that people were so lackadaisical about settling their legal accounts. Were everyone to pay him what they owed tomorrow, he would be a rich man, comfortable at least. But they did not. It had to be said that his father, John Crawshaw Brandon, had been somewhat dilatory on the work front. He'd been far more interested in catching char and pike from the lake than sitting at his desk. Fascinated by points of law he may have been, yet he had shown little head for business, certainly none for turnover. In consequence, matters had suffered interminable delays, clients had grown restless and ultimately taken their business elsewhere.

It had all been most unsatisfactory.

It had fallen to him, Philip, to build the practice up again. Not an easy task. Sometimes he was so busy he was fortunate if he had time to prepare any bills at all, let alone reminders. Even when he put Miss Henshaw on the task of ringing people up it brought a poor response. They were happy enough for him to solve their problems, their disputes with neighbours, convey their house or dispose of their dearly departed, but balked when it came to paying the bill.

So he had taken the matter into his own capable hands. Here and there, not too much and only where there was no risk of it being noted, he managed to keep his pockets fat and his own bank account healthy.

It was while serving in the army that he had learned there were short cuts to everything. One did not have to tread the twisting and thorny path when there might be a smoother, more advantageous route. Great care of course, must always be taken.

The McArthur estate had been unusually easy since the nephew was as flexible in his code of conduct as Philip himself.

McArthur had no more wish than his solicitor to declare the true extent of his aunt's estate. A sum had been agreed upon which would satisfy the Inland Revenue and leave the nephew nicely in pocket. Should the beneficiary of this good fortune choose to show his appreciation by way of a small gratuity, was that any fault of Philip

Brandon? No indeed. It was no more than common business practice, after all.

Even were the client not amenable, he usually found a way to benefit, without ever stepping too far outside the grey fringes of the law. Thanks to the two wars there was no shortage of widows and probate always proved delightfully lucrative.

Certainly more so than divorce, which he disliked as it was messy and troublesome. Philip hated disagreement of any kind, and rarely recommended such a course of action for his clients. Divorce was bad for society. A woman's duty was to her husband. Yet there was something about a vulnerable woman that appealed to him, and he was always happy to counsel and advise.

The day passed much the same as any other, sunnier than most which added to his unusually cheerful mood. It was one of those rare, brilliant Lakeland days when the lake glimmered, the mountains were wreathed in a soft blue mist, which made you think summer might actually arrive at any moment. It would be a pity, he decided, to waste it.

At lunchtime, instead of eating his sandwiches at his desk as usual, Philip decided to take them down to the lake.

On Fridays he usually treated himself to a ham salad at the Marina Hotel where one had a grand view of the lake. His budget, however, did not stretch to making this a daily ritual. One day he meant that to change.

He was sitting on a bench, quietly enjoying his fish paste sandwiches and trying to avoid the rapacious ducks, when he saw her.

She was not alone, but Philip cast the other girl scarcely a glance. His gaze was riveted upon a mass of black curls. Some attempt had been made to hold the hair back from her face with a scarlet ribbon but tendrils of curls were determinedly springing free, bursting joyously all across her brow and upon the curve of each soft round cheek. His gaze shifted to the smooth golden skin, the dark, violet eyes like great bruises in a perfect, heart-shaped face. She moved with such grace it was a joy simply to watch her.

He heard her voice, light and musical, sensed it like a thrill deep inside him as she laughed at something her friend had said.

They were climbing the wooden steps up to an old boathouse and the wind was pressing her straight black skirt about slender, shapely legs. Philip became acutely aware that he was holding his breath.

He sat for a full half hour waiting for them to come out, well past the time he should have returned to the office, but he would have waited twice as long if necessary. An incongruous figure on the bench in his double-breasted, black pinstripe suit, fully buttoned as was right and proper, he tapped one polished toe and then the other.

When he had almost given up hope she burst

out of the boathouse like a small explosion of colour. She wore a bright red duffle-coat, swinging open over her skirt and blouse, and he caught a tantalising glance of a slender figure, voluptuously ripe and blossoming. The outfit, obviously new, looked well against her black hair, and he felt a hard knot of excitement deep in pit of his stomach.

She was laughing as she locked the door, then as she swung round to hug her friend, he saw that she was younger than he had thought by a number of years. The realisation brought a sharp edge of disappointment. How very foolish of him. He should have realised at once. She couldn't be more than seventeen or eighteen. Less perhaps.

Loneliness swamped him and he moved not a muscle as he watched her walk away.

He had to fight hard to pull back his shoulders and get up from the bench, dusting off his immaculate trousers. Carefully folding his empty sandwich paper, Philip slipped it into his briefcase, ready to use again tomorrow. He told himself he was scarcely into his thirties and not unattractive to women.

He thought of Felicity. Sweet, darling Felicity with her pale blonde beauty, her illness and fragility making him love her all the more. Felicity had been pure as well as beautiful not like most of the women he came across through his work, who played fast and loose with some poor fool of a husband.

But Felicity had died, leaving him alone in an

unfeeling world with a memory that remained a raw wound. What was he thinking of even to be looking at another girl, let alone one so young?

He had his practice, didn't he? His home may be a touch too modest and further from the lake than he would like, but it was bought and paid for and one day he would improve upon it. No mortgages for him. Too disagreeable. Then there was his sailing dinghy. He was thinking of having a new one built, something classy and fast. He'd never yet won in the annual Yacht Club races but he meant to, very soon.

Philip Brandon told himself he was going places. All he needed was a touch more security.

He straightened his shoulders, replaced his trilby hat so as not to disturb his carefully combed dark hair, and without a backward glance walked smartly from the lakeside and back to the sanctuary of his office. He might make eating his lunch on the lakeshore bench a regular feature of his routine. When the weather was pleasant.

'Leave? How can you leave? Your dad wouldn't hear of it, I can tell you that for nothing.' Renee's orange mouth drooped at each corner, making her look like a comical clown as she gazed woefully from one girl to the other. The budgie in the corner started to squawk, reacting to the alarm in her voice.

'I can please myself what I do,' Jan said, flicking back her hair and raising her voice above the din.

'You didn't ask my permission when you moved in here, did you?'

'I didn't have to. Your dad wanted me to marry him, so that was that.'

'You wanted an easy life.' Jan stormed over to the cage and flicked the cover over it. Blessed silence fell.

'What if I did?' Renee dropped her voice to a belligerent mumble. 'My dad thought it part of his daily routine to batter the walls with my head. So what if I did want to get away from that? It's not a crime, is it? And Jimmy loves me.' She gave a great gulping sob.

Both Renee and Jan were so close to tears that Lissa instinctively put out a hand to each of them, wanting to calm the situation. 'Have you thought, Renee, that it might be for the best? You and Jimmy need more time on your own. We feel a bit in the way with you two so obviously in love.' She cleared her throat. 'Anyway, we won't be going for a week or two. There's a heap of work to do on the boat-house before it's habitable. Cleaning it out for one thing, then painting it and finding something to sleep on and cook with. Simple things like that.' She laughed as if she'd made a joke. 'You'll have plenty of time to get used to the idea.'

Renee's eyes filled with a sudden gush of tears, the effect upon her mascara-coated lashes quite catastrophic. Black rivers ran down her face, adding to the clown-like effect. 'What about me then, after you've gone? I can't cook,' she sobbed.

'I've never so much as boiled an egg in me life. Even me mother didn't do much cooking. Bread and dripping, sausage and HP beans, that's what we were brought up on. He'll kill me, he will. You know how Jimmy likes his food.' She opened her mouth into a wide orange oval and began to wail.

Incensed, Jan almost shouted her response. 'He won't do any such thing. My dad would never hurt a flea, let alone a woman. You should have realised you'd be expected to do cooking and cleaning and such like,' she said, astounded by the state her teenage stepmother was getting into, howling like a banshee and shaking her head in despair.

'He said I didn't have to worry my pretty little head about such things,' Renee sobbed, 'cause you'd never get wed. You're too plain, he said, what with your straight brown hair and squinting at folk all the time.'

There was a small stunned silence, although Renee, blithely unaware of the insult she had voiced, continued to howl, working herself up to a fine pitch. Her face looked like one of the new zebra crossings.

Seeing her friend quite bereft for words, Lissa spoke for her. 'Jan is not at all plain. As for the cooking . . . well, I could teach you.'

The wailing stopped instantly and they all sagged visibly with relief. 'Could you?' Renee asked, wonder in her voice.

'Of course. Meg taught me. She's a very good

cook is Meg. Steak and game pie, Cumberland sausage, mutton and tatie hot pot. Gingerbread. Oh, and her Rum Nicky Pudding is to die for.' Lissa stopped. Both girls were standing gazing at her open-mouthed.

'You a chef or summat? How can anyone have so much food with the war and the rationing and all?'

'I lived on a farm. We produced our own.' Her mouth was watering and her heart beating fast at the memory of the big warm kitchen at Broombank. She was back sitting at the huge scrubbed pine table, Meg laughing as she whipped and stirred, Tam tasting and teasing.

What was she doing here? She belonged with them, on her very own fells where the wind blew free. Where you could swim in the tarn, stay out all night, and drive your foster mother to a miscarriage. Lissa shook the image away. This was her new life and she meant to make it a good one.

Over the following weeks Lissa taught Renee all she knew. It became clear that no one had ever troubled to teach the girl anything in her life before. And judging from what Lissa learned of her home background, was it any wonder if she had grabbed the first kind man who had come along?

Lissa searched her mind for Meg's recipes and soon Jimmy thought himself the luckiest man in Carreckwater.

'All I want is a quiet life,' he kept saying, tucking into his food with relish. To be fair, he was most appreciative of Renee's efforts, patting her cheek fondly if she burned something or the meat was tough. 'Better next time, my poppet.' Which increased Renee's confidence and made her more adventurous.

'I'll have to buy meself one of those striped pinnies like Philip Harben,' she said.

In an odd sort of way, seeing their happiness made Lissa feel more insecure. Would anyone ever love her so completely? Jan was happier though, as she no longer felt so put upon.

A letter came from Meg, asking her to visit, but Lissa wrote back saying that she was too hard at work renovating the old boathouse and converting it into a flat.

They scrubbed and scoured, painted window frames and doors and sewed rag rugs from scraps of old clothing. The panelled walls needed little more attention than a good sweep, banishing cobwebs and running spiders by the score.

Furniture was still hard to come by so Lissa scoured house sales and auction rooms and came up with a bed each, two chairs, and a small table which they covered with green oil cloth. The cooker was the most difficult but they found an old one on a stall in the market, along with a few pots and pans.

It was well into the summer season by the time the boathouse was ready for occupation and they moved in with great anticipation. 'Isn't it lovely?' Jan cried, pink cheeked with excitement. 'I'm so glad you came to Carreckwater, Lissa. So glad we're friends.'

'Me too,' she said, pleased with their efforts, wondering if at last she had found somewhere to put down roots. Lissa could scarcely believe their good fortune in finding it. She loved it already. They could sit in their tiny living room and gaze out across the lake to Wetherlam, Tilberthwaite Fell and the Langdales. They could watch the visitors bobbing up and down in their clinker-built boats, see families picnicking on the small island. Life was suddenly fun again and Lissa wanted to sing with joy.

'I just know we are going to be happy here.'

'Oh, me too,' echoed Jan, giving her impish, triangular smile. 'This is a new beginning, a new life.'

Yes, thought Lissa. A new beginning sounded good.

A second letter came from Meg and this one made Lissa sit up and take notice. She read it in the stock room while she had her morning coffee break and found herself gaping with shock. She had to read it twice more to be sure that she had it right.

Ashlea belonged to her. Meg had written, plain as day. Jeffrey Ellis, the man she had always referred to as an honorary uncle but was in fact her grandfather, had left her the freehold.

Meg's letter gave the details:

It has only this moment come to light as the family solicitors, as trustees, have written to ask if you wish the rent to be reviewed. It is a safe tenancy, still in my father's name of course, and he couldn't be got out unless you wished to live there yourself. I know, darling, that you would never deprive Sally Ann and her family of a home. But it could be purchased for Nick, in Sally Ann's name of course, and she wonders if you would consider selling? Are you planning on coming on a visit soon? I do hope so. It seems so long since we saw you. You could tell us your decision then. Are you enjoying your new job? I must come and see your boathouse.
All my love, Meg.'

So her grandmother had kept this secret from her? A creeping sickness came over Lissa at the thought. Not that she wanted Ashlea, or any other farm, but the thought that Rosemary Ellis had callously deprived her of her inheritance, and Nick of an opportunity to purchase his home, out of pure spite, was quite beyond imagining. Nor did she feel any more inclined to trust her grandmother's solicitors, who only had Rosemary's interests at heart.

Lissa folded the paper and thrust it into her

pocket. She thought about this news all day, then as they walked home that evening, asked Jan for help.

'Who is that solicitor Derry works for?'

Surprised by the question, Jan gave her an odd look. 'Why do you want to know?'

'I need some advice. Family stuff, you know.'

Jan was at once sympathetic. 'Oh, sorry. He's called Philip Brandon. Has an office near Benthwaite Cross. Bit of a stick-in-the-mud but I doubt he'd overcharge you, being a friend of Derry's. Shall I ask him to fix an appointment for you?' Her brown eyes were troubled, filled with curiosity.

Lissa decided the less either of them knew about this, the better, If she started talking about an inheritance, they might get the idea she was rich and nothing could be further from the truth. 'That's OK. I'll call in one lunchtime. See if he's got a minute.'

CHAPTER 5

Philip couldn't believe his good fortune. 'Please take a seat, Miss Turner.' His mind whirled through the possible reasons for her visit. Close to, she was even more attractive than his first glimpse of her by the lake. Young and fresh, with her hair in a swinging pony tail, the same wayward tendrils framing her face in a most beguiling manner, her beautiful slender body prettily decked out in a pink shirt-waister dress. 'What can I do for you?' He offered her his most charming smile. 'Coffee?'

'No, thank you. I don't have much time as I must get back to work.'

She looked uneasy, embarrassed by whatever had brought her here. Philip Brandon's heart sank. Surely she couldn't be married, seeking a divorce from a rake of a husband? No, she was far too young. He held out a chair, not taking his eyes from her as she sat. Her legs were sweet perfection, long and smooth-skinned. He slipped his spectacles into his top pocket and realised with a jolt that she'd launched into some tale and he had missed it.

'I have no wish to keep it. What would I do with a farm? But Nick is an old friend. There was a time when he might have liked . . . Anyway, I want him to have Ashlea.'

Very gently Philip took her back to the beginning and piece by piece, with the very gentlest questioning, he had the entire life story from her. He guessed that she told more than she'd intended but then he was a sympathetic listener. It was a shock to learn she was only sixteen. Clearly mature for her age. He was astute enough to guess the effect the stigma of illegitimacy would have upon her.

He came round to sit upon the edge of the desk. Pansy eyes looked up into his, brimming with unshed tears and his heart clenched. 'It must have proved such a burden for you. Heart-rending for a sensitive child to feel rejected at birth.'

'You do understand. Oh, I'm so relieved. Few people do, you know.'

He gave her his wise, compassionate smile, debated whether he might take her hand but decided against it. 'Ah, but I am different. Rather like a father confessor or family doctor. You can tell me anything, anything at all and I would not divulge a word of it.'

She warmed to him instantly. 'I'd really like Nick to have Ashlea. He works the land and lives in the house so he deserves it. Can that be done?'

'Nick is presumably your own age, so too young for a mortgage. No bank would consider him.'

'What about Sally Ann?'

'Of course. You could offer her a private mortgage, though farmers are notoriously irregular payers, preferring as they do to deal strictly in cash.'

'Nick is very reliable.'

'I'm sure he is. I should warn you that property with a sitting tenant has a very poor sale value.'

'I don't care about the money. I don't want anything that belongs to the Ellis family. Nothing at all. Do you see?'

'I do. Absolutely.' He paused, hooked his thumbs in the pockets of his waistcoat then went to sit behind his desk again. 'Pardon my saying so but that is a rather short-sighted view. There may be other property, or funds, to come.'

Lissa thought of Larkrigg and of her hard-hearted grandmother. Where would she leave her money? To a daughter whom she considered wicked and undeserving? To a granddaughter she refused to acknowledge? What did it matter? Lissa straightened her spine, smoothed her short white gloves and gave a dry smile.

'It's possible, but unlikely. My grandmother is more likely to leave her property to some charity or other. Probably the church. I sincerely hope so.'

'Not to your mother?' Eyebrows raised in query as he had become very still.

'Who knows? They haven't seen or spoken in years, which gives you some idea what I'm up against.'

'Indeed,' he said thoughtfully and gave a gentle smile. 'How very sad for you.'

'It's all in trust until I come of age and I wondered if there was anything we could do about that?'

'Certainly there is. I could write to the trustees and ask them if they could deal with the matter in this way. They may even agree to transfer the trusteeship of Ashlea to my firm, if I persuade them.' He smiled, as if she had favoured him in some way, then became at once brisk and businesslike as he explained to her, most carefully, the ins and outs of the transaction but finished with a smooth word of advice. 'You should perhaps reconsider your view of the future. Sell Ashlea to your friend by all means but income, from any source, is a valuable asset in today's rapidly changing world. Is there no chance of a reconciliation with your grandmother?'

Lissa stood up, face tight. 'No. That is quite out of the question. She would never . . . Neither would I. Please arrange this matter for me and send me your bill. I have a little money to pay the fee.'

He had offended her. Damn!

Philip led her to the door and risked taking her hand. It felt small and soft. The urge to raise it to his lips was almost overpowering. 'I will carry out your wishes to the letter.'

'I don't want anyone to know about this. Not even Derry. I work with his sister and I'd rather

104

keep my affairs private.' She half glanced through the glass panel, thankful she had chosen a time when he was out at lunch.

'You may rely upon my absolute discretion.'

She smiled at him then, a brilliant, wide, shining smile that revealed perfect white teeth and the smallest, pinkest, most delightful tongue.

'Thanks,' she said, issuing a deep sigh. 'I do appreciate your help. It's a real joy to be able to do something for Nick.'

He gave a light laugh. 'You must be fond of him.'

'Oh, yes. We've always been close. Like family, you know.'

'I can see that you are a girl to whom family is important.' A shadow flickered across her face and he was at once all contrition. 'Oh dear, I seem bent on offending you. How very clumsy of me.' He lifted the hand now and pressed his lips against it. Her skin tasted delicious but he would need to be very patient. 'Forgive me,' he murmured, smiling into her eyes.

Quite unable to help herself, Lissa found herself smiling back, responding to his charm.

As she hurried back to the shop she decided that Philip Brandon was really far more attractive than Derry had led her to believe. And so kind.

It was Derry's idea that they go on a day-long hike the following Sunday, and Lissa and Jan readily agreed. The weather was calm and settled, the sun shining like a big soft round cheese and there were few holidaymakers to disturb the peace so early in the season as they caught the bus out to Skelwith Bridge.

The three of them were sensibly dressed in slacks and warm sweaters, for mountain weather can change even as you are wondering if it might. On their feet the girls wore strong shoes, Derry his favourite boots for he was a keen climber.

Lissa cast him a glance from beneath her lashes. He looked different today in his windcheater and rough cords, woollen socks replacing the hideous lime green, more approachable somehow.

'Do you really go rock climbing?'

He pushed back his shoulders, preening himself, brown eyes glinting with such a cocky arrogance she almost wished she hadn't asked. What a peacock he was. 'Sure, would you like to try?' Lissa haughtily assured him that she would not.

They got off the bus and walked along the lanes to the bridge where there were a few people sitting about having picnics. Where only a short while ago there'd been limp dead grasses, the verges were now clotted with yellow primroses thick as cream. Violets, bluebells and meadowsweet filled the clear mountain air with their fragrant scents. In a few weeks the scene would change yet again and foxgloves, wild roses and ox-eye daisies would have their moment of glory.

Lissa felt the excitement of a day free from the dusty confines of the old fashioned draper's shop.

They walked up a dusty lane by the river that

led up through the quarry work sheds. A few shirt-sleeved men sat joking and whistling as they worked the stones, splitting them on the grain with their special tools.

'This is where they quarry the blue-green slate that makes Westmorland famous,' Derry told her as if she'd never seen such a thing before.

She almost told him that they quarried stone on her fells too, but it sounded too petty. Besides, she'd no wish to think about quarries, or the roads that led to them. Not today.

They stood on the huge flat rocks at Skelwith Force and watched with wonder as the small waterfall rushed down in a cloud of white froth into the river below, swirled around huge boulders which forced it to gush and froth and gather in deep dark pools. It was like a fairy glen, a magic place where a water sprite would be sure to live, reminding Lissa suddenly of that other day in early summer when she and Nick had played their wishing game.

For a moment, homesickness claimed her. It didn't happen so often nowadays and she knew it was foolish for she could visit Broombank at any time, only she rarely did. Transport was a problem and she felt instinctively that she wanted to make a place for herself here first, before she dared risk it. Or she might never have the courage to come back.

After a while they left the force and walked on up the rough footpath, across flat water meadows where the river widened and spread out until it reached Elterwater. Ahead lay some of the most dramatic scenery in Lakeland. Blue-grey crags jagged against the pale sky, dark rocky grandeur dropping precipitously to a thickly wooded fringe of trees below.

'It's like Switzerland,' she said, breathing deeply her delight. 'Or how I imagine Switzerland might look.'

'It's the Langdales, a special place,' Derry said.

They reached the village of Chapel Stile and went on past the school and the post office, and up the big hill. When they grew hot from their walking they pulled off thick sweaters and settled in the lea of a drystone wall to eat their lunch. It felt cool and sheltered, whorls of yellow lichen rough and scratchy on their bare arms. They watched an Orange Tipped butterfly light on a bloom of lady's smock and laughed in delight as a tree pipit descended like a spinning top in a graceful spiral of song.

'Not used to walking?' Derry teased as he saw her catching her breath, and Lissa was infuriated with herself for giving him another opportunity to show off.

'Hardly, I grew up on the fells.' she said scornfully. Her annoyance was made worse by the fact she could feel her cheeks growing warm under his amused gaze. Turning quickly to Jan, she offered more sandwiches, a piece of cake, a sip of water.

Derry made a sound very like soft laughter. 'We

won't go as far as Bowfell today. I don't think Lissa is quite up to it.'

Flushing a deep red Lissa longed to deny it but dare not, for she was indeed tired. It had been a hard week in the shop. Jan settled the matter.

'Thank heaven for that. My legs are like jelly already.'

Proving her worth on a high mountain peak must wait for another day. They set out from Stool End to walk up the broad smooth incline, and after a while Derry made sure Jan was striding ahead, as she so loved to do, so he had Lissa all to himself.

'You don't say much, do you? Are you always so touchy?' he asked. 'Or have I done something to offend?' His voice sounded so genuinely concerned that she was quite taken by surprise. He thought her standoffish, a bit uppity, when all the time she was simply – simply what? Nervous of possible rejection? Something of the sort. She didn't like to think too deeply about it. Lissa only knew that she felt better, safer, when there was a certain distance between herself and others.

'I don't know what you mean.'

'Is it because you think I'm a Ted? It's only a style, you know, not a way of life. I don't beat old ladies over the head with my comb.' Despite herself, Lissa giggled and he gave her an answering grin, lopsided and so full of impish good humour that she very nearly laughed out loud. Derry Colwith might be a bit too full of himself, but he surely wouldn't hurt or offend anyone.

Then he spoiled it all by starting to tell her about the climbs he'd done and how difficult they were.

'And you, being Mr Wonderful, managed them with no difficulty whatsoever,' she said dryly.

He blinked innocently at her. 'How did you guess?'

'Pity you didn't land on your head. Might have knocked some sense into you.' She flounced away, walking so fast he had to run to catch up. He said nothing for a while and for some reason, perhaps to fill the silence, Lissa found herself talking about Broombank and the sheep, Nick and Daniel, and how they had played in the beck as children. Derry listened, asking questions from time to time as if he were really interested. Perhaps he wasn't so bad after all.

Once, he took hold of her hand as she stumbled and a series of tiny shocks ran right through her. Instinctively she lifted her face up to his, violet eyes coaxing and teasing. His stunned expression warned her that she trod on dangerous ground and quickly loosed his hand. But she regretted its loss.

'I think we'd better hurry and catch up with Jan,' she said, increasing her pace. 'What a speed she walks at.'

'Jan loves walking, as I do. We spend days out on the mountains in the summer.' He was staring down at his boots, as if something was troubling him.

'Oh, so did I once,' Lissa agreed.

'Once? Why not now?'

She hesitated, feeling she'd blundered. 'I mean when I was at home.'

'You'll soon get to know and love it here too,' he said sympathetically and she felt emotion suddenly block her throat. She couldn't deal with sympathy.

'I'm not really homesick. Well, sometimes, but it passes.'

'You are going to stay? You won't go home yet, will you?' he asked, sounding suddenly so anxious she glanced up at him in surprise. As their eyes met Lissa felt something warm unfold inside. He seemed to be passing some sort of message to her and her cheeks flooded with heat. Embarrassed, she quickly turned her attention back to setting her feet carefully on the stony path, and for the next several minutes ignored him completely, just to prove to herself that she could.

At the summit they sat on the wiry grass to catch their breath and admire the panorama of mountains. Lingmoor and Wrynose Fell, Tilberthwaite beyond, and Bowfell Links above, achingly green beneath a clear blue sky.

'Isn't it grand?' Jan said, and Lissa, hugging her knees and drinking it all in, had to agree.

'You'll come on another walk some time?' Derry asked, sounding so hopeful she simply couldn't find it in her heart to say no. He rewarded her with a wide beaming smile.

'Great. I knew we'd get on. Knew it the first moment I saw you looking in the shop window.'

111

'Hark at him?' Jan laughed, getting up and dusting down her jeans which were bright green and cropped just below her knee. 'Right, last one down pays for tea.'

'Oh, no,' Lissa mourned, all pride gone. 'I can't rush, really. I'm shattered.'

'There're some clouds gathering,' Derry said. 'Time to make tracks.'

Jan won, of course. She looked like a tiny fairy perched on a stone by the lane. But Derry held his pace to match Lissa's, for which she was truly grateful. She never enjoyed going downhill.

'Don't you think we get on OK? I can see you're not really stuck up. You're just shy. I know you like me, so stop pretending you don't.'

Lissa might have thumped him for this patronising remark but he'd taken her hand again, as if to prove the sincerity of his words and she quite liked the feel of it. He held it tenderly, tracing each of her fingertips with his own. 'Such lovely pearly nails. I certainly like you, Lissa. I like you very much.'

Lissa expelled her breath on a tiny sigh and then his lips were on hers, warm against the cool mountain breeze, tender and deliciously soft. She leaned against him, startled by the pleasing sensations swirling through her.

Somewhere high above a lark sang and her heart lifted with each climbing note.

When the kiss ended he squeezed her fingers,

very gently, and smiled at her with that lovely secret message again passing between them, his brown eyes seeming to dance over her face. She wished, with a piercing sweetness, that he would kiss her again and swayed gently towards him, her head giddy with longing, then quickly pulled back, shocked by her own wantonness.

And when he held on to her hand for the rest of the way down the steep mountain track, Lissa did not pull away.

Afterwards they ate scones and jam and drank tea at the Old Dungeon Ghyll Hotel, which Lissa poured from a silver pot. It was the perfect end to a perfect day.

Summer passed in the blissful pursuit of uncomplicated happiness. It seemed to be filled with raspberries and ice cream, happy laughter and daring pursuits.

They often took one of the many footpaths or trails that traversed the heights around Carreckwater, Ambleside and Rydal. From those windy tops the visitors looked liked ants, riding the toy steamer up and down the lake.

Derry's friends would often come along too, bringing their girlfriends to form a happy, relaxed group. They would spend whatever spare time they had either on the lake messing about in boats and dinghies, or high on the fells. Loughrigg was a favourite walk. Or they would explore the eastern sides of the lake, even so far as Jenkyn's Crag, from where they had a wonderful view of the whole Windermere valley. Once they climbed right to the summit of Wansfell Pike, relishing the sparkle of clear fresh air after the dusty days confined to shop and office.

Derry made no move to repeat that magical kiss, which proved how little it had meant to him. Lissa took care to studiously avoid being anywhere alone with him, preferring to keep a safe distance between them at all times. She watched the other girls hang on his arm and told herself Derry Colwith was not her sort at all.

If she saw something like disappointment in Derry's eyes she refused to let it trouble her. He was only playing a game, wanting to notch her up on his belt along with his other conquests. She was not so stupid.

In July she paid a fleeting visit home to Broombank, and found she could return quite happily to Carreckwater. She worked hard in the shop during the week, and the Sundays she wasn't out with the gang she spent tidying the boathouse, or resting by the lake where she loved to hear the slip-slap of water against the shingle. Cooking a good meal for herself and Jan.

Once Lissa saw Philip Brandon eating his lunch on a bench by the lakeshore and she stopped for a chat. He seemed embarrassed to be caught doing anything so human as eating and she very nearly giggled out loud, only that would have been unkind.

'I've been meaning to call upon you,' he said in a rush and she took him to mean concerning the sale of Ashlea.

She was anxious suddenly. 'I should have called on you. I'd rather you didn't come to the shop.'

He looked attentive and sympathetic. 'Of course. Then perhaps you could call at the office one evening next week?'

'No problems I hope? Meg wrote to say that Nick was happy with the price.'

'Everything is splendid. I need you only to sign some papers. Though I'm sure you could have got a touch more for it.'

Lissa shook her head. 'I told you. The family have lived there for donkey's years. It wouldn't have been fair.'

Mr Brandon very kindly assured her that she might call upon him at any time, should she feel the need of advice. Lissa thought how much smarter he looked now summer was here. He'd stopped wearing that old fashioned trilby and given up the dull black suits. Today he was wearing pale grey and looked quite dashing.

'You'll soon think of me as a friend, I hope,' he said, and Lissa felt grateful and humbled that he could spare her so much time from his busy schedule.

But even as she talked to him, her eyes lifted to scan the path that led out from the church yard through St Margaret's Walk, in case Derry should appear as he sometimes did at lunchtime. 'Must get to work,' she said, backing off. 'I'll settle my account with you next week, if you'd like to have it ready.'

Then she whirled about and skipped away on light steps, looking so young and carefree it made his heart ache to watch her. He wished he'd thought to ask her out. What was the matter with him? He'd missed an ideal opportunity. Wished she'd look back and give him a bright wave then he could call her back, perhaps offer to take her for a sail.

But Lissa was too busy wondering where Derry was and feeling ridiculously disappointed that he hadn't come.

But then why should she care? He was far too interested in himself anyway, in her opinion. If he wasn't talking about his music and his guitar he was planning how he would win the Yacht Club races which were held every year in the first week of September.

'Have you ever won one'!' she had asked him.

'No,' he'd said, the light of battle in his eyes. 'But I intend to. This is my year. I can feel it.'

When September came and the races were held it was Philip Brandon who won, as apparently he usually did. His yacht was so smart and fast Lissa didn't wonder at it. Derry was disappointed, and vowed to persuade his father to help build him a better boat for next year.

'I'd give anything just to win one race, so he

couldn't lord it over me in the office and make me feel so small. If I got a boat like his I could enter in the same class and maybe beat him.' Derry's eyes lit up. 'God, that would be something.'

'He wouldn't like being beaten by his clerk,' Jan warned. 'I should stick with your dinghy if I were you.'

Lissa kept quiet, not understanding all the fuss. Later, Jan asked her to come to the Yacht Club dance and hear Derry and his group play but she refused.

'I don't think it's really me.'

'Aw, come on,' Jan urged. She moved about their small home, closing windows against the growing chill of the September evening, clicking the latch on the door then shutting it firmly against the world. Lissa had lit the lamp and it was cosy here, by the fire. 'He won't take no for an answer, not this time. The group has never played at the Yacht Club before and they've been asked to fill in at the interval while the main band is taking a break. They're a bit toffee-nosed up there, more into trad jazz, and he says he needs all the support he can get.'

'Do you mean that rock 'n' roll stuff?' Lissa asked, feeling herself weaken. She wished Derry no harm, for all his arrogance.

'They play skiffle mainly, but some rock 'n' roll too. The dancing is pretty much the same.'

'You go. I'll be quite happy here. I could start to crochet that cover for the old arm chair.'

Jan pulled a face. 'Or knit socks?'

Lissa's lips curved into a smile. 'Don't mock. People in my dale are good at knitting socks. And sweaters. Meg and I spent hours each evening doing it. Sally Ann too.'

'What a talented family you have.'

Lissa grinned. 'Not really, there's not much else to do up there.'

'Well, we don't knit socks in Carreckwater. In the evening we jive and rock. So do come, you'll be an old woman in bed socks soon enough.'

'But I don't know how.' There was a tremor of longing in Lissa's voice and Jan burst out laughing.

'Is that what this shyness is all about? Right, no time like the present.' She selected 'Hound Dog' from her collection of 78s and put it on the record player. The music rang out with a tinny fervour, echoing wonderfully in the wooden building. What followed was the most hilarious hour and a half of Lissa's life. She twirled and shook, jived and rocked, till her head was spinning and both girls fell gasping on to the rag rug.

But she agreed to attend her first dance.

CHAPTER 6

T he dance floor was crowded when they arrived at the Yacht Club and Lissa very nearly changed her mind and went straight home again. She hadn't wanted to come in the first place. Now they'd actually arrived, fighting for space against a tide of other girls in a stuffy cloakroom, Jan was urging her to put on some pink lipstick.

Lissa looked doubtful. 'I've never worn lipstick.' But seeing Jan's expression, obediently took out a small mirror from her bag and complied. She did feel rather good in a lavender linen dress that had a small Peter Pan collar and turned back cuffs on the short capped sleeves. Its skirt was full, the waistline fitting snugly, nipped in with a broad black belt.

Jan nudged her. 'Look at these toffs coming in, all dressed up to the nines in their little bow ties. Lord, they look like penguins.' She started to giggle. 'I can't see them getting up and dancing to our Derry's racket, can you?'

Since Lissa hadn't yet heard him play so felt unable to comment but they did seem somewhat forbidding, very stiff and formal. The two girls put their cloakroom tickets inside their shoes and headed for the dance floor.

It was crowded, hot and stuffy with a big silver ball hanging from the ceiling that sent little coloured lights all over the walls as it turned. The band was playing 'Love Is A Many Splendoured Thing', and a host of stout dowagers in stiff taffeta and satin were dancing, elbows at 45 degrees, with even stouter men in evening dress.

There were girls in long dresses with elbow-length gloves and matching satin slippers, and others like themselves in bright summer dresses. Such a rainbow of bouncy net petticoats that Lissa wondered how some couples could get near enough to dance together.

When the dance ended everyone stood about gossiping, as there weren't enough chairs for everyone to sit down. Then the band struck up a cha-cha and there was much chatter and laughter as people started following each other to pick up the steps.

Jan went off to dance with a young man with a toothy grin while Lissa hid in a corner, hoping no one would notice her. It was a world far removed from the quiet fells of Broombank. Would she ever have the courage to get on to that floor herself? The prospect seemed too daunting.

A waltz followed, then a succession of quicksteps. Lissa could see Jan changing partners, clearly enjoying herself while she herself declined every offer. Privately she wished Derry would come and ask her to dance but knew he was too busy getting his skiffle group organised. She longed for the interval when she would see him up on stage.

The memory of that kiss rose in her mind, making her stomach go all wobbly. Yet she knew for a fact he'd been out with several girls since, so it was just as well she hadn't thought too much of it.

Even so, she wanted tonight to go well for him and didn't envy the skiffle group facing this lot. Lissa hoped he wasn't dressed too outlandishly. Somehow she knew that she would be embarrassed if he looked too much the Teddy Boy.

'Would you do me the honour of this dance?'

Startled, Lissa was about to refuse when she looked up into a familiar face. 'Oh, Mr Brandon.' He looked different, smartly attired in evening dress with a silk shirt and cummerbund. His best bib and tucker, as Jan would say.

'It's a slow waltz, not too difficult. I noticed you don't seem too keen on dancing but you look far too lovely to hide away in a corner. Perhaps you would care to try? I'll be most gentle with you, I promise.' He smiled, which made him look younger somehow. Very debonair.

'I'm not really hiding,' Lissa protested, smiling shyly up at him. She didn't want to appear a complete fool. 'Well, perhaps I was, a bit. Thanks. I'll give it a try if you don't mind my two left feet.' She placed her hand in his and let him lead her out on to the dance floor.

'No legal matters tonight. Agreed?'

'Agreed,' she said, her smile warming.

He guided her with perfect expertise right around the floor, not once crashing into any other couples. Nor did he step on her toes or attempt to take liberties by pulling her too close. Lissa began to relax and enjoy herself, clinging tightly to his shoulders as he whirled her around. She couldn't help noticing that his dark eyes rested upon her in a most admiring way.

When the music ended he didn't take her back to her seat as expected but stood smiling down at her, chatting about the weather, saying how good the band were, waiting for the music to start again.

He talked to her all through the next dance and listened most carefully to her replies, as if he were truly interested. Though what he asked and how she answered Lissa could not afterwards recall.

'You must remember something,' Jan insisted as they exchanged notes over a Coca-Cola in the bar. 'You do realise who you were dancing with, don't you?'

Lissa looked puzzled. 'Yes, of course. Philip Brandon. What of it?'

'He's not normally one for dancing. You must have caught his eye.'

'Don't be silly.' Lissa felt herself flushing.

'He's a very good dancer as a matter of fact. A real gentleman.'

'He never goes out these days, though he used to at one time. Or so Derry says.' Jan pulled Lissa close to whisper in her ear against the loud chatter of voices all about them, and above the music coming from the other room. 'He was engaged, just after the war, to a girl called Felicity. Only she had some mysterious illness or other. Very highly strung and delicate apparently. He was supposed to be absolutely devoted to her but she died.' Jan's myopic eyes were wide as she nodded at Lissa's expression of horror. 'Found her drowned in the lake, just like the poor mad girl in that fairy story.'

'What fairy story? You mean Ophelia? That was Shakespeare, not a fairy story,' Lissa laughed. 'Are you telling me the truth, Jan?'

'Course I am.' Jan looked affronted. 'Just because I'm not informed on books and stuff, like you, doesn't mean I don't know the truth about life and death.'

'Sorry. When did she die?'

'About three years back.'

A wave of compassion for Philip Brandon washed through her. Why was life filled with pain? 'How terrible. No wonder he looks sad.'

As they walked back on to the dance floor Lissa's eyes circled the room and found him gazing across at her. She turned quickly away, blushing in scarlet confusion.

'He's been a lonely bachelor ever since, so watch out. Don't get mixed up with him,' Jan said.

'Why not? He looks harmless enough.'

Jan wrinkled up her tiny nose. 'He's thirty.'

'Then he's probably learned a bit of sense,' Lissa smartly replied.

As luck would have it, Philip Brandon chose that moment to ask for another dance. 'How are you on the tango?'

'My favourite dance for getting in a muddle,' said Lissa, and cocked a cheeky grin at Jan's stiff-faced disapproval as he led her out on to the floor.

'But have you any sense, lass?' Jan murmured.

The band departed at the end of the square tango. Lissa and Jan held their breath as Derry's Skifflers sprinted on to the stage. Would he be successful? Would the Yacht Club members like him?

Lissa's heart swelled with pride. He was dressed in smart narrow black trousers topped with a red silk shirt shot with silver thread, and a black bow tie. He carried a guitar which he started to pluck with something he held in his hand. Jan explained it was a pick, to save his fingers.

'You should have seen them when he first started to learn. Made them bleed it did.' But Lissa wasn't listening. She was swaying to the lilt of the music, a Lonnie Donnegan number, thrilled by the skill with which Derry played, the way his hips swayed to the beat of the music. He looked so good up there, different from the young man in cords and sweater. It was hard to work out what kind of a person Derek Colwith really was.

Her eyes shone, her smile widened, and she nodded her head and tapped her pointed toes in time to the music. It was pulsing and irresistible. Yet the dance floor remained empty.

There were five in the group. One other guitar, played by Tony who strummed the chords while Derry picked out the melody. John, who rattled a washboard with dancing fingers tipped with silver thimbles. Another boy was getting a surprisingly rhythmic and pulsing beat from a single string attached to a tea chest and broom handle, while the fifth member of the group played his heart out on a set of drums. Even if Lissa had not known the hours they'd spent in practice she would have been able to tell. They were good, no doubt about it, they deserved to be appreciated.

'Why didn't I come before?' she shouted to Jan, clapping her hands in time to the beat. 'They're great.'

Jan grinned delightedly. 'Told you. Think of all those dances you've missed, sitting at home being sad.'

Lissa realised Jan had guessed her unhappiness but had made no comment on it. But she wasn't miserable now. Oh no, this was glorious, this was living. Just to listen to this music made you feel happy.

She glanced about the room and found that the stuffy, over formal Yacht Club types were not even paying any attention to the skiffle group playing their hearts out. They stood about in tight little groups, their backs to the stage as they chatted to each other and laughed too loud. It was as if the group didn't exist.

'Why aren't they dancing?' forgetting that only

a short time ago she had been the retiring wall-flower, reluctant to join in.

Jan's face was grim. 'They wanted a trad jazz group in the interval and since they didn't get one, they're determined to make their feelings known. They like to imagine themselves above this sort of music. Derry was afraid it might be like this. If no one dances, the MC will get fed up and could sack the group on the spot. Then they mightn't get paid and certainly wouldn't be asked again.'

The prospect of Derry failing, of not being liked by this crowd, had not until that moment occurred to Lissa.

'Then we must do something.'

'What can we do?'

'We must *make* them dance,' Lissa said.

'Oh, yeah? How? Brought your magic wand, princess?'

Lissa spoke without even thinking, aware only of the expression of pain and discomfort that was tightening Derry's face, of the faltering beat as unease began to affect his confidence. 'If no one else will dance, then we must. We'll shame them into it.'

'Go out there alone, you mean?' Jan sounded appalled.

'Come on, don't just stand there. Action is called for.' The two girls' eyes met and mischievous excitement bubbled out of Lissa. She could have been that young girl again, daring Nick to catch her a jar of fish.

Jan hesitated, glancing anxiously at the empty

dance floor, the stiff backs turned resolutely away. 'We'd look a proper pair of clucks dancing out there all on our own. All eyes upon us.'

Lissa tilted her chin. 'We won't be on our own though, will we? Your brother is out there already.'

A slight pause, then a grim smile. 'Too right he is. OK, you're on. Let's see how good my teaching was.'

The two girls stepped out on to the floor and began to jive. Not a moment too soon it seemed. The MC was already looming close, the music having lost its excitement, and everyone was expecting Derry's Skifflers to be evicted at any moment. The whole room held its breath with anticipation, liking nothing better that a little fracas to liven up the evening.

Derry, who a moment ago would have welcomed being struck down by a bolt of lightning, missed a beat as the girls came on to the floor. Then, beaming his delight, yelled, 'Come on, lads, let's give it to them.' He started singing and thrumming for all he was worth, backed by the renewed enthusiasm of his group.

'We'll give it everything we've got,' Jan gasped, crooking her arm and catching Lissa expertly as she spun her round. They made a colourful, arresting sight in their pretty cotton frocks and can-can petticoats showing just the right amount of shapely leg as they twirled about. Not a male eye in the room missed one moment of the dance.

By the time the two girls had rock 'n' rolled a

second time around the dance floor they came close to the dais where Lissa caught the full force of Derry's lopsided smile. He winked at her and she felt again that lovely warm feeling flow within her, that secret message flash between them as if only they existed.

Now some of the audience were smiling, picking up the beat as they started to clap.

'They think we're the floor show. We ought to get some of them up,' Jan whispered, gasping for breath as they swirled and rocked and skipped about the waxed floor.

'Oh, goodness.' Lissa hadn't bargained for this. 'D'you think we should?'

'Come on. Don't weaken now. I'm game if you are.'

So they split up, Jan dashing off to choose a rather good-looking young man who had danced with her earlier. For a moment Lissa felt stranded, alone in the centre of the floor with all eyes upon her.

Then she became aware of a particular pair of eyes, of a dark, familiar face, and she crossed the floor in a whirl of floating colour to stand before Philip Brandon.

'Would you do me the honour of this dance?' she asked, very properly, face alight with laughter.

In the normal course of events Philip Brandon would have refused instantly. Not for the world would he ever risk setting himself up as a stooge. For him to rock 'n' roll was unthinkable. But this girl was giving him such a radiant smile, such a delightful beckoning in her beautiful eyes that he could not refuse. Besides, he was flattered that she'd chosen him, and wanted everyone to see that.

'You must show me what to do,' he groaned, taking her hand and following her on to the floor.

'I'll be very gentle with you,' she teased, and they both laughed at her repetition of his own words. As she turned into his arms he noted the firm roundness of her young breasts, the smiling pink mouth that he had a sudden urge to kiss. His arm felt extremely comfortable around her trim waist. 'Take my hands. I'll show you the basic step,' Lissa said. 'It's very easy. Lean on this foot, then back on the other and do a kind of wiggle. Like this. Do you see?'

'Yes,' he said, eyes on her swaying hips. 'I do.'

Moments later the dance floor was filled with happy, laughing people. Even the fat dowagers in regal satin and swinging pearls were attempting to learn the steps of this new-fangled dance and loving every minute of it.

'Thank you,' he said at the end, dark grey eyes on her flushed face. 'I really enjoyed that. You made me feel young again.'

She looked surprised. 'You are young. At least . . .' She shrugged her shoulders in a captivatingly elegant gesture. 'I never think age is of any importance, do you?'

He held her close for just a shade too long, the pressure of his fingers at her waist strangely compelling, before letting her go with obvious reluctance. 'You don't know how happy it makes me to hear you say that.'

Lissa was thoughtful as she watched him walk away. Were the idea not entirely silly she might have imagined be was making a pass. But then Derry and the group bounded up and she forgot all about Philip Brandon.

'How about that?' Derry cried. Lissa was astonished to find herself gathered into his arms. The scent of his hot skin against her cheek was heady and for a moment she wondered if she dared hug him back but he'd let her go before she'd made up her mind. 'That was great. Thanks.'

He hugged Jan with even greater vigour, face flushed with triumph. 'That was brave of you, Sis.'

'It was Lissa's idea You can thank her, not me.'

Derry cast Lissa a thoughtful glance then took out his comb and started to adjust his quiff as if the embrace had ruffled it. 'They loved it, didn't they? Did you see the young girls come up to the stage afterwards? Screaming and crying, some of them were.'

'We saw them,' Lissa said, an unusual tartness to her tone, eyes upon his laughing face.

He winked at her. 'Didn't make you jealous then?'

'Why should it?' Deliberately cool,

The pressure of his strong body against hers had felt delicious, better than she had ever imagined. It really felt quite good to be wanted. If only for a moment.

She longed for Derry to stay, to ask her to dance and hold her close again, but from the corner of her eye she saw Philip Brandon approaching. He took hold of her hand as if he owned her and she very nearly protested. But remembering what a good sport he had been she bit her lip, smiled, and went meekly with him on to the dance floor, acutely aware of Derry's eyes piercing her back.

She could barely wait for the dance to be over before excusing herself and hurrying to Derry. Only she was too late, he had gone. To get changed, Jan said.

'They're to play again later. The MC has arranged a second interval specially. They're going for a quick pint now, Derry says.' She raised disbelieving brows. 'Never had a quick drink in his life, mind.'

Keen disappointment bit into Lissa. 'That means we won't see them until after the dance then?'

Jan raised surprised eyebrows as she glanced at her friend but said nothing, even when Lissa, catching the expression, blushed furiously. Then suddenly he was there, at her elbow, and her heart jolted, shocking her by the astounding affect he had upon her.

'Hi,' he said. 'How was the dance?'

'Fine, thanks.' She could feel herself shaking. Not that Derry noticed. A group of young girls hovered close and half his attention was upon them, a smile curving one corner of his mouth, self-satisfaction lurking in the deep brown eyes. 'Coming for a drink?' he asked, his gaze suddenly switching to Lissa, then flicking over to include his sister and back to Lissa again.

Heart beating rapidly, she was about to accept when she saw one of the girls, a blonde with forget-me-not blue eyes who couldn't be a day over fifteen, edge closer. Derry turned his head and winked at the girl who gave a tiny squeal of delight and at once came to hang upon his arm. When he turned back to Lissa, he was grinning from ear to ear.

'We have to be quick because Tony's broken a string so we must fix a new one and tune it in with mine before we go on again.'

'Then don't let me keep you.' Lissa's tone was frosty, as if she couldn't care less what he did.

His smile faded. 'What's biting you?'

She saw him shake his arm free of the girl but it was too late. Lissa had seen the pleasure it gave him. 'I don't drink beer,' she said, in her loftiest tone.

'Fine. Well, I haven't brought any champagne.' Then he glanced down at the blonde still hovering close. 'Come on then, love. I bet you drink beer.'

'Ooh, yes,' she squealed, in a poor imitation of Marilyn Monroe. Derry glared at Lissa for another half second then took a step back, evidently itching to be gone. 'If you two want walking home you'll have to wait. It'll be late by the time we've changed and cleared away.'

'And you've signed autographs for all your adoring young fans,' Lissa said, while Jan watched the growing tension with amusement.

132

'Yeah, maybe that too. Any objections?'

'You can take as long as you like. It's no concern of mine. We certainly don't need you to see us home,' Lissa haughtily informed him, determined to let him know she wasn't hanging around waiting for any favours.

His eyes narrowed as he glared at her. 'Maybe you've got an offer already?'

'Maybe I have,' she said, hating him for letting her down, wishing he'd take her in his arms and tell her he wanted to be only with her, not this foolish young blonde. But she was done with wishing, wasn't she? 'I haven't gone short of partners so far.'

'So I noticed. Suit yourself.' And pushing back his ridiculously wide shoulders, he strolled away, the fifteen-year-old blonde scurrying after him.

'Arrogant young fool,' said Jan, crisply. 'Still, at least we saved him from a dire death, eh? Fun, wasn't it?'

'Yes,' Lissa said, swallowing bitter tears of disappointment. 'At least we did that.'

So when Philip Brandon asked her for the last waltz she accepted, and afterwards let him walk her home.

He judged the moment of their meeting with a perfection that owed more than a little to careful planning. But then Philip Brandon approved of planning, of order and organisation. He liked perfection.

Lissa was perfection. From the sweet oval of her

133

face, the curves of her slender body, to the last curl on her beautiful head.

He could see her sitting on a stone wall by the lake, her head bent over a letter she was writing as he willed the fickle breeze not to change direction at just the wrong moment. The yacht tacked bravely across the lake as if knowing its own destiny, skimming fast and sure across the waves.

Philip swung the jib round and brought the little boat safely to shore with well-judged skill.

'Ahoy there,' he called. 'Fancy a sail?'

She glanced up from her work, her expression vague and unfocused. Then as they fixed upon him, the smile of recognition that followed was his reward. 'Mr Brandon.'

She seemed lost for words and he longed for the ability to make some witticism, a little quip that would remind her of the fun they'd had in their attempts at rock 'n' roll, and of his prowess in the yacht race. But he was not good at quips. They were not his forte.

'It's a lovely evening,' was all he could manage. He was quite close to her by this time, the tiny yacht bobbing gently up and down, the clear water slapping against the boat's sides. 'I did promise you a sail and this is probably the last chance we'll get. I'll be laying her up for winter soon.'

She looked confused, pursing her soft pink lips. Was that what he had talked of at the dance? His yacht? 'I – I'm not sure.' She half indicated the letter in her lap.

'I can see you're busy,' he said, playing on her sense of guilt. 'But a spin across the lake and back wouldn't take more than a few minutes. Bring some colour to your cheeks.'

Such wonderful cheeks, and a perfect straight nose. If she would only stop dithering. All he needed was an opportunity to give her a sample of his charm.

He could see she was tempted. Her gaze kept straying across the lake, ruffled gently by the breeze, perfect for a sail on this lovely September evening. With summer gone and the quiet of autumn approaching, the water was the colour of amber, sky and lake melding together like molten gold.

Then she was climbing into the boat, laughing with delight as it rocked beneath her feet, and Lissa couldn't have said quite when the decision had been made. Or why. Perhaps she wished to show Derry Colwith, and herself, that she was her own woman.

Whatever the reason she longed suddenly to feel the spray in her face, the keen wind in her hair, to trail her fingers in the rippling chill of the water. Lissa wanted to experience the hard thump of the waves scudding beneath the hull of the boat and banish the blues from her mind.

'I can finish the letter at any time, so why not?' It was to Meg and could wait.

'Good.'

She laughed when a swan took off, beating its wings in temper, flurried by the winter geese newly arrived from the north.

Their eyes met. She had such wonderful eyes. Exciting, mysterious, sensual. If he saw any hint of rebellion or stubborn independence in them he chose to pay it no heed. If a wildness came into her expression he interpreted it as fear. She was young, and therefore impressionable, malleable, he was sure. And he knew that soon, very soon, his patience would be rewarded. The thought excited him almost beyond endurance.

White sails cracking in the wind. Dare he land on the island? Should he risk mooring the boat and make love to her with a passion that would have her begging for more? He could feel his arousal and busied himself with the jib and the sheets.

'Ready about,' he called. What was he thinking of? He mustn't blow it, not now he was so close.

As Lissa climbed out of the boat, cheeks aglow, curls bursting loose from the restraints of the bobbing pony tail, he asked her for a date. 'Would you care for dinner one evening?'

'Oh, that was wonderful, thanks a lot, I loved it. And for the offer of a meal only . . .'

'You're pretty busy?'

She smiled, flushing pinkly. 'Yes.'

His dark eyes looked sad as she walked away and Lissa almost regretted her refusal. But Philip Brandon was reminding himself of the need for patience. She was young still. He could afford to wait.

1957

CHAPTER 7

Carreckwater, like many another of its kind in Lakeland, was a town with a split personality. For most of the year it was a quiet, sleepy place where people walking up and down its slate cobbled streets would smile or say good morning to everyone they met. In the summer they thought themselves lucky if there was room to walk on the pavement let alone see a familiar face.

Lissa loved the hustle and bustle. She enjoyed the clatter of walking boots even if bulging haversacks did constantly bump her off the narrow pavements. The visitors came in droves down the mountain paths which descended like the spokes of a wheel into the little town. Lunchtime and late afternoon were popular times, when they came to partake of a substantial lunch or a high tea in the many cafes and hotels along Carndale Road. They tramped their mud in and out of every establishment, bought a few postcards to send back home, explored the many little shops and picture galleries, replaced a broken pair of boot laces and went away thinking they had done the town a favour by bestowing their meagre business upon it.

At Stevens Drapery they were rushed off their feet. Lissa soon discovered there wasn't time in the summer to do anything but deal with customers and their endless enquiries. Often these were not at all concerned with the goods in the window, which grew increasingly dusty since there was no time to change it. More often than not the visitors asked the most unlikely questions, like where Beatrix Potter had lived, what time the next steamer left, and if they sold fishing nets.

'The fish shop.'

'Half-past two.'

'Far Sawry.'

June had been pleasant but July was heavy and sultry with the heat. It made Lissa almost long for a cold snap. Perhaps all this rush and her long working hours was the reason she hadn't seen Derry lately. The streets were so crowded she'd missed him. Not that Lissa had seen much of him through the winter either. He always seemed so busy, what with his work as clerk during the day, his evenings devoted to skiffle practice and weekends given over to playing at dances. The group travelled half across the county in their little van at weekends.

She only had herself to blame in a way, she supposed. Frozen him out, as she always did. She'd given up going to dances, certainly those at which Derry played. Not that there were many dances in Carreckwater itself but she couldn't bear to watch the crowds of screaming females all clamouring around him. Derry seemed to revel in their silly attention. Even Jan had told him off for letting it all go to his head.

'You're turning into a prig,' she'd said, with her usual lack of sisterly affection, but he'd merely grinned and told her he couldn't help it if he was popular, puffing out his chest all the more.

Lissa would not have minded so much were it not for that other Derry she'd caught a glimpse of, and the memory of a kiss that still haunted her.

So by and large she was glad she was busy. That way she could maintain her resolve to keep him at a distance.

Lissa brought her wandering attention back to the reality of a long, hot and tiring day, pushing back damp tendrils of undisciplined curls as she bid good day to yet another grumbling customer who had taken thirty-five minutes to choose two yards of lace trimming.

'Why doesn't Miss Stevens spend more time in the shop?' Lissa groaned, propping herself on a stool so she could massage her aching calves. 'We've been run off our feet from the moment we opened. One minute she's in the middle of serving that plump lady with some Lyle stockings and the next she's vanished. I was left with a queue of not very happy customers to attend to.'

Jan raised her eyebrows. 'Best not to ask too

closely when it comes to our Stella,' she advised, wrapping braid back on a reel with alarming dexterity. 'It doesn't do to upset her.'

As if on cue, Miss Stevens stuck her head around the stock room door, hair awry, looking faintly flustered with flags of colour lighting each prominent cheek bone.

'Ah, there you are Jan,' she said, as if it were a surprise to find her two shop assistants still behind the counter. 'Kindly take a selection of brassieres along to Mrs Elvira Fraser. She has sent a request for some in this morning's post.'

'But she lives right up on the Parade,' groaned Jan, thinking of the long hot trek staggering under a weighty parcel. 'We're run off our feet. Why can't she come here?'

'Because she's quite old and rich enough to do as she pleases. A state of affairs which will never be a problem for you, girl, if you don't jump to it, as you will be unemployed and expire of starvation before you reach twenty.'

Jan hung her head. 'Yes, Miss Stevens.' Studiously ignoring Lissa's giggles, she gathered up a suitable selection and set out.

Stella Stevens returned to her office, staring at the wad of unpaid accounts in her hand and reaching for her bottle of Milk of Magnesia. Her nervous stomach was really giving trouble this morning, a little sip or two might help.

She was a large lady with a healthy appetite, a low-slung bosom and hips that were a walking

142

advertisement for her corset department. Her 'nerves' were aided and abetted not by the worthy Milk of Magnesia but by whatever liquid the innocent blue bottle actually happened to contain. Today it was brandy.

'Something must be done,' she informed the Kangol beret poster stuck on the wall above her desk. 'Clients no longer seem to have the good taste of former years. Turn their noses up at true quality, they do. "Is it in fashion, my dear Miss Stevens?" they say.' Stella mimicked the warbling tone of a customer and took another sip from the Milk of Magnesia bottle, found it empty and threw it in the waste paper basket. Then realising what she had done, took it out again and went to her washroom to refill it. She was not herself this morning and could do with a bit of comfort. Surprising really how bad her stomach got after the monthly bank statement arrived.

'This is a good little business, no matter what the customers might say,' she declared to Jan and Lissa as she faced them later that day with the unpalatable truth that despite the high volume of people passing through the door, the takings in the till were pitifully small.

'Course it is, Miss Stevens,' Jan hastily agreed.

Lissa privately thought Stevens Drapery had not moved with the times. It fell very much between two stools. The clothes were neither stylish nor classic, merely old fashioned. Admittedly they did well with a few useful bits and pieces of haberdashery, but not enough to sustain a thriving business.

'What I wouldn't like to do with this place!' Lissa said, as Miss Stevens retreated to her office like a crab scurrying sideways to bury itself in sand, safe from the harshness of the world.

'Burn it down?' And they both burst into fits of giggles.

The girls were thankful when five-thirty came and they could lock the door, hand over the takings and return home to the little boathouse where they took it in turns to make the evening meal. Then they would sit outside by the lake in the evening sun and talk about how blissful it was to be seventeen and free.

Occasionally Derry came over, declaring himself in need of some fresh air, though he always managed to make a point of rubbing Lissa up the wrong way. Tonight was no exception.

'Not going out then?' he asked, staring almost accusingly at her.

'No,' Jan answered for her, eyes closed as she sat sprawled in a deck chair, her neat figure clad in a blue and white swimsuit that sported a dashing skirt about the hips.

Derry was dressed in a blue check shirt, open at the neck to show off his tan, and tight blue jeans that no doubt sent the young girls crazy, Lissa thought, averting her eyes from his neatly shaped rear.

'Wouldn't get me leading such a dull life. It isn't cool to stay in,' he loftily informed them, and started skimming stones across the lake, yelling with delight when he got a high number of bounces. 'Out every night, me.'

'Good for you,' said Lissa dryly. 'How would you know what we do, since you're never around?' She lifted violet eyes to his, a challenge blatantly written in them, and felt a curl of delight to see the swaggering arrogance slip slightly into doubt as he frowned at her.

Lissa's swimsuit was a two-piece, of a modest cut but revealing enough to give Derry pause for thought.

'You could come with us on our gigs.'

'Perhaps we have better things to do.'

'Who would you go out with?' He preferred to imagine her sitting serenely here, by the lake, waiting. For him? He wasn't quite sure. He'd thought at one time that she quite fancied him, now he'd given up hope. Almost.

'None of your business.' Violet eyes met brown, and held.

For the first time Derry looked uncertain, almost as if he wished he hadn't asked. He skimmed a stone with such fierce vigour it bounced half across the lake before sinking.

'Did you see that? Thirteen.'

'Unlucky,' said Lissa and sank back in her deck chair, closing her eyes as if she wasn't interested.

He took out his comb and flicked at his quiff

with quick, agitated gestures. 'This town is boring. You won't find me hanging around here much longer. I'll be off and away. Starting to make real good money with the group now.'

Despite herself, Lissa's eyes flew open and saw the triumph register in his eyes as he recognised her interest. The thought of never seeing Derry again sent her heart plummeting. 'Go where?'

'Haven't decided yet. Manchester. London. Who knows?'

'You were born and brought up in the Lake District. How could you ever be happy anywhere else when you love it so much? There are no mountains to climb in London.'

He looked thoughtful for a moment then shrugged his shoulders. 'Life goes on. I'm going up in the world. Good as this is, I could do better. Renee's a pain, though her cooking has improved, and Dad isn't too bad. He's building a boat for me, you know. So I can win the races this year.'

'You're staying on at Nab Cottage because you get well fed and Jimmy is building you a boat? You selfish, arrogant . . .'

Jan lifted her hands in her favourite conducting gesture. 'Now children, no more squabbling. Why don't we go for a row on the lake? A little gentle exercise will do us all good. Cool us all down.'

Lissa was still stinging from his accusations of dullness as they dragged the wooden row boat over the shingle. 'Where's your fan club tonight? Deserted you already?'

Derry stopped tugging at the boat to grin at her, his face so close to hers that to Lissa's immense fury her heart gave a little flip. Why won't he stay out of my life completely then I could forget him?

'They do tend to wear a bloke out, it's true. But I'm between dates, as you might say.'

A wave of sickness hit her and Lissa would have liked to knock the supercilious expression off his face.

With strenuous efforts on Jan's part, good humour was restored as they puffed up and down the lake and were soon squealing with delight every time they 'caught a crab' and were splashed with the ice cold water.

'This is fun, we should do it more often,' Lissa gasped, on a sudden burst of enthusiasm.

Derry glanced at her in surprise. 'My, take care. Dangerous to unstuff your shirt and mingle with the peasants.'

'*Derry!* What a thing to say.' Jan was horrified.

He said he was sorry but didn't look it. Lissa decided she'd been right about Derry Colwith all along. He was perfectly horrid.

With the fickleness of Lakeland weather the skies had turned iron-grey, promising rain, held off only by the wind which tore through the valley, turning the leaves upside down on the trees, churning the waters and scurrying the ducks into flustered huddles.

It was a day to be indoors. Renee was spending it defrosting her fridge.

'Drat the thing,' she screamed, jabbing her knife into the huge lumps of ice stuck fast to its shining surface.

'There's more water on your kitchen floor than in the lake,' said Jimmy, watching her wring out cloths and shift bowls about. 'Our Derry'll have to swim in for his tea tonight.'

'All the food's going off.' Renee almost sobbed her frustration. 'Why didn't that salesman tell me it'd take half a day and a night to defrost the damn thing?'

'He told you to do it every week. You do it once every two months, and the ice builds up.'

'Looks like the bloody north pole. I wish I had one of those huge American fridges, like on "I Love Lucy".'

Jimmy groaned and got up from the kitchen table where he'd been enjoying a bacon and egg breakfast. 'Aw, don't start, Renee. Not summat else. Enough's enough.'

'I only want what I deserve, pet. What I've never had.'

'I know, sweetheart, but there's only so many working hours in a day.'

'We could get it on the Never-Never.'

'Aye, and never bloody pay for it? I thought you wanted a gramophone?'

'I do.'

'I'm not a walking bank, Renee.'

Tears were streaming down her face and Jimmy watched her with a sad expression. It was the nearest they'd come to a quarrel. 'I'd give you the earth, love, you know I would, but it'd cost too much.'

The knife jerked in her hand and flew off into some distant recess of the kitchen. Renee doubted she would ever see it again, and didn't rightly care.

'To hell with it. Oh, Jimboy, I'm sorry. I wanted things to be real nice this evening when they all came.'

'They will be nice. Don't you always make things nice?' Then she was in his arms and in seconds the quarrel was forgotten. He was lifting up her skirt, grabbing like a teenager with eager hands. He took her there and then, slipping and sliding in the pools of ice on the kitchen floor.

'I'll get you a telephone installed, so you won't feel so alone,' Jimmy gasped, when he could breathe again. 'How about that?'

Renee screamed her delight and hugged his tousled head close to her soft round breast. 'Oh, I do love you, you soft old fool. Now get off to work, and take care.'

He smacked a kiss on one damp nipple. 'When do I not?'

When he was gone Renee sat for a minute longer on the damp floor, eyes glazed with soft love.

'Mind you,' she said to the budgie as she went off to change. 'It's all very well being a modern woman and Jimmy working hard to buy the latest gadgets, but there's so much to learn to operate the damn things you need to be a trained mechanic.'

The little gate had been given a fresh lick of green paint and the tiny garden was crowded with blue delphiniums, hollyhocks, pink rambling roses and pale crinkly honesty as the two girls walked up the path to Nab Cottage.

Renee loved to invite them for a meal. It gave her a chance to show off her latest culinary efforts, and they were always glad to accept. The electric fire was not switched on since the rain had stopped and a fitful sun was warming the August day, but the little blue budgie was still squabbling noisily with its alter ego in the mirror.

'You're cooking is really getting very good,' Lissa told Renee as they all tucked in to delicious lake trout, baked to perfection with smoked crispy bacon. There were plump ripe strawberries to follow, piled high on a meringue nest.

'I've you to thank for that. No one else has ever bothered to teach me anything.'

'You'll have to teach her to knit socks next,' Jan said.

Renee looked puzzled, as well she might. 'Why socks?'

'Lissa's family are experts but haven't the first idea how to dance.'

Nobody else quite understood their hilarity. But that's the way they were: silly and careless. Joking all the time. Life was fun and Lissa wanted to keep it that way.

Jimmy Colwith let his eyes rest on his young wife with pride. Dressed in her usual black pencil skirt which flattered her shapely figure, she wore a pink top with raglan sleeves and a wide vee neck that kept slipping off one lovely bare shoulder. Ripe as one of those luscious strawberries she was. It had been a lucky day for him when she'd walked through the door. He'd quite forgotten she'd ever had any connection with his son.

Lissa hadn't. She was letting her own gaze stray to Derry's face and found his warm brown eyes riveted upon his young stepmother. Her heart plummeted. So that was why he was reluctant to leave home? He still wanted Renee. The thought filled her with a sick dread. What a foolish innocent she was.

'She'll be running the Marina Hotel before she's done,' Derry was saying. The expression in his eyes was filled with laughter and admiration and Lissa almost hated him for being happy. But when they turned to her, instinctively sensing her gaze upon him, the eyes narrowed and noticeably cooled. 'She could hold dances for the Yacht Club set. I'm sure Lissa would love to attend. She likes men in penguin suits.'

'They certainly wouldn't let you in wearing that jacket.' she tartly responded. 'Not to mention the purple shirt. Where did you find it? At a fancy dress party?'

She lifted her chin with haughty disdain, turning her attention to the dessert as it was placed before her, then found the lump in her throat would not allow her to eat it. She really shouldn't waste time on him. But Lissa knew, even as she chastised herself, that it wouldn't have made any difference. Despite all her efforts to keep him at a distance she was falling for Derek Colwith and there wasn't a damn thing she could do about it.

There was a balmy warmth to the evening air as Derry walked the two girls home later that evening. The black mountains huddled about the shoreline seemed to protect them in a secret world all of their own. Soon summer would be over, the visitors would leave and the quiet riches of autumn would be theirs to enjoy, unfettered by overwork.

Contentment warmed Lissa. What did it matter if Jan had a good looking, infuriating brother? On the whole, taking everything into account, she was happy here in Carreckwater, for all she still missed Broomdale, and Meg. 'What more could we ask for but a job that puts money in our pockets and friends to enjoy life with?' She really mustn't let Derry guess how she felt. She would fight her emotions every inch of the way. If he still had a thing going for Renee, that was his problem. And Jimmy's. He was the one she should feel sorry for.

'I could think of one or two other things I might ask for.'

'I can guess,' teased his sister. 'A Vespa scooter maybe, or a recording contract with Decca?'

He cast a glance at Lissa across Jan's head as if trying to judge her reaction. 'We're buying a bigger van next week, then we can travel further, to play at other places. Maybe go as far as Manchester.'

Lissa stared at the ground, not wanting to show that it mattered whether Derry stayed in Carreckwater or not. But the rapid beat of her heart told its own tale.

'What about your job?' Jan asked. 'You can't take too much time off from that.'

'He's too grand to be a clerk,' Lissa said, hating the way her voice sounded peevish. But Derry agreed. 'I'd give it up tomorrow for one chance at the big time.'

'Jan laughed. 'Fat chance.'

The boathouse was bathed in a pool of pale moonlight as Jan turned her key in the lock, still chuckling over her brother's foolish dreams.

The soft lapping of water slipping over stones echoed magically in Lissa's ears. Pewter grey, its polished surface reflected a half moon and the need to be alone with Derry was suddenly so compelling that the blood hummed in her veins. She wished Jan would go to bed so she could walk with him along the shore, hand in hand, gazing at that moon, talking softly together, perhaps feeling his lips on hers. Lissa shook the dream away, knowing it to be false and dangerous, and then as if she'd spoken out loud, Jan declared she was tired and would go at once to her bed.

'If you two don't mind? Goodnight.' She flashed them a cheery wave then went up the spiral staircase to her tiny bedroom in the eaves.

Now the very opposite emotions ruled. Cold fear gripped Lissa's heart. She was alone for the first time with Derry. He stood in the tiny living room smiling at her, hands in pockets, and to her complete shock and dismay she felt her limbs start to tremble. Foolish as it might seem the sensation persisted, filling her with a sudden panic. How ridiculous.

'I'm tired too,' she blurted out, more harshly than she intended. He considered her for a long moment in silence, and Lissa saw his shoulders tense.

'I'd best be on my way then,' he said at last, not making a move.

'Yes,' Lissa agreed through stiff lips, and after a moment found the strength to walk to the door.

Derry took his hands out of his pockets, wiped the palms on his trousers and slowly followed her. She held open the door, stiff-backed, as she waited for him to leave. Then the panic dissolved into a wave of shyness as he brushed past her and Lissa lowered her chin, unable to meet his shrewd gaze. She was aware that he'd paused in the doorway, that he was looking down at her, waiting for her to say something. But she dare not move, dare not return his gaze. Couldn't think what to say.

'Good night then.'

'Good night.' Lissa sounded falsely bright, moved as if to close the door. Derry stopped it with his foot, then catching her chin between finger and thumb, tilted her face up to his.

'I don't understand you.' There was a grating quality to his voice that she'd never heard before.

'What do you mean?'

'Think about it. Sometimes you give me the real come-on. Slanting those delicious smiles when there are other people around and I can't do a damn thing about it. The next minute you're as cold as ice and don't want to know. You've avoided me for months. What is it with you? I hadn't thought you a tease but it's looking that way.'

'I – I really . . .'

'I'm only human, Lissa. Its not fair to lead a bloke on, then freeze him out.'

She was appalled. 'I never led you on.'

'You let me kiss you on that walk. You said you'd come again but never did. You danced for me and saved the group from certain death. Then you went off with Philip Brandon. Now you've hardly a good word to say to me.'

Lissa remained silent, hanging her head with shame. She'd never considered the situation from Derry's point of view and it was unsettling. She'd never thought that he could be hurt by her blow hot, blow cold attitude.

He was accusing her of being a tease, which must be true. '*You'll end up wicked like your mother,*' her grandmother had told her.

Lissa had no wish to be wicked. She didn't mean to be a tease. Oh, what was wrong with her? Why did she behave in this way, so cold and heartless? Everything that had ever happened to her was all her fault. Her mother abandoning her, Meg losing her baby, now even Derry hated her. Lissa felt so certain nobody really liked her she wanted to lay her head on his shoulder and burst into tears.

'I'm sorry.' Her voice was barely above a whisper. 'I didn't mean to . . . I was just protecting myself.'

'From me?' His voice had softened and the anger in his face eased a little. 'Do I look such a villain? OK, so I wear fashionable clothes. That doesn't mean I carry a flick-knife and knuckle-dusters. Bit of a swank but Honest Jack, that's me.'

She met his frank, open gaze and was troubled.

'Yet you love to encourage all those females to hang about you. I mean it when I say I've no wish to be numbered among your fan club, Derry Colwith. A notch on your gun.'

'Is that what you think you'd be?' His hands grasped her shoulders, the weight of them burning through her thin dress, and he gave her a little shake. 'You really believe those girls matter to me?'

'I don't know what to believe.' The warmth of his hands were having a strange affect upon her, making her feel wanton. Like her mother.

'Miss Henshaw told me you'd been up to the office once or twice. Were you looking for me, or developing a schoolgirl crush for my boss?'

Lissa tossed back her hair on a spurt of temper.

'Don't you dare call me a schoolgirl. Why on earth would I look for you? That was family business.'

He glowered at her, disbelief in his brown eyes. 'Was it family business when she saw you walking by the lake, or sailing in his boat?'

Lissa felt herself grow pale. Office gossip. Drat Derry Colwith, and his nosy secretary.

'I really don't see that it's any concern of yours,' she said, in her haughtiest tone.

He was so close she could smell the aftershave he wore, fuelling her desire for him to stop talking and kiss her.

'No wonder you're so cool towards me. My wallet not big enough?'

'Perhaps I'm just careful and don't trust any man.'

'Known a lot, have you?'

Without stopping to think, Lissa lifted her hand to slap him across the face but he caught it and held it fast with his own, a white line of anger showing above his full top lip. Lips she still longed to kiss, even now.

'Don't class me with the likes of Philip Brandon.' His voice was no more than a low hiss. 'Not ever. There's more to him than he lets on.'

'You're jealous,' she taunted, and laughed, delighted to have the upper hand again.

His mouth came down upon hers, hard and demanding, bruising in its intensity. A great giddiness swept over her, desire so overwhelming she couldn't help but give in to it. She melted against

157

him, holding fast to his broad shoulders in an effort to steady herself. Then just as abruptly he stepped away from her, leaving her bereft. 'Don't worry, I'm not interested in competing with the likes of Philip Brandon, except in a yachting race. He's welcome to you.' Then turning abruptly from her, Derry slammed the door so hard it rocked on its hinges.

Lissa leaned her head against the door panel and cried. What had she done now?

CHAPTER 8

A rumble of thunder echoed over the lake and Philip Brandon shuddered. There were times when he would like to escape this small community, were his fortunes not so firmly tied to it. Crowds irritated him, the happy bustle of the visitors only intensified his intrinsic loneliness. Particularly today when a summer storm seemed to be brewing and the air grew heavy. Huge purple and grey clouds gathered above the lake which lay like an amethyst in the fading afternoon light. Neither poet nor artist, yet he was aware of its beauty from his vantage point in the bay window of one of the more flamboyant Victorian villas on the Parade.

He allowed the voice of Elvira Fraser, his esteemed client, to flow over rather than into his consciousness. She would run out of steam soon, or her maid would turn up with the long promised tea, then he might bring her to the point.

Philip adjusted his gaze to the fine mouldings and carved cornices, giving every appearance of attending whilst thinking how much he appreciated a house of style. This one would suit him nicely, though it had about it the stale smell of a house occupied by the old.

He'd made good progress over the last year and his bank accounts were looking modestly healthy, but his patience was wearing thin.

'So you see, *dear* Mr Brandon, I do depend upon you absolutely. My father made his fortune in the cotton mills but times are not what they were.' Elvira emitted a heavy sigh. 'Too many imports, don't you know? Yet my family would rob me of my last farthing given half a chance, I am quite sure of it.'

Philip smiled, not unsympathetically. He was so accustomed to hearing the woes of distressed gentlefolk whose ample funds had first brought them to the Lake District and were not now quite so abundant, that his concern was limited. Poverty was relative.

Reaching across the small table set between the two chairs he patted the old lady's hand. The flesh was soft and papery and made him cringe. 'You may rest assured that I have your best interests at heart, Mrs Fraser.'

'Dear boy,' she said, dabbing at a tear with a lavender-scented handkerchief. 'It is so rare these days. Everyone has become so greedy since the war. Do you not think so?'

The door opened and a tiny maid staggered in carrying a loaded tray. Silver teapot, silver milk jug and sugar basin, and of course a tea strainer. Cups and saucers of the very finest porcelain, he noticed. Even one of those old fashioned cake stands dangling from her arm to set by her mistress's right hand. Philip considered the peaked ridge of cucumber sandwiches and wondered how quickly he could conclude the small ceremony and be out of here in the fresh air, bank books in hand.

It took less time than even he had anticipated. Mrs Elvira Fraser, having been vilified once too often by an indiscreet son-in-law, was only too pleased to hand over her financial affairs to *dear* Mr Brandon without any fuss at all. It took no more than two triangles of cucumber sandwich and one slice of seed cake and the deal was done.

'I shall be only too happy to invest your funds for you, Elvira.' This concession had been granted with the second sandwich. 'A sum of interest will be paid each month into your bank account, more than sufficient for your needs. The balance will grow and add to your securities.'

'Oh, what a relief.'

He leaned forward and rested his hand on a stout, tweed-clad knee, allowing it to linger until a slight stain of colour touched the sagging cheeks. He could feel the elastic garter just above her knee that held up the thick Lyle stockings.

Elvira Fraser was perfectly enchanted. No one had paid her this much attention since her own darling Charles who had departed this life believing her to be very well provided for, though that had been a full twenty years ago, before this last war. It was a different world today and one's children never turned out quite as one hoped.

Philip Brandon's dark good looks set her old heart racing, and for a moment Elvira quite feared for her health. 'So charming,' she said, showing her yellowed teeth as she simpered at him. 'And so dependable.'

'Certainly you may depend upon my services,' he beamed, leaning back in his chair, glancing at his watch as he did so. The air in here was growing stifling. 'I've enjoyed our little chat but unfortunately, Elvira, I have other clients demanding of my time.' He stood up.

Hastily, she set down her cup and saucer with a clatter and did the same. 'You will call again? I must see you regularly, mustn't I? Now that we are doing business together.'

'But of course. What a pleasure that will be,' he murmured solicitously. At the door he turned and regarded her with all due seriousness. 'Now if you have any worries, any little thing bothering you, you have only to call.'

'Oh, yes, I do know that, Mr Brandon,' she sighed.

'Philip, please, if we are to be friends as well as business colleagues. You may rest assured that your affairs will be in safe hands. You need never worry again.' Taking her wrinkled hand, he kissed it. It was the final accolade. Sometimes he made himself sick with such sycophancy.

''Oh,' Elvira breathed. 'Oh, dear me.'

'Good day to you.' Bowing himself out of the room while she shooed away the little maid, declaring that she would show *dear* Mr Brandon to the door herself.

'You must call at twelve o'clock next Thursday,' she informed him. 'We'll enjoy a small sherry and partake of a light luncheon.' It was a summons not to be ignored. Far better than sandwiches on a bench. But then a picture of black curly hair and a scarlet duffel coat lit like a beacon in his head and he wondered. The memory prompted a question. 'Are you by any chance acquainted with a family by the name of Ellis?'

'Ellis? Dear me, now let me think.' Elvira Fraser and her family had lived in the Lake District for almost a century. If the Ellis family held any status locally, then she would know of it.

'Of Keswick?' she brooded, struggling to bring her recalcitrant memory to heel. It was not so biddable these days.

'The south eastern part of the county, I believe. High on the fells?'

'Ah, that would be the medical chap, Jeffrey Ellis. Charming man, charming. Played golf sometimes with my darling Charles. Married some jumped up daughter of a quarry owner. Pretty little piece, but opinionated I seem to remember.'

'The family owns a fine house, I believe,' Philip prompted her. 'Yes, Larkrigg Hall, over Broomdale way. Had some wonderful parties in that house as a girl I do recall.' Elvira's eyes glazed, her mind slipping back to pleasanter times and then as quickly sharpened. 'Why do you ask?'

'Met someone who claims to be related. I was curious.'

Elvira Fraser's own curiosity was well and truly aroused. 'No family to speak of, so far as I can recall. No, wait a moment. They had one daughter. Left home over some scandal or other.'

'What kind of scandal?'

'An affair, I shouldn't wonder. Always having affairs, young girls, eh? Particularly during the war.' She cackled with laughter and offered him a leer that in younger days might have been alluring. Philip shuddered.

'This person claims to be the grandchild.'

'Indeed? Well, it might well be so. We never saw the Ellis girl again, but then we wouldn't, would we, if she'd gone off to have this child? What is it?' she asked, as if speaking of a puppy.

'A girl. A lovely young girl.'

'How sad. Jeffrey would have enjoyed a granddaughter. A darling man. So kind. Handsome too. Wasted on that creature he married. Dead now, or so I'm told.'

'Mrs Ellis is still very much alive.'

'She would be. Hard-faced madam.' There was nothing Elvira loved more than a good gossip, and today was proving to be most fruitful, in so many ways.' This granddaughter will come into a tidy sum one day. Violet, no . . . Rosemary, that's the woman's name. I remember it was something silly and flowery. She's the one with the real funds of course. Family made a fortune in copper mining and slate quarrying.'

Philip's mind was racing. The only grandchild of a wealthy woman. Better and better. Pity about the illegitimacy, and disturbing that Mrs Ellis still refused to acknowledge her, but they might be persuaded into a reconciliation yet. He smiled at Elvira Fraser. 'Now if there is any little thing, don't hesitate to give me a call.'

He had such a delicate touch with old ladies.

The storm finally broke just as the two girls had got the fire blazing and the sausages were only half cooked. A whole group of them had been enjoying a barbecue by the boathouse. It would probably be the last of the season so they were determined to make it a good one.

The reflection of the fire's flames dancing in the waves was shattered suddenly by a warning shoreward breeze, broken into a million sparkling remnants of light. Lightning tore open the sky, thunder rolled and the lake seemed to heave like a live thing. The roar of it rumbled endlessly along the valley followed by sheeting rain that put out the fire and drenched everyone in seconds. There were squeals and shouts of laughter as pans and bread rolls were grabbed and people ran for cover into the boathouse.

The girls found towels and dried their hair then got on with frying the sausages in the little kitchen while Derry picked up his guitar and started to strum and sing, trying to outdo the noise of the thunder. 'Singing the Blues', 'Love Letters in the Sand' and Tab Hunter's hit, 'Young Love'. These were his current favourites.

His singing sounded good, making Lissa's heart do funny acrobatics, that despite her determination to have nothing more to do with him, she was tempted to abandon the sausages. She sat by his feet, looking up into his face as he sang. Would like to stay there for ever.

They drank several bottles of Coca-Cola with supper and there was much speculation about the coming yacht race, a major event at the end of the season.

'This is going to be my year,' Derry boasted and they all laughed.

'To justify your poor old dad spending all his free time building you a fancy boat?'

'This boat is a winner. I'll come zooming in first, you'll see.'

Lissa saw everyone hide their smiles behind their hands even as they offered to help him spend the winnings. She guessed this must be an annual resolution.

After supper, since it was still raining, Tony suggested they play some party games, winking at a little brown haired girl called Helen he'd had his eye on all evening. An empty Coca-Cola bottle was found and spun.

Lissa was amazed how often it pointed to Derry

whenever it was one of the prettier girls who had spun it. She found herself counting the minutes he was out in the kitchen with them, thinking it grew longer every time.

Once it stopped at her and it took all her courage to walk out of the room with Dave and let him put his cold lips against hers. She quickly returned to her place, complaining about the draughty kitchen, and everyone laughed.

Derry didn't look quite so amused. He was frowning, probably disappointed in her for not being a good sport. So what? She hated these silly parlour games. Who wanted to be kissed by this lot?

Then it was Derry's turn to spin the bottle. At that moment Sam offered her another Coke and almost spilled it as he popped off the metal cap. Laughing, Lissa turned back to find the bottle pointing at her. She could feel her cheeks start to bum as she got up and followed a silent Derry out to the kitchen.

They stood face to face in the darkness, saying nothing, not even looking at each other. She could feel her lips tingling with the expectation of his kiss which confused her somewhat since she'd taken fright the last time. But there was no denying that her heart was hammering against her rib cage so loud she was sure he must hear it. Was he never going to speak? Never kiss her?

It occurred to Lissa with sickening disappointment that perhaps he didn't want to. He was letting this time go by so that everyone would think he was kissing her, imagine he was playing the game when really he was seeking a way out. The very idea obviously repulsed him.

'You don't have to,' she said, her voice sounding weak and unconvincing even to her own ears.

'I know.' It was not at all what she had wanted to hear. 'I don't suppose you want to.'

'I didn't say that.' Did she sound too forward? she worried. Lissa stared at the floor and decided, inconsequentially, that they really should have varnished these floorboards which were all scratched and splintered. Maybe if they put down lino . . .

After a further long moment she could bear the suspense no longer and of its own volition a tiny agonised cry came from her throat. Lissa half turned to the door, desperate suddenly to escape. 'Let's go back,' she mumbled, wanting to die on the spot, wishing this old wooden floor would open up and swallow her.

'Wait.' Then his hands were on her arms. He was pulling her towards him and the next instant he was kissing her. His mouth was soft and compelling, warm and coaxing, not cruel and hurtful, every bit as exciting as that first time. Except this was different. This time she was kissing him back. They wrapped their arms about each other and clung as if neither would ever let go. The kissing went on far too long of course, and they returned to the living room looking flushed and rumpled, anxious to avoid each other's eyes and the knowing grins of their friends.

It was a long time before Lissa slept that night. She went over and over the kiss in her mind till a thousand pains of sweet agony pierced her, all mingled with uncertainty, confusion and regret. It had shocked her how much, in that moment, she'd wanted him. Why couldn't she make up her mind about him? He could leave any day.

Well, she could leave too.

It was reported that two thousand people a week were emigrating to the Commonwealth; to Australia, New Zealand and Canada. Maybe if she'd gone out with them, gone to look for her mother, she could solve this stupid sense of insecurity.

Maybe she could still go.

What a fool she was. Lissa thumped her pillow and squeezed her eyes tight, trying to shut out the picture of his tender smile, the memory of his touch searing her skin, the excitement of his mouth against hers.

She enjoyed her work, had found in Jan the friend she'd always wanted. Jan was sweet and funny and kind. Practical and sensible and easy to get along with.

They both loved the boathouse, had money in their pockets to spend on fun things, such as a new lipstick or a hooped petticoat which were all the rage. Each week they considered most seriously which singer's latest record to bestow their hard earned shillings upon. This week it might be Guy Mitchell, the next Johnnie Ray or Elvis. Then they would carry the prize home with pride and play it on their record player till they knew every word by heart. Life was good.

Now she was risking all of this for a few kisses. Derry only took his music seriously, nothing else. He had every intention of leaving Carreckwater to follow his crazy dream to be famous, and he certainly had no intention of taking her with him when the music world was full of silly screaming girls. She was simply an amusement, to pass the time.

But how could she avoid him? He was Jan's brother, for goodness' sake. When he left, she would feel abandoned all over again, no doubt end up an old maid sitting on some shelf or other.

Lissa gave up trying to sleep, and throwing off her sheets lay on her back to stare miserably up at the ceiling. The storm rumbled in the distance, moving away, leaving the air still warm but slightly fresher in its wake.

Did she never learn? But then if you couldn't trust your own mother what hope was there? Hadn't that fact sunk in yet? Hadn't she packed her heart away, where no one could damage it ever again? Not well enough, obviously.

There had been no word from Kath in years, no suggestion that she would ever wish to see her. The rejection still rankled, deep down, so all things considered Lissa felt she'd made the right decision in staying in Lakeland. This was her home, where she belonged. Yet she'd wasted years longing for something she couldn't have. Her mother hadn't wanted her, Meg had probably only taken her in out of loyalty and duty and because she had no child of her own. Yet here she was, risking rejection all over again by falling for a swollen-headed young clerk with his heart set on fame and his eyes on any girl who happened his way.

Lissa turned her hot pillow over and curled up, willing sleep to rescue her tortured mind. She told herself firmly that his kisses were part of a game, just a giggle at a party. Nothing more. The fault lay in her own naivety. She'd never been kissed by anyone but Derry. She was an innocent, with no experience at all.

Why, for two pins she'd accept a date with someone else. That would show him. Yes, she thought, that might be the answer. And on this comforting thought, Lissa fell asleep.

For some reason Lissa couldn't quite explain, the day of the races brought a flutter of nervous tension to her stomach. It was a perfect day for a sail, warm and sunny. Puffy white clouds danced across an azure summer sky while the prevailing wind seemed almost eager to fill the white sails and power the little boats along by the unseen miracle of aerodynamics. The lake had never looked more inviting with lacy tips to a blue-grey ruffle of waves.

Competition at the Yacht Club races was always fierce. There were several classes taking part from small dinghies to huge, spanking yachts. Great kudos was attached to winning.

She and Jan had walked down to the little jetty early to watch events, though Derry was already there, trimming sails, checking his mast and rigging, oiling, scrubbing and greasing since dawn.

'It's tricky, sailing these lakes,' Jan told her. 'The mountains affect the wind currents which are constantly changing. It's important to know how to play it, how to use the wind, whether to put the spinnaker up or not to get the most speed from the boat. One mistake can slow you down and lose the race.'

'Will Derry win?' Wanting him to, very badly.

Jan considered a moment. 'He's a good sailor, decisive, but perhaps a touch impulsive at times.'

They found a space on a low wall where they could get a good view of proceedings.

'Wish me luck,' Derry said, appearing at her elbow with a wide grin on his face. He looked so young and eager, handsome in his white T-shirt and navy shorts. Too young and inexperienced compared with the rest of the entrants, Philip Brandon among them. Lissa could see Brandon's yacht with its showy blue sails standing serenely at anchor some way off shore. Derry will never beat that, she thought, and wished it didn't matter.

'Good luck then,' she said, resisting the urge to kiss his smooth tanned cheek.

'Now if I were a knight in shining armour going into combat you might offer me a favour.' For all he was smiling his brown eyes were serious, almost intense.

'Depends what kind of favour.'

He reached out a hand and before she could guess what he was about, slid the ribbon from her hair, releasing her pony tail. The wind caught her black curls and whipped them about her face but she only laughed, instinctively lifting her face to his. And as her gaze slid to his mouth she watched it move slowly towards hers.

'That won't help. No pretty ribbon will win you this race.' The deep voice cut in and they broke away, pretending they hadn't been irresistibly drawn to taste each other's lips.

'Mr Brandon. What a surprise.' Lissa covered her confusion by desperately trying to gather her hair together and bring it under control. 'How's the jiving these days?'

'I've given it up. Sailing is much easier.' .

'It's a fine yacht. I've been admiring it.'

'You must come out on it later,' he said. 'I'll let you take the tiller.'

Derry said, 'There's no need for that, Mr Brandon, thank you. As you can see I have one exactly the same, *The Fair Maid.. My* father built her for me. If Lissa wants a sail she can come out on mine.'

Philip Brandon smiled, though it didn't reach his eyes. 'Perhaps she may be permitted to choose for herself. She certainly enjoyed it the last time, did you not, Lissa?'

Lissa's cheeks fired, disturbed by the gleam of admiration in Philip Brandon's eyes and by the undercurrents she could feel flowing between these two who were to be adversaries in this race. 'Dry land is my favourite place. I know nothing about boats.'

Philip chuckled. 'Nor does my clerk, truth to tell.'

Derry was glowering like a sulky child. He longed to say that he didn't care if Lissa had sailed in Brandon's yacht, that he'd grown up with boats and his father had taught him to sail almost as soon as he could walk, but this was his boss, and he had no wish to lose his job.

Lissa, sensing his problem, spoke up on his behalf. 'You don't need to feel sorry for Derry. He'll manage well enough. I'm not sure you're right about the ribbon though. An emblem of good luck never did any harm, particularly if you believe in it. My own family puts great store in a simple Luckpenny.'

'And Dad is crewing for him,' put in Jan, eyes hot with pride.

Now it was Philip Brandon's turn to look annoyed. 'It isn't luck that wins a race but skill, evaluation of all the relevant factors such as wind and current, and perfect planning. Something I am adept at.' There was a small, awkward silence.

Lissa tried to smile. 'Let the best man win, as they say.'

Dark eyes met brown and for a moment the air crackled with tension. Then Brandon relaxed, his smile at its most urbane. 'It should be an interesting contest.' Bowing slightly to Lissa, he gave her his most charming smile. 'That dinner invitation still stands, by the way,' and walked away, leaving Lissa bright red and Derry furious.

The start of a race, Derry knew, was of vital importance. Get this wrong and precious time would be lost, not easily made up. He checked his stop watch so he could keep an eye on those first vital minutes. He knew the distance he must tack away, and at what moment he should turn so that he was crossing the starting line exactly as the starting pistol sounded. He knew how and when to trim his sails, had worked out his plan for tacking to the first marker buoy to the very last detail.

And it seemed that everything was working well. Derry got off to a flying start and *The Fair Maid* hummed along, pointing well into the wind.

What he hadn't properly taken into account when he devised his plan was Philip Brandon.

It was Jimmy who noticed him first. Brandon had taken the opposite approach, going first to port as Derry tacked to starboard, so when Derry went about on to the port tack, he came about too on a starboard one and was heading straight for the *Maid*.

'He's coming a bit fast,' Jimmy called to his son, indicating the approaching yacht sailing at a killing angle in the wind.

Derry scarcely glanced at it, too busy judging how closely he could risk running behind the buoy. 'Don't worry. We'll be well past by the time he reaches us.' He lifted his voice above the slapping waves. 'The rules allow him to come pretty close and try to unsettle us. Only he won't unsettle me.'

'So long as he doesn't risk a collision,' Jimmy muttered, not entirely mollified by his son's confidence.

'Ready about,' Derry shouted, as he saw they were approaching the buoy.

Jimmy slipped the sheets from the cleat and held the rope ready, waiting for the next call when Derry had swung over the tiller, then he would let the jib sheet go so that the boom and mainsail could follow it. But before that could happen his attention was caught once again by Brandon's boat.

'Bloody hell, he's cutting it a bit fine. What the . . .? He's letting his sail out. Watch it, Derry, he's swinging this way.'

Derry's face was as white as the sails as he watched Philip Brandon deliberately alter his course so that instead of crossing safely some fair distance behind Derry's yacht, he cut right across the bows, narrowly risking collision. The spray hit Derry in the face, running down him like a cold shower and the boat lurched, very nearly over-turning in the wash.

'You damn fool,' he shouted.

'Scared of a bit of competition?' Brandon called back, and neatly turned about ready for the next tack. 'I told you that bit of ribbon wouldn't help.' His laugh rang out and Jack Callan, who was crewing for him, likewise grinned while the scrap of scarlet, tied to one of The *Fair Maid's* main ropes, waved bravely in the wind.

The next few minutes needed Derry's entire concentration if he was to stay on course and not lose the advantage of his flying start. Anger curdled within. Had he not been an experienced sailor he could very easily have been overturned.

When they were on an even keel again, Jimmy was the first to speak. 'You should bloody well report him for that. Bad sailing, that's what it was.'

Derry only shook his head. 'Who would believe me, a mere clerk complaining about his boss? And Brandon's a real big-wig in the Yacht Club.'

'It was deliberate.'

'We can still win, which is all that matters.'

The teamwork of father and son was superb, working as one, anticipating the other's thoughts and actions, horn hard hands on sheet and tiller, keeping the weight right, the sails at the proper tension and swinging over at exactly the right moment. At one point Philip Brandon tried a bit of serious blanketing to rob The *Fair Maid* of vital wind for her sails, but it did no good, she flew over the line several feet ahead, with both Derry and Jimmy yelling for joy.

'We've won.'

Derry was jubilant, barely able to wait to see the girls' faces and wallow in Lissa's admiration. He'd won the race for her, hadn't he?

It was much later, after everyone had moored and anchored, that he was called to the committee room. Philip Brandon and several other members were already there, and a very sad-looking official. 'I'm sorry, son, but I have to disqualify you.'

'What?' The blood seemed to seep from Derry's veins. For years he'd dreamed of winning this race. 'I don't understand. I won it easily.'

The official looked even more uncomfortable, clearing his throat, smoothing a hand over his bald head. 'These matters are always difficult. As you know it's not possible for the committee boat to be everywhere at the same time, to see what's going on, particularly at the start of a race when everyone is so spread out. Mr Brandon here has reluctantly put in a complaint.'

Derry stared blankly at his employer. 'What kind of complaint?'

'He says you cut too close. If he hadn't taken evasive action you and he would have certainly collided.'

'But he . . .'

'I was on the starboard tack, Derry,' Philip gently

pointed out, his face sad, as if he hated to be the cause of these ill tidings. 'Thus had right of way.'

Jimmy opened his mouth to protest, anxious to point out the finer points of the ruling. Right of way or not, Philip Brandon had been the one on the attack. Hell-bent on collision, if he was any judge. But his son kicked his ankle so he shut his mouth again, remembering the particular relationship of these two antagonists. Losing a yacht race was preferable to losing a job. He cast a hasty glance at Derry's face, pale but inscrutable, and surprisingly calm. You had to admire the lad for holding his temper.

'Nobody else saw what happened?' Derry asked, quiet as you please.

The official looked embarrassed. 'As I said, Derry, it's very difficult . . .'

'Thanks. I understand.' Derry nodded to them both and, turning on his heel, walked out of the room. Once outside he found he was trembling. He thrust his hands deep in his pockets and drew in several harsh breaths to regain control. After a moment he became aware of Jimmy standing quietly beside him.

The two men exchanged a long speaking glance, each telling the other that they understood perfectly what had happened. Philip Brandon had failed to overtake Derry so had put in a fallacious complaint to get the result squashed. And there wasn't a damn thing they could do about it.

'Come on, son, I'll stand you a pint.'

179

Later, the girls wanted to know what had gone wrong. Derry considered telling them the truth then changed his mind. It would only sound like the gripes of a poor loser. 'I lost. That's what went wrong.' What else was there to say?

CHAPTER 9

First thing the next morning, holding fast to her determination not to risk rejection from Derry, and astounded by her own daring, Lissa telephoned Philip Brandon at his office. 'Is that offer of a meal still open?'

'Of course,' he said, sounding slightly breathless.

'I'd like to accept then, thanks very much.'

He picked her up on the dot of seven and took her to a very smart little restaurant in Fisher's Gate. What a relief, she thought, that she'd worn a smart little navy and white polka dot dress that just skimmed her knees.

Even so, she felt ridiculously nervous. Lissa told him she'd never been in such a place before, its clientele being the kind of businessmen and visitors who had been least affected by war and the years of austerity since, perhaps even profited from them.

'We've moved into more prosperous times,' he agreed as Lissa looked about her at the plush atmosphere and candlelit tables. 'Never had it so good, isn't that what Mr Macmillan tells us?'

The waiter came and Philip ordered for them

both without even consulting her. Lissa felt relieved and strangely irritated all at the same time.

'I could never imagine coming to a place like this with my friends,' she laughed, feeling self-conscious.

'You count Derek Colwith as a friend?'

Lissa smiled across the small table at him, quenching the curious disquiet she felt in talking about her feelings for Derry. 'His sister is my best friend.' She saw by his expression that he was not convinced it was quite so simple.

'I would have thought a girl like you could do better than my clerk,' Philip's handsome face took on a scathing expression which did not suit him. 'He's a young tearaway who thinks too much of himself. Take the yacht race, for instance.'

Perversely, though Lissa had said the very same thing about Derry, she now defended him. 'I felt rather sorry for him actually, coming so close. But you were the better sailor, evidently.' She smiled, to show how sporting she was.

'I can also win without cheating. The trouble with young Colwith is that he is so determined to be the best he is perfectly unscrupulous.'

For a moment Lissa was stunned into silence. 'What did he do?'

'He cheated.'

'I don't believe it.'

But by the time Philip had finished explaining his version of events she had no choice but to believe it.

Lissa was horrified. She'd come out on this date to prove something, to herself perhaps, and to make Derry jealous perhaps. To make him want her so much he'd give up on the blond fan club. Now she felt sickened by this new aspect of his character. 'You say he deliberately tried to cause a collision?'

'Someone could easily have been injured.'

Lissa's eyes were bleak, her mind so distracted she did not notice when the waiter placed a dish of prawns and salad before her.

'May I pour you a glass of wine?' The conversation moved smoothly on to safer topics but her appetite had quite gone. She couldn't stop thinking about it.

Seeing her face, Philip slid a hand over hers. 'You mustn't fret over Derry Colwith. He's a young fool with his head in the clouds. You are far too beautiful to waste time over him. You deserve better. Someone to care for you as you should be cared for.'

The hand gently squeezed hers and she lifted her eyes to his, reading a message she could not deny. Heavens, he fancied her. And he thought her beautiful. Surely this charming, good-looking man couldn't be jealous, could he?

As they ate he got her talking of Broombank and Ashlea, smiling over tales of her childhood with Nick and Daniel. Lissa felt quite at ease with him, almost sorry when the evening ended.

A perfect gentleman to the last, he took her to

the door of the boathouse, unlocked it with her key and bade her a polite good night. No fumbling attempts at a goodnight kiss.

'I have so enjoyed our evening. Perhaps we may repeat it some time?'

'I'd like that,' she said, and was surprised to realise that she meant it.

'Who's a pretty boy then?' Renee poked a finger between the bars of the budgie's cage only to be met with a loud squawk and a vicious nip from the sharp beak.

'Bloody hell.'

She pulled the finger away and ran to the kitchen tap. No blood appeared but tears stood out in her childlike blue eyes. 'What a day,' she mourned, switching on the electric fire, kettle, radiogram and television set all at once in a fit of pique, unmindful of the huge electricity bill Jimmy had recently received.

Music blared out from the one while the television set blinked blankly at her, too early for its programmes to have begun. Peeved, she switched it off again.

'Waste of money, that was,' she said and went to glare out of the window instead. It was, in Renee's view, a typical Lakes day, grey and miserable with rain coming down in stair rods. Poor old Jimboy. He'd hoped to get a bit of fishing in later.

'Anyone would think it was November instead

of September,' she mourned. 'And nobody to talk to half the time, what with Jimmy working long hours and Derry never in.'

She'd been glad at first when Jan and Lissa had taken the boathouse. Give Jimmy and me more time on our own, she'd thought. But in the twelve months since she'd found it hadn't worked out as she'd hoped. Jimmy worked all hours and she was more and more alone. Derry still hung around, making a nuisance of himself.

'Not that he isn't still fanciable,' she admitted, mouth lifting into a knowing smile. 'That's part of the problem, isn't it, Peter?' she said, addressing the budgie. 'Don't do to have two gorgeous men in one house. Particularly when you wouldn't mind sleeping with either of them. Not that I would, you understand. But thinking about it can have a funny effect on a girl.'

She sat with her hands cradling a mug of tea, her skirt pulled up over bare thighs to warm her cold legs by the glowing bars of the electric fire, and began to plan.

They were having a nice pair of lamb cutlets tonight, baked with a sprinkle of rosemary on top, accompanied by mash potatoes and some nice Batchelor's peas out of a tin. Amazing really that she had taken so well to cooking. There'd never been the opportunity before, not at home where you were lucky to get a bag of chips. Nor at the Marina Hotel where she worked, skivvied more like, as a waitress and general dogsbody.

Renee hated working at the hotel. Jimmy hated it too. He felt threatened by all the young men she met there.

'Just because I like to dress with a bit of flair,' she constantly assured him, 'men think they can take liberties, cheeky buggers. Forever pinching my bottom they are, and I don't like it. No respect for women, that's what it is. Not like you, pet.' Then she would kiss him and in no time at all he would feel better. He was a good man, her Jimmy.

'Deserves the very best, don't he, Peter darling?' She reached for her packet of cigarettes and lit one.

Having beaten out its ill temper on its companion in the swinging mirror, the budgie chirruped back, quite equably.

Renee pulled out her own small spotted mirror from her crocodile plastic handbag and, holding it in one hand, started to titivate her hair with the other, cigarette stuck between orange lips, eyes creased against the ensuing curl of blue smoke.

'I'd hand in me notice only I enjoy a bit of money of me own, d'you see? Point of fact, we could do with a bit more.'

The budgie attacked its millet spray, quite unconcerned.

'Jimmy works hard all day at the boatyard, comes home knackered and a tired man ain't no good to woman nor beast.' She laughed. 'You know what I mean, Peter boy?'

He blinked at her through the bars then bashed

his bell, just to assure her that he understood perfectly.

'I fancy one of them new Hotpoint washing machines. A Hoover vac and a new electric cooker. So clean they are, you wouldn't credit. We might even save up enough for a Hillman Minx.' She blew smoke rings up to the yellowed ceiling. 'Ooh, that would be lovely, don't you think?'

Sometimes she could hardly sleep, she was that busy planning. She stubbed out the half-smoked cigarette and set off up the stairs to investigate the bedrooms.

There was hers and Jimmy's, the biggest in the house. Next to that was Jan's which she'd shared with Lissa for a time. At the end of the landing, next to the bathroom, was Derry's. That was only a single but it was a good-sized one all the same. You might fit a three-quarter bed in it if you got a smaller chest of drawers.

She took a tape measure out of her skirt pocket and started to measure.

With these three bedrooms in operation she could take in two, four, maybe five, guests at ten shillings and sixpence a night bed and breakfast. She started doing sums in her head, got lost and went searching for a bit of paper on the kitchen mantelshelf.

Back upstairs again, satisfied with her arithmetic, she faced her major problem. Jimmy.

First off she'd have to persuade him to convert the loft into a bedroom for them to use. It had a proper staircase to it, that was one good thing, narrow but solid. But the room itself was a junk heap with cracked floorboards that didn't quite reach the plastered walls, and no electricity. She stood rather gingerly on the floorboards and stared out of the small attic window.

The rain had stopped and though the mountains beyond were still wreathed in mist a faint sun was attempting to break through the grey cloud, sending shafts of sunlight down on to the grey water. Needing no further indication of a brighter day ahead, she could see two elderly couples taking to the lake with gusto, pulling up masts and sails, swinging jibs about, wheeling dinghies down the slipway.

You get a good view of the lake from up here, that might appeal,' she announced to the empty room, so used to talking to the budgie she hardly noticed when it was absent.

But she'd have her work cut out to persuade him. It wasn't so much the joinery in the loft that would be the problem. Best craftsman in Carreckwater, Jimmy was. Had built their kitchen cupboards easily and with the same spit and polish as the clinker-built boats he worked on for his boss at the yard. They could spend the winter getting it ready for next season.

Oh, no. It was the idea of having strangers in his house. She'd have to prove her figures, show him how much money they could make with bed and breakfast. How tourism was the coming thing.

Renee upturned an old box, licked the tip of her pencil and sat on it to tot up the figures again, just to make sure she'd got them right. It was true. She could make more money out of letting three bedrooms than she could working four nights a week at the hotel.

But then she came to the most difficult problem of all, which could put a stop to all her plans. Derry. Renee thought about this for some time, chewing on the pencil till it was a frayed soggy mess, as she had used to do with the pencils the teacher gave her at school. Got a right telling off for that she had.

But she was a married woman now, not a schoolgirl, for all she was only seventeen. She could make her own decisions. If she wanted to chew pencils, she would chew pencils. If she wanted Derry out, then out he would go. And she could handle Jimmy. When had she ever not been able to handle Jimmy?

B and B. That was the future.

The solution came to her. Mr Brandon. He could tell her about any possible regulations the council might throw at her. And he might also be able to help with Derry.

The rain had stopped and the sun was glinting on pale pebbles, lapped by the waves on the shore. A breeze shuffled across the water and the reflections of cloud and boats and sunbeams broke into a brilliance of disorganised fragments then pieced themselves together again, like a jig-saw. It made Derry feel quite light-hearted as he hurried to the boathouse. The two girls would have finished early since it was half day closing and he'd made it his habit to take lunch with them every week at this time. Whether there'd be a welcome for him today was another matter.

He couldn't quite make Lissa out, one minute all friendly, the next cool and distant. Jan said she had family problems needing dealing with. And he always managed to say or do the wrong thing when she was around. He might like to give the impression of the tough, swaggering man-about-town, but in truth he was as shy and very nearly as inexperienced as Lissa herself. He knew she was jealous of the attention he got when he was singing, which excited as much as it irritated him.

How could he not enjoy it when all the girls screamed at his music, or hung around waiting for him afterwards? Gave him a good feeling, that did. Made him look real cool to his mates. But he couldn't quite see himself as a lothario. Was that the word? Up close they unnerved him with their long nails and bright pink lipstick. Girls liked you to spend money on them, which he didn't have.

And Money was something he'd never have if he stayed at Brandon's, a small, down-at-heel solicitors.

In any case Derry believed he could afford to

be choosy. He was going to be famous, wasn't he? Some days he thought the right girl might be Lissa Turner. When they quarrelled, he thought not. She'd thawed a bit recently but still kept him at arm's length. And they never had a minute to themselves. He thought she deliberately encouraged Jan to hang around, perhaps only tolerated him because he was Jan's brother.

Once he got a recording contract, then the money would really start rolling in. Derry had no doubt that he could make it big. She'd take more notice of him then, wouldn't she? The fact that half the teenage boys in the country had the same dream did not occur to him.

He clucked to the ducks as he swung along, whistling happily, his natural optimism restored. He took no notice of the people sitting upon the green benches as he sprinted up the steps to the boathouse. His heart was racing, and he bounced impatiently from one foot to the other as he waited for Lissa to open the door.

Five seconds later there she was, as lovely as he had imagined.

'Hello.'

'Hello.'

Tongue-tied, he simply looked at her. He could scent the sweetness of her skin, longed to run his hands over the slim curves of her back and up into those silky black curls. She still hadn't let him cross the threshold, nor had he noticed.

'It's turning colder.'

'Yes.'

'Winter coming on.'

'Hm.'

They talked like strangers and looked at each other like lovers. 'Sorry about the other night.'

'Family business, that's all,' she said, wondering why she felt the need to explain. 'I over-reacted.'

'No, like you said, none of my business. Right blockhead I am. Won't do it again.'

'It's OK.'

'Will you be my girl?' he blurted out. Oh God, he thought, I've messed it up again. What's the matter with me? No wonder she was staring at him. Probably wondering how to let him down easy and get rid of him without giving offence.

As he set one hand at each side of her head on the door frame, she blushed hotly, feeling oddly trapped. Yet she could easily walk away into the living room. Not that she wanted to. She couldn't seem to move a muscle. Her legs had quite turned to jelly. 'I – I don't know,' she said, looking up at him through lowered lashes. Waiting. When the kiss came, with only their lips touching, she felt a shudder of desire run right through her like an electric current. It was as if her mouth had found sanctuary and yet opened the rest of her body to an excitement she had never believed possible.

'Lunch is ready,' Jan called from the kitchen and they broke hastily apart. Gave a half laugh. Embarrassed, as if she had actually caught them.

But if Jan had missed the kiss, more than half the people on the lakeshore benches certainly hadn't. They'd thoroughly enjoyed the moment, sighing as they remembered sweet young love. Save for one man in a pinstripe suit, who sat frowning with displeasure into his uneaten sandwiches.

Renee Colwith stood before Miss Henshaw wearing what could only be described as a mulish expression. 'I'll wait,' she said.

'Mr Brandon has appointments well into the afternoon,' replied Miss Henshaw through pursed lips. It wasn't true but she didn't believe it gave a good impression for the General Public to imagine they could simply walk into a solicitor's office and be seen right away. Particularly a madam such as this who was clearly no better than she should be.

'He will see me,' Renee insisted, bending her knees slightly so she could peer under the gold lettering on the glass panel of the inner office door to see if anyone was inside.

Miss Henshaw was incensed by such impertinence and got up, ready to bar the way with her own frail body if need be. 'You should have rung for an appointment,' she chided.

Renee laughed. 'The only bells that get rung in our house are in the budgie's cage.' She resented the secretary's hard gaze, judging, making assumptions. And after she'd put on her best pink fluffy wool coat and black gloves too.

The stand-off might have gone on indefinitely had not Philip Brandon chosen to return early from lunch. Disturbed by the sight of Lissa in the arms of his own clerk, his appetite had gone.

'Yes?' he barked at the girl with the orange mouth, bright pink coat, and the most ridiculous bleached blonde hair, hopping about on her stiletto heels that were drumming holes into his office lino.

Vera Henshaw made plain her disapproval of this unexpected visitation. 'This girl wishes to speak with you. I told her you were engaged, and offered to make her an appointment later in the week.'

'It'll only take five minutes.' Renee batted her spiky eyelashes, which usually did the trick where men were concerned. This one, however, wasn't even looking at her.

Short on patience in his current mood, even with his secretary let alone a potential client, Philip stormed past both women, burst into his office and flung off his coat in a single movement of fluid rage. 'I can spare you two.'

It was enough.

Renee's wriggled with delight as she cast Miss Henshaw a sweetly venomous smile and sashayed into the inner sanctum, shutting the door with a cheery wiggle of her fingers through the window.

When she had finished telling Philip Brandon her plans, he reached past her and drew the green blind down over the glass.

'Sit down please, Mrs Colwith. You and I should talk.'

Derry had been given the task of calling upon Elvira Fraser to ask her to sign a document for the bank. The old lady was disappointed that it wasn't Philip himself, but warmed instantly to the fresh-faced young man who was shown into her parlour.

'Would you care for some tea? Indian or Earl Grey?'

Derry politely declined. If he got this over with quickly he would have time to call and chat with the girls, assuming the old dragon wasn't anywhere about. He explained his need to hurry to Mrs Fraser in more diplomatic terms.

'Mustn't be seen to be wasting time,' and brought a smile to the old lady's drooping mouth.

'Not all young men would see it in that light. Mr Brandon must inspire loyalty in his staff.'

Derry made a non-committal grunt. 'I've brought you a form to sign, something to do with releasing funds.'

Elvira hooked her glasses on her long nose as he handed her the papers. 'Ah, this will be concerning my investments. Should I read it?'

Derry inwardly groaned. If the old dear read every word on these two closely packed pages they'd be here all day. 'I shouldn't worry,' he said, anxious to be off.

'Will I have enough income to keep on my dear

housekeeper, do you think? Then there is the man who does my garden. I really couldn't manage it on my own.'

She fiddled anxiously with the rings on her plump fingers and Derry felt suddenly sorry for her. Old and vulnerable, Elvira Fraser reminded him of his own gran. Never missed a trick, his old gran. But she'd been poor, Elvira Fraser was rich. House by the lake, servants. What was she worrying about? She was loaded.

And if he explained it all wrong, he'd be the one to get it in the neck. 'I'm sure Mr Brandon will explain it all properly when he calls next time.' Derry held out the pen.

Elvira smiled at the charming young man, thinking it would give her a lovely excuse to invite Philip to luncheon. They could have salmon mousse, and finish with a nice glass of port. 'Of course. Where do I sign?'

It was the Monday following Renee's discussion with Philip Brandon that Derry burst into Stevens Drapery, his face crimson with outrage. 'What do you think she's put me in the garden shed.'

Jan and Lissa stared at him for a moment, nonplussed. 'Who has done what?'

'Renee. She says she wants my room and she's put my bed in the shed. I either sleep in there or get out.' Both girls exchanged a long glance, then burst into peals of laughter.

'It isn't funny.' Derry sounded deeply hurt. 'It'll be cold out there come winter.'

'Buy a paraffin lamp. Weren't you a boy scout?' his unsympathetic sister suggested.

Derry took out his comb and began to smooth back his quiff as he always did when he was agitated. 'I wondered if I might kip down on the floor at your place?'

'Think again,' Jan told him as Lissa's heartbeat quickened, though whether from fear or excitement she couldn't rightly say.

'Why is she throwing you out?' Lissa asked.

'Would you believe she's going to do B and B? It's all your fault, Lissa. You started her on this cooking lark.'

Lissa couldn't help but giggle at the look of outrage on his face. 'Why shouldn't she do bed and breakfast? Sounds like a good idea to me. But that isn't till next season surely?'

'Claims she needs to redecorate and refurbish. She's got Dad doing up the loft to use as a bedroom for them.'

'Fumigate your room, more like,' Jan laughed, backing away to avoid any retaliation. 'You'd best get out of here before the dragon catches you. The last thing I need is my notice because of your troubles.'

'I might catch pneumonia in that shed,' Derry mourned. 'I'd rather stay at the boathouse.' He'd taken quite a fancy to the idea. He'd get all his meals made and see Lissa every day. A nagging landlady clocking him in and out was not Derry's idea of a peaceful life.

Jan rolled her eyes. 'Why should we help?'

Because if he couldn't find a room, he might leave, Lissa thought. But Jan wasn't for backing down. Derry was on his own. The subject, it seemed, was closed.

CHAPTER 10

Autumn was coming to Carreckwater and the numbers of visitors declined. Families had gone home, children returned to school, and elderly couples who enjoyed a little gentle walking occupied the narrow streets. Gentlemen in good sound windcheaters, ladies in sensible twin sets and tweed skirts, woollen socks and walking shoes. Both sexes sporting cherry wood walking sticks and warm woolly hats.

Locals breathed a deep sigh of relief, pulled down the shutters on their guesthouses, and returned to their winter activities of bell ringing, flower arranging, photography and amateur dramatics.

With the promise of a restful, quiet autumn and winter ahead, now was the time, Lissa decided, to pay a visit home. She readily accepted Derry's offer of a lift in his new van, knowing it was only an excuse to show him off, and Jan too. She was almost sure that Meg would like her new friends. How could she not?

Meg and Tam came running down the fells from where they'd been checking the sheep, to greet them. There were tearful hugs and kisses which set the young dog Ruff, grandson of Rust, into a frenzy of barking.

'Oh, it's so lovely to see you all,' Lissa declared on a happy sigh. She gazed around at the mountains thick with fronds of bracken like a matted bronze beard. Heard the familiar sounds of hens clucking about the yard, sparrows squabbling in the hedge, the moan of the wind through the ash trees. Relished the dearly loved scents of green grass and woodsmoke.

When she returned her gaze to Meg, it was to find her eyeing the two smiling visitors with a query in her grey eyes.

'Sorry, this is Jan Colwith, my best friend.' Lissa felt proud to introduce her as such.

Jan stepped forward, hand outstretched. 'Pleased to meet you, though I feel I know you already.'

Meg smiled an acknowledgement but her eyes slid to Derry.

Lissa had grown so used to Derry's outlandish style, knowing it didn't give a full picture of his complex personality she'd come to ignore it. It certainly didn't affect the way she felt about him, particularly when he kissed her.

But looking at him now through Meg's eyes, her heart shrivelled a little inside. He cut an odd-looking figure in leather jacket, narrow black trousers, huge crepe-soled shoes and string tie. A skiffle king with a fancy to be a cowboy?

Is this the best my darling girl can do? the grey

eyes said. Is this why I brought her up with such care, to have her throw herself away on the first dandy that crosses her path? All this was evident, and more, in the set of Meg's mouth, the tightness of the skin around her shrewd eyes, the whole stance of her body.

Lissa could see that Derry too had noted the disapproval for he adopted a defensive, insolent look.

Lissa drew in a quick breath as she introduced him. 'Jan's brother Derek, though he prefers to be called Derry.'

There was a long awkward pause as Meg made no move towards him. Then Derry, responding to a nudge from Lissa, held out his hand. Howdy,' he said, as if he were a US Marshal. Lissa inwardly cringed.

'Good afternoon,' Meg coolly responded, not taking her hands from the pockets of her jeans. For a moment the awkwardness deepened before Tam slapped Derry on the shoulder and ushered them all inside.

'So good it is to see you we're forgetting our manners, are we not? I'll put the kettle on. Meg, you fetch that fruit cake you made the other day, since we haven't got a fatted calf.'

Everybody laughed and the moment of tension passed.

An hour drifted by pleasantly enough with Lissa learning all the latest news and gossip, though the conversation grew stilted at times. Derry didn't say a word and nobody spoke to him. He sat and gazed upon them all with impudent arrogance on his face and Lissa chewed on her fingernails and worried.

Tam finally excused himself, saying he'd catch them a rabbit for tea. 'Would you be wanting to come with me, lad?' he asked Derry, who blenched and shook his head.

'N-no thanks. I'm OK here.'

Tam chuckled and went off whistling.

Lissa recognised a flicker of annoyance in Meg's eyes, as if she'd been hoping that Derry would disappear in a puff of smoke, so she started to talk about the draper's shop, anything to lighten the atmosphere.

'You wouldn't believe how old fashioned it is, and Miss Stevens spends all her time in the office though what she does there I can't imagine. I'd love to be let loose on the place,' Lissa declared, suddenly realising that she would.

Meg, scraping potatoes for lunch at the kitchen sink, looked up in surprise. 'Why, what would you do with it?'

'I could make it profitable.' Lissa's sudden flush of excitement increased as she considered the idea. 'I'd get rid of all that old stock for a start.'

'Paint the front,' Jan suggested, coming to sit at the pine table with her. 'Get rid of that awful pea green.'

'And turn that draughty old stock room into a

second display area, and fitting rooms. There's plenty of space upstairs for stock.'

'Why not open two floors while you're at it,' Jan quipped.

'Why not?' Lissa laughed.

Meg rinsed the potatoes, put them in a pan and set it on the stove with a clatter. Then checked the progress of the meal. A casserole of pork in cider was bubbling nicely in the oven. For afters she'd made a lovely apple pie, spiced with a pinch of cloves. It would go down well with a hunk of home-produced, crumbly cheese. She wiped her hands on a cloth and took off her apron.

'You seem happy anyway,' she said, forcing her voice to sound pleased and wondering why she wasn't.

'Oh, we are. Life's great.'

Meg wanted Lissa to be happy, she really did. If only Carreckwater were nearer, and they saw a bit more of her. And if only she wouldn't pick up every bit of rubbish she felt sorry for, such as this Teddy Boy. Meg felt the familiar fear in the pit of her stomach. Didn't Lissa realise how unreliable men were?

After lunch Lissa offered to show Jan and Derry around her home. They were halfway out the door when Meg stopped them.

'We're a farm, remember, and the lanes are muddy,' eyeing the pretty blue shoes with the kitten heels.

'Oh, sorry, I didn't think.

Meg tried to make a joke of it but felt awkward, as if her own daughter had become a stranger to her. 'Not really suitably dressed, are you? You look so different.' She hadn't meant to say anything of the sort. But looking at this newly minted, coolly sophisticated young miss who had replaced her own laughing, lively country girl, Meg felt suddenly faded and tired, and old. But then that girl had vanished long since, in a muddle of adolescent angst. It was sad really that daughters had to grow up at all, Meg decided.

Lissa was bridling at the implied criticism. 'I wanted to look smart for you, that's all.'

Now all the wrong words came tumbling out. 'What in fancy shoes, lipstick and eye shadow. Is that mascara on your lashes? And what makes your skirt stick out?'

'A paper nylon petticoat. Do you like it? I starch it with sugar.' Lissa spun about to show it off then flushed slightly as she saw Derry's smile.

'Paper nylon? Whatever next?' Meg said, wiping the table top with unnecessary vigour. 'You must be earning plenty of money then?' She bit her lip, realising she sounded silly and mean.

'I earn enough.'

Tam laughed in his cheery way, as if it were all great fun and the air was not crackling with an undercurrent of tension. 'I think we're a bit out of touch with your young world,' he said.

Wellingtons had to be found for them all since

Jan's shoes were even sillier and Derry's were quite beyond the pale for farm lanes. But there was no shortage of sensible footwear in the Broombank kitchen. Yet the fact that she had forgotten to come properly shod seemed to be a black mark in some way. Lissa felt hurt by this unspoken criticism, seeing it again as a form of rejection.

Lissa stood on the knoll gazing up at Dundale Knot, breathing deeply of the clear air, letting it bubble inside her like champagne. She'd taken her friends to visit Sally Ann and Nick down at Ashlea, which had gone quite well and she'd left them talking while she went for a walk with Meg. 'Carreckwater is pretty, and great fun but I do miss all this majesty, this freedom of space.'

'You can come back any time,' Meg said at her elbow.

Lissa smiled. She thought Meg seemed quieter these days, a rather sad and lonely figure. No more babies had come and she would be forty next year. She wanted to wrap her arms about her foster mother and say how sorry she was to have caused the loss of that precious burden, but Meg was moving away from her, saying something that brought Lissa's wandering attention to heel quite sharply.

'What did you say?'

Meg turned to her. 'I said where on earth did you find him? He's not at all the sort of boy I would've expected you to bring home.'

'Derry?'

'Yes, Derry. Even the name is rather silly.'

'Why? What's wrong with it, or him?' Lissa was instantly on the defensive.

Meg gave a self-conscious laugh. Too late she realised she'd spoken her thoughts out loud when really she shouldn't. She ploughed on, hoping to make Lissa understand how anxious she felt. 'I should have thought that was obvious.'

'Not to me.'

'Look at his clothes. We may live on the remote fells and not yet have the wonders of television, or even electricity. But we read the newspapers, listen to the radio, so we're aware of the trouble such people are causing.'

'Such people?' Lissa could feel a cold sensation creep into her stomach. Why could they never be friends as they used to be? 'Derry isn't a separate breed. Anyway, what sort of trouble?'

'Teddy Boys. Ripping up cinema seats, that sort of thing. We've read all about it.'

'Derry never ripped up a cinema seat in his life. He wouldn't know how to start.'

Spots of colour marked each high cheek bone but Meg's lips remained tight and thin, determined to stick to her point. 'Nevertheless, he seems unreliable. Not at all the sort of boy we would have chosen for you.'

'Then it's a good thing I can choose for myself,' said Lissa tartly, feeling the gulf between them widen. And she had hoped to bridge it today, to bring them close again.

'You're too young to make choices,' Meg unwisely remarked. 'It's too easy to make mistakes when you are young.'

Lissa struck back in the only way she knew. 'Like you objected to my writing to my own mother?'

Meg's face was the colour of cold ash. 'I was afraid for you. I wanted to keep you, yes, I'll admit that. But I was afraid that it might not work out with Kath, and her rejection would hurt you.'

It was a fair assessment of what had actually happened, but Lissa was no longer receptive to reason. Meg had disapproved of her clothes, Jan's silly high heels, and worst of all, she'd criticised Derry. 'I need to understand why I wasn't important to her. Why my mother didn't simply drop everything when she realised she was having me.'

Meg did not reply. It all seemed so long ago now. How could she explain the hurt, the passion, the lost hopes and fears of a past generation to this young woman who saw everything in black and white, and only as it related to herself. Lissa was self-obsessed as all young girls were, as Kath had been. But it would be unkind to say so. She had often thought how unfair it was that the major decisions of one's life had to be made when one was too young to make the right ones.

'There was a war on,' was all she could say. 'It changed things.'

'I don't believe that.' Lissa spat out the words, stepping, as if wanting to distance herself from the simple truth. 'Anyway, the war has been over for years. Everyone is entitled to know who they are, where they come from, and what makes them behave in a certain way. You never gave me that chance.'

'I did my best. I told you about Kath, about both of us, and about Jack. I told you what happened.'

'Eventually you did, but much too late. The damage had been done.'

Meg looked Lissa squarely in the face but she did not beg for understanding now. She showed annoyance at fighting this unjustified attack. 'What damage? I loved you. I wanted to protect you.'

Lissa gave a grunt of disbelief, hot tears standing proud in her eyes, wanting to extricate herself from the terrible hurtful words pouring into her head and out of her mouth but unable to do so. 'If that were true you wouldn't have needed a baby, would you? But you did, so you couldn't possibly have loved me.'

Meg jerked with shock and at last did raise her voice, the anger in it sharp and acrid. 'That's a terrible thing to say.'

'It's the truth. I have this memory,' Lissa cried. 'Of me crying in a cot. I'm holding on to the sides and you look as if you are about to pick me up, then you turn and walk away, leaving me screaming. Was that true? Did that really happen?'

Meg was gaping at her. 'No one can remember so far back. Someone has told you.' It was the worst possible thing she could have said, for it proved Lissa's point.

Lissa stared at her for a long, silent moment, shaking her head in bewilderment. 'So it did happen. You really didn't want to pick me up.' It was a statement, cold and bleak.

'I was young. Hurt and betrayed by my best friend and the man I'd hoped to marry. I was afraid . . .'

'For yourself,' Lissa cut in bitterly, not wanting to hear any more. She turned and started to walk away. Meg hurried after her and grasped her arm.

'Don't go, Lissa. Not like this, angry with each other. I do love you. I know I have my faults, being obsessed with the sheep the main one, but I've been the best mother I could be. I loved you as if you were my own child. I also knew that I might lose you, that Kath might come back at any time and take you from me. Can't you imagine how that felt?'

There was a desperation in her voice, one that suddenly Lissa longed to respond to. But too much had been said, too much hurt inflicted. 'You stopped me going with her when I was seven. You stopped me writing to her. Now you want to stop me from seeing Derry.' Lissa shook off Meg's restraining hand. 'You criticise me, tell me which friends I should choose, decide my life for me, but you really have no rights over me at all, have you? You never even adopted me, not officially. *You are not my mother.*'

It was the final cruelty and Lissa's heart clenched

as she saw the spasm of pain that came into Meg's face at these words. What had she said? What had she done? She hadn't meant to go this far. But all the disappointments, the broken promises she'd suffered over the years had boiled up and spilled out of her like a hot tide of evil lava, destroying everything in its path.

'Oh, Lissa,' Meg said, putting her hands to her face in a helpless gesture of despair. 'I didn't realise . . . I never believed it was so important to you. You should have said.'

'I *did* say, but you weren't listening, were you? You only heard what you wanted to hear.' Lissa's voice grew thick with unshed tears and not a little self-pity while Meg, knowing there was too much truth in the accusation to deny, bit on her lip and said nothing.

Then Lissa tossed back her head, eyes blazing, and in that moment she had never looked more like Kath, with the same wild, devil-may-care beauty about her. 'As for Derry, he's good and kind for all his odd notion of fashion. More importantly, he's my friend.'

She very nearly said that she loved him but decided against it at the last moment, her instinct for self-protection too strong. 'I choose my own friends even if I couldn't choose my own mother. I'm free to make my own decisions now, and one day I'll marry whom I damned well please. Not that you'll be interested, since neither you nor Kath wanted me at all really, did you?'

And she walked away, not waiting for Meg's reply.

Lissa wept as they drove along the lane out of the dale. She knew she'd hurt Meg badly and wanted it not to matter. Knowing that it mattered very much.

'Didn't go too well, did it? Suppose I shouldn't have worn this pink shirt. Bit much, was it?'

Lissa wiped her eyes to look into his warm brown eyes and felt herself melt inside. 'Wear whatever you like, Derry. People should accept you for yourself, not what or who they think you are. Stop. Stop here.'

He slammed on the brakes at the urgency of her request and stared at the rain streaming down the windscreen. 'You're not getting out in this?' But she was.

Lissa was out of the car in a trice, gazing out across the rain swept fells.

'What's she doing?' Derry asked Jan, disbelief in his voice.

'Haven't the faintest.' Jan tried calling through the window but Lissa didn't even turn her head. Then she darted an agonised glance at her brother and on a mutual decision they both sighed and climbed out of the car, stepping gingerly through the puddles to go and stand beside her. Derry turned up his collar as the rain flattened his hair and ran down his face and neck, soaking the front of his best pink shirt. His shoes would be quite ruined, he thought.

Lissa was lifting her face up to the rain as if she loved it.

'What are you looking at?' he asked, following her gaze into the sweep of mist that cloaked the fell.

'There. Don't you see it? High on that ridge?'

Derry squinted through the rain, trying not to think that he could be somewhere warm and dry, enjoying a pint in the King's Arms with his mates maybe. 'There's a house,' he said in surprise. 'Surrounded by tall trees.'

'Larkrigg Hall. Yews and oaks all about it.' Lissa smiled. 'Or yows and yaks as Grandfather Joe would say. That's where I might have lived, if my mother had kept me. It's where my grandmother still lives.'

'Saints alive!' Derry said, forgetting all about the rain as his mouth dropped open. 'That's some pad.' No wonder she'd appeared so stuck up at first, with a place like that behind her.

'I suppose it is. But I hate it. I hate my grandmother too. She doesn't want me and I don't want her. Any more than my mother wanted me. Any more than Meg wants me now.'

They were both staring at her, not daring to challenge her words because of the venom and desperation in her voice.

'I don't care. I don't need anyone. Not Rosemary Ellis, not Meg, not my mother. No one.'

'Everyone needs someone,' put in Jan quietly.

Lissa only shook her head, flicking back the wet

curls from her face with a defiant gesture. 'I'm a woman now, not a child, and can cope on my own.'

'Hear hear,' murmured Derry, though not with any great conviction. Her mood bothered him, as it clearly bothered Jan.

Lissa turned away suddenly and if either of them noticed her dash a hand across her eyes, they put it down to the rain. Best not to question her any more today, Derry decided. He put an arm about her shoulders. 'Come on, you're wet through. We all are. Let's go home and put the kettle on.'

She smiled up at him, slipping her arm into his. 'Yes, let's go home. I've looked my fill for today, perhaps for a lifetime. There's nothing for me here.'

There was a note pinned to the garden shed door when Derry got back that Sunday evening. It was from Renee. 'Mr Brandon called. Wants to see you in his office, first thing.' There followed several exclamation marks.

Had the old lady complained because he'd failed to explain the papers to her. Oh, crikey!

The thought of the interview kept him awake half the night, worrying himself into more discomfort than usual in the narrow bed that just about filled the small wooden shed. A cold wind blew through the gap under the door, lifting the newspaper he'd used to block it and giving Derry cause to wonder what he was doing here. Why didn't he find somewhere better to live?

The cold light of Monday morning found him tapping politely on the glass panel of the inner office door, his heart in his boots as he prepared for the worst.

He was wearing his sober grey office suit, pristine white shirt and blue tie with silver diamonds down the middle, half wishing he'd found the courage to wear his new blue silk waistcoat. It wasn't strictly businesslike but it might've given his confidence a boost. Derry was shocked to find his hand actually shaking as he turned the knob in answer to the command to enter. He thrust back his shoulders and swung into the room. Nevertheless, it was a pale imitation of his usual swagger.

'Renee said you wanted to speak with me.' Whatever he had to face he'd do so with courage. Even so he was shocked by the cold anger in Brandon's face.

'You've gone too far this time. There's no excuse for such loutish behaviour.'

Derry hastened to his own defence. 'I thought you'd want me to leave the legal explanations to you. It's not really my job, is it?'

Brandon glared at Derry in perplexed fury. 'What you are jabbering about?'

'The old lady, Mrs Fraser, who else? She didn't understand all those long words and to be honest,' he flushed beetroot red,' neither did I.'

'I'm not talking about a foolish old woman, nor any dratted document. I'm talking about my boat.'

Now it was Derry's turn to gape. 'Your boat?'

Brandon leaned across the polished mahogany surface of his desk to glare at Derry. 'Why did you do it? In revenge for the yacht race, I suppose.'

'D-do what?'

'Don't play games with me, I'm not in the mood. You holed my boat in revenge.'

'Holed your . . .?' An awful realisation dawned. 'Good God, are you saying someone has damaged your yacht?'

Brandon rolled his eyes up to the ceiling as if for assistance. 'Stop pretending, Colwith. I've no time for your lies.'

'I'm not lying.' Every vestige of colour had drained from Derry's cheeks, leaving them almost as white as his shirt. 'Why would anyone make a hole in your yacht?'

'Why indeed? You had the motive and no doubt the opportunity, as you know where I moor it. Who else could it be?' He let the words hang in the air and in the long moment that followed Derry desperately searched for an answer.

'One of your clients, someone with a grudge?'

Philip gave a mocking laugh. 'I don't take that kind of client on, as you well know. This isn't a criminal practice. You don't suppose Mrs Fraser goes in for vandalism, do you? Or perhaps Mr McArthur? Come, Derry, admit to it. Your air of innocence doesn't convince me and it certainly won't convince the police.' He reached for the phone.

Derry's was filled with alarm. 'Don't ring the

police. I didn't do it, I swear. I didn't touch your damn boat. It hasn't sunk, has it?'

Brandon's fingers drummed on the telephone. 'Fortunately not. But you've made a mess of the hull. It'll cost a small fortune to repair.'

'Oh, God. I didn't do it, I swear.' Derry stood transfixed with horror, appalled by the accusation. 'I wouldn't do such a thing. Why would I?'

'Save your winsome charm for your lady friends, it cuts no ice with me. We both know why you did it. Because I beat you in that race.'

Derry was desperately trying to pull himself together, to think, but his mind refused to operate beyond the horror of his predicament. 'I did win, you know I did. It was you trying to ram me, not the other way round.'

'Can you prove it? I was on the starboard tack, remember. Therefore I had right of way.'

'In theory. I'm innocent and that's the truth.'

Barndon's voice almost purred. 'If you're so certain of being able to prove your innocence, you've nothing to fear from police questioning, have you?' He lifted the receiver. 'Assuming they would take your word against mine.' Charcoal eyes seared into brown.

'I wouldn't stand a chance,' Derry said, hopelessness in his voice. 'They'll call me a Ted, a rabble-rouser, a trouble-maker.'

The telephone receiver slid back into its cradle. 'Very well, I will agree not to call in the police. But I feel bound to terminate your employment.'

216

Derry gasped. '*Why?* My dad could repair the boat.' His offer was treated with silent contempt, as if he hadn't spoken.

'On numerous occasions you've been given warnings for insubordination. You cavort all over town when you should be working. Pester Miss Henshaw and Christine, and play foolish games in the office. Now you've gone too far. I'm perfectly justified in having you sacked, Colwith. My patience is exhausted.'

'But . . .'

'I strongly advise you to leave town,' Philip mangled a paper clip to little more than a crumpled piece of wire in his fingers. 'Go and seek this fame and fortune you talk so much about.'

Derry was appalled. 'You've declared me guilty without a trial. That's not fair.'

'Take a week's notice, or we'll let the local constabulary decide the matter. The choice is yours.'

CHAPTER 11

Lissa felt oddly nervous as they stepped off the bus. There'd been no problem with Jan as she'd claimed to have plans of her own, so here they were. Just the two of them. She could feel her heart beating fast at the prospect of a whole day alone with Derry on the fells. Clothed in their tawny brilliance, they looked so achingly inviting Lissa could hardly wait to get up there. With a pale, shining sun and clouds too high for rain, it seemed a perfect autumn day, an opportunity to prove she wasn't as frozen and stuck up as Derry imagined.

The bus dropped them close to Troutbeck and they didn't speak as they started to walk up through the village. Lissa shyly kept several feet of track between them as they made their way past farmsteads, seventeen-century statesman houses with their quaint spinning galleries, along narrow walled lanes and beside the bubbling beck that gave the village its name.

As they laboured uphill the distance between them shrank to a matter of inches.

'I need to talk to you,' Derry said, and Lissa was

surprised to hear a nervousness in his voice even greater than her own. Then a farmer stopped and offered them a lift.

'It's a bonny day.'

'Aye,' Derry agreed.

'Going up the fell?'

Derry agreed they meant to walk up to High Street by way of the Tongue.

'Jump in then. I'll save thee the boring bit up this road. Then you'll know where you're at.'

And so he did. Lissa sat with Derry on the bumpy leather seat and thought how lucky she was to be here with him now, alone. It was all very exciting. And what could he possibly want to talk about?

The farmer dropped them above Troutbeck Park Farm, saving them two or three miles. They thanked him and he waved them off, warning them to take care.

'Watch the weather. It'll come in from the west.'

'Thanks.' They set off through the gate to cut across country, over rocks and through thick clinging bracken. They climbed stiles, bridged the beck and negotiated boggy ground which sucked at their boots. Yellow loosestrife bloomed and the sedge grass and rushes were thick beneath their feet. A family of meadow pipits 'pheeped' crossly at being so rudely disturbed. When they finally reached firmer ground with Ill Bell rising above them, they stopped by mutual consent for a rest and a sip from their water bottle.

'It's a tough, steep haul of two and a half thousand feet. Think you can make it?'

Lissa gazed up at the steep climb, Thornthwaite Crag to the left, Ill Bell to the right, and grinned. 'Of course.'

'We'll take it slow.'

'What was it you wanted to talk to me about?' Lissa asked, as they set off up the track.

'Philip Brandon.'

Violet eyes sparkled. 'Every time we talk about your boss, we quarrel. I want nothing to spoil this wonderful day. I've shown you my favourite places, now you can show me yours.'

'Maybe you won't enjoy my company as much as you do his.'

'Oh, for goodness' sake. Didn't I say we'd quarrel? I won't hear another word on the subject of Philip Brandon.' And she strutted ahead in high dudgeon, forcing him to hurry to catch her up.

Derry was in despair. How could he explain about him being forced to leave if she refused to let him explain? Not that Lissa would necessarily believe him. She hadn't believed him about the yacht race. Accused him of making it up and of being a bad loser. So why should she believe him innocent now? He sighed. Girls! You couldn't understand them.

But he'd no wish to spoil this day either. He straightened his spine, eased the rucksack on his back and decided he'd tell her later. It'd taken him months to get her alone like this, he wasn't about to mess it up now.

They stopped for a much needed rest half way up to admire the view. 'Isn't it utterly breathtaking?' Lissa said, rubbing the cramp in her calves, though the walking was getting easier as she found her second wind.

'This is the same path the Roman soldiers would have taken from the Windermere valley to reach High Street, where they marched right across the tops in their quest to get to Scotland. They fought a battle here with the Britons, on Scot's Rake. Can't you just see it?' His brown eyes shone and Lissa had to laugh.

'I wouldn't like to do this climb in full armour, with breastplate and sword.' They both gasped at the thought. 'I'm sorry if I've been a bit – well, blow hot and cold, as you put it, Derry. I've had a few things on my mind lately.'

'I'd like to think we've called an end to our own battles,' he agreed.

Lissa smiled at him, feeling the warmth of his response flow through her, setting her blood surging. He did like her, he really did.

It came to him then, with a jolt, just how much he would miss her when he left. But he had his career to think about, didn't he? Which was more important? He wished he could decide.

'I've thought about that question you asked me,' she was saying, 'and I've decided. I will be your girl, if you still want me to be.'

She was blushing furiously and Derry was puffing out his chest as if she'd told him he was the most handsome man in the universe. Yet inside his heart was sinking, knowing this made it worse. But what could he do if he stayed in Carreckwater? Be a waiter at the Marina Hotel? Build boats that fewer and fewer people wanted to buy because they preferred the new moulded plastic and fibreglass. And how could he give up his music? He leaned forward and kissed her softly upon her lips. The thrill of it ran through her like a forest fire as, hand in hand, they walked on up the track.

When they reached the beacon on Thornthwaite Crag, a solid chimney of stones fourteen feet high, they were breathless and stopped to eat their sandwiches.

'Isn't it beautiful?' Lissa breathed, the freedom of the fells soothing her soul, as it always did, the undulating surface of the summit stretching out invitingly all around them, just waiting to be explored.

'Makes you feel a bit insignificant though, doesn't it? As if your own troubles are slight by comparison with those nature has to contend with.'

Spread out below them, beyond the fans of scree and craggy boulders, lay all of the Troutbeck valley. The silver thread of the beck could be traced right down until it disappeared around the hump of the Tongue, dwarfed by the sweep of greater mountains all around. And beyond that, could be seen the blue ribbon of Lake Windermere and the smaller Carreckwater.

Derry wondered if he could tell her his troubles now, then bit hungrily into a thick cheese sandwich. Lissa did the same.

They ate in companionable silence. When they'd finished, Derry rolled over and cupped his chin in his hands to stare up at her. 'So tell me what you intend to do with your life?'

Lissa stared at him in surprise. 'I've never really thought about it.'

'Everyone should have a life plan.'

He'd tell her now. He'd say, quite casually, 'I'll be away for the next few weeks, trying to get a recording contract.'

'Plans don't always work out,' she said, with such sadness in her voice that he bit back the unspoken words.' Long ago, when I was very young, I vowed to have no more plans, no more wishes. It's too disappointing when they don't work out. What about you? Do you have one?'

She looked so beautiful, so trusting, gazing at him out of those soft, entrancing eyes. His courage failed. 'Oh, you know me,' he joked. 'I intend to be rich and famous. Make a million records and have my skiffle group play on television. The usual stuff.'

Lissa tried to laugh, though she found it surprisingly difficult. 'You'd have to leave Carreckwater to do all of that. Go off to London to seek your fame and fortune?' She smiled up at him, waiting for him to deny it.

'Would you blame me if I did?' He was watching her carefully.

Lissa frowned, cautious suddenly. 'Everyone has the right to pursue their dream. It's no business of mine what you do, is it?' She longed for Derry to assure her that he would never leave, that his only dream was to stay with her. But he was chewing on a piece of grass, saying nothing.

The black knuckle-bone rocks, the cry of a lone curlew in the silence seemed to intensify a sudden and intense sense of loneliness. As if Derry had slipped from her in some way when really he was still beside her, reaching for her hand, urging her to move on.

Why hadn't he denied it? Oh, she didn't want him to go away. The very idea opened up a deep void that frightened her. Head in the clouds. A dreamer, that's all he was.

They walked on, hand in hand. Perhaps because of the silent sweep of mountains all around, which made Lissa feel as if they were the only two people in the world, she told him of her illegitimacy. She brandished it like a weapon, so he could stab her with it if he wanted to. 'That's why I hate my grandmother.'

'I know all about that,' he said, as if it were of no consequence. 'Jan told me. So what? It's not your fault. is it?'

Violet eyes opened wide and she pushed back

the wayward curls with an impatient hand. 'Don't you understand? Can't you see how rejected it makes me feel? It's not as if Meg went along to an orphanage and *chose* me. Kath, my own mother, didn't want me at all, and got rid of me at the first opportunity. She left Meg literally holding the baby. *Me.*'

Derry considered this for a moment as he helped her negotiate a pile of fallen rocks, the peat cracked and brown underfoot. 'So because you hate Kath for dumping you, you blame Meg? That's not very fair.'

Hot fury rose in her breast. 'Fair? For all I know, Meg might've driven Kath away, as punishment for stealing her fiancé. How do I know what happened?'

'Exactly. And it's so long ago, does it really matter?'

'Of course it matters. Don't blame me, I'm the victim here.'

'What sort of victim?' He gazed at her, genuinely puzzled that she was so close to losing her temper, simply because he didn't see her point of view.

'Nobody wanted me. None of them. Don't you see?' Lissa longed for him to tell her that he wanted her, would want her for as long as he lived.

Derry had been watching her face, reading the expressions that flitted across it in the space of a few seconds. Hope, pain, disappointment and disillusionment. 'You know your trouble, don't you?' He grinned at her, crooked and teasing. 'You don't know where you're going because you're too busy looking where you came from.'

'What?'

'In climbing we're taught never to look back. Onward and upward, that's the thing. Look, I'll show you something.' Lissa very nearly refused but then let him take her hand and lead her to where a drystone wall lay tumbled across their path. She stood and looked over, gasping at what she saw. It was the most amazing sight.

A whole new vista had opened up before her eyes. She looked out on to a complete new set of dales and mountains, lit by the sun in brilliant green and gold patches like a magical stage set with a backdrop of blue mountains and the glimmer of yet another silver lake.

'This is known as Threshwaite Mouth, probably because the mountains yawn wide open, giving you a grand view of the Northern Lakes. If we carried on walking we would reach Patterdale and Ullswater. There's Ullswater, every bit as beautiful as Carreckwater and the Windermere valley we've just left.'

'It's magnificent. Takes my breath away.'

'We could stay in the softer valleys for ever of course, in the lush intake land, taking no risks whatsoever. We don't have to come up these mountains. We could venture on through the rigours of Skiddaw forest. We could choose to climb Helvellyn or Scafell, or go right over the border and up into the highlands of Scotland if we wanted. Or we could take a bus and play it safe. It's up to you. But if you want to know what lies beyond the next mountain and the one after that, and find out your own worth at the same time, then don't look back, look forward. It's the only way to succeed.'

He turned to her and found she had tears in her eyes. 'Oh, crikey, listen to me playing the philosopher. Still, life isn't about where you came from, only where you're going.'

'I can't believe that. I believe who you are and where you start out determines where you are going.'

'But a lot of it's up to you. When my mam was dying,' he said, fixing his eyes on the middle distance. 'She told me not to remember her as sick and unhappy. "If you must look back," she said, "think of the happy times when I was healthy and full of life. Better still, look forward. Live your life to the full. Live for tomorrow."'

He was silent for a moment, then he said. 'So that's what I try to do. Much as it hurts at times.'

Lissa gazed at him, and at the land before her. Could he be right? Had she spent too much of her life looking back, worrying about other people? Should she push herself forward more? Anything seemed possible with Derry beside her.

He was looking at her with the kind of intent gaze that made her shiver with longing. 'I wish I could be brave like you. Dream. Make plans. Do anything I wanted.' She slanted a glance up at him. 'Perhaps I even wish I dared to let myself love you.'

Lissa wanted to take back the words the instant they were out of her mouth. But they were spoken now, bursting out of her, answering a need in her.

His response was everything she might have hoped for. He pulled her into his arms and kissed her, a deep, loving kiss that went to the heart of her. 'Why can you not?' he softly asked. 'If you want to?'

'Because I'm afraid.'

'Of me?'

'Of rejection. I expect people not to want or care for me, except out of duty. I've decided they're really only concerned about their own feelings, not mine.'

He looked shocked. 'What, because your mother didn't want you, you imagine everyone else is the same? Even Meg? Even me? That's a bit strong.'

'It's how I feel. So unwanted.'

He was cradling her in his arms, smoothing back tendrils of hair from her brow, kissing the tears from her cheeks, telling her that he loved her and would do so for as long as he lived. Excitement mounted inside as his words soothed her, making her grow weak with the need to surrender to the compulsion of wanting.

Their kisses were growing ever more passionate and he suddenly stopped, to put her firmly from him. 'Hell, we'd best stop now. We've a long way to walk yet.' His eyes were warm and loving and she reached for him, kissing him of her own volition, heard his groan, and her own soft sigh of pleasure as they sank upon the sweet grass.

'I won't hurt you,' he murmured against the fevered warmth of her skin. 'I won't do anything you don't want me to.'

'I'm not cheap,' she said, aware in that moment that there was little she didn't want him to do.' I want you to respect me.'

'I do respect you, silly.'

Her heart exulted when she felt the muscles in his arms tighten about her. Lissa had never felt more alive, more wanted in her life before. They rolled and clung together like young puppies, teasing, touching and kissing as they explored and discovered the joys of love. She stuffed bracken down his neck and he tickled her mercilessly, stopping her squeals with increasingly demanding kisses.

It was meant to be no more than harmless fun. They'd neither of them intended to take it too far but Derry couldn't disguise his hunger for her, nor she her need for him. Though he was a young and inexperienced lover, a little clumsy in his eagerness, they came together quite naturally and made love without restraint, pulling off clothes which got in the way, ignoring others till a tide of passion took them over and the laughter faded. Their loving seemed right, the most natural thing in the world. Lissa gave herself to him freely and with all her love, cleansing herself of the pain of broken promises. There was a tender sweetness and sensitivity in their loving that moved her to tears and brought Derry to a shuddering climax.

★   ★   ★

Afterwards they lay upon the yielding bracken staring into the wide arc of a brilliant blue sky, stunned by their emotions and shaken by the result. 'I shouldn't have let you do that,' Lissa murmured, filled suddenly by the enormity of what had happened. What had she been thinking of? She hadn't been thinking at all, that was the trouble. Now that the passion had faded she began to worry. 'I can't think what came over me.'

'Me neither.'

A dreadful thought struck her and she sat up, all hot and bothered. 'Oh lord, what if I get pregnant?'

Derry took her hand and squeezed it consolingly. 'You won't get pregnant. I'm not daft. I was careful.'

Violet eyes gazed pleadingly into his. 'But what if?' It didn't bear thinking about. 'I'd die. I'd just *die.*'

He pulled her into his arms and kissed her brow with great tenderness. 'I promise you, Lissa, you're quite safe. I'll look after you.'

'I love you,' she said.

'And I you.'

'For ever?'

'And ever.'

They were sitting on Kidsty Pike. Not too far, had they but known it, from where Jack Lawson had proposed to Meg nearly twenty years before. Where he'd given her his mother's engagement ring and she'd kept by her promise to wait for him throughout the long years of war that followed, through all the pain and suffering, the realisation of his betrayal and her love for another man.

Lissa and Derry were children of a different world. There was no fear of their young lives being torn apart by Hitler's ruthless ambitions. They believed it would be an easy world to live in because of that simple fact.

'We should go,' he murmured, kissing every contour of her delightful, beautiful face. 'How smooth and silky your skin is.' She felt warm and languorous, heady with the joys of the tenderness that flowed between them, pushing aside her niggling worries. She wouldn't get pregnant, she wouldn't. Not from just one mistake.

Neither could bear to break the spell, and as they were quite exhausted, they fell asleep, wrapped in each other's arms.

Lissa woke to find the clouds had gathered and darkened, clotting the skies like thick cream. She looked beyond his beloved face and stared into a blank, soft white nothingness. Then she was pushing him away, trying desperately to wake him and examine the seriousness of their situation.

'Do wake up, Derry. The mist has come down. We're smothered in cloud.'

He sat up and rubbed his eyes, gazing about him as worried as she. The last thing anyone needed on a mountain walk was to be engulfed in mist. He cursed quietly under his breath though the face he turned to Lissa was reassuring, fixed with a careful smile.

'It'll be all right. We'll just have to sit it out until it's gone.'

'Sit it out? Here?' She was pulling her sweater over her blouse, reaching for her coat. The golden moment had faded, leaving cold reality in its wake. 'We must go home, before we freeze to death.'

'We can't see where we're walking. One wrong step and we'd be tripping down the cliff into Riggingdale. That's a fair drop and I'd prefer not to make it, if you don't mind,' he said, making a joke of his anxiety.

Lissa hesitated, understanding the sense of what he said but unwilling to accept it. 'We can be careful.'

'It's easy to lose any sense of direction in thick mist like this. Much safer to stay put.'

The argument went on for some time, but in the end Derry won. They put on every item of clothing they'd brought with them and waited, cuddled up together for warmth.

'It's lifting.'

'I don't think so.' A soft rain had started, sweeping in, as the old farmer had warned, from the west. 'I'll keep you safe, I promise. All night if need be.'

'All night?' The last time she'd stayed out all night Meg had lost her baby. Lissa felt the same cold panic. 'We shouldn't have fallen asleep. It's all your fault,' she accused, with no sense of reason as fear took root.

'Oh, sure. I ordered the mist by mail order and told it not to be late. Calm down, Lissa. You're getting hysterical. Come here, love. You can have my coat as well if you're cold.'

She hated to be told to calm down. She'd been a fool, she told herself. He'd coerced her here, persuaded her to believe in him, *seduced* her, but how could she trust his promises? How could she trust anyone, even Derry? Oh, what had she done? What had she been thinking of to let things go so far? 'If we stay here all night everyone will know. It'll be all around town that we've slept together.'

'Well, it's true. We have.' He laughed and she felt suddenly exasperated with him, almost crying with frustration.

'I don't want anyone to know.'

'Why? Are you ashamed of me?'

'Don't be silly. It should be our secret. Just between us. What will people think? They'll say I'm no good.'

'To hell with what people think. That's their problem.'

Now that the sun had gone and the beautiful green grandeur of the fells swallowed up by ghostly mist, Lissa felt cold and vulnerable and alone. All her worries exploded in her head, numbing her with their implications. 'Oh, what if I do get pregnant?' She was as bad as her mother. Wicked.

Wanton. A harlot. She'd proved her grandmother right.

'You won't get pregnant. I promise, Lissa.' He was stroking her hair, smoothing her cheeks, trying to reassure her. 'It's all right, love. You're quite safe.'

But she wasn't listening. 'What will Meg say? She must have guessed I was really wicked inside. Just like my mother.'

'It's not wicked to love.'

The mist seemed to be thickening, pressing against her like soft padding hands. Lissa was slapping his hands away and the next instant she was on her feet, running and stumbling in her desperation to find her way back.

He called out to her, urging her to take care. To one side of her, smothered by the thick cloud, was the perilous drop to Blea Water, two hundred feet or more below. She ran the other way to avoid it, became disoriented, then her foot caught on something, there was a loud crack and blackness closed in.

'Lisa. Wake up, Lissa. Are you all right? Please open your eyes.'

Derry's voice came as if from a great distance, then his face swam into view before her eyes.

'Thank God,' he said when he saw her blink. 'You tripped and hit your head against a rock. Are you all right?'

He helped her to her feet and they huddled

together, wrapped in each other's arms in a small hollow they found beside a rock until she felt recovered enough to go on.

'I'm sorry I panicked,' she murmured, snug against his hard chest. 'Only shows my foolish insecurity. I will learn to trust you, really I will.' Her teeth were starting to chatter with cold. 'You're very special to me, Derry Colwith, d-do you know that?'

'We'll have to risk going on now,' he said, trying not to show his concern. 'You're cold and it's starting to rain. Come on, love, hold on to me. If we can find the cairn that marks Nan Bield pass, there's a shelter there and we can rest up for a while, until the weather improves.'

But search as they might they missed the cairn, smothered as it was in the mist. With visibility so bad and the rain running down their necks it soon became plain they had gone too far and were almost on the Longsleddale ridge which went ever higher and miles out of their way.

'I should have brought my compass,' Derry mourned. 'There's nothing for it but to go back and try again.'

Lissa almost sobbed with tiredness and frustration. What was she doing on this mountain top with Derry Colwith who didn't seem to have the first idea where he was? Could she really trust him with her life? For that was what this could amount to. Worries about lost virginity seemed small by comparison.

'Can you find it this time?'

Sure.' Less certain than he sounded.

Turning back and retracing their steps was the worst thing Lissa had ever done. The rain was in their faces now and the grass grew slippy underfoot. After another hour Derry admitted they must have missed it again.

'We'll have to go down the scree into Kentmere valley,' he suggested, and Lissa's heart jolted. Scree walking was dangerous at the best of times. In mist, late in the afternoon, it was very nearly foolhardy. She said as much, protesting vigorously.

'This bit isn't too steep, I promise.'

Lissa said she didn't wish to hear any more promises. Not right now. But he wasn't listening.

'We can't go west over Kirkstone in this weather and Longsleddale would be a long, hard walk in the opposite direction. Much too far. Kentmere is the best bet. There are farms down there, houses and people. Trust me.'

What choice did she have? Lissa slid her hand in his and gave it a little squeeze. 'All right, I will.'

It took them three hours to get down off the fells. It was the worst three hours of Lissa's life. Sometimes the mist lifted, giving them tantalising glimpses of the way ahead. At other times it blanketed down, sweeping them with rain so that they were soon soaked to the skin despite thick woollen sweaters and waterproofs. It ran down their necks and into their socks, making puddles between their toes. It soaked right through their clothing and plastered their shirts to their backs.

Underfoot it was treacherous, slipping and sliding over rain-slicked grass, patches of scree, and jagged stones where a cricked ankle seemed inevitable and could have been a life-threatening catastrophe.

Lissa felt certain they would never reach the soft meadows of the valley below, but at last they did, almost stumbling with relief on to the long flat road. Drenched and shivering, Derry knocked at the first door where a light showed.

'Eeh, na then,' said a warm friendly voice as the door opened, letting light spill out into the gloaming. 'What have we here?'

'I wondered if perhaps you could provide us with a cup of tea?' Derry held fast to Lissa's hand, shaking violently in his.

The farmer's wife stood on her slate doorstep, her mouth agape, and gazed at the two miserable young figures before her. 'Well, I never. George, see what we have here. Come in, the pair of you, afore you turn into a couple of puddles.'

Mrs Bowker wouldn't hear of them settling for anything less than a substantial spread. Fresh bread was brought and scalding hot soup, followed by thick slices of ham, pickle, spiced sausage, and enough tea to float a battleship.

Their clothes steamed on the rack above the big farmhouse fire while Derry and Lissa snuggled sleepily into huge blue-checked dressing gowns that smelled of pipe smoke and cold cream respectively.

'I've made up two beds,' she told them, whisking away empty plates and gathering up the tablecloth to flick the crumbs out the back door for the hens.

'Beds?' Lissa managed weakly.

'Thee doesn't think I'd send you bairns out on a night like this, do you?' She grinned at her husband. Happily ensconced in the chimney corner he had said not a word, happy to leave these domestic matters to her judgement. 'It'll be right by morning, George, won't it?'

'Aye,' he said, and returned to his pipe.

'I'll take the young lady up first then,' Mrs Bowker said, in a voice which said she would stand no nonsense, not in her house, thank you very much.

'We're truly grateful,' Lissa said as she followed her up the broad oak staircase.

Lissa was sure she wouldn't be able to sleep a wink. She wanted to go over in her mind everything that had happened that day, and its possible implications. But the moment her head touched the pillow, she was fast asleep.

Derry, however, lay wakeful for some time. He couldn't help wondering what he had got himself into. He did love her, at least he felt almost sure that he did. But he was young, with all his life and his ambitions before him. He wasn't ready for responsibility. Not for himself even, let alone another person.

How can I tell her now that I've lost my job? How can I say I'm leaving, after all of this? he worried. She'll think it sure proof that I didn't mean what I said, that I don't care for her. His eyelids began to droop. Perhaps next week, he thought, when I've finalised everything in Manchester. It'll be time enough to tell her then.

And so they each slept, with reasonable contentment, in their chaste beds.

CHAPTER 12

'How did the walk go?' Jan wanted to know as they polished the windows and swept out the shop. Lissa made no reply, merely smiled as she worked.

'Ah, that good, eh? About time you two got together.' Jan spoke if she had arranged it all. 'And you only got home this morning? Well, well.' There was a question in her voice and Lissa flushed, unable to prevent herself from looking guilty.

'There was a mist and we got lost. Derry thought it safer to go down into Kentmere where we were offered accommodation by a very proper farmer's wife. Mrs Bowker, she was called. She was lovely, dried our clothes, and wouldn't even take payment for the accommodation, and excellent breakfasts she provided. Said it was a poor do if you couldn't do someone a good turn.' Lissa knew she was over-explaining, but somehow felt she should fill the silence.

Jan's eyes danced. 'I'm sure. Very sensible on the hills our Derry.'

'Weren't you worried when we didn't come

home? We thought you might call out the mountain rescue.'

'Er, I stayed over at a friend's house myself,' Jan said. 'So, come on. Tell all.'

'Stop it, Jan. It was very . . .'

'What? Innocent? Sweet? Passionate?'

'Stop asking questions,' Lissa complained, rubbing vigorously at the glass, already sparkling with her efforts.

Jan tucked her hair behind her ears and grinned. 'So nothing happened then? How very disappointing.'

Lissa marched away, chin high, to beat her duster on the door post, setting both girls into a fit of coughing, well mingled with laughter.

'To more mundane matters, have you seen the dragon this morning?'

Lissa shook her head, not really concentrating on what Jan was saying, her head too full of the delights of her Sunday walk and the way Derry had lingered over his goodbye kisses this morning at the bus stop.

'She isn't usually late. And she has the stock room key. Until she comes we can't get in there, not even to make our morning cuppa.'

Lissa frowned. 'How did you get in the shop then?'

'Oh, she trusts me to keep a key for that, so we can get in and start cleaning. But we can't serve anybody until we get the change from the safe.' Jan was looking worried. 'I think I'll nip to the post office and telephone her. She might be ill or something.'

Moments later she was back, looking more anxious than ever. 'No reply. What do you think can have happened? This isn't like her at all.'

'She's probably on her way right now.' Lissa started to polish the glass counters. She felt so good this morning, as if a new life had begun, which in a way it had. She and Derry had made arrangements to meet again this evening and her stomach was churning already with the agony of anticipation. How could she wait a whole day before seeing him?

It was when she carried some old stands out to the narrow dark corridor which ran behind the main shop that Lissa heard the sound. No more than an echo it made her spine prickle, and she wondered for a moment if she'd imagined it. She froze, one hand caught in mid-air. When it came again she knew it must be real.

It was a groan. Miss Stevens was locked in the stock room. Dropping the stands with a clatter, Lissa ran for Jan.

'I should have realised,' she mourned. 'I felt sure something like this might happen one day. She's probably drunk as a lord.'

'Drunk?'

'Likes a little nip does our Stella. She's discreet, I'll give her that, but she can't count. And she has a bad stomach. Oh, what if she's been there all weekend?'

They banged on the door, tried to force the lock but it wouldn't budge and there was only silence now from within. The two girls gazed at each other in horror.

'What ought we to do? How can we get her out without a key? Is there a back door?'

Jan shook her head. 'Nope.'

'Who will have a spare?'

Jan thought about this for a minute then her face brightened. 'Her solicitor. He has a complete set as a precaution, since she's a maiden lady with no relatives. I remember her telling me soon after I came to work here.'

'Which solicitor?'

'Derry's boss. Philip Brandon. There we are then, since you know him so well and have been given the privilege of a sail in his spanking yacht, you can have the pleasure of informing him that his esteemed client is three sheets to the wind.'

Lissa giggled but then quickly sobered. 'This isn't funny. Miss Stevens could be in dire difficulties. Perhaps we should call the police, or an ambulance?'

Jan looked alarmed. 'They'd break down the door and she'd be furious. No, fetch Philip Brandon. He'll have a key and know exactly what to do.'

Lissa was already putting on her coat.

'Anyway, give you the chance to see our Derry again, won't it?' Jan said, grinning wickedly, and Lissa's cheeks flamed.

'Really, Jan, there's a time and a place.' And she dashed off, trying to ignore the fast beating of her heart which had very little to do with Miss Stevens' predicament.

When Lissa reached the offices of Brandon and Brandon, there was no sign of Derry. Probably out on one of his many errands.

Miss Henshaw showed her straight in, and when Philip heard her tale he put on his coat right away.

So it was that as Derry turned the corner of Benthwaite Cross on his return from the post office where he'd been making yet another of his long-distance calls, he saw Lissa climbing into Philip Brandon's car. She was smiling up at his ex-boss, apparently thanking him most profusely, and Brandon was preening himself, as he usually did.

Derry felt as if he'd been kicked in the teeth.

He hid in a doorway to watch as the car drove slowly past, his face tight with misery. To think he'd actually felt sorry for her, and been nervous about admitting he was going away. She wouldn't miss him for more than a minute.

Miss Stevens was found in a crumpled heap in the corner of the stock room, an empty bottle of Milk of Magnesia clutched tightly in her hand and vomit all down the front of her best fair isle jumper. She was still alive, though how she had survived all weekend was considered a miracle.

After the ambulance had carried her away both girls gave way to weeping.

Philip held them gently in his arms, patting, soothing, paying particular attention to Lissa.

'If I hadn't heard her,' Lissa mourned, 'how long might she have stayed there? Oh, I do wish we'd found her earlier. We were so busy talking we never thought.' And she was off again, borrowing his great white handkerchief and sobbing her guilt into it while Jan recovered sufficiently to pull down the blinds and lock the door.

'We'd best close for today, out of respect,' she decided. 'Will she be in hospital long, d'you think? How will we manage?'

Philip took it upon himself to supply the answers. 'Who can say? You must carry on as before. I shall leave you with a complete set of keys, and you can bring the takings to me each evening when you lock up. I'll keep a watch on matters for Miss Stevens, never fear,' he reassured, delighted with this turn of events that would give him the opportunity to see more of Lissa.

I'll bet you will, Jan thought, but only smiled, and agreed to do as he asked.

The letter was waiting for her when they got back to the boathouse. It lay on the mat, and Lissa picked it up with a soft smile on her face.

'It's from Derry.' She hurried off to her room to read it in private.

'Lissa, Lost my job. Can't explain everything now but am on my way to Manchester. We've a

245

chance of a recording contract. Who knows where it might lead? Can't believe our luck. Will write later and let you know when I'll be back. Derry.'

She read the letter through several times before the full meaning of the words finally penetrate, seeking a word, a hint of his feelings for her.

He hadn't even signed it 'with love'. Only his precious recording contract seemed to matter. Yet he promised he'd be back. Lissa, grasping at straws, read the letter for a fourth time. Yes, it definitely stated, *Will write later and let you know when I'll be back.* So it wasn't over between them. She simply had to trust him, and wait.

During the following weeks the note almost fell to pieces, so often did she read it. Jan kept on reminding Lissa how he would write to tell her when he'd be home. Lissa would smile and wonder why a letter never came. But then she knew all about promises written in letters.

'Don't give up on him. He's not the best letter writer in the world but he's honest. Believe in him.'

'I do.' Lissa said, trying to be convinced. Wasn't that what you were supposed to do when you loved someone?

Not that Jan was around as much as Lissa would have liked. Most weekends she went off to visit this new friend she'd acquired, and since she volunteered no further information on him, Lissa didn't like to ask for details. But she felt the loss of her company, and a slight coolness sprang up between them for the first time.

Miss Stevens made good progress following an operation for a stomach ulcer, but would be away from business for some months, recovering. Philip Brandon informed them that she was happy for the current system to continue until she'd decided what best to do about the shop.

'You mean she might close it?' Lissa asked, stunned.

'She may well decide to retire. She is well past fifty and not in good health. But there is no immediate cause for concern,' he assured them. 'I trust you will not desert her for some other employment in her hour of need?'

Lissa was shocked. 'Of course not.' But if she lost her job, she could go with Derry. Manchester, London, anywhere. What did it matter so long as they were together, and he wanted her?

But still there was no word.

Then one day Tony's mother came into the shop and told them the recording deal had been a flop, and the band were all coming home. 'He and Helen are engaged, so we have a wedding to look forward to in the spring.'

'Oh, how lovely!' Lissa gazed enviously at the woman, so obviously pleased with herself. 'They're coming home, you say?'

'Yes, dear. Next Wednesday, on the midday bus.'

'Derry too?'

'Of course Derry too. He said for you to meet him at the bus station. Since it's your half day.'

When Mrs Courtney had gone, making them promise to come to the wedding, which was certain to be the most spectacular event Carreckwater had ever seen, Jan gave a loud cheer and Lissa lifted shining eyes to hers. 'He's coming home.'

So thrilled was she, that she even told Philip Brandon the moment he walked into the shop that evening.

He'd called every day, as agreed, for the takings and to check they locked up properly, often walking the girls home afterwards. Jan's presence irritated him but he hadn't quite worked out a way to avoid her. Today she'd left early for once, and gone off somewhere. Nor had Lissa yet agreed to go out with him again, though he'd asked her a couple of times. Now he saw the excitement in her face at the prospect of his ex-clerk's return.

Philip felt a deep resentment thinking how patient he'd been, waiting for Lissa to grow up. Then when he'd seen her fix her attention on his clerk he'd set out to beat him in the yacht race and for her heart. In the end he'd been forced to give Derry the sack. Lissa didn't seem to know about that. Perhaps it was time that she did. Hadn't he been patient long enough?

Taking her elbow, Philip steered her across Carndale Road. 'I hope he's achieved whatever he set out to achieve.'

So that he'll stay in Manchester indefinitely, came the thought.

Lissa pulled a wry face as she shook her head. 'Apparently not. Maybe this will bring him down to earth. No more chasing rainbows.'

'You think Colwith will settle down to a steady job?' There was disbelief in his tone which caused Lissa to bridle.

'I believe he will.'

'He'll need to find a job first.'

'Oh, but I thought you'd take him back.'

'I'm afraid I took on a replacement clerk. He told you, I dare say, that I'd been obliged to sack him?'

'What?'

Lissa couldn't take in what he was telling her. That Derry, her Derry, would carry out such a criminal act as damaging a boat was unthinkable. 'He would never do such a thing!'

Philip looked sad. 'I'm afraid Colwith is not quite the innocent you seem to imagine. Those clothes he wears speak volumes. You mustn't let yourself be fooled by his boyish charm.'

'I don't believe it. I won't believe it. He wouldn't touch your yacht.' But her voice trembled, momentarily uncertain. Derry had always disliked Philip Brandon, swearing he'd do anything to beat him and win that race. But he hadn't won the race, he'd been disqualified, accused of cheating. Was all this because he was jealous of Philip's attentions to her?

Tears filled her eyes and Philip handed her a large white handkerchief. 'I didn't mean to upset you. Let me buy you a drink.' And before Lissa had time to protest, he was leading her into the Marina Hotel, settling her into a comfortable chair and handing her a brandy.

It shot like fire through her veins, making her head spin. 'Oh dear, alcohol on an empty stomach.'

A meal was duly ordered and brought, and Philip was all attention, smiling, handsome, charming, nothing too much trouble. He was really very kind, she thought, if a bit too serious for her taste. He talked a good deal about how Carreckwater was developing as a town, due in part to tourism, and partly to old money and how those people must never be forgotten. She tried to sound interested but her mind was elsewhere. She must keep her faith in Derry. She must. What else did she have? Even Jan had deserted her these days.

He walked her home, held her hand briefly as he unlocked the door of the boathouse then smiled into her eyes. 'I've enjoyed this evening. Perhaps we may repeat it some time?'

Lissa smiled vaguely, not quite seeing him. 'That would be lovely.'

What would Derry's explanation be? He must surely have one. She wouldn't think the worst until she'd heard his version.

When Wednesday arrived Lissa was so excited she could hardly sit still. She'd treated herself to a smart new suit with a straight skirt and box jacket in a soft powder blue, a small hat to match, with white gloves and handbag. She brushed her hair till it shone and applied a new lipstick in a bright coral, the most daring colour she'd ever tried. She would have set off a good two hours early had Jan not prevented her.

'I'll put the kettle on.'

'No, it'll spoil my lipstick. What time is it? Why didn't he write himself?'

'Derry hates writing letters.'

'But what if he no longer cares for me?'

'Of course he still cares. Stop worrying.'

Jan settled herself in the armchair and picked up the knitting that was rarely out of her hands these days while Lissa went to the window to look out along the shore just in case he should arrive early, though how he could manage that until the bus came at noon she wasn't sure. 'You aren't going out today, are you?' Lissa asked. 'He'll want to see you too.'

Jan smiled and shook her head. 'No, I told my friend I couldn't come today.'

At the sight of Jan's face, Lissa forgot her own affairs and, sitting beside her, gathered Jan's hands in her own. 'Won't you tell me who he is, this man?'

Jan set down her knitting and gazed at the floor, eyes half closed in her familiar squint. 'We decided to keep it secret for a while.'

'Why? He isn't married, is he?' Lissa waited with

trepidation as Jan raised brown eyes, so like Derry's, to meet her questioning gaze and laugh.

'Heavens, no. It's Nick. We've been going out ever since we met that day we visited your family. We love each other and he wants to marry me.'

'Nick? *My* Nick?' Lissa could hardly believe her ears.

'Not *your* Nick any more.'

'Oh, that's wonderful.'

'You don't mind?'

'Why should I mind? I'm delighted. You're really going to marry Nick?'

Jan nodded, a wide happy smile lighting her face, giving it a new radiance. 'He wants the wedding to be as soon as possible.'

Lissa squealed in delight. 'I can't believe it. It's wonderful. But why keep it a secret? Why didn't you tell me?'

Jan gave a shamefaced little shrug. 'I know he had a crush on you for years. He never stopped talking about you the first few times we went out. I had to be sure he really liked me and wasn't just using me to reach you.'

Her eyes were bright and Lissa's heart clenched. 'Oh, Jan. I'm sure Nick would never do such a thing. We were just good friends, family.'

She blinked. 'I know that now. He says he does love you, as an honorary cousin, always will. But his feelings for me are . . .' She blushed bright red. 'Different.' They were laughing now, squealing with delight.

'Heavens, Derry! What time is it?'

'Go on. Don't be late. He'll be as impatient as you. Make sure I'm chief bridesmaid, and you can do the same for me.'

They hugged one last time then Lissa set off, heels clicking on the slate pavements, a spring in her step, face shining with happiness. Oh, she was so thrilled about Nick and Jan, her two dearest friends. How good life was.

Bus station was rather a grand term for two shelters and a newsagent's that doubled as a small booking office. These simple structures linked Carreckwater to the outside world. The railway had never got beyond Windermere, despite valiant efforts by eminent Victorians, so without a car, the bus was the only means of transport. It ran several times a day in the summer. But in the winter, as now, it came twice. If you were lucky. The driver had been known not to bother if he couldn't rustle up enough passengers. Lissa worried that this might happen today. What if he were left stranded in Windermere?

She paced restlessly up and down, wishing she'd put on a coat over her new suit for it was bitterly cold. The wind swept down from the hills, swirling up toffee wrappings, discarded bus tickets and dried leaves and depositing them in untidy heaps in the open road, before blowing them all away again.

Would the bus never come?

And then she saw it. Small, red, and dearly familiar, it rumbled along as if it had all the time in the world. As if she were not waiting for her life to begin, her heart beating twenty to the dozen. Helen came running up, at the last minute as usual.

'Is it here?' she gasped, flushed and excited, and Lissa tried not to glance at the sparkle of diamonds on the third finger of her left hand.

The bus drew up and then Tony was leaping out, Helen was squealing and flinging herself ecstatically into his arms.

Lissa stepped forward, looking for Derry's dearly loved face, eager for her own turn.

A touch on her elbow brought her spinning around, face alight with love. But it was Tony, pink with embarrassment. He was holding out an envelope and Lissa was staring at it as if it were poison.

A letter? She looked into Tony's eyes and knew that her own were pleading. Tell me he's here, they said, but Tony only shuffled his feet, thrust the letter into her reluctant fingers and gathering Helen close, walked quickly away into the wind.

The conductor rang the bell, the gears of the bus grated loud in the empty street and slowly the vehicle moved off. Lissa stood alone, staring at the envelope in her hand.

With trembling fingers she slit it open and quickly scanned the few words on the single page. He wasn't coming. There it was in black and white. He was very sorry but there was no work for him in Carreckwater. Since he'd failed to realise his dreams in Manchester, he thought he might as well try London.

She felt her heart shrivel and her hopes crumble to dust. The pain in her breast was so bad she thought she must be dying.

'I'll be in touch,' the letter said.

In touch? How? With a card each Christmas?

He'd signed it in his usual casual way. She must have imagined that he loved her. She must have dreamt those hours out on the fells when he'd made love to her with a passion that said he didn't want to let her go, even for a moment. Imagined that he'd promised to love her for ever. Derry Colwith had broken his promise and rejected her, just like everyone else.

A wildness came over Lissa following the receipt of that letter. The subdued, withdrawn Lissa had gone. She wanted to be on the go all the time. She redecorated the boathouse, went dancing every Saturday night, worked far longer than was necessary in the shop, cleaning out corners of the stock room that had never seen the light of day. But she could not eradicate the pain and misery in her own heart.

Christmas came and both she and Jan visited Broombank.

Meg and Tam were delighted to have the family about them again. Lissa played the old harmonium and even Joe joined in with the happy carolling. His wife Connie came, as she always did for Christmas, however much she might avoid farm life for the rest of the year. Sally Ann and Meg put on a huge spread and everyone ate too much and laughed too loud and took turns with the endless washing up. Almost as if life were normal, Lissa thought.

She did her best not to feel envious of the lingering looks, the secret whispers and stolen kisses of the two lovers. Their happiness shone from them like a radiance. Sometimes Sally Ann would whisk her daughter-in-law-to-be off into a corner to talk about weddings and dresses and flowers.

Meg found she had a new audience who had not heard her sheep stories. Given chance she would talk endlessly about her beloved land, and the different qualities of staple in the wool she produced. Grandfather Joe told how he had won the war without leaving his own fireside.

The result was that Lissa felt more than ever an outsider in her own home. She didn't seem to belong anywhere, or to anyone. Jan might tell her not to worry, that Derry's crazy ambitions might take him off chasing rainbows but that he still cared, deep down, and would return. Lissa didn't believe a word of it.

And there were no more letters. A Christmas card, as expected – to keep in touch. It carried no address and said little beyond the fact that he still had several agents to see.

* * *

Lissa didn't know where she would have been during those first miserable weeks without the kindness of Philip Brandon. On his daily calls when he checked the shop and reported on Miss Stevens' slow return to health, he also found time in his busy schedule to stop and chat, and try to cheer her up. He showed concern over her health and the fact that she looked so pale.

Lissa appreciated his concern. He sent her flowers and a box of chocolates. He often bought her a coffee in The Cobweb, a new coffee bar that had opened by the shore. He was so attentive that on occasions she found herself very nearly flirting with him, deciding he was really quite attractive, for all he was older than she.

But when he asked her for a date, she refused. 'You must eat.'

'I don't ever seem to be hungry.'

'He isn't worth it, Lissa.'

''No,' she said. 'He isn't.'

'I would never let you down, I promise.'

'Ah,' she said, a sad smile on her lips. 'Promises.'

When he asked her out to dinner again, she thought, to hell with it, why not? Recklessly she spent far more money than she could afford on a new dress in a daring off-the-shoulder style. She tucked up her hair into a stylish French pleat, wanting to look elegant. She'd been out with Philip Brandon before, and knew the kind of places he liked.

It proved to be a wonderful evening. He was

charming and flattering, if not quite so amusing as Derry. He treated her as if she were made of Dresden, which right then was how she felt, so fragile she might break. He soothed her jangled nerves and told her not to blame herself for Derry's defection. But she did. If she'd been worth loving he would still be here. As would her mother.

'I don't intend to trust you either,' she told Philip, slanting her violet eyes up at him in her most bewitching manner.

'What have I done?' His handsome face looked so bleak she couldn't help but laugh. 'I only want you to be happy, Lissa.'

If she couldn't trust Derry, who could she trust? But then she had loved Derry, and that was why it hurt so much. She had loved Meg and presumably her mother. She didn't love Philip Brandon so how could he ever let her down?

CHAPTER 13

The winter months passed and the first green shoots of spring appeared. The lilac-veined white blossoms of wood sorrel crowded the woodlands, wild daffodils lined the fringes of the blue-grey lakes. Wheatears and chiffchaffs were, as usual, the first birds to arrive for the summer months, followed by the willow warblers. Lissa sat at her window in the boathouse and wondered if Derry would fly home too. She ached for him so much the pain of her longing made her feel quite ill at times. But he didn't come. Nor was there any news of him beyond one scribbled note.

'Not the greatest letter writer in the world, is he? The young fool. It's his pride. Won't write till he's something wonderful to tell us. He wants to prove himself.'

'He doesn't have to prove anything to me.' Except that he loves me. Lissa firmed her lips, outlining them with a bright, red lipstick, remembering the time not so long ago when she'd watched Jan get ready to go out while she played Cinderella and stayed in all the time. Now the reverse was true. Jan complained she'd changed and was never home. Lissa preferred it that way. Staying in was bad for her. It gave her too much time to think.

Nor did she care how much make-up she wore. It helped somehow, to see a different face in the mirror than the one Derry had loved. She felt reckless enough to try anything, even going so far as to paint each of her nails a different colour. It was quite the rage, as were her pale blue nylon stockings, snapped seductively in place with a mere scrap of lace.

'Oh, Lissa. How hard you've grown.'

Lissa blinked away the prick of tears that stung the backs of her eyes. 'Not hard, self-protective. Necessary if one is to survive in this world. Or so I've discovered. I've certainly no intention of writing to Derry when he's the one who failed to keep his promises. Let him pursue his dream. I come very low on his list of priorities.'

If I don't stop talking about him, I'll cry, and ruin all my careful composure. Snapping shut her mascara case she flung it into her bag.

Then she calmly smoothed the blue satin of her short evening dress with its hip hugging skirt, picked up the beaded black bag and smiled serenely at Jan in the mirror. 'Will I do?'

How could anyone deny that Lissa Turner was beautiful? 'I think you're playing with fire. Please stop seeing Philip Brandon. He isn't right for you, really he isn't. Too old for one thing.'

Lissa stared at her friend with cold, unseeing

eyes. She didn't care to be told what to do any more now than when she was as a rebellious adolescent. She certainly felt old enough to make up her own mind.

She'd partnered him for the New Year Ball at the Yacht Club, causing quite a stir amongst his friends. But why worry? He was good-looking, enjoyed her company and made her feel more confident about herself. He never seemed short of money, and if he wished to spend it on her, take her to the very best restaurants and order the finest wines, why shouldn't she accept? He said it gave him enormous pleasure to see her happy. With Philip Brandon she could have fun without worrying about love and heartache and all of that dangerous nonsense.

And he made no demands upon her. Once, in his car, he had kissed her, and with too much champagne singing in her head she'd very nearly encouraged him to go further. Derry had taught her that loving could be delicious, so would it matter if she did? She'd already proved how wicked she was.

'Unlike your foolish brother, I'm not a child with my head in the clouds, playing childish games in childish clothes. I gave up such nonsense years ago. I'm a woman and I enjoy the attention of an attractive male, particularly one who is reliable and courteous, gracious and charming and with impeccable manners. Philip is all of those things and I like him. Is that so wrong?'

261

Jan banged the kettle on the stove. 'You're a cruel, unforgiving woman with a heart of stone. Derry has lost everything and now he's about to lose you.'

Lissa started as if Jan had struck her. 'That was his choice, not mine.'

'He's doing this for you.'

Lissa's violet eyes blazed with sudden fire and she swung about to face her friend, more furious than Jan had ever seen her. 'Don't give me that! He's doing this for himself. Your brother isn't to be trusted, Jan. He let me believe he loved me. I certainly fell for his line of chat and gave him everything a girl can give. So there, now you know. He's no good, and I don't ever want to see him ag . . .' Her voice choked on a strangled cry.

'Oh, love, I didn't know.' Then Jan was holding her in her arms and Lissa was biting hard on her lower lip to stop the tears which would surely come if she lost control for only a second, From outside came the sound of a car's horn.

Jan clicked her tongue with impatience and pulled aside the curtain to peer out into the darkness while Lissa searched frantically in her bag for a powder puff. 'Why does he never come to the door in a civilised fashion?'

'Perhaps he senses your disapproval.' Lissa slipped into high stiletto heels, collected the cashmere stole Philip had bought her and moved to the door. 'Don't wait up, I might be late. He's taking me to the theatre at Keswick and dinner afterwards.' If she didn't get out of the room fast, she would burst into tears. 'In any case, Jan, I really don't think it's any of your business. Do you?'

'Well, look who the wind's blown in,' Renee said.

He stood on her doorstep trying not to look shamefaced. Renee blew on her bubble gum and cracked it. 'You'd best come in.'

'Thanks.' She hadn't changed, he thought.

Over a cup of very welcome tea and several ginger biscuits that went some way towards abating his hunger, Derry briefly told his tale, trying to make a joke of how he'd dreamed of seeing his name on a record label and having it played on Radio Luxembourg, and failing miserably.

'Poor love,' she said, as if she were years older and wiser than him. 'All that effort with nowt to show for it.' She watched him pick up two more biscuits. 'Have you eaten lately?'

'Not today.'

'This week?'

He smiled. 'Not that I noticed.'

Less than fifteen minutes later Derry was sitting down to a plate loaded with lamb chops, baked beans and chips.

'By heck, Renee, you're a treasure,' he said, tucking in with gusto. He couldn't remember when a meal tasted so good.

'Generous to a fault, that's me,' she said. 'Eat up. I'll make a fresh pot of tea.'

Later, as he sat replete on the opposite side of

263

the brown tiled fireplace, Derry thanked her. 'You're all right, Renee. I'll forgive you for nabbing my dad. Though he's too good for you.'

'Thanks a bunch. I'd've waited forever for you to get round to it.' She grinned happily at him, content with her lot. 'You thought you'd got young Lissa in the pudding club, did you? Then ran away, to avoid trouble?'

Derry's cheeks flamed bright scarlet and he was on his feet in a second. 'No, course I didn't.' He stopped, appalled. 'She isn't, is she?'

'Ooh, not far wrong, was I? Well, well. She wouldn't be the first it's happened to.' Renee smiled, orange lips clashing horribly with the shocking pink of her sweater. 'Happen I'm only teasing.'

'What?' Colour rushed back into his ashen cheeks. 'You rotten . . . You mean she isn't?'

'Not unless she's carrying it in her handbag. Thin as a rail she is these days. Mebbe Philip Brandon likes her that way though.'

'Philip Brandon?'

'Aye. Your ex-boss, no less.' Renee took an age to light up a cigarette. 'Escorts her everywhere, or so I'm told. Not that I see much of her these days. Quite the gad-about-town. Wouldn't recognise her, you wouldn't. Come out of her shell good and proper. Ain't that right, my pretty Peter?' she finished, directing her last words to the budgie, busy bashing its mirror, as usual.

Derry stood in the tiny, overheated parlour and

looked so stricken that a wave of maternal sympathy washed over Renee. 'Oh, poor cherub,' she gushed, wrapping her arms about him to pull his head down to her rounded breasts. 'She's cheated on you, the rotten madam.' Renee thought how good he felt against her breast. But then he'd always had a good body, had Derry. She wriggled closer. 'And you were a wonderful lover, she must be mad.'

He tried to pull away from her clinging embrace but the scent of her was so familiar, of strawberries and lipstick and summer days, and he felt so wretched that when she put her lips against his, he didn't protest. She reminded him of a time long past when he hadn't a care in the world. She placed his hand on the soft cushion of her breast and it felt so comforting he forgot for a moment that it was Lissa he wanted, not Renee.

The front door banged open and the scent changed to wood shavings, rain and the acrid taste of varnish.

'Oh, bugger me,' Renee calmly said, pulling away from his arms. 'Now the cat's among the pigeons, ain't it, Peter my pretty boy?' Derry found himself staring into the furious eyes of his father. It was some moments of scarlet-faced embarrassment before he managed to speak.

'Christ! This isn't how it looks.' He wished he'd died of starvation in those awful lodgings. Fallen in the Thames or under a London bus.

Renee was the only one still in possession of her voice. 'Just giving the poor little love a step-motherly cuddle.' And going over to Jimmy she gave him a smacking a kiss. 'Had a bit of a dis-appointment, our Derry. Come home to lick his wounds. Are you ready for your tea, love?' Jimmy neither moved nor answered. 'A stiffener, mebbe? I think we've got some sherry somewhere. Celebrate the return of the prodigal, eh?'

She went to the new sideboard and poured out three glasses, placing them on a small, tile-topped coffee table. Two stood untouched while she took her own back to her chair by the fire and beamed at her husband and stepson.

'Well now, isn't this cosy?'

Jimmy glared at his son. 'Out.'

'What?'

'Out. This is *my* home, *my* wife, and I'll not have that sort of behaviour here.'

'But I never . . .'

Jimmy pulled open the front door, every taut line of his wiry body declaring he would stand no argument. He emphasised his words by ominously pushing up his sleeves. 'Don't make me any madder than I already am, Derry. I'm not a man given to violence but I have my limits. You've never shown any respect for Renee. Now you've gone too far. Out.'

'OK, I was going anyway. I only came back to see how you all were.' Derry swaggered to the door.

'Go and see her,' Renee called as he marched off down the front path.

Derry didn't reply, didn't look back. But he winced when he heard the door slam and wished he could turn back the clock and make it all come out different. Now he was at odds with his father, on top of everything else. Dear God, what was happening to him?

It was one of those beautiful clear nights that often come in early spring. The sky was studded with stars while a pale moon floated in the black waters of the lake. Lissa stared at it through the windows of Philip's car and wished she could float into a magic world where everything was beautiful and there were no more bitter disappointments.

'You're not cold?' he asked, ever considerate, and she turned to him with a smile.

'No, I'm fine. Thank you for a wonderful evening. Would you like a cup of coffee?'

He glanced across at the boathouse, in complete darkness. 'What about Jan?'

'She'll be in bed by this time.'

He smiled. 'Fine.'

He stood and watched her as she moved about the small kitchen, enjoying the sway of her slender hips, the rise and fall of her breasts. How patient he'd been. He was really quite proud of himself. But not for much longer. He could feel he was winning.

'It was a good meal, wasn't it? I love trout. And

the play was superb. Time we enjoyed some culture. Next time we'll try a concert in Lancaster.'

He was growing ever more proprietorial, making decisions for her. Lissa never protested, it saved her the trouble of making them for herself. What did it matter where they went? She smiled her agreement. 'That would be lovely.' Philip knew so much and she so little. She appreciated his efforts to educate and entertain her. And he made her feel safe.

Miss Stevens had decided to sell the shop and take early retirement so she mightn't have a job for much longer. The prospect of starting again, seeking new friends, a new job, perhaps a new home, chilled her.

Nor did she wish to return home to Broombank. Jan was happily planning her wedding and Lissa couldn't bear the prospect of watching her glowing happiness. It would be too much. It would make her feel even more of an outsider and unwanted.

'You don't know what these evenings have meant to me,' Philip was saying. 'You've made me the happiest man on earth.'

Lissa glanced at him in surprise. 'Have I?'

He reached for her, pulling her into his arms, smoothing his hands lingeringly down her spine and over her hips, the sensuality of the gesture catching her unawares. 'You must guess how I feel about you, Lissa. You've filled my rather dull life with joy. You can't imagine how much I needed someone like you, only I never thought I'd be so lucky. Since Felicity died . . .' He stopped and seemed to take a minute to collect himself. Lissa's heart filled with sympathy. She knew about pain.

'It's all right. There's no need for you to talk about it. I understand how you must have felt when she died in that tragic way.'

His dark eyes swam with gratitude. 'Of course you do. Because you've known pain too. Darling Lissa, what can I say? You humble me by your beauty. I want you never to suffer pain again. We both of us deserve so much more, a new beginning. To have you here, beside me, makes me the richest man in the world. All I ask is to spend the rest of my life making you happy. I believe you feel exactly the same way.' He was taking her hand, slipping something into it.

She glanced down, surprised. 'Philip?'

'I've decided it's time we made it official.'

She opened the box in a daze and stared at the ring, no more than a glittering blur in her hand.

'If it isn't the right size I can get it altered. You do like diamonds, don't you, darling? Let me put it on for you. There, perfect. Flawless, like you, darling.'

'I am far from perfect.' Diamonds. Ice cold. Many-faceted. Diamonds are right for me, she thought.

'To me you are.' He kissed her cheek. Chaste and undemanding. 'I thought June for the wedding. Far the best month for weather. A reception at the Marina Hotel. You have no objection to June?'

She gazed up into his face, his eyes filled with a quiet eagerness to please, anxiety to make her happy. Offering the stability and security she craved.

'I need you, Lissa.'

It was what she most wanted to hear. No more broken promises, no more rejection. A simple and uncomplicated relationship, dependable and caring, untroubled by too much emotion.

'June would be perfect,' she said.

Lissa was upstairs showing Jan her ring as Philip had suggested when the knock came. Philip crossed the room and opened the door. Derry stood on the step, mouth dropping open in shock.

'Mr Brandon.'

Philip half glanced back over his shoulder, then stepping out, pulled the door closed behind him. His voice was low with unspent anger. 'What the hell are you doing here?'

Derry's brain was spinning so fast he could hardly find the words. 'I want to see Lissa.'

Philip jabbed one finger in Derry's chest, pushing him backwards down the steps and on to the shingle. 'The last thing Lissa wants is you hanging around, creating trouble.'

'I'm not here to make trouble. I need to talk to her, that's all.'

'She's no wish to talk to you.'

'How would you know?' Derry wanted to ask what Philip Brandon was doing in the boathouse at past eleven o'clock at night but couldn't seem to get his tongue around the words. Maybe because he was too afraid of the answer. 'Isn't that something she should decide for herself?'

'You promised to stay away. You know what'll happen if you don't.'

Derry stiffened. 'Is that some kind of threat?'

'My boat is still undergoing repairs.' Quietly spoken, with undertones of menace.

Derry gulped. 'I never touched your bloody boat. Maybe I'll face the police and tell them that.'

Philip's dark eyes raked over Derry from the top of his tousled head to his dusty shoes. 'You could try it, but think of the risk. I see you haven't made your fortune yet. Quite the reverse in fact. Scruffier than ever, if you ask me, in that old leather jacket and Teddy Boy jeans. The world is moving on, Derry. It really is time you started to grow up.'

Derry wanted to yell that his jacket cost fifteen quid and wasn't scruffy at all but he'd worn it every day for months, so he ground his teeth together and held his temper with difficulty. And he really had no wish to get involved with the police. Not the way his luck was running at the moment. 'Where is she?'

Having reasserted control Brandon was gracious. 'You are history so far as Lissa is concerned. I'll tell her you called.'

'What will you tell me?' A familiar voice from the door. A beloved figure silhouetted against the light that spilled out on to the shingle. As she

271

moved involuntarily towards him so that the moonlight captured her in its radiance, he gazed up at her, speechless, awed by her ethereal beauty.

'Hello,' he said. Renee was right, he thought. She was too thin. Her eyes were like dark bruises in her face. Oh, but so lovely, and surely that light which suddenly sparkled on her face was happiness at seeing him?

'Derry?'

Philip put his arm about her waist. 'I was telling Derek that it was rather late for social calls, but he's leaving on the first train from Windermere in the morning, so he's in a hurry. Aren't you?'

'Er . . .'

Lissa cleared her throat, her brain surging with so many questions she could hardly think. What was he doing here? What did this mean? Then reality sank in. 'Train? You're leaving already?'

'Well, I had a bit of a barney with Dad so . . .'

'But why didn't you tell us you were coming?'

'He has his fortune to make, my dear. Have you not, young sir?' Philip said in a jokey voice. 'Shall we tell him our good news, darling?' He pulled her closer as he smiled triumphantly upon Derry. 'Lissa has done me the honour of agreeing to become my wife.'

A stunned silence during which there was no sound but that of the waves noisily slapping the shore.

'Your *wife*?' Derry's voice had sunk to a whisper, as if he was afraid of disturbing that silence. But there was fury in it. And cold shock. 'Did you say *wife?*'

'Show him the ring, darling.' It was Philip who held out Lissa's hand, since she seemed reluctant to display quite the right degree of pride in it herself. 'Rather lovely, don't you think? A well-cut stone. Only the best, of course, for my own sweet love. We thought June for the happy day. Let us have your address when you get settled, then we'll maybe send you an invitation.'

Derry stared at Lissa, bemused, a question in his brown eyes, but she was looking up at Philip and the expression upon her pale face was quite unreadable.

'I doubt I'd be able to manage it,' he said stiffly, fighting the tremor in his voice. 'Congratulations. You must be very happy.' Only then did she look at him and her eyes seemed distant, unforgiving, empty.

'Yes,' she said. 'I must, mustn't I?'

1961

CHAPTER 14

A coating of rust lay upon the mountains. Mist hung in the valley, trailing ethereally over the glass-calm water. There were fairy rings in the woodlands that clustered along the shoreline, and heaps of leaves in gold and amber and bronze. The mallards hustled together on the lake in restless groups, sometimes springing up into the air, instinct telling them that soon their feathers would be ready for flight to the winter nesting grounds further south. One pair came waddling across the road, as if returning from a shopping expedition in the quiet streets of the town.

'Raarb!' called the showy drake, bossing his dull brown wife, but she refused to hurry, holding up traffic, making people curse or smile as their mood took them.

Lissa tried to smile too but the sight was almost painful. She felt at one with the plain little duck, following on in the wake of her mate, his brilliance outshining hers.

It was three years since she had married Philip Brandon. It had taken less than three months to realise her mistake. A sobering thought.

It served her right of course. No one else had been in favour of the match. Certainly not Jan.

And when Lissa had asked Meg and Tam for permission to marry since she was still under age, Meg's reply had been to urge her not even to think of it until she was at least twenty-one.

'You're too young, sweetheart. Do you truly love him?'

Love? What was love? Lissa didn't trust love. Love let you down. It had no substance. It lasted only for, a moment and was all tied up with duty and selfish need. Why should she expect anyone to love her when her own mother and grandmother hadn't even bothered to try? Meg had tried, she supposed, until she'd started wanting her own babies. Derry hadn't. Derry had let her down like all the rest. No, best to steer clear of love. It was unreliable.

So Lissa had married Philip Brandon one sunny day in June, 1958, and twelve months later almost to the day the twins had been born. Only in that moment, when her babies were put into her arms, did Lissa learn about love. Sarah and Elizabeth were two precious scraps of humanity with soft downy hair, curling fingers tipped with pearl, and bewitching blue eyes. Even at birth Sarah seemed especially alert and enquiring, while Beth, as she at once came to be known, contentedly smiled. They were a part of her and Lissa knew that their birth had changed her life for all time. She could pour all of that frustrated love upon them without fear of rebuff.

Not that it was quite fair to blame Philip for whatever it was she felt their marriage lacked. He adored her and told her so all the time. The failure must be in herself. She should be the happiest woman on earth. As well as her beautiful children she had a lovely home on the Parade with a fine view of the lake and the mountains beyond. Beautiful clothes to wear, an interesting social life with a good looking husband, and money in her purse. Philip gave her everything a woman could possibly desire. So what was the matter with her? She could surely expect no more?

'Come along, darlings, throw the crust to the ducks. We must get home.'

The two year olds squealed and giggled as the ducks clustered about, gobbling up the pieces of bread they'd thrown with such verve but which had landed only inches from their feet.

Sarah suddenly took it into her head to set off after one unfortunate duck, running on unsteady legs down the shingle to the water. Laughing, Lissa snatched up Beth, who protested vigorously, and ran after her.

The duck took evasive action while Sarah plonked down on to her bottom, missing the water by inches.

'Duck, duck!' she shouted.

'Take care, darling. Mummy doesn't want you to fall in.' She gathered her children to her, one at each side, while she knelt on the shingle and gazed at her own reflection in the still waters. It surprised her sometimes to see how young she still was. No more than twenty-one, for all she felt like a mature married woman. 'Can you see your faces, darlings? Look, there's Sarah with her snub nose, and little Beth with her sweet smile and new tooth. Can you see?'

The twins hunkered down beside her in their matching cotton frocks and gazed very seriously at their reflections, so similar and yet so different. They were not identical. The hair was changing colour now, even the eyes had lost their baby blueness.

'When I was a girl we used to wish by the water every spring for whatever our hearts most desired.' Lissa laughed at the memory, pushing back the errant jet curls that still tumbled upon her brow for all the care she took to pin them back in a tidy fashion as Philip liked. She never wore it in a girlish pony tail any more and he did not like to see it flying free.

'Me want to wish,' Sarah announced, sticking out her jaw in determined fashion, making Lissa laugh.

'You want everything, darling, even when you have no idea what a wish is. What do you want, Beth?'

Beth slid her arms about her mother's neck and kissed her damply. 'Sweetie,' she said, at her most alluring, and Lissa laughed all the more, letting them tumble her backwards on to the shingle and search her pockets until the hoarded treasure of two jelly babies had been found. Then she dusted the children down and took their hands in hers, her spirits sinking in that familiar way as they turned towards home.

Sometimes she did wonder why Philip had chosen her. Just as one might wonder why the showy mallard was happy with its dull brown mate. Perhaps it was simply because it had no choice.

Was that how Philip saw her? As the best choice he could find at the time? He was certainly always striving to improve her. And she was grateful for his assistance, oh, she was. How else could she know the correct knife to use at a grand dinner, or which dress was quite appropriate? She depended upon his opinion absolutely. If she felt inadequate sometimes, the fault must be entirely hers.

Where was it they were going tonight? The Yacht Club, or something to do with the Town Council? She couldn't quite recall but there was plenty of time. It was lovely to saunter by the lake in the September sunshine. And what was there to rush home for? The house shone like a new pin, and was entirely empty.

They passed the benches and as she passed the old boathouse, tears sprang to her eyes. What was the matter with her today? She could remember those happy times as if they were yesterday and not a million years ago.

'When I was a teenager,' she told the twins, her voice brightening for their benefit. 'We used to have parties and barbecues on the shore here, with Coca-Cola and burnt sausages. What fun we had!'

She remembered the night of the storm and the Spin-the-Bottle party when Derry had kissed her in the kitchen.

She remembered how he would pull a comb from an inside pocket and flick the already tidy quiff into place. Did he still dress in those ridiculous long jackets, tight jeans and brightly coloured shirts? Had he ever got his recording contract? she wondered. His dream?

She recalled the night he'd stood on this very spot and Philip had told him of their coming marriage. She would never forget the expression in his brown eyes till her dying day.

A ripple of emotion coursed through her body, shocking her by its intensity. It did no good to remember. She was a mature, married woman. Those glorious youthful summers were over. Strangers lived in the boathouse now. Jan was at Ashlea with Nick, busily knitting for the expected arrival of their first child. Tony and Helen had two. Where the other band members had gone, she had no idea.

Lissa had no dream, only a confusing jumble of unsatisfied needs. She'd never felt Derry's driving ambition to succeed, would have been happy with more modest achievements. Someone to love her and never let her go.

Yet more often of late she had felt dissatisfied, had started to ask herself questions. Am I happy? Am I fulfilled? The Russians had more control over their rockets flying through space than she had over her own life. The days seemed so long. She had the twins, of course, and they were such darlings she could eat them. But Philip had insisted on employing a nanny. A plain, stolid woman of uncertain years who dressed predictably in starched overalls and had all the right qualifications. Which meant Lissa was left with too many empty hours to fill, too much time to think.

They had reached the bandstand when Sarah squealed in delighted fear. 'Duck chasing me, Mummy.'

Lissa laughed. 'No, darling, they're greedy, that's all.'

A hopeful troop of ducks had come waddling behind in search of a forgotten crust, so the twins must be permitted to bend down and talk to them, explain how they would be back tomorrow with more. Suddenly a car came, too fast, along the narrow shore road. The birds whirled up into the air, wings beating madly, crazy with fear before skimming into the water in a flurry of injured pride and flustered panic. Scattering all the other ducks in a squawking mass of feathers. In an equal panic Lissa grabbed the twins, heart beating wildly as she leapt to one side, shouting at the retreating car. 'How dare you? Road hog! Have you no consideration?'

The ducks flapped their wings, shook their stubby tail feathers to restore lost dignity and at once began to preen and groom themselves to settle their nerves.

Sarah was screaming. She had fallen down and grazed her knee. Beth was sucking her thumb and crying around it, wide-mouthed, in sympathy.

'Oh, dear Lord.' Lissa held them both in her arms, soothing, kissing, mopping up blood and tears. What would Philip say?

The sun was dropping behind blue-misted mountains by the time she reached home. He met her at the foot of the stairs in his dressing gown, face tight with anger.

'Where have you been? What have you done with the children? Nanny?' He yelled up the stairs and a starched white overall came instantly into view. Nanny Sue came running, clucking her tongue in disapproval, and bore the children away for hot chocolate and baths and the joy of an Elastoplast.

Lissa's heart sank. She so hated to displease him. 'It's all right. It's only a graze.'

'They shouldn't have been out so late. What were you thinking of? I came home to find the house empty. You weren't here, Nanny on her afternoon off, the twins not in bed and my bath not even run.'

Reaching up she kissed his cheek, hoping to placate him. 'We were feeding the ducks.' Smiling, she brushed past him and walked up the stairs to the blue and white bedroom they shared at the front of the house. Ten minutes in the bathroom, she dare waste no more time, and she was standing before her dressing table in her slip, dabbing her face with cream when he entered.

'Is it the Yacht Club dinner tonight?'

'No, that's next week. Don't you ever listen? We are due at the Cheyneys on the dot of seven-thirty.'

'The Cheyneys. Of course.' Nothing to do with either the Town Council or the Yacht Club. Don Cheyney was a magistrate of some standing, so the talk this evening would be of legal matters. 'How delightful. It won't take me long to get ready.' It would be boring in the extreme. His wife would be no help at all since she was at least fifteen years older than Lissa and constantly trying to persuade her to join some worthy ladies' group or other. Lissa stifled a sigh and started to pull the pins from her hair.

'I'll do that.' She looked up, catching sight of his expression through the mirror, and felt her stomach clench.

Lissa stood unresisting as he released her hair, spread it upon her shoulders and combed his fingers through the tumbling curls from scalp to tip. Then he lifted it with one hand so he could kiss a bare shoulder. Lissa suppressed a violent urge to slap his hand away. 'You said we were in a hurry.'

He half glanced at the clock but his eyes were already glazed, the pupils darkly dilated. It was an expression she had come to dread. 'Not that much of a hurry,' he said thickly, letting his lips linger over the silky skin. His hands slid to her buttocks. 'Damn, you're not wearing suspenders. Did you go out in those ankle socks again? Haven't I told you always to be properly dressed?'

Lissa said nothing. She had learned the art of silence.

But he made her put them on now, and as she did so, she was aware of his growing eagerness. She watched him taunt himself by making her remove the silk slip and walk around the bed to him. He could barely wait for her to come to him before he was running his hands over her firm body and pushing her back on to the bed. He dropped his own robe to the floor, spread her legs and the next instant he was on top and inside of her. The pain of it was unbearable and she tried to lift her knees in order to ease it, putting her arms about him. His impatience was always at its worst when she had displeased him. 'Wait for me, Philip. Give me time.'

'Keep still, for God's sake. You're so clumsy.' He shook her arms away, took hold of her wrists and held them back while he pounded into her, pouring out his frustration till moments later it was all over. For which she was deeply thankful.

'God, that was good.' He slumped against her on a great gasping groan. Lissa eased herself from beneath him. He never asked if she had enjoyed it, didn't seem to require it. At least it spared her the need to pretend.

'I'll have to shower again now,' he said, sounding irritable as if it had been her intention to distract him with unplanned sex.

He pulled on his robe and went into the bathroom while Lissa rolled over on the bed and curled into a tight ball, her hands between her legs, testing the sore tenderness there. But she did not cry. She never cried.

When they were first married, his love making, if that was the right name for it, had pleased her. He'd certainly behaved with more consideration, being gentle and kind, calling her his darling virgin bride, and she'd taken care not to disillusion him on that score. But she'd been young then and was so grateful to Philip for choosing her as a wife that she'd been eager and anxious for love, not minding if they didn't quite reach the heady heights of ecstasy she'd found with Derry.

It was all her own fault of course. Somehow she'd failed in that as in everything. As time went by Philip became more ardent and demanding. No matter how hard she tried, she could not please him. Her inadequacies had at first distressed and then annoyed him. She was either too slow, too clumsy, or too tired. In the end he'd lost patience, accusing her of being frigid and abandoned all consideration for her.

'Some women find no pleasure in sex,' he told her on countless occasions, and were it not for the dreams which haunted her at night of reckless young love on empty golden fells, she might well have believed it to be true. 'But *I* must have it, Lissa. You do understand that, don't you, my darling? It's a physical necessity for a man.'

'Of course, Philip,' she would assure him. 'I want so much to make you happy.'

And he would smile and pat her cheek as if she were a child not able to understand such adult mysteries. 'Of course you do, my darling.'

In their everyday life together he remained everything she could wish for in a husband, she told herself now. Exquisitely caring, in his own way, helping her to cope with the complexities of life. But in the bedroom his charm too often vanished, replaced by a driving need. He took what he required as and when he required it and her own needs were forgotten or ignored. Sometimes, as today, she made an effort to respond, to kiss or caress him. But it rarely worked.

She had learned it was better to damp down her emotions when he was in an impatient mood, and not think of what he did to her. Sometimes it took all her courage simply to stay ice cool in his arms, waiting for him to be done, glad when he was.

And really he was not unkind, Lissa thought as she struggled to pull the hair brush through tangled locks. Sometimes he could be charm itself, sweet talking and caressing her, making her feel like a young bride again, precious and beloved. He would often let her massage his shoulders and bring him breakfast or supper in bed, then read snippets of his newspaper to amuse and educate her. She loved to make him happy for that made her happy too, and they had grown used to each other, developed a sort of contentment.

So if she found little pleasure in their love making, how could she blame him? She was the one with hang ups about love, and belonging, as he very reasonably pointed out.

'Wear the burgundy suit with the navy trim,' he told her later as she reached for her favourite silk dress in lupin blue, which so suited her eyes.

'It makes me look old,' she demurred, but he took the blue silk from her hand and hung it firmly back in her wardrobe.

'Let me be the judge.'

She put on the suit with its pleated skirt of a demure length, and short fitted jacket, and he told her how beautiful she looked.

'Perfect. The very thing for a magistrate's dinner.'

She couldn't help but smile. 'How fussy you are, Philip. But I'm glad you like it.'

He'd thrown away all her pretty cotton dresses and rainbow net petticoats, declaring them too young and frivolous. It was a new decade and a new era in her life, so she had made no protest.

Lissa called in to kiss goodnight to the children and Philip did the same. 'We should have a nurseryful,' he said, gazing on their sleeping faces. 'Girls are very pretty and appealing but a man needs a son.' As if in some way this would prove his virility or perhaps his status. Lissa made no reply. It had been a difficult pregnancy carrying two babies, a prolonged labour and worse delivery.

It had taken her months to recover from the exhaustion and she had no intention of repeating the experience. Not until she had sorted out the problems in her marriage.

He led her out to the car as if she were a princess. 'You will be the most beautiful woman there, and you know how much that means to me. I'd be lost without you.'

'I know,' she said, smiling radiantly up at him, loving this evidence of his adoration.

'I may decide to join the Golf Club. Don Cheyney is the Vice Captain this year.'

As he pulled the front door closed he happened to glance at the coloured patterns in the pane of glass in the top of the door and ran his finger along the strip of black lead that divided each portion. He stared at the tip of his finger, grey with dust. 'Have you cleaned this door recently, my sweet?'

Lissa's heart sank. 'I'll do it tomorrow.'

'Tomorrow never comes though, does it, darling? We've discovered that before, haven't we?' He glanced at his watch. The fingers stood at twenty past seven.

'You'll have to hurry. We mustn't be late.'

Lissa was appalled. 'You can't mean that I do it now?'

Dark grey eyes opened wide. 'Why not? No time like the present. I wonder sometimes what you do all day. Wasting time feeding the ducks. And keeping the children out far too late.'

'The children like the ducks and . . .' What was

the use? 'I'll do it first thing in the morning, Philip, I promise. I can hardly start cleaning windows in my best suit.'

He was unlocking the door. 'You should have thought of that before, my pet. It won't take a moment to get a damp cloth. Wear an apron and rubber gloves. We don't want you to spoil those lovely nails.'

He stood on the doorstep, tapping his foot impatiently while Lissa hurried into her pristine kitchen, smartly decked out with every modern appliance, and collected the necessary items. She was flushed and flustered by the time the task was done to Philip's satisfaction, and tendrils of carefully lacquered hair were already escaping to lie with clammy heat on her brow.

By the time she'd hurried back to the kitchen with the bowl, wrung out the cloth and hung the gloves on the taps to dry he was calling for her, a note of hard impatience in his voice. 'It's twenty-five to eight.'

'The fault is all Lissa's,' he informed their hosts as they arrived twenty minutes late with everyone else well into the soup course. 'You know how women are. Such perfectionists.'

All she could do was bite on her lip and try to smile so that the tears that blocked her throat would not betray her.

Lissa cleaned the house from top to bottom the next day. Not that it needed it. Every surface gleamed, the mahogany table in the hall reflected a carefully arranged copper bowl of gold chrysanthemums as if it were made of glass. The pristine white paintwork glistened in the sun. Even the tastefully plain blue carpet looked brand new. Indeed she kept out of the drawing room for fear of marking the pile with her footprints.

But she knew that once Philip had spotted an imperfection he was likely to go on the hunt for more. It made her feel dreadful when he found her wanting in some way. It simply wasn't worth the risk.

When she had vacuumed every square inch of carpet and dusted and polished the furniture till it glowed, she switched on the electric kettle and settled herself with a thankful sigh on one of the lemon yellow kitchen chairs, a magazine and a plate of biscuits to hand. She felt more comfortable in the kitchen, where she wouldn't mess things up. Lissa pulled the pins from her hair, fluffing it free with her fingers, the way she preferred it.

When Nanny brought back the twins from their shopping expedition she would play with them in the nursery until it was time for their afternoon nap. That was her escape. The twins made her life worthwhile.

Even so the day stretched endlessly before her. There were times when she longed for the heady freedom of the drapers shop with Miss Stevens calling them 'my dear gels' in that frosty manner she had. You knew where you were with old

Stevens, dragon though she undoubtedly was. Lissa was never quite sure with Philip.

But Stella Stevens had long since retired. The old drapery was now a not very successful Gifte Shoppe, providing the increasing numbers of visitors who crowded the streets of Carreckwater with rather tacky souvenirs. And even if it had still been there, Philip would never have countenanced her working. She was a wife and mother, that should be enough. Lissa wondered why it wasn't.

He'd been quite shocked once when she'd suggested she might take a part-time job. Almost as outraged as if she'd suggested taking a lover.

'I hope I can keep my wife without her needing to demean herself by clocking in every morning.'

'But the house doesn't fill my day and it would only be in the mornings. Nanny is with the children in any case.'

'I won't have you worn out when I come home from the office.' Since then he had perversely made sure that her day was filled to capacity. If she could not find sufficient tasks, he found them for her, or make her do them all over again.

It was a large house. Six bedrooms, attics, cellars, and three reception rooms all on different levels. Spacious lofty rooms filled with old fashioned furniture, cornices, picture rails and stained glass windows that were all difficult to clean. The fact that most of the rooms were never used did not prevent the necessity of their having to be turned out regularly. Certainly not in Philip's view. He was punctilious in keeping her up to the mark, as he put it.

'They still get dusty,' he told her. 'What if someone should call or come to stay?'

'Who?'

'I've no idea. Does it matter? We must be prepared for all contingencies.'

'I could cover the furniture with dust sheets in the rooms we don't use.'

'I'll not live in a museum.'

'Oh, sorry, I didn't think.'

He shook his head with a sigh of exasperation. 'You never do. Leave the thinking to me, darling.'

It was easier to agree. Lissa hated conflict and Philip could cap every point she made with another, and never lose his cool. While she would end up hot with frustrated temper.

The house had apparently once belonged to an old lady. Farquar? No, Fraser, that was it. She had kept a maid and a gardener in happier days, and probably a cook, Lissa thought, with some displeasure. She'd now retired to a home for the elderly and Lissa was expected to attain the same standards with the assistance only of her modern appliances which seemed to break down every time she looked at them. Renee might worship at the feet of vacuum cleaners, they left Lissa perfectly cold.

As she sipped her second cup of tea that morning, Darjeeling from the very finest porcelain, she experienced a deep aching need to be back in a corner of the stock room with a mug curled in her hand and Jan's ceaseless chatter in her ears.

She went to the phone and dialled a number. Meg's voice rang out, as clearly as if she were in the next room.

'Broombank.'

'Hello, it's me.'

'Sweetheart! When are you coming to see us? We haven't seen the terrible twosome for weeks.'

Lissa laughed. She and Meg had become a little closer since the birth of the twins and Lissa was anxious to build on this progress. 'They nearly fell in the lake yesterday, got chased by the ducks and almost run over by a car. Status quo really.'

Meg chuckled, not taking this dire list too seriously. 'Jan's pregnancy is well advanced now. Not long to go. She misses you,' Meg said, the tone of her voice changing slightly.

Lissa propped herself against the telephone table and agreed that she'd been thinking the very same thing. 'I miss her, but she'll soon have her hands full.'

'Like you, sweetheart.'

'Yes,' said Lissa. 'Like me.'

The front door opened and two tiny figures in neat canary yellow coats and bonnets burst in. 'Ah, here they are. Must go.' She hurriedly rang off, repeating her promise to visit.

'Hello, my darlings.' Lissa knelt on the hall carpet to sweep them both into her arms, nuzzling against their soft cheeks, breathing in the sweet baby scent

295

of their skin. Her heart soared with happiness. How lucky she was. Nothing to complain about at all. 'What shall we do now? Play soap bubbles? Or paint pictures to take to Granny Meg?'

Nanny's hand came down upon each small head. 'The children must have their lunch and go down for their nap.'

'Of course. How silly of me. I'd forgotten. Run along then, darlings. Nanny's waiting.'

She remained kneeling on the carpet for several moments after they had gone.

It was late afternoon when they woke and Lissa spent a riotous hour or more in the nursery right at the top of the house, playing Ride-a-Cock-Horse, daubing glorious pictures in red, yellow and purple on pieces of old wallpaper, and building huge brick towers which the twins knocked down with screams of delight.

She was telling them a story when Nanny Sue came in, clicking her tongue over the mess they'd made, just as if Lissa were a child too. The clock chimed down in the hall.

'Lordy, it's five o'clock, and I still haven't decided what we're eating this evening.' She hurriedly finished the story, attempting to placate the protests and prevent tears. Then after raiding the kitchen larder and flinging together some scraps of pork and vegetables into a casserole, she flew back upstairs to bathe and change, paint her nails and attend to her hair.

At six-thirty precisely Lissa was waiting in the

drawing room for the sound of his key in the lock, his gin and tonic already poured and standing on a silver tray on the walnut sideboard. She might have been Grace Kelly waiting for her prince to come, were it not for the deep and abiding unhappiness that was eating away at her soul.

CHAPTER 15

The Yacht Club held a formal dinner every year in the Marina Hotel at the end of September. Afterwards there would be dancing for those so inclined. The band would be a classic trio and there would be no skiffle in the interval. The craze had long since died. Lissa was glad about that.

She sat at the long, white-clothed table in her little black dress, shorter than she was used to wearing but slim-fitting, expensive and flattering, with a red silk rose bud pinned to one shoulder. Philip had wanted her to wear a long one in heavy white satin, as if she were a debutante, but for once she'd refused. Lissa could sense waves of disapproval emanating from him as he took the chair next to hers and slipped his hand proprietorially over a black-stockinged knee.

'Please, Philip,' she whispered, anxious someone might see. 'Not here.'

'In a dress so short you are clearly inviting such attention, and I am your husband.' He slid his fingers under the dress right up to her stocking tops and then back to the knee, much to the

298

amusement of the man on Lissa's right who, catching her angry glare, hastily addressed his attention to the woman on his left.

Lissa gently removed the hand and attempted to appear unconcerned, smiling into the mild gaze of Doctor Robson, seated opposite. 'Good evening, Lissa,' the doctor said. 'Looking as lovely as ever, I see.'

'You're looking rather spry yourself.' Lissa liked Charles Robson. A patient, rotund man, rather old fashioned but unshockable, like the rest of his profession. Yet he managed to maintain an affable quality that made him entirely approachable. Lissa had visited him on several occasions, and he of course had delivered the twins.

They chatted for a while about the health and beauty of her two offspring, a subject Lissa never tired of.

'Ah, Robson old chap.' Becoming aware that a man was monopolising his wife, Philip smiled expansively. He had already enjoyed several whiskies, though not of the best quality. He was not normally one to indulge in alcohol but felt he needed to relax this evening. It had been a tedious day. Now he poured himself a second glass of a rather fine claret, hoping to soothe his irritation which had increased with Lissa's obdurate stubbornness. It occurred to him that this might be the very opportunity he'd been seeking to discuss a matter of some importance with the good doctor. Man to man. Fellow professional and all that.

'When are you going to help my wife, you old duffer?' he asked. 'Came to you months ago and you've achieved nothing.'

The doctor looked startled, though not half so startled as Lissa. She attempted to laugh it off, then flinched as once more Philip's hand fastened upon her knee. 'Please, Philip. Doctor Robson is enjoying an evening out. He has no wish to discuss medical matters.'

Philip rarely relinquished an argument once begun, certainly not when his inhibitions were at their lowest. 'He knows well enough what I mean. What sort of a quack are you? Damned inadequate in my view.'

'I'm sorry you're dissatisfied, Brandon,' the doctor said, quite equably, lifting his soup spoon. 'Whatever it is I've done, I hope you're not about to sue me for it.' Several people tittered, partly from amusement, partly embarrassment.

Lissa could hardly contain her shame. She could feel her cheeks firing up, acutely aware of the growing interest about her. Voices deliberately lowered as people waited to hear what it was the doctor had failed to do. Waitresses pretended not to listen to what sounded very like the start of a matrimonial dispute, which they would be sure to relate with relish in the kitchen the moment they returned from handing out the dishes of asparagus soup and bread rolls.

'How long is it now that you've been treating her? The twins are two and a half years old and still no sign of another child. You incompetent old fool.'

Lissa's cheeks flared to bright red. 'Philip, please! Not now. You're embarrassing me.'

Hush, woman, I'm talking to this nincompoop.' The hand on her knee gripped tighter and Lissa let out a tiny whimper.

Doctor Robson turned to her, a frown on his round face. 'Come and see me in the morning, Lissa. We'll talk about it then, see what we can do for you. This isn't the moment, Brandon.' So saying, he applied himself to his soup.

Philip leaned forward across the table, pushing his flushed face as close to the doctor's as he could and speaking in a loud whisper that not a soul in the room could miss. 'Are you suggesting the case is hopeless? That my wife has turned barren?'

In the loud and dreadful silence which followed, all movement ceased. Not a hand moved, not a soup spoon lifted.

Except for one red-headed waitress who chose that precise moment to place a bowl of soup before him. Perhaps Philip moved or jolted her elbow, no one could be entirely sure, but the bowl missed the edge of the table and hot soup poured all down the front of his black evening trousers.

Pandemonium broke out, and low-pitched, stifled laughter. Philip leapt to his feet, shouting his rage and agony, demanding the waitress be dismissed on the spot. Bringing the manager scurrying.

'I'm going,' she said. But not before she had placed one hand on Lissa's shoulder and given it an affectionate squeeze. Lissa looked up into Renee's sympathetic face.

'Common as muck, that's me, but I don't let nobody push me around. Certainly not a jumped up, full of himself, no good tyke like Philip Brandon.' Renee's hands stilled in their kneading of bread dough as she stared, appalled, at Lissa. 'Crikey, what've I said? I didn't mean it like it sounded. He's your husband, for God's sake.'

In bright tartan trews and an emerald green T-shirt, the whole covered by a huge white apron, and her once bleached hair now a bright orangey red to match her lips and backcombed to within an inch of its life, Renee looked the very picture of a fulfilled and happy woman. Apart from the fact that her voluptuous figure filled the clothes a touch more tightly, gone was the lethargic, whining creature who had never moved from her fireside. Lissa felt a pang of envy at her obvious contentment.

'It's all right. I do understand what you're saying and in a way I agree with you, it's just that . . .' Lissa searched her mind for a way to explain the complications of her marriage. 'Philip needs me, and I want to make him happy.'

'Except in this. You don't want another kid?'

'No.'

'But they're gorgeous.'

They both gazed at the two girls, happily swathed in tea towels and rolling out grey pieces of dough on the end of the table.

'And all my maternal instincts are quite satisfied, thank you. I don't need to go through it all again.

'So tell him.'

'I can't. He's keen to try for a boy.'

Renee glanced sharply at her. 'You've been using summat. Right?'

Lissa, hunched on a tall stool, nodded her agreement. 'A diaphragm. Doctor Robson didn't know Philip wanted another child. Until last night.'

'Now the fat's right in the fire.'

Lissa nodded.

Renee sucked in her breath, then picking up the lump of dough flung it back on to the floured board and began pummelling and rolling it with fresh vigour. Clouds of flour flew up and settled in drifts on her red hair. In her mind the dough might well have been Philip Brandon's head. She wished it was, for the contempt with which he'd treated Lissa at the dinner last night. Humiliated her, rotten toad, fondling her before everyone and then revealing her private business. 'So what did the good doctor say when you saw him this morning?'

Lissa, an incongruous picture of elegance in the untidy kitchen in a sleeveless dress of ice blue linen, hair hanging in a single plait down her back, gave Renee a woebegone look. 'He expressed his surprise.'

Both girls' eyes met and held while the dough was neglected. 'I'll bet he did. Let me get this straight. Your husband thinks you've been going to the doc for help to get pregnant again, only the doc has actually been helping you stop babies from coming? Is that the way of it?'

There was a glint of merriment now in Renee's eyes and for the first time that morning Lissa began to see the funny side of her predicament and twisted her lips into a smile.' It does sound a bit odd, I suppose, put like that.' She glanced at the twins, stopped Sarah from putting some of the disgusting mixture into her mouth and helped Beth stick currants into hers.

'No, darling. We must cook it first.'

'I'd say it was pretty confusing for any chap to understand, even someone as clever as a doctor. A woman now, would catch the drift right away.'

'Oh, Renee.' Laughter was bubbling up in her throat. Where it came from, Lissa couldn't imagine. She certainly hadn't felt like laughing earlier when she'd faced Doctor Robson's glowering disapproval and listened to his lecture on wifely duty. It had taken all her courage and skill to persuade him not to divulge this information to Philip, which he'd threatened to do for all it would mean breaking a patient's confidence. Now she was holding her sides as if it was the funniest thing in the world.

Renee was screaming with laughter, flour going everywhere as she circled the kitchen gasping for breath. The twins, entranced by the sight, started to shout with laughter too though they had no idea why. 'Oh Gawd, what a laugh. Crikey, I'd love to see his face when you tell him the truth!'

Lissa tumbled from the stool and grabbed hold of Renee, shaking her slightly to make her stop laughing and take the matter more seriously. 'Philip must *never* know. That's the whole point. I don't *ever* want him to find out. Do you understand, Renee?'

Renee stopped laughing to look deep into the violet eyes, darkly shadowed in an unusually pale face. She could feel the very slightest tremor in the hands that held hers, the wrists seeming so frail and thin they might snap in two at any moment. 'I'll put the dough to rise then I think we might have a drop of sherry. For medicinal purposes.'

'Maybe I should be getting back. Nanny Sue will wonder where I am.'

'Let her. Old po face. Come on, you two whipper-snappers. You can go and sleep on my big bed while I bake your dough men. OK?' She swept Sarah into her arms while Lissa followed on with Beth.

Ten minutes later they were more comfortably seated in Renee's living room, still untidy with newspapers and discarded clothing. Exactly as Lissa remembered, except that the chirping budgie seemed to have departed, for the cage stood empty.

Renee did not remark upon this, so neither did she.

She was suddenly glad to be here, in Renee's uncomplicated company, and for the first time in months felt herself relax. She wondered why she'd kept away so long.

Renee took a sip of the sherry, sighed with pleasure then set her glass on the mantelshelf.

'Why did you marry him then?' The bluntness of the question took Lissa by surprise.

'I-I'm not sure. I liked him, I suppose, he was charming and kind and good looking. He seemed a safe bet.'

'So what's gone wrong? Come on, lovey, let's be having it. Has he been knocking you about? Because if he has . . .'

'No, nothing like that.'

'What then? You and me have a lot in common, y'know, both being married to older men like. Mind you, Jimmy could give your Philip a few years and he's a long way behind in the looks department. Is it the age thing that bothers you?'

Lissa shook her head. How could she explain the depths of the terrible mistake she'd made by marrying Philip? She'd made her bed, as they said, and must lie in it. With him. But she couldn't talk about all that, not with Renee, not with anyone. It was too intimate.

'I never did understand why our Derry left the way he did,' Renee was saying. 'Mind you, what a mess when he came back that time! Took me days to calm Jimmy down.' She hurried on, not explaining how he'd found his son in his wife's arms. 'You two seemed made for each other.'

Lissa pressed her lips together and stared out of the window on to the back garden. She could see the shed at the bottom of it, the one where Derry had presumably slept for several months at Renee's instigation. But he hadn't left Carreckwater simply because Renee had asked him to move out. He could have found other digs in town. Even after all this time Lissa had come up with no answer except the obvious.

'His head was full of his own ambitions. I couldn't compete with a guitar or the promise of a recording contract.'

'He never got it, poor mite.' Renee looked mournful as she reached for her sherry. 'Played his socks off all over Manchester and London to no avail.'

Where Derry was, or what he was up to, was no longer any concern of hers. 'What is he doing these days?' The words came of their own accord.

'He's gone abroad, hasn't he?'

'Where?' She didn't care. She only hoped he was miserable as hell, as miserable as she was.

'America, would you believe? Do you think he might meet Acker Bilk? Ooh, I love that record don't you, 'Stranger On the Shore'?' She began to hum the tune.

'I'd believe anything of Derry Colwith.'

'That's men for you. Never there when you want

307

them.' Renee took several sips of her sherry. 'Broke Jimmy up it did, his only son and heir going off like that at a moment's notice. Mind you, we've decided against kids of us own. 'Jimbo's had enough of all that, and I don't want the responsibility. I fancy this new pill, don't you? I'll give it a try when they get it sorted out.' She stared at the cage. 'I might get a parrot.'

Lissa felt a sudden spurt of laughter but managed to restrain it. It would be too cruel. Renee might be brash, greedy, oversexed, possibly verging on the amoral judging by the gossip there was about her guest house, but no one could doubt that her heart was in the right place. She meant well for all her clumsiness on occasions, and was the only person Lissa had found in an age who was prepared to be on her side now that Jan had gone.

'I'll never forget the look of shock and outrage on his face when the soup poured down his legs,' Renee said, spluttering over her sherry.

'Oh, golly, yes.' And they were both off laughing again. It made Lissa feel so good to feel young and carefree. When they'd mopped up their tears and more sherry had been poured she said,' I shall continue to lie, about wanting more children. If it saves an argument.'

Renee looked doubtful. 'You can't keep it up for ever.'

Lissa turned her face away, not wanting to meet the inquiring gaze.

'So what is it? What's really wrong? I'm not daft. I can see there must be summat else.'

'I don't know. Maybe I'm bored.' Lissa felt her heart jump as the words popped out and realised for the first tune how true they were and how much that bothered her. She took a deep breath and began to pour out her heart. 'Philip expects me to be the perfect little wife. Beautiful, charming, hosting his dinner parties, entertaining him each evening with a gin and tonic and adoring attention.' The sherry had loosened her tongue and she warmed to her theme.

'I don't even get to spend much time with my own children, except for an hour or two each afternoon. He expects his house to look like something out of the Ideal Home Exhibition with me devoting my entire life to achieving such a miracle. He's so very particular and has such high standards yet treats me like Dresden china, or a weak fool incapable of intelligent conversation let alone holding down a job.' She lifted clenched fists in helpless appeal. 'He goes out to meetings most nights and sometimes I think I'll go mad, with no one in the house to talk to but two babies, a starchy nanny and the vacuum cleaner. Can you understand?'

'Oh, yes,' said Renee, nodding wisely. 'I understand perfectly. That's why I miss my Peter since he passed over. Jimmy's never away from that boat yard. Mind you, I have my guests, in the summer at any rate. The long winters can be a bit of a drag. That's why I help out at the Marina Hotel now and then. Bit of company like, as well as a few bob in the pocket. You should try it.'

Lissa shook her head in despair, an expression raw with lost hope on her drawn face. 'There's nothing I can do. Philip wouldn't allow it. I'm a possession, like a sofa or a fine picture. And if I'm not careful, the bearer of an increasing brood of children which will keep me very securely within doors.'

The familiar sensation of fear beat slowly in her stomach, the sickness sweeping right up into her gullet. She felt like a prisoner. Yet how could she ever escape without a job, without money of her own? And did she really want to? 'Philip needs me at home. He's said so a million times.' And she wanted him to need her, didn't she? What else did she have? She couldn't risk losing him.

'I wouldn't let that stop me.'

Lissa drew in a trembling breath, aware she must remain composed. 'Simply not on the cards, he says.'

'Bugger his cards,' said Renee, reaching for the sherry bottle and refilling the glasses for a third time. 'If you can lie about the baby thing, why can't you lie about that too?'

Lissa blinked. 'What are you saying?'

'How will he know if you're working, if you don't tell him? So long as you're home by the time he is and the house is done and dusted, he'd never notice. Men never see what's right in front of them, everyone knows that. Anyway, you could employ a cleaner. Surely you can afford one?'

'He expects me to look after our home myself. Anyway, Nanny would tell. She's very proper. Likes to do everything by the book.'

'Not if you bribed her not to.'

'Bribed?'

Renee smiled. 'Threatened her with the sack if she split on you.'

Lissa looked shocked. 'I couldn't do that.'

'Ask her nicely then.'

'I'd never get away with it. Would I?' Why was she even considering it? The idea was utter madness.

Renee propped her feet on the mantelshelf while she considered. 'Pretend to take up charity work. Most ladies of your class, if you'll pardon the expression, are out and about all day and nobody has a blind idea what they're up to. Take up good works. The Lissa Turner – sorry – Brandon, Save-Her-Sanity Committee.'

They were both hooting with laughter again. Before the sherry bottle was halfway down they had begun to devise a plan.

Following the evening's débâcle, which he blamed entirely on the clumsiness of the stupid waitress, Philip insisted that the hotel pay for his dinner jacket and trousers to be dry cleaned. He returned three days later to collect them, repeating his annoyance at the incident and his hope that the waitress, whoever she was, would pay out of her wages. When he'd vented his wrath he agreed to be mollified by a glass of malt whisky in the bar, courtesy of the management.

'Got to keep them on their toes,' said a voice at his side. Philip swivelled round to find himself addressed by a young man with fair, floppy hair and tortoiseshell spectacles that kept slipping down his nose. His dark grey suit was clearly brand new and the white collar he wore looked odd against the pale grey of his shirt, giving him an almost clerical appearance. A clipboard and measuring tape reposed on the bar counter beside a half empty glass of beer.

Philip said, 'Very true,' and returned to his whisky.

After the usual discussion about the weather and the failings of hotels in general, a subject close to the man's heart apparently, he informed Philip that he was a consultant. 'Andrew Spencer.' He held out a hand which Philip reluctantly shook. 'For Manchester Water Board. They're the bogeyman round here, in case you didn't realise.'

Philip gave a dry smile. 'I believe so.'

'They've learnt a bit since Thirlmere were built. That's what started it all off.'

'Indeed?'

The Manchester man warmed to his theme. 'The mistake they made then was to concrete the shoreline. Too hard and unnatural, d'you see? Then they stopped folk from using the new lake, which again didn't endear them to the natives, as you might say. They don't make those sort of mistakes these days.'

'I see.' Philip tried to look interested though his mind was on Lissa and how she had actually refused his essential needs these last three days and nights. He blamed it all on that doctor. If he didn't set her right soon, Philip meant to go and tackle Robson himself, women's complaints or no. A man was entitled to a son if he wanted one, to carry his name forward to the next generation. He never loved Lissa more than when she was soft and vulnerable with pregnancy, smelling of babies with breasts swollen with milk. He felt an ache start up in his loins even now at the thought and hastily took a large swig of whisky.

The man was still talking. 'Eighty million gallons of water are pumped from the Lakes area each day. Trouble is, Manchester could do with another fifty at least. Industry must have its water, eh?'

'Quite.' God, what a bore he was. Philip drained his glass, preparatory to making a hasty departure, but the man clung.

'The demand goes on. Industry versus tourism, I suppose. I've to speak at a meeting tonight, in fact. You'll read all about it in the local paper, how Manchester Water Board is on the lookout for another site. Most of it is scare-mongering of course. Rumours abound.' He rolled his eyes and laughed. 'People panic and come up with all sorts of daft notions. They'd have everyone believe we're ploughing up half the Lake District to hear some talk.' He continued with his tale without pausing to draw breath.

'But if we don't find a suitable valley for a holding reservoir soon, we'll have to extract from the main lakes, and folk won't like that any better, now will they? Think they're holy, those waters, and it's my unenviable task to help find the right spot. Do preliminary survey work before calling in the geologists and the rest of the engineers. I don't mind telling you this is my first big job, so it'd be a feather in my cap if I came up with the goods, so to speak.'

'I see,' Philip said, suddenly thoughtful.

Andrew Spencer puffed out his chest with self-importance then took a swallow of beer, wiping the froth from his upper lip with the back of his hand. 'No doubt I'll be questioned by the local big-wigs and the press *ad nauseam.* I've given two interviews this morning already.' The man sighed at the trials of unwanted fame. 'Not my favourite task, I can tell you.'

Philip was back on the bar stool by this time, dark eyes alert. He glanced at the empty beer glass. 'Can I get you the other half?'

'Aye,' said the Manchester man. 'I wouldn't say no.'

Lissa stood in front of the shop windows which someone had painted white on the inside and felt a stir of excitement. Renee had been right. The

Gifte Shoppe people had packed up and gone. Miss Stevens' old drapery was looking sadly neglected. The paintwork was chipped and there were posters and sale tickets peeling off the filthy windows.

Of course the idea was preposterous. How could she take on the lease? Who would arrange it for her? Where would she find the money? Nor could she hope to keep it a secret from Philip. That had soon become apparent, even to Renee when she'd talked to her about this mad idea.

'Don't you think someone might notice me behind the counter?' Lissa had said, giggling over their usual glass of sherry. She made a point of calling in at Nab Cottage regularly now. Renee was good to talk to, and their friendship had deepened.

'Wear a disguise. Buy a wig and a pair of dark glasses.' Renee had been off again, opening wide her orange mouth and letting the laughter ring out. In the end, however, common sense prevailed and new strategies were devised. 'Sex. That generally gets you what you want,' she'd bluntly suggested. But on seeing Lissa's face muscles tighten and a shudder ripple down her spine, did not pursue the subject further. 'Sweet talk then. Worked with my Jimmy when I first thought of doing B and B.' Her face had softened. 'But then he's a pet, bless him. Wouldn't refuse me a thing.'

'Philip isn't like Jimmy.'

'No, and even Jimbo has his limits. I'd like us to sell this place and move to somewhere bigger.'

315

Her expression grew dreamy. 'We could do with the money and we can only take five guests here, six at a pinch, so it'd be grand to have a couple more bedrooms, and a separate dining room. Feeding them is a problem. At the moment we have to put up tables every morning in the front parlour. Bit of a fag that is, I can tell you. We did try them in here, but Jimmy didn't like it. He likes his privacy, you see.'

Lissa, remembering how the pair had seemed to be permanently glued together, didn't doubt it.

'The poor lamb deserves his little pleasures. He works hard enough. He's a creature of impulse. We both are.' She winked outrageously, the spiky eyelashes wriggling like spider's legs. 'But you can't go having it off on the rug if some old dear could walk in at any minute for her cornflakes, now can you?'

Lissa flushed, then giggled. 'Do you never take life seriously?'

'Not if I can avoid it. Jimmy does, bless him.'

Funny how she and Renee got on so well when they were as different as chalk and cheese. Renee so robust and unashamedly sexy, and herself having forgotten what it was to really love a man. Well, almost. And now was not the moment to recall it.

Then when Renee had switched on the electric fire and drawn the curtains, the gesture had reminded Lissa of the time. 'Golly, I must go.' She'd hurried to find her coat which matched the pale blue dress exactly. Renee smoothed her hand admiringly over the soft fabric as she helped her on with it.

'You're so good with style. Not like me. I buy summat because I like the colour, then throw things together and hope for the best. I like bright colours, d'you see?'

Lissa thought about this remark now as she stared at the peeling paintwork. Was it possible? Could she run a shop, build a career for herself? Would Philip agree? Dare she ask him?

CHAPTER 16

'I've been thinking that I might start a business of my own.'

Philip stared at her, then laughed. It would almost have been better had he shouted at her. But he simply put back his head and roared with laughter, as if she'd said the funniest thing. 'What do you know about running a business?'

'I could learn.' But he only laughed again. Then he lifted his head, smiling and handsome, and sniffed the air. 'Is that the dinner I smell burning?'

Lissa dropped the knives and forks she was carefully laying on her best white lace tablecloth and flew to the kitchen to rescue the steak and mushroom pie which she had baked especially to please him this evening.

'The Cheyneys will be here at any minute,' he warned, getting in her way as she flustered about with oven gloves. 'You are utterly incompetent, Lissa. Why can't you be more organised?'

Because I've been run off my feet all day cleaning this place from stem to stern, she thought furiously, but said nothing. Perhaps he was right. Mortified by failure as the kitchen filled with acrid smoke Lissa decided that she probably was incompetent. She did seem to make a dreadful mess of everything: marriage, their sex life, even apparently her own children. What made her think she wouldn't make a mess of a shop as well?

He came to stand beside her at the kitchen sink, watching as she tried to salvage the pie by scraping off the worst of the blackened pastry. It always made her feel worse when he watched. 'How silly of me to forget it,' she apologised. 'I've some cold duck left in the fridge. We could have that and I'll do a salad instead.'

'I would prefer the pie. This only proves you must keep your mind on your true purpose in life, being a good wife to me. What can be more important than that? Business indeed.' And his handsome face filled with derision.

'I would so like to be a success at something,' Lissa said, turning pleading eyes to his, the oven cloth still in her hands. There was no sign of compassion in his face, not a trace of understanding, and in that moment she truly hated him. 'Can't you see, Philip? I need a life of my own.'

'You have a life, looking after me and the children.'

'I need some independence. More than that, I need to feel proud of myself, build my self-esteem. I want to be a real person, not a shadow of what I might have been.'

'How terribly melodramatic you sound.'

'Only because it's true.'

319

All she had to say was, I've got a business in mind already, but somehow the words wouldn't come. Lissa flushed at the very thought. Quite impossible.

'Is this supper ever going to be ready? You do care enough about me to give my friends a decent meal, I suppose?'

She gazed at the pie in despair. Hilary Cheyney was a wonderful cook. Lissa went and stared in the fridge, seeking salvation.

'You want to abandon your children and a loving husband to play at being a businesswoman, and you can't even manage one simple dinner.'

Lissa was becoming increasingly flustered. 'If you'll just let me get on with it, I can manage very well. Anyway, I'm not asking you for any money,' Lissa said, very quietly. 'What if I grill this pair of trout, add a bit of a bacon and a nice sauce?' She started to chop lettuce.

He pushed his face close to hers and spoke to her in staccato fashion as if explaining something to an idiot. 'You need capital to start a business. Did you not realise, my sweet innocent child? It isn't a new toy to play with and throw away when you get bored.'

He took the trout from her and put it back in the fridge beside the cold cuts of duck.

Anger rose hot and sour in her throat. Lissa wanted to shout that she knew all of that, that she did have money. Money which had been left to her, and she could manage very well without him. But some part of her made her hold this piece of information back, as if she needed to keep the knowledge secret, for protection.

How could she defy him? Philip loved her. Wasn't it her duty to make him happy?

'You're probably right,' she sighed, shutting the fridge door. The anger had faded, swamped by depression. There could be no escape. Philip would have his way in everything, not understanding her desire for independence.

Lissa reached for the cloth but he took it from her with finger and thumb, grimacing with distaste as he dropped it to the floor and gathered her in his arms. 'You are young, and vulnerable. I want only to protect you and keep you safe. I need you here, Lissa, my darling. What is so wrong with that? For my pleasure alone, free from all outside troubles and influences. Forget the pie,' he murmured against her ear. 'I'll ring the Cheyneys and tell them you're not well. I find I'm not hungry this evening after all, not for food anyway. Perhaps it was meant that you burn it. A lucky omen to make us take an early night.'

He was leading her from the kitchen and a tide of panic flooded her. She couldn't face it, not now, not tonight.

Unbidden, the image of Derry came into her head. She saw his smile, heard his laughter and his cheerful chatter, remembered the smoothness of his skin, his loving arms about her as they had been on that day at Kidsty Pike. The truth was that she still wanted him, as much as ever.

'No,' she said, very firmly, removing herself from Philip's grasp. 'Not tonight.' Then picking up the oven gloves Lissa calmly proceeded to carry the pie dish into the dining room. Philip blocked her way, his face dark with anger.

'I've told you I'll ring and cancel. Go upstairs.'

'Cancel the Cheyneys by all means, if you wish, but I said no, not tonight.'

'Are you disobeying me?'

She laughed as she adroitly side-stepped him, and though Lissa quailed at her daring she secretly revelled in the shock that came over his face at her temerity. 'I suppose I am.' Feeling the exhilaration of her defiance soar through her veins. 'I'm hungry and rather tired. I've had a busy day.' She drew in a deep breath and sat down, arranging her skirts, more composed than she had felt in a long while.

What had come over her?

Where was she finding this courage? From fear? Or an echo of that old Lissa, not quite dead after all?

Philip towered above her, angry, menacing, and Lissa lifted her chin to smile up at him. 'Do stop huffing and puffing, darling. Are you going to ring them or not? The pie will go cold.'

He lifted one arm and swept it from the table. The dish broke as it hit the floor and rich gravy and pieces of blackened crust spilled out on to the blue carpet.

'There now,' said Lissa, with not the faintest

tremor in her voice. 'Now we can't possibly have the Cheyneys to dinner. Not until we buy a new carpet.'

It was an insubstantial victory. Philip rang and put off the Cheyneys till the following Friday. Lissa spent an hour on her knees cleaning the carpet. But she had learned never mention the subject of taking a business ever again.

A cold winter changed into an indifferent spring and then into a summer of sweet scents which lightened her heart. She loved to see the boats bobbing on the lake, their masts bristling with importance, white sails flapping, children squealing with delight. It made her think of that long ago joyous summer when she too had felt her blood sing with the promise of youth, all her future before her. Lissa constantly needed to remind herself that she was still young, even as the thought of growing old with Philip somehow made her shudder.

She felt as if time was slipping through her fingers and she had no control over it. But then she had no control over anything. And every time she passed the old drapery she felt that it symbolised in some way the loss of her freedom.

She devoted more time to her children, much to Nanny Sue's annoyance. Any change in routine was strictly frowned upon but Lissa took to impromptu picnics, to longer walks by the shore, and bus rides to neighbouring towns. Anything to keep her occupied and out of the house. Not that she could stay away too long. Philip rang regularly to check how she was. And though he smiled in fond amusement when she told him of little incidents that had occurred on her walks, he expected her to be home in good time to be ready for him.

'My own sweet darling. You mustn't do too much,' he would say, kissing her brow. 'Is my drink ready?'

The twins loved these little adventures, as they called them. But however much she might fill her days, there was no escaping the nights. Each evening Lissa found herself filled with an increasing dread. Partly from the fear of his unremitting interrogation about her state of health, and the sense of ruthlessness that was edging into his lovemaking. He still hoped for a son.

Clad in her silk robe, hair brushed and face cleansed of make up, she looked like an innocent young girl and Lissa found herself trembling as she walked into the bedroom. Today the humidity had developed into a summer storm, wrecking her plans and keeping her within doors, making her edgy.

'I'm so tired,' she said, the moment she saw Philip's face. 'It's been a hot, trying day. The twins were fractious because the rain spoiled their walk.' It was still beating now on the window panes, emphasising her claustrophobia.

'You do look a little pale,' he agreed, his voice

warm with consideration. 'Are you well? Is there no sign yet?'

'I'm afraid not,' trying to disguise the tremor in her voice.

'You must see Doctor Robson again.'

'Yes.'

'And take more care. We don't want you over-doing things.' There were times when he wanted her to appear sensual and sophisticated, when he liked to invite men to dinner and watch them drool over her beauty and their wives grow cold with envy. He loved to sense their need, bask in their jealousy. But in the bedroom he preferred her to exhibit a more virginal appeal. 'You must rest more. I shall insist upon it.'

She saw at once her mistake. If she became too tired to please him he would confine her to the house even more.

'I'm just ready for a good sleep, that's all,' she said, sounding bright and cheerful as she went to draw the curtains. 'What a dreadful night.'

He moved up behind her and slid his hands over her hips and down between her legs, making her jump, loving it when she gasped. 'I need a contented wife. Willing and loving.'

Lissa eased herself gently from his grasp to attend to the other window.

'I thought I might take the children for a drive tomorrow. I promised Meg. I haven't seen her in ages.'

'A drive? Alone?'

'Why not? May I use the new car?'

He looked doubtful. 'I would feel happier if I were to drive you.'

'I can drive. I took lessons and passed my test, remember?' It had been one of her minor successes.

She'd finished attending to the curtains and moved back to the dressing table. Philip watched every nuance of the way the silk gown clung to her slender body, the peak of her nipples thrusting against the flimsy fabric. The need in him was growing and he revelled in the anticipation, only half aware of her words. 'You are such an innocent, my darling. Driving a car is a serious business.'

'I'm perfectly capable.'

'We'll discuss it later, shall we?' He smoothed his hands about her throat, kissing the nape of her neck.

Her chin came up, neatly evading his hand. 'No, Philip, we'll discuss it now. I want to go. I'm perfectly capable of driving myself.' Rebellion was crisp in her voice and he felt a flush of irritation that she should spoil this sensuous moment for him.

'Dear me. You sound like a sulky child.'

'I mean to go.'

'Perhaps your little adventures have gone to your head?' He kissed her bare shoulder and she shrugged it away. A look of irritation came to his face. 'I'll take you on Sunday if you wish, and we can fit in a visit to Larkrigg at the same time. More effort on that score wouldn't come amiss.'

Lissa bit down on a sigh of vexation but said no more, taking her frustration out on her hair as she dragged her brush furiously through tangled curls.

Philip smoothed the curls with his fingers, noting how she shivered at his touch, how she really wanted and loved him to touch her. 'I can understand how you might have a problem with families, having been rejected by your mother. I know Meg claims to have loved you, but you've failed to keep her love, haven't you? My own mother, now, was a wonderful woman, absolutely devoted to me. But you have me to take care of you now. I will never let you down, my darling. A visit to your grandmother wouldn't come amiss, as I have told you many times. You could make more effort to build a relationship.'

'Perhaps.' Lissa was tired of the argument, wishing he didn't make her feel so inadequate, knowing the subject would be brought up time and again until in the end she would be forced to agree for the sake of peace. I dare say you're right, Philip.'

'Of course I'm right.' He laughed. 'Aren't I always?'

Lissa closed her eyes in despair. How could she fight him? It was like hitting a marshmallow that bounced and clung to you, resolutely sticky and sweet. Once she had longed to be loved devotedly, to feel she belonged to someone. And there was no doubt that Philip loved her. He couldn't bear her out of his sight. Yet now she longed only for freedom.

'We should give Rosemary a great-grandson. That would do the trick.'

'I very much doubt she would care. Even if it were possible.'

His tone sharpened. 'Most women find no difficulty in conceiving. Yet you're dealing with this matter with your usual degree of incompetence. You don't try.'

'That's not fair,' Lissa cried, spinning about to face him, feeling the pain of his accusation as if it were really true, as if she didn't spend hours each day dealing with revolting jelly from long white tubes. 'I have tried. I never resist you, do I?'

He looked surprised at the very idea. 'You make it sound as if you're doing me a service.'

'Sometimes I feel that I am.' Reckless words, bravely spoken. Philip was not pleased. Dark eyes sparked with a quiet fury, the expression she most feared, as if he enjoyed these little spats, as if they added to rather than detracted from his arousal.

'I need no favours, Lissa. I need a son.'

She fought for breath, for courage. 'And I need a little more consideration.'

'I devote my entire life to loving and caring for you.' He took the brush from her hand and tossed it impatiently away, then gripping her wrist led her to the bed, urgent now, stripping his clothes off as he went.

'Take off your nightdress. No, I'll do it. I'll teach you how to please a husband as a good wife should, then there'll be babies. Just do as I say for once. No protests.' As Felicity had used to do so very nicely, he thought, meekly obeying his every whim as a woman should. Dear, sweet Felicity.

'Philip, please, you're hurting me. Give me time.'

He had hold of both her wrists and was pushing her back on to the green silk cover. Then he took one of her hands and thrust it down between his legs, closing her fingers about his member. He felt her stiffen and flinch. Her resistance filled him with annoyance, firing the anger in him. He tried to push her head in the same direction but Lissa wriggled free, pretending she didn't understand what he asked of her.

Hot temper showed itself in a white line above his tight upper lip. 'What's the matter with you? I'm your husband, dammit. You should be happy to love me, to do as I ask. Instead of chasing after independence and stubbornly resisting me at every turn.'

She knew he was right. She should want to love him. But she didn't. Lissa could hardly bear to be near him any more, let alone touch him. 'Please. Not tonight, Philip. Not like this. I'm very tired.'

'Damn you, woman!' If she didn't become more amenable to his needs, he might have to consider chastisement, a touch more discipline. If he did ever resort to such actions, she could blame no one but herself. He pushed open her legs and drove himself into her, enjoying the sound of her cries. It gave him the proof he needed that he could control her body if not her obstinate mind.

Two days later Lissa went to call upon Miss Stevens. Her former employer lived in a cottage clinging half-way up Benthwaite Crag, its precipitous garden held in place by a border of clipped laurel, surrounded by a thicket of hazel and beech that stretched across the hillside and hid other, similar properties. A glass conservatory fronted the little house, offering a magnificent view of the lake and it was here that Lissa found her, busily watering plants. She smelled of damp earth and dahlias and welcomed Lissa as if she were an old friend. 'How lovely to see you. How is Jan?'

'In rude health, as they say. Produced a beautiful baby boy.'

'Oh, how wonderful. I must send her a card.'

Once Lissa had enquired about Miss Stevens' own health, admired the geraniums, commiserated over the loss of a favourite rose due to the notorious black spot and exchanged other family news she came eventually to the point of her visit. 'I'm interested in taking on the lease of your old shop.'

'Goodness me. Really?' Miss Stevens looked startled. 'But I thought you were married, to Mr Brandon?'

'I am.'

'With lovely twin daughters?'

'I am, but . . .'

'Then surely a lady in your station in life has no need to work.'

Lissa cleared her throat. 'I would like to. I need to feel more fulfilled.'

'My dear, isn't marriage to a wonderful man fulfilment enough?' Miss Stevens would have given anything for such joy.

Lissa took a deep breath. 'May I speak in complete confidence?'

Miss Stevens looked suddenly panic stricken, having little knowledge of matrimony. 'Oh, my, well of course, only – Mr Brandon is my solicitor and . . .'

'I need to do this, Miss Stevens.' Lissa nervously tapped the hanging bell petals of a pink fuchsia. 'I need something of my own, and for my girls. I think my marriage may be in trouble.'

'Oh, my dear.' Shock registered in the other woman's eyes. 'Has he left you? Oh, my goodness.'

'No, nothing like that. We are not particularly compatible, I suppose.' How to explain her feelings of being held in a trap? That although her husband plainly adored her, he insisted on controlling every part of her life, even in bed, and she couldn't bear it. But Lissa felt quite unable to explain all of this to Miss Stevens. 'He is too possessive,' she said, on a falsely bright laugh.

Stella Stevens set down her watering can and considered her ex-employee more seriously. She had suffered enough romantic disappointments in her own life to recognise distress when she saw it. She could see it in the haunted expression in the girl's eyes, the pinched quality of the skin about the mouth, the darting glances and quick gasps for breath.

'I believe a cup of tea is called for.'

'That would be lovely.'

The tea was made and brought, along with triangles of cucumber sandwiches with the crusts neatly cut off. Lissa struggled to eat one. This meeting was even worse than she'd expected.

'It is no concern of mine, my dear, but have you seen a doctor, for your nerves at least? And you'll do that fuchsia no good at all if you don't leave it alone.'

Lissa guiltily relinquished the flower petals and pleated her fingers tightly together in her lap, trying to keep them still. 'Could we discuss the shop, do you think? I don't have much time.'

'Of course. I hadn't really done anything more about letting it. It's very rundown, you know.'

'It doesn't matter.'

Stella Stevens liked Lissa. She was lovely, sensible and intelligent, though at this moment her beauty had taken on a brittle quality quite at odds with the liquid, golden grace of the young girl who had first come to work at her drapery. She warned herself not to get involved, that it was no business of hers if Philip Brandon was proving to be a possessive husband. For all she knew he may well have cause. He was certainly not a man to cross for all his outward charm. He was a professional, a man of affairs. And a gentleman. A thought struck her.

'Goodness me, you weren't considering . . .' she paused, breathless with horror. '*A divorce?*'

The word jolted Lissa. She hadn't gone so far in her thoughts. It seemed rather too daring for her. 'I shouldn't think so,' Lissa admitted, and Stella grasped her hand in a gesture of relief.

'Oh, thank goodness.' And lowering her voice to a confidential whisper, 'Divorce is not at all the done thing, you know. Very vulgar. You would lose your reputation, my dear. It is only for those scandalous women who are no better than they should be.'

Lissa stared at Miss Stevens in distress. Would this be how everyone would view her if she did leave Philip? Vulgar. Scandalous. *Just like her mother.* She could almost hear Rosemary's purr of satisfaction at being proved right. 'I'm sure it won't come to that,' she said. 'I have my children to consider.'

'Of course you have. I appreciate your confidence in telling me of your troubles, and not a word of it shall pass my lips, but I really think you should consider the matter most carefully before making any rash decisions. There is great stigma attached. Why, every week my magazine implores women to be good wives and mothers. It is up to the woman to make a marriage successful, is it not?'

Lissa set down her uneaten sandwich with a small sound of exasperation. 'Then they are living in the past. You'd have thought the war would've changed all of that, wouldn't you? Yet here we are, years later, as tied as ever. Duty. Obedience. Responsibilities. Making our husband's happy. What about *our* happiness? Are we not entitled to some of that ourselves?'

Miss Stevens looked flustered by her cry for independence. 'I know nothing of marriage, dear. As a maiden lady.'

'You are a woman, Miss Stevens.'

'Quite so, quite so.' To cover her confusion she got up from the small table and, picking up a small pointed trowel, dug it into a pot of begonias, the soil as rich as fruit cake. 'I must say I don't necessarily agree with these opinions but they are generally held. I did have a young man myself, once.' Her faded old eyes grew misty for a moment as her mind slipped back to those early days of her youth, before the war. 'But Mama decided he wouldn't be suitable. I'm sure she was right.'

Lissa squared her shoulders. 'I'm only asking to rent the shop, that's all. I can't go on like this with nothing of my own, I really can't.'

Or the girl would break. Any fool could see that. Miss Stevens nodded, looking thoughtful. 'I shall give your request careful consideration, but I make no promises. And you would do well to remember that the law is not easy to face for a woman alone shunned by society.' The dragon could still roar. And speak utter sense.

The weeks dragged by and Lissa heard nothing from Miss Stevens. Gradually she lost hope, nor did she find the strength to ask Philip again. The idea died, stillborn.

'Don't give up,' Renee told her. 'Tell him you want to be a typhoon like Mr Woolworth.'

'Tycoon. I'm not sure that I do.' Lissa would laugh and change the subject. She enjoyed her visits to Nab Cottage. Renee always managed to make her smile. And Lissa did decide to take up one of her suggestions. Surely there must be something useful she could do. It wasn't exactly the kind of freedom she'd had in mind but it was a start.

'I thought I might take up some voluntary work,' she said one evening as she handed Philip his drink. 'Just an hour or two a week.'

'Excellent,' he said, his attention on his newspaper.

'I thought perhaps I'd ask Hilary. She might know of something I can do. Would you mind?'

She kissed him on his forehead and he glanced up, surprised. It was rare for her to be demonstrative and the gesture touched him. 'Of course not, darling. The woman always seems to be dealing with some good cause or other.' And it would do him no harm with Don Cheyney.

Lissa smiled, as if he had offered her a gift. He loved her best when she was weak and gentle, showing her dependence upon him. She'd turned out to be surprisingly stubborn, not at all like dear, sweet Felicity. Far less malleable than he'd expected or hoped for. There was the matter of her grandmother, for instance. He still had great difficulty in persuading her to visit Larkrigg Hall, with no sign of a reconciliation between them. Not that he had given up hope of winning that one. But then he always did win, in the end.

'Did you see Doc Robson again today, as I asked?'

Lissa turned away, busying herself with arranging flowers that were already immaculate.

'Yes.'

Philip wanted to know what treatment he'd offered to help her to conceive, if she must go into hospital for it, which would demand yet more lies. Lissa's head was spinning with the complexity of the web of deceit she was weaving. The prospect of even more duplicity were she to acquire the shop, was daunting. Perhaps it was just as well nothing had come of that.

One of the old school, Doctor Robson had been unsympathetic when she tried to explain her problems. 'You are depriving your husband of a son.'

'As he tries to deprive me of my freedom, of any say in my own life, even in whether or not I want to make . . .'

'Make what?'

Lissa, blushing with embarrassment, had stared at the worn carpet in the doctor's surgery and pretended she'd forgotten what she was about to say. She couldn't talk about sex, not with the doctor. 'He seems obsessed. He must have me near him at all times. Constantly checking on where I am and what I'm doing. It's unhealthy.'

'It sounds as if you are a very lucky young woman. Few men care so much for their wives.'

She'd looked at him then with pleading eyes, begging for him to understand. 'I was too young when I married, too inexperienced. I don't know what I expected, but not this. I didn't realise what I was taking on.'

Doc Robson had looked very sternly at her over his spectacles. 'Then it is time you grew up, Lissa. You have made your bed and you must lie in it. Match your expectations to suit your husband's requirements. That is your responsibility as a wife.'

She'd argued no more. There seemed little point. More worryingly he'd refused to refurbish her contraceptive supplies.

'I think I'd like to discuss the matter with you both together,' he'd decided, and Lissa had felt herself go quite white and shivery.

'That would be too embarrassing.'

'Don't be silly, Lissa. He's your husband.'

Taking her courage in both hands she'd tilted her chin and outfaced the doctor with a courage she did not feel. 'I thought patient confidentiality meant these things should be private?'

'Having, or preventing, children is something you should decide together, dear girl.'

'I'm not ready to have any more babies yet. I had thought about trying this new pill which a friend told me about.'

He'd been so shocked Lissa thought he might have a heart attack there and then. Then he'd proceeded to give her a long lecture on sinful promiscuity, as if it automatically went with the pill. But she'd stuck to her guns and got the prescription she needed. Victory was sweet. How long it would last was another matter.

Now she faced Philip with another lie. 'He says there's nothing wrong with me. It's just one of those things. We must simply be patient.' She went to him and put her arms about his neck, wanting to distract him. 'If we're meant to have another child, one will be given to us. The twins are young yet. Doctor Robson says I'm a perfectly healthy young woman.' That, at least, was true.

CHAPTER 17

By February Jan announced that she was pregnant again. In late March, around the time of Lissa's birthday, Philip insisted they visit Larkrigg Hall. She always protested vehemently but it was hard to deny Philip anything once he'd set his mind to it. And she wanted to see her family, so what excuse could she give?

They sat now in the shrouded sitting room, Lissa's heart filled with dread as usual, Philip at his most charming. It was like a scene from her childhood bringing back all her old feelings of rejection.

Rosemary Ellis poured tea brought by Mrs Stanton, the housekeeper, more ancient and crabby than ever. She responded to Philip's attempt at small talk with such a frosty politeness they might well have been strangers, instead of a part of her own unacknowledged family.

Lissa made no effort to join the conversation, having learned long ago that any remark from her was rarely granted the courtesy of a reply. She wondered why the woman even received them. As always, Lissa fixed her gaze on the panorama of mountains through the trefoiled windows, which brought their usual comfort, trying to detach herself from the scene being played in the stuffy drawing room.

She sipped her tea, not tasting it, longing for the agony to be over so she could return to the warm cocoon of Broombank kitchen and gather her children on her lap.

'I'm glad to see you looking so well after your difficult winter,' Philip was saying. He really could appear a most charming, handsome man when he wished, she thought.

'I'm old,' said Rosemary starkly. 'Prone to colds and chills. Which no doubt pleases you.'

'My dear lady, you have no idea how it distresses me.' Philip set down his cup and saucer on the polished table and edged closer. 'Forgive me for saying so, but you should not live alone in this big house, now that you are reaching your most vulnerable years.' His voice seemed filled with genuine concern so that even Rosemary paused before barking out her reply.

'Vulnerable years indeed. And I do not live alone. I have Mrs Stanton. We do very well.'

'I'm sure you do. But there is really no necessity for it when you have a family only too ready to care for you. You could come and live with us, or we could move in here, if you prefer?'

'I do not prefer,' she snapped.

Thank God, thought Lissa, horrified by Philip's unexpected suggestion. She certainly had no wish to live with Rosemary Ellis. But he was oddly persistent. 'You would love the twins. Perhaps we could bring them to see you one day?'

No response.

'Did we tell you that Melissa and I are trying for another child? A boy this time, hopefully.'

'There's no hurry,' Lissa interjected, then flushed as Philip frowned at her.

She had said the wrong thing. Yet again. But sensible thought seemed to desert her when she had the eyes of these two people resting so critically upon her.

For the first time that Lissa could recall, Rosemary turned interested eyes upon her. For a full half minute grandmother and granddaughter's gaze locked and she saw a terrible bleakness in the faded eyes. She's unhappy, Lissa thought, and lonely.

A part of her ached to reach out and put her arms about the old woman, beg Rosemary to forgive her for whatever it was that had turned her so firmly against her in the past. She wanted to ask for her love, her acceptance at least, but then the face seemed to close and turn away, and Lissa felt the familiar rebuff like a slap.

Her grandmother had never wanted her, not when she was small, not now. She would never accept her. Even as a child when Lissa used to clamber on to Jeffrey's knee and he would give her sweets and presents, laugh and play with her, Rosemary had never unbent a fraction from her rigid disapproval.

Now Lissa stiffened in the straight-backed chair, staring into the empty grate as she remembered doing as a child. Could that be the same cobweb? The very same spider? She would not allow the woman to see that she cared, that her words could still hurt.

'There seems to be a problem, but we'll resolve it,' Philip said.

'At least you are respectably married,' Rosemary commented, glaring accusingly at Lissa. 'I suppose we should be grateful for that small mercy, in view of her undisciplined, hoydenish youth.'

Philip laughed. 'Hoyden? Hardly a word I would use to describe my wife.'

Rosemary stared at him without expression. 'Then you do not know her very well. Or she has disguised her true character from you, as Katherine did from me. You have my utmost sympathy.'

Lissa felt a tremor come into her limbs. He would interrogate her later, ask what Rosemary meant. And she would feel guilty even though there was nothing to feel guilty about. She felt a prick of annoyance that they should talk about her as if she weren't there. Lifting her chin, she outfaced them both.

'I was no more a hoyden than any other child. Nick and I fell in the beck a few times it's true, as children will. No other terrible misdemeanours that I can recall.'

Rosemary fixed her with the same cold unblinking stare while continuing to address her remarks to

Philip. 'I used to see her riding the fells on a pony, reckless and alone. Or wandering about on foot. Staying out all night on one occasion, up to goodness knows what. Meg exercised no control over her. None that I could see. She ran wild and free. It is a relief to see you using some discipline over her. She has long been in need of it. More tea, Mr Brandon?' Rosemary twisted her face into what might pass for a smile.

Red hot fury was pouring through Lissa's veins. How *dare* Rosemary Ellis talk about her as if she were a child needing correction, or a dog who needed to be trained? She found herself on her feet, limbs trembling, and two pairs of eyes swivelled to hers, surprised that she had dared move without their permission.

'I think it's time we returned to Broombank, Philip,' Lissa said in her stiffest manner. 'I must see to the twins.' If she relaxed her control for a second she would burst into tears and shame herself before them both. 'Meg will be wondering where we are.'

'Sit down,' he said, in his quiet voice. 'Finish your tea and treat your grandmother with more respect.'

'But . . .'

'Sit down.'

Rosemary Ellis smiled, if only with her cold narrow lips.

Lissa was shaking, the cup and saucer clattering in her hand as she searched blindly for the table. The cup wobbled, fell over and rolled to the floor where it snapped into two pieces. The sound was like gunfire in the still room.

Lissa stared appalled at the broken flowered porcelain, then at the two coldly furious faces. 'I-I'm sorry,' she whispered, her throat constricting with fear and shame. But the anger was still there, deep inside, burning right to the heart of her. Then she started to speak, the words spilling out. 'I won't have you treat me like this, as if I'm some sort of problem to you both. I'm a living, breathing person who needs to be loved. Can't *either of you see that?*' She looked wildly from one stiffly blank face to the other, then she was running from the room and the sobs were coming from her in great tearing gulps.

Philip did not speak to her for days. And when he did it was to demand she write her grandmother an apology, which she absolutely refused to give.

'I've done nothing wrong. I'm not a wilful child in need of discipline.

'That is exactly what you are.'

'I won't do it.'

'I say you will. Old ladies sometimes say foolish, hurtful things but she is your grandmother.'

'She doesn't think so.'

'All the more reason for you to try harder to be pleasant to her and then she will.'

'I won't do it.'

Philip's dark eyes glittered with anger though his

tone remained as cool as ever. 'You will if you wish us to remain friends.' He brought pen and paper and stood over her, instructing her what to write, blotting the angry marks of blue ink, folding the paper, slipping it into the envelope with resolute fingers and taking it to the post box himself.

When he had gone, Lissa hammered the desk with her fists in a moment of rare fury then sobbed out her despair. But what else could she have done? His control was absolute and she couldn't bear him to be angry with her.

Hilary Cheyney was delighted to acquire a new volunteer with her charity work but though Lissa might fill an afternoon with a rummage sale, or spend a morning serving coffee, it did not make her feel any more fulfilled. She even felt an outcast from her own children.

The twins seemed to grow with each passing day and Lissa found herself competing for every moment with them, asking Nanny Sue if she might take them to the park or to feed the ducks, or if Beth might be spared egg for tea since she did not care for it. It was as if she had no say over her own children's welfare. Philip saw little of them but laid down a strict routine which he was adamant must be kept.

And Nanny must answer to him if it was not kept. What hope did Lissa have of changing anything? She grew increasingly frustrated. Yet any resolve to defy him was demolished by his continual criticism of her. He was like a tightly coiled spring, barely restraining his anger. Each month he would bark out his disappointment at the regularity of her periods which seemed to mock his manhood. His increasing complaints and demands left her too numb to argue, made her question her own self-worth and wonder if she had anything of value to offer anyone, let alone her own children.

Nevertheless Lissa went on taking the contraceptive pill. She refused to contemplate bringing another child into this less than perfect marriage.

And every time she walked past the old drapery her heart clenched, as if it somehow represented the depth of her captivity. Dare she contact Miss Stevens again?

Whenever she could, Lissa escaped to Nab Cottage. She and Renee would drink sherry or Coca-Cola, and gossip. Those times were a blessed relief, an oasis of warmth in a life stultified by frozen emotion and a growing fear that things would never be any better.

'You shouldn't let your husband dictate your life to you,' Renee insisted. 'Make a stand for women's rights. It's 1963, for goodness' sake.'

Lissa was sitting on the rug in front of the electric fire, playing with the twins who were happily engrossed emptying Renee's capacious beige plastic handbag and filling it up again, trying out comb, powder puff and hair pins as they did so. Sarah had daubed lipstick on Beth's mouth and was pretending to be a hairdresser and put rollers and pin-curls in her baby soft hair. Lissa, for once, was laughing and happy, Nab Cottage seemed to be the only place where she could relax and enjoy her children.

'I mean to, one day.'

'Huh. One day.' Renee was washing out the budgie cage in preparation for its new resident. A hot pot was bubbling in the oven and Jimmy would be home in an hour or two but for now she was concerned about Lissa. Renee had grown quite fond of her over recent months, and the terrible twosome, who were delicious and not terrible at all.

'Look, love. If I thought he was making you happy I'd say bugger the shop, have another kid and be done with it. Except that nobody but a one-eyed catfish could call you happy. I can see that there's more to this than you're telling. No, it's all right. None of my business. It's your life. Only don't let things drag on too long. Make up your mind to put it right, one way or the other. Everyone deserves to be happy. You only get one shot.'

'Derry used to say that.' The unexpected admission brought a blush to Lissa's cheeks, and a wry smile to Renee's bright lips.

'I know you've never got him out of your system, but I won't tell on you.'

The doorbell rang and she swore silently under her breath, annoyed by the interruption. 'Who the hell can that be? It's too early in the season for paying guests.' She peered through the lace curtains. 'Oh my God, it's your beloved himself. In person. What the hell is he doing here?'

Lissa leapt to her feet, reaching for the twins. 'He must be looking for me. Oh, Renee, he mustn't find me here. He'll stop me coming again.'

Renee didn't pause to question why, or feel offended by the implied criticism. She was too busy finding the twins' coats and bonnets, bundling the three of them out the back door. The doorbell rang again.

'Won't be a minute,' she shouted. 'Down the garden and out the back gate,' she hissed. 'Takes you directly to the lake path.'

Renee closed the kitchen door and hurried back to the parlour with the sound of continuous ringing in her ears. Drat the man. Had he no manners? Moments before she opened the door, her eyes alighted on the spilled contents of her handbag, all over the rug.

'Mrs Colwith?'

'What is it?' she snapped. 'Am I on fire or summat?'

Philip Brandon looked startled by the question. 'I beg your pardon?'

'All that damned ringing. Thought it must surely be the fire brigade.'

He gave a half laugh. 'Very droll.'

'Didn't you hear me call? I was out the back.'

His face tightened and the smile vanished. 'I don't have all day. My friend here is looking for a room,' indicating a bespectacled young man who might have been a vicar, fidgeting beside him. 'I seem to recall you are in that line of business.'

'I do bed and breakfast for summer visitors. I don't take lodgers.'

'He'd be no trouble. A professional man who must visit the area from time to time for the purpose of his work, which may take two or three weeks on each occasion. The Marina Hotel is somewhat expensive for a long-term stay.'

Ah, so that was the way of it. She'd had those sort of folk before. Travelling salesmen who pretended they were staying in an expensive hotel, wanting her to bill them as if they were, so they could claim extra on expenses while paying her cheaper rates.

'I don't think so,' she said, giving the man a scant glance of disapproval. 'I never take folk this early in the season. My husband doesn't like it. Sorry.' She started to close the door.

'Let's see if I can change your mind.' Philip brushed past her, as if she were of no account, and marched into the front parlour. As she told Jimmy later, it was as if he owned the damned place. The young man followed like a spaniel at his heels.

Renee had always thought him a real charmer, a proper gent. He was smiling at her now, though something about it caused her to suppress a shudder. She could see he was weighing her up, starting with the hair.

'Well, well. You're the red-headed waitress who tipped soup down my trousers. I didn't recognise you at the time, Mrs Colwith, being otherwise occupied.'

Renee didn't feel too happy about being recognised now, but carelessly shrugged her shoulders, trying to show that it didn't trouble her one bit. 'These things happen. I nearly lost my job over it.'

'Nearly?'

'They're very fair at the Marina Hotel,' she said, meeting his stare with her own. And if you humiliate Lissa in public again, I'll do the same again, her eyes said. Job or no job.

'You do seem rather accident prone.' He was staring at the jumble of items on the hearthrug. Purse, bus tickets, spare stockings, safety pins, an open lipstick, powder everywhere, all spilled from her bag. Then his gaze took in the rest of the untidy room. 'Housekeeping not your forte?'

Renee shrugged, not troubling to reply. She wouldn't be bullied by him. He wasn't her husband. Though despite herself a feeling of intimidation was creeping over her and she felt vaguely uneasy with these two men in her parlour. 'Jimmy'll be home in a minute.' She didn't know why she needed to say that. Something about the expression in his eyes. 'There's nothing I can do for your friend. I've told you. I only take summer visitors.'

That would show him she wasn't scared of his high-handed tactics. She half glanced at the young man, pale and freckle-faced, skinny, glasses sliding down his nose. Probably single and lived with his mother, she decided.

But Philip Brandon didn't seem to be listening. He circled the small room as if he owned it, filling it with his tall, lean, pinstripe presence. He poked a finger at the budgie cage and laughed, picked up newspapers and tossed them down again. Even walked into the kitchen and inspected her cupboards.

'Here, where d'you think you're going?' Cheeky bugger.

He turned to her with a dry smile on his thin mouth. 'I was told you were a good cook. Is that so?'

Renee drew in a deep breath and puffed out her chest. 'There isn't lighter pastry in Lakeland.'

Philip was rubbing the bridge of his narrow nose with the tip of one finger, his dark eyes measuring her. The woman was proving obstinate but he had little patience to waste on persuasion. Time was of the essence. Money went nowhere these days, what with nannies and children, the new car he had bought, enormous fees for the Yacht Club and the Golf Club next year. Not to mention all the entertaining that was expected of a man in his position. He needed a fresh injection of capital and thought he'd found the way to do it. No blowsy female too big for her stocking tops was going to get in his way. 'I once recall doing you a favour,' he said.

'Eh?' Renee was startled, wondering for a moment what he meant.

'I remember you coming to me for advice on how to rid yourself of Derry Colwith. Isn't he your brother-in-law?'

'Stepson, as a matter of fact.' Uncertainty crept into Renee's voice. 'I wanted him to move out, that's all. And I asked your advice on doing bed and breakfast.'

'That's right. I suggested you put him in the garden shed and leave the rest to me. Now it's time to repay the favour.'

Renee stared at him, appalled. 'I only asked you to pay Derry more money so he could afford his own place.' Somehow the conversation had got out of hand. Philip Brandon had offered to persuade Derry to leave town, though how he'd intended to achieve that, she hadn't asked at the time. She wished now that she'd never interfered. If Lissa, or worse, Jimmy, found out that she'd been to see Derry's boss who'd then sacked him, they'd blame her for everything. 'Oh, hecky thump,' she said.

Philip smiled. 'Your husband wouldn't be too pleased to learn how you conspired to drive his son out of town, now would he?'

'Conspired?' Renee wasn't good on long words, but she understood this one. And when she was beaten.

'Look, it doesn't matter,' the young man said, speaking for the first time. 'If there's a problem I can go elsewhere.'

They both stared at him, as if they'd forgotten his presence.

'There's no problem,' Philip said, suave and confident. 'Mrs Colwith will be only too pleased to take you. Mr Spencer here is a consultant for Manchester Water Board. A respectable man. He requires a clean, comfortable bed, a substantial breakfast and an evening meal. You can manage that, I'm sure?'

'I don't do evening meals.'

'You do now. You can provide him with a monthly account to send to his employers but the exact sum will be settled in cash, privately. Is that clear?'

As crystal. 'Jimmy might object,' Renee mumbled. 'He likes his privacy.'

'I'm sure you can persuade him, if you put your mind to it. Well, that's splendid.' Taking her agreement for granted. 'It is so much easier when people are obliging, don't you think?'

He's nuts, Renee thought, finding herself suddenly feeling sorry for the young man who looked as bemused as she felt. But she agreed to take him, evening meals and all.

CHAPTER 18

Lissa stayed away from Nab Cottage for a while, just to be on the safe side. She'd gone home in trepidation that day, expecting the usual lectures, but rather to her surprise Philip had said nothing. Nevertheless, his visit had made her jumpy. How often did he follow her? Did he watch everything she did? Surely not, he was far too busy to concern himself with her mundane routine.

For two pins she would leave him, start a new life of her own. Then almost before the thought had formed she would quash it with a sigh of despair. Look at the scandal there would be if she did. She would be looked upon as a loose woman. Wishing to be liberated was one thing, carrying it out was quite another matter. Lissa did not think she could face the shame of the whispers, the sly looks and comments which Miss Stevens had rightly warned her of. Her case was hopeless.

She concentrated on keeping busy, filling her life with good works as if that would solve everything. So when Hilary Cheyney rang and asked her to visit an old folks' home, Lissa was happy to oblige.

The Birches seemed better than most, being a spacious, rather sedate, ivy-clad building, set in its own grounds. It looked like a grand country house hotel and the residents appeared lively and occupied. She talked with several, listening to their stories, admiring photographs of grandchildren and beloved, long dead husbands looking impossibly fresh and young in smart WWI uniforms.

Lissa approached one frail old lady who sat apart from the rest, in a corner all alone. Her head flopped oddly to one side, the mouth twisted, and Lissa's heart flooded with pity. How dreadful to be overset by old age and abandoned by one's family. It made her own problems seem insignificant by comparison.

'Hello, how are you today?' she asked, taking the old woman's hand gently in her own.

'Charles will be home soon,' the woman said. 'He's in the war, you know.'

'Really? So was my husband. Perhaps you know him? He's a solicitor. Philip Brandon?'

Lissa did not at first associate this rather sad woman with the one-time owner of her own gracious home. Elvira Fraser, locked in her own confused world but still clinging to a fragment of that indomitable spirit, struggled to make the connection.

'Brandon? Do I know you?' The faded grey eyes focused a moment as if struggling to capture a wayward memory, but as quickly became blank again, the effort too much. The next instant she spoke in a loud sharp voice that made Lissa jump. 'I won't stay here a moment longer.'

She leaned forward to speak in a loud confidential whisper. 'The people here steal my things, don't you know? Taken my bank book and savings certificates, every one. But I'll find them.'

Lissa was so troubled by this outburst that she called over a nurse.

'Don't worry, Mrs Brandon. Mrs Fraser is easily upset. Tomorrow it might be her slippers or her liberty bodice that she'll claim has been stolen.' A lowering of the voice. 'The poor lady gets very confused.' Smiling cheerfully, the nurse went on her way.

Lissa flicked an uncertain smile at Elvira and prepared to do her best. 'I'm sure you will find your bank book soon. Philip likes to have things tidy too.'.

'You know him?'

'Who?'

'Philip.'

'He's my husband. Didn't I say?'

Irritation flashed. 'No, Charles. My husband is called Charles. When he arrives he'll sort this muddle out. Never stands any nonsense, doesn't my darling Charles. He'll take me home. I'm not staying here.'

'Of course he will.' This was the craziest conversation Lissa had ever experienced. Yet she'd taken a liking to the old lady, the way she kept her shoulders square with a certain regal air, dignity in her bearing for all the obvious disability of a recent stroke. Here was a woman who must once have been a beauty, with a position in the world and proud of it.

'I have a lovely house, don't you know?' Elvira said, in a rare moment of clarity. 'On the Parade.'

'Mrs Fraser, of course. I hadn't made the connection.' Lissa was delighted. 'I believe we bought it off you.'

The old lady glared fiercely. 'Bought it? Nonsense. I'm going home soon. How can they sell my house? It's mine.'

Lissa stroked the old lady's hand, filled with compassion. 'You must have been sorry to leave it.'

'I haven't left it. Call that silly maid to bring us lunch. We'll have salmon. I love salmon, and sherry trifle to follow.'

'Did you live there for a long time?' Lissa interrupted, trying to keep her in the present.

'Live where?'

'In your house on the Parade?'

'I'm here now, aren't I? Silly child. Lived here all my life. Born here. Father would never hear of my leaving it. Certainly not now that I've married my darling Charles.' She smiled, as if she were an excited young bride.

How terribly sad, Lissa thought, moved almost to tears by the blank confusion in the old lady's eyes.

Elvira suddenly grasped Lissa's hand in a fierce grip. 'Wait for Charles. He'll sort this muddle out.

No money indeed! He left me plenty of money. They come in the night and take my things. Won't stand any nonsense, my darling Charles. He's in the war, you know. He'll be home soon, when it's over.' And she was off again, round and round the same senseless conversation. Lissa exchanged sad glances with the nurse who hurried back, offering lunch and Mrs Fraser's favourite bread pudding.

Lissa said her goodbyes and left, wondering if she'd been at all successful in her visit and thinking that perhaps voluntary work was not her thing, after all.

It was when she was coming out of The Birches that she ran into Stella Stevens.

'How fortuitous, I was only just thinking about you the other day,' Miss Stevens said. 'What on earth are you doing here?'

Lissa told her and Stella shook her head sadly. 'I remember Elvira Fraser. We were in the WVS together during the war. I call in to see her myself every now and then, to try to cheer her. Poor old soul. Had a terrible stroke, you know.' Then, brightening, she took Lissa's arm. 'Come along, let me buy you lunch.'

'Oh, there's really no need . . .'

'There's every need, I wish to talk to you.'

How could she resist? Besides, Philip wouldn't be home for an hour or more yet. She had plenty of time. 'Lunch sounds good.'

'Splendid.' Miss Stevens took her to a charming little cafe on Carndale Road which still had lace tablecloths on polished mahogany tables, instead of the newly popular Formica. They ordered ham salad and a pot of tea.

Stella at once adopted a businesslike pose. 'Now, are you still interested in the shop? I rather expected you to call back.'

Lissa flushed. 'I thought it would be a waste of time.'

'Good heavens, girl, you'll need more stamina than that if you are to be a successful business-woman. As you can see, it remains empty, but I now have a serious offer for it. However, I wished to give you first refusal.'

'Oh.' Lissa's attention sharpened and she felt that familiar buzz of excitement.

'If you really want it, I see no reason why we couldn't come to terms.'

'That would be wonderful. Thank you.' Happiness shone from Lissa's face and the transformation almost took Stella's breath away. Then a cloud dark-ened the heart-shaped face and the brilliance instantly faded. 'Would there be much in the way of legal documentation? It's only that I've no wish to involve Philip – at this stage – until . . .'

Miss Stevens gave a polite cough. 'I prefer not to discuss the state of your marriage, Lissa, though, as you will appreciate, I have given your problem a good deal of thought. You once saved my life. Had you not discovered me that day senseless in the stock room, who knows what might have been the outcome?'

The waitress arrived with their salads and they were both able to cover their respective embarrassment with passing salt and salad cream.

'I appreciate the fact that you did not broadcast the reason for my indisposition on that occasion. The hospital realised, of course, but no one else seems to know. Which is a great relief. I'm quite over that now,' she hastily added. 'Never touch the stuff. No more trouble with my stomach necessitating Milk of Magnesia bottles.' A wry smile, to which Lissa responded, understanding perfectly.

'I'm so glad.'

'You gave me a second chance, so I think I owe you one. Take the shop. Do with it what you will. But make it a good business. Give it your all.'

Lissa was thrilled. 'Oh, I will. I will.' She could hardly believe it.

When she'd set out today on an act of charity, she'd never guessed that someone would do the same favour for her. Now she could begin to build a future for herself and later, if life with Philip became too much of a strain, she could turn the two rooms above the shop into a small flat for herself and the girls. Lissa's head buzzed with ideas and her smile turned into one of beaming delight.

Stella Stevens, a shy woman with few friends, was nonetheless an astute judge of character and resolutely set her own misgivings aside as she watched the expressions of joy flit across the girl's enchanting face, as if she'd been given the whole world.

'I'll never forget this. Thank you so much,' Lissa said.

Clearing her throat and paying excessive attention to her ham, Stella felt quite moved. But she judged it best to bring Lissa down to earth. 'I've no wish to pry into your plans, but in view of your other – um, confidences, may I point out that you will need money to set up a shop? People never realise quite how much. There's stock and new fittings, and decoration will be considerable. Then there'll presumably be wages for an assistant, electricity and advertising, rent and rates, and working capital is vital. It will take some time before you move into profit. Can you manage all of that, without your husband's assistance?'

Lissa smiled. 'As a matter of fact I can. It was a gift from my grandfather. Not a fortune by any means but enough, I believe, and I've added more to it over the years. I was told to save it for a rainy day.' The smile changed to a grin. 'It's rained quite a lot recently.'

Stella sipped quietly at her tea, then set down the cup with a decisive click. 'Taking everything into account I see no reason why you shouldn't begin your little enterprise in an unofficial sort of way. So long as the rent is paid regularly I shall be perfectly happy. Later, once you are successful, which I'm sure you will be, we can settle all the legal niceties of leases and so on. You may even prefer to take on the freehold in time. We'll see, shall we?'

'Oh, I can't tell you how grateful I am.'

Miss Stevens cleared her throat. 'As to that other matter, think of your children. Do nothing hasty. Did you see your doctor?'

'Yes.'

'Ah, no good, eh?'

'Not a lot.'

'Lawyer then. Take some advice on the matter.'

Lissa bit on her lip and promised that she would certainly think about it.

She ran all the way home and arrived breathless but relieved to find that Philip had rung to say he would not be home for lunch. 'Have the children eaten?'

'Of course. It is after one.' Nanny Sue sounded offended.

'Then I shall take them out. Let's get them ready. Come along, darlings, find your cardigans.'

Lissa ignored protests that the twins had not yet taken their afternoon nap, and, bubbling with happiness, grasped their small hands and marched them off. They giggled and skipped along with her, delighted to find Mummy in such a happy mood. They sang and laughed all the way through Fairfield Park, past the ducks on the lake and along Fossburn Street to Nab Cottage.

'I've done it,' she announced, the moment Renee opened the door.

'What, left him?'

Lissa looked startled. 'Not yet. No, I've taken the shop.'

'Well, strike me down with a feather, I never thought you would.' Renee's mouth fell open as Lissa hugged her. 'I've never seen you so full of yourself. Have you told himself? Has he agreed?'

A small silence.

'Ah, like that, is it?' Renee shrugged. 'I've always been of the opinion that the less men know, the better. Time for a celebration then?' She wore strawberry pink lipstick today and the bright mouth widened into a smile. 'Shall I fetch the sherry?' She grinned at the two smiling faces below her. 'How about ice cream for you two? I just happen to have some in the freezer compartment of my fridge. So long as the door isn't gummed up with ice.' She laughed as the twins screamed their delight and galloped off into the kitchen. 'Don't stand on ceremony your two, do they?'

There was a choice between vanilla, strawberry or chocolate, and since a decision was quite impossible, a small amount of each was put in two dishes and the little girls sat happily on the back doorstep, eating.

'They'll be covered in the stuff soon.'

'I know,' laughed Lissa. 'I'll stick to Coca-Cola. Philip might smell alcohol on my breath.'

Renee brought two glasses and they sat at the small kitchen table, a plate of coconut cakes between them. Then going to the dresser Renee brought out a bottle of rum and added a dash to each fizzing glass. 'It's Jimmy's really but he won't mind us having a tot. Your husband won't smell that little bit.' She picked up a glass. 'So what do we drink to? What's this shop to be called?'

'Good Lord,' said Lissa, stunned. 'I haven't the first idea.'

Renee roared with laughter. 'Well, there's a good start. Here's to it, anyway.'

The new incumbent of the budgie cage, bright green this time, bashed his bell and squawked joyously in the front parlour. Both girls laughed.

'I'll let him out in a bit. He likes a fly round. This one's called Mickey.'

'Hallo, Mickey. I'm glad you let him out,' Lissa said. 'I hate to think of a bird in a cage, like a prisoner.' She went oddly silent, dipping her head to her glass.

They munched their way through several cakes, drank another Coca-Cola, though Lissa positively refused any more rum. Then they chewed over several ideas and Lissa rejected them all. The germ of an idea was growing in the back of her mind, perhaps it had always been there, waiting to be picked up, but she didn't feel quite ready to bring it out into the open yet and examine it.

Renee frowned at her over the rim of her glass. 'What did you mean when you said, not yet?'

'Pardon?'

'We've finished our ice cream, Mummy. Can we play in Renee's garden?'

'Course you can, Poppet. Go play at house in the shed.'

Squeals of delight, and more when Renee went to the under-stairs cupboard and brought out scarves and hats and bags in riotous colours. 'Here you are, my pets, get dressed up and enjoy yourselves while your mum and I have a bit of a crack.'

'Ooh, I want the pink one,' cried Sarah. 'You can have the blue hat, Beth.'

'That Sarah, chippy little sprite. She'll organise you all one day,' laughed Renee, shaking her head as the two skipped happily away, small bottoms wriggling with self-importance.

She turned back to Lissa, eyes shrewd. 'So, when I asked if you'd left him, why did you say "not yet"?'

Silence, which grew and lengthened. Lissa chewed on her lip and Renee quietly waited.

'You'd feel better if you talked about it.'

'Would I?' Violet eyes like bruises in a pale face gazed into hers. Lissa knew, deep down, that although Renee might be right, she simply couldn't. It was too private, too personal. 'It's just that I feel such a failure. You and Jimmy seem so well matched, so happy, always laughing and kissing, making love without a thought. While I . . .' Then the question burst out, unbidden. 'How do you know when you do it right?'

Lissa flushed deeply and Renee laughed. 'When it feels good. There aren't any rules. So long as you're both happy in what you do.'

'I see.'

'You're not?'

'I don't think either of us are.' She manufactured a laugh. 'Perhaps I was a silly romantic girl expecting too much. Philip is very kind to me.'

'So long as you do what he says.'

The smile trembled a little and faded. 'He never seems quite satisfied with my performance. As for my feelings . . . Oh, hell, I would so like to succeed in something.'

It all poured out then, her dashed hopes for a happy secure marriage, the way he controlled her every move, made all the decisions, liked to keep her at home, told her what to wear, how to clean, what to cook, how to think even. But she could say no more about the intimate side of her marriage.

'Sometimes my brain goes numb with all his instructions.'

Renee quietly sipped her rum and Coke and listened. 'So when?' was all she said when Lissa finally fell silent, the tears mopped up, deep breaths taken. 'And how?'

'What?'

'You can't go on like this, Lissa. You have either to leave him or make him change his ways. I can see that wouldn't be easy. Loving a man is good. Sex is good too, smashing with the right fella. Everyone deserves to be happy and treated well.'

Lissa was calm again. 'I couldn't really leave him. He's good to me in so many ways. And there are the children to consider. They would miss him terribly.'

'Children would rather have one happy parent than two unhappy ones. I'll vouch for that. Mine drove each other crackers then took it out on me.'

'Oh, Renee, how sad. Maybe I will pluck up the courage to leave him one day, who knows? One step at a time. I told Miss Stevens a little of my problem, no details, but she'll keep my confidence. She says it will bring shame on my head if I divorce him.' Lissa gave a bitter little laugh.

'And happen worse if you don't.'

Lissa squared her shoulders and looked Renee straight in the eye. 'I don't want him to know anything about this shop. Not yet. Not until it's a success and I have some money coming in.' Her eyes became distant, narrowing on some future plan. 'Then we'll see.'

Renee sipped her drink, reading Lissa's faraway thoughts. 'D'you think he'd let you keep them?'

Lissa frowned, not understanding. 'Keep what?'

Renee jerked her head in the direction of the garden. 'Them two. The lively duo. Would he give them up if you did leave him?'

Lissa looked stricken. 'Oh God, I hadn't thought, I mean . . . why shouldn't he? I'm their mother?'

'No reason,' Renee put in hastily, thinking for a moment that Lissa was going to pass clean out. 'You could move in here you know, any time.' But Lissa shook her head.

'No, you have a lodger.'

'My Water Board man? He comes and goes. We have another room.'

Much as Lissa enjoyed Renee's company and was glad of her support, the thought of sharing a house with her and the rapacious Jimmy did not appeal.

'I saw an old lady today. The one who used to have our house. Poor thing has gone quite senile.'

Renee looked sympathetic. 'My gran went that way. Loved the old so and so, I did, for all she was nutty as a fruit cake in the end.' She blinked hard, batting her spiky eyelashes. 'So what about this old dear?'

'It was so sad. She kept on talking about her husband, long dead in the war, I'm afraid, whom she obviously adored and thought would arrive at any moment to carry her away. What romantics we women are.' Lissa got up to glance out of the window. 'I hope the children are all right.'

'Course they are. Made you think about how you'd feel about giving up that grand house on the Parade, did she? Or growing old with a man you don't love?'

Lissa gave a wry smile. 'I didn't say that I didn't love Philip.'

'But you don't.'

'No, I don't. She made me think how fleeting life is. What little time we have. Troubled me a bit, actually.' Lissa took a deep breath. 'Anyway, Philip doesn't ill treat me. If I can improve my life, win back some pride and self-esteem, I can cope well enough.' She turned to Renee with a grin. 'No more self-pity. It's bad for me. What about this shop then? Shall I risk it?'

'Absolutely.' Renee grinned. 'How will you manage to keep it a secret? Till you get it going, I mean. You can't work behind the counter yourself, or everyone will know and tell him.'

'I've thought about that. I shall work in the office upstairs and employ a shop girl. Why not? I can deal with the ordering and buying, while she can do the selling. It should work. I may need more than one assistant eventually, if the shop gets busy.'

Renee considered, then set down her glass, looking unusually bashful. 'I don't suppose, I mean . . . How would you feel about . . .? Nah, forget it. Daft idea.' Renee picked up her glass again, looking flushed and embarrassed.

Lissa smiled quietly to herself. 'The sort of person I really need is someone I can work with, someone I can trust. Initially to help get the place ready. Too late for this season but perhaps in time for Christmas. After that I'll need a manageress, someone reliable and honest to be in charge of the day to day running of the shop, train new seasonal staff and so on. I have the twins to take care of too, you see. Ideally I need a person who is good with people and of course likes clothes. Someone, for instance, rather like yourself. It's a pity really that you're so busy.' She cast Renee an enquiring glance.

Renee's eyes opened as wide as her mouth which

formed into a perfect strawberry oval. 'Ooh, I'd kill for a job like that. All dressed up and in charge of a shop. Crikey!'

'Then the job's yours. If you want it. But what about your bed and breakfast?'

'Hang the B and B! Jimmy never liked it anyway. And I have the lodger. Not that I wanted him, but the money's useful, I can't deny that.' She thought it best not to mention how she'd come by him. 'Oh, Lissa. It'd be grand to work in a lovely shop. I'd never have to serve soup to pawing old men again.'

Then they were laughing and shrieking their delight, hugging each other and jumping up and down with excitement like the young girls they really were.

Later they stood at the front door, the twins looking exceedingly grubby after their afternoon's adventures. Sarah's dress was torn and Beth had lost her hair ribbon.

'Lord, look at them. Philip will kill me.'

'It's all good clean muck, isn't it, kids?' laughed Renee.

'He can't bear to see them dirty. I'll have to scrub you both in the bath before your daddy sees you,' Lissa warned and their small faces looked so doleful she couldn't help but laugh. Then Lissa turned to hug Renee again.

'I'm so glad it's all worked out. I must visit my family, and Jan, of course. Long past time I did. This plan that's growing in my head won't work without their help. We'll see what they have to say about it. If their response is positive, then we'll get cracking. You can come too, if you like? OK?'

Eyes shining. 'Just say the word and I'm your girl.'

Philip was waiting for her when she got home and tore into her about the state of the twins' dresses.

Nanny's obvious satisfaction at seeing her scolded as if she were the naughty child, infuriated and embarrassed her. Lissa fought to maintain her dignity. 'They are children, Philip, and must be permitted to play.'

Ignoring her he ordered them to the bathroom at once. 'And there will be no supper for you two,' he shouted. 'You naughty girls.'

Both children started to cry in unison and Lissa grabbed hold of his arm as he would have walked away. 'How dare you? They're only four years old. I may have to put up with your bullying, but not my children. Do you hear?'

'What nonsense. When have I ever bullied you? You are hysterical, Lissa, as usual.' Even so, her unusual vehemence shocked him, and even silenced the twins. 'Perhaps I shouldn't have shouted at them, though discipline is important. Look after them better in future.'

He still refused to let them have supper and later Lissa crept upstairs with a tray when he had gone to the Yacht Club and Nanny wasn't looking. The twins thought an eiderdown picnic was a wonderful treat and the bad feelings were soon smoothed over and forgotten, by them at least.

To Lissa it seemed a portent for the future. As they grew older, would he treat his children with the same mocking contempt with which he treated her? Dear God, please not. It sealed her determination more firmly than ever.

She spent the rest of that week secretly drawing up plans. She paid a visit to the shop, making notes as she walked through the dusty rooms, talking to herself, planning. Her mood lifted with each passing day and never had she felt so positive about life, so filled with new hope.

CHAPTER 19

The sky was eggshell blue over Broombank, streaked by ice pink cloud, the mountain air so crystal clear that Lissa drew great healing gulps of it into her lungs. She was always surprised, and calmed, by the peace of the place, loving the way the humps of grey mountains blended into the blue haze. Lissa looked about her with sweet relief, glad as always to be home.

The harvest had been brought in and the lower fields were already showing flecks of fresh green between the stubble. The leaves on the wild cherry tree in the garden were beginning to change colour and drop. Soon the mellow days of autumn would be upon the dale, Meg's favourite time of year.

Lissa could see her, halfway up Dundale Knot with the dogs, moving among her sheep, checking the feet of any that were limping, making sure they stayed healthy, and probably deciding which ones must go in the backend sales.

'Do you never sit down for a minute?' Lissa called up to her, laughing as Meg waved madly, hurrying down the hill arms outstretched to hug her. Lissa forestalled the embrace by offering a cheek which Meg kissed, rather awkwardly, before picking up her giggling granddaughters. Ruff and the rest of the dogs smothered Lissa in a moist and joyous welcome, rolling over onto their backs so they could be tickled and petted and admired.

'How did you get here? Where's Philip?'

'He let me come alone for once. Even lent me his precious car. I was so afraid of scratching it I've driven all the way at twenty miles an hour. Tea would be a life saver. This is my friend Renee, by the way.'

'Hello Renee. You must be exhausted.'

'Walking would have been quicker,' Renee agreed, grinning.

Meg chuckled. 'The kettle's already on.'

'You're going to sell children's clothes? But that's a wonderful idea.' They were all seated about the big pitch pine table in Broombank kitchen, Meg pouring tea from a huge brown tea pot, Tam smilingly watching her every movement, and Sally Ann stoutly content, hands appropriately busy with her knitting.

Jan and Nick sat as close together as they could get, arms full of babies. Robbie, who at fifteen months was already showing a mind of his own, one moment content to sit in his father's lap, the next wriggling free so he could chase after the twins, squealing with delight. And the new arrival, Alice, cooing happily in Jan's arms.

The remains of a ham and egg meal littered the

table and cheeks were flushed, eyes sparkling, voices light and happy. It was good, Meg thought, to have her family all together again. If only she could feel they were enough for Lissa, she would be the happiest woman alive. But she could see that her darling girl was unhappy, and finding it harder to disguise the fact.

'I need to be occupied. That's why I want a business. I feel it's time for things to change.' They all stared at her, waiting, listening, while Meg nodded, her head teeming with questions, asking none of them. Except one. She was striving to give the impression she was a happily married woman. While inside lay a still, grey pool of pain, which Lissa dutifully hid from view. Or thought she did.

She told herself that life couldn't be filled with joy every day. The lake often looked grey. It was only when the sun shone that it glistened like silver. Life was like that. So all she had to do was bring some sunshine into her own life, then she would glow again.

Oh, Derry, why did you leave me? Life could have been so different with you. She pushed the thought away. Concentrate on reality, the way things really were.

'What does Philip think of all this?'

Lissa dare not meet Meg's shrewd gaze in case it should carry disapproval. It was suddenly so very important that she gain her support. If she lost that, what would she have? 'I haven't told him.

Not yet. He's a bit – over-protective – and not in favour of my working.'

A small explosion of exasperation from Meg that made Lissa glance at her in surprise, and then laugh when she read her expression. 'Of course. You must have struggled once, so you'll perhaps understand how I feel?'

Meg gave a rueful smile. 'You could say so! I hoped things had changed. Apparently not.'

Sally Ann gave a deep chortle of pleasure. 'Used to eat bank managers alive, this woman did.'

Everyone was smiling, trying to disguise their concern.

'I know it's wrong to keep secrets but it would only be for a little while. Till I've proved it's possible.' Lissa paused. 'Then I'll sort everything out.'

'I've kept secrets,' Meg mused. 'It took me ages before I admitted to my father that I'd been given a dog. As for when I got you, well . . .' She could laugh now, remembering Joe's reaction to the unexpected arrival of a baby. 'But keeping secrets from your own husband, that's another matter entirely. I couldn't fool Tam, could I now?' She glanced across at her husband who merely shook his head, his eyes on Lissa.

'Are you sure, lass, that it's a good idea?' he asked.

'Yes,' Lissa said, tight-lipped. 'For the moment it is necessary.' She looked about her at the many serious faces, all of whom wanted the best for her. 'Renee and Jimmy are sworn to secrecy too. I'll tell him soon, I promise. As soon as the time seems right.'

They shifted their feet, glanced at each other, then Meg spoke for them all. 'Very well. We'll ask no more questions. We want only your happiness. I just hope it's a great success.'

'I'd give my virginity, if I still had it, that it will be,' Renee said, and they all burst out laughing.

'Renee, I like you,' Meg said, eyes suddenly growing misty as she glanced at Lissa. 'I'm glad my daughter has you for a friend. She looks sorely in need of one.'

A small silence, for no one present had missed the pride in Meg's voice as she'd called Lissa 'my daughter'. Meg simply smiled, blithely unconcerned.

It was good to see Jan again, and how happy she was with Nick. The two friends stole a few moments to chat alone as Meg and Tam went off to do chores, assisted, or hindered, by Renee and the children. Lissa sat quietly watching as she prepared a bottle for the new baby.

'Are you all right?' Jan asked. 'You aren't still worrying over being illegitimate and your mother dumping you, are you?'

'Lord, no. I never think of it these days.'

'You're not jealous of me then? Being here with your family?'

Lissa shook her head. 'They're your family too now, you and your lovely children.'

'What about you and Meg? Have you made your peace yet?'

When Lissa avoided her gaze, Jan persisted, 'It's long past time you did. It would make Meg so happy.'

Despite her embarrassment, Lissa felt warmed by Jan's concern, and gave a wry smile, then softly musing. 'It's ironic really. I've spent so much of my life fighting this feeling of rejection, wanting to belong. As a result I made hasty judgements, rash decisions for which I must now pay the price.'

'What sort of rash decisions?'

Lissa shook her head. 'Don't ask. I now seem to have quite the opposite sort of problem. Isn't that silly? Serves me right, I suppose.' There was a hint of bitterness in the falsely bright tone, a bleakness in the flashing eyes that Jan did not miss nor feel able to comment on.

Somewhere deep in the house a clock struck six, the notes chiming endlessly on, and a log fell in the great hearth. When silence fell again Jan asked, 'Have you ever heard anything from Derry?'

'You're his sister. He'd write to you, not me.'

'I did think at one time you two might . . .'

'Don't say it, Jan. I don't think I could bear to hear you say the words.' Lissa was on her feet, pushing her chair back so hard that it grated on the slate flagstones and almost fell over. 'I think I'll get a bit of fresh air, if you don't mind.'

'Yes, do that, and speak to Meg.'

'Are you happy?' Meg and Lissa had walked up

to Brockbarrow tarn. Now they were sitting on the windy heaf as if there wasn't still the prickle of past differences between them. 'I like to have you to myself for a while. But you look tired, a bit peaky. Aren't you well?' Meg cast her a sideways glance. 'You're not pregnant?'

'No.'

'Isn't little Alice a treasure?'

'Absolutely.'

'You wouldn't care for another?'

'Not at the moment.' High above, the small blue outline of a merlin falcon flying low and fast in a passing air stream swooped and dived, seeking a wandering mouse or vole who might have escaped Meg's harvesting. Lissa changed the subject. 'It's so lovely to be at Broombank again. I don't visit nearly often enough.'

'No, you don't,' Meg agreed. 'You haven't been near since your birthday in March. But I know you have your own life to lead.'

'There were – reasons.'

Meg stifled a sigh and turned her head away to stare at the horizon, not wanting to ask if it was herself who had kept Lissa away. Nor did she wish to let her daughter see the hurt in her grey eyes. The distance between them yawned as wide as ever, hurting her more than she cared to acknowledge. But it had to be bridged. One of them must make the first move. 'Do you want to talk about it?'

Summoning all her courage, Meg put an arm about Lissa's shoulders. She expected her to move away or shrug it off, as she usually did, and was glad when she didn't. But the slender body seemed somehow frailer than usual.

'There's nothing to say.' Head down, lower lip quivering. The misery etched in her daughter's profile cut her to the heart.

Was this man making her daughter happy? Philip Brandon had seemed so very sensible and caring, a suitable person for Lissa to marry despite his being older than they would have liked. Certainly an improvement on that young Teddy Boy she'd once taken up with. Not that Tam had agreed with that. He'd been quite taken with young Derry, but then he was a soft-hearted Irishman. Philip got on well with them all, fitted in at family events. Only there was something wrong now, Meg could smell it. How could she be sure he was being good to her lovely girl?

'You'd tell me if there was a problem? If you were distressed about anything, wouldn't you?'

Lissa gave a half laugh, blinking away the prick of tears. 'I'm fine. Don't worry about me.' The shoulders stiffened and Meg let her arm drop.

'And Philip?'

'He's fine too.' A light, jocular tone. 'Overworked and underpaid he says, but otherwise fine. How very motherly you sound all of a sudden.'

'Why not? I am your mother, in all but name.' The sharp words faded into silence and the two gazed upon each other for a second before both looked away, awkward and embarrassed.

Something inside Meg seemed to snap and she tossed back her hair in a characteristically defiant gesture. 'I'm the best mother you're ever likely to get.'

A long pause, then a reflective smile at the circling merlin. 'I dare say you are,' Lissa agreed, an edge of resignation in her tone. 'And I should make the best of that, eh?'

Meg felt as if she'd been slapped. She stood up, kicked a small pebble with the toe of her boot so that it rolled down the bank and fell with a plop into the tarn. The ripples widened and spread, just as Lissa's remarks spread within her like a canker, making her heart bleed. It was hard to know where you were with her. Meg tried to tell herself that the young tended to make these pithy comments without thought of their effect. Yet Lissa made too many, and too often for Meg to shrug them all off.

'Do you still write to Kath?' She dreaded the answer.

'Once. I never got a reply. No point, is there? She's made her position clear.' Lissa gazed out across the ruffled water. 'I used to come here when I was a child, against all your rules, to make wishes. I called it my Wishing Water. Grandfather Joe told me of a silly ritual he used to do when he was a boy. I thought it would be sure to bring Kath hurrying home to see me.' She smiled now at her own youthful folly. 'Kids have such wild notions, don't they? All fantasy and foolish fancies.'

381

'There's nothing wrong with a bit of fantasy. It would be a dull old life without it. I wish I could have made your dream come true, Lissa, but I couldn't. I even swallowed my pride and tackled that dragon of a grandmother to make you happy.' A rueful smile. 'But I failed you. Perhaps I should have let you go when you were seven, when you took a fancy to going with Kath back to Canada. I see it was selfish of me not to consult you.' She hugged herself with arms that suddenly ached. 'When you were very small, I used to ask how much you loved me. More than all the world, you'd say.'

'I remember.'

'I couldn't risk losing that, you see. I was so afraid. Afraid that you might not come back. I didn't even have Tam at that time, didn't know if he would ever come back to me. I'd no one but you.' There were tears in her eyes, in her throat, which as ever she refused to shed.

Tears glistened too in Lissa's eyes as she stared up at Meg as if seeing her for the first time, seeing her as a young woman, vulnerable and alone. When she spoke again it was in a hauntingly quiet voice. 'I didn't know about Tam. And I'm glad you didn't let me go. How can a seven year old choose what's right? I just fancied the horse she promised me. Probably wouldn't have kept it any more than her other promises.'

Her eyes pricked but she didn't want to touch them in case Meg thought she was crying. Yet the tears rolled down Lissa's cheeks nonetheless. 'Then I made you lose the baby.'

Meg looked shocked. 'Heavens, that wasn't your fault.'

'I thought it was, because you were worried over me staying out all night after we had that row.'

Meg was shaking her head, her face warm and alight with sympathy and love. 'That didn't make me lose the baby. It was an accident, nature's wisdom perhaps.'

'I wanted to hurt you. I was so cruel, so jealous.'

'You were young, an adolescent rebelling against a world that had hurt you. I just got in the way of your anger.' Meg came to sit beside her again. 'I tried to explain the baby wouldn't have made any difference to us, to you and me. You weren't ready to take that in.'

Lissa looked at her, her face a picture of agony. 'I've wasted so much time in foolish wishing. I'm sorry I ever blamed you for Kath's deficiencies. Now that I'm a mother myself, now that I can perhaps understand human nature a little better, I realise how lucky I was. It's taken me a long time to say it, but I'm so glad I had you for a mother, Meg.'

Meg gazed in wonder at this girl who she'd always loved as if she were her own, even though she'd fought against it at first, fearing it would hurt too much when Kath returned and reclaimed her. In the end she'd dug her heels in, and, rightly or wrongly, had kept her. 'You're right. It has taken you a long time.'

Lissa swallowed. 'Have I left it too late? For us to be friends, I mean?'

Meg felt her heart swell with happiness and pride. 'No, my bonny lass. Never too late. I've picked up and started again more times than I care to count. It's the way of the world between mothers and daughters. It's what binds us together. It's called love.'

Then Lissa was putting her arms about Meg and they were hugging and laughing and crying together, wiping each other's tears away, drawing closer than they ever had before.

'It'll be all right,' Meg said, patting Lissa's back as if she were a small child again. 'You'll see. It'll be all right. Never say die, eh?'

And somehow Lissa knew that it would be. She did have the love of a mother. She'd had it all along and never realised.

The winter following was long and cold and filled with a million pinpricks of frustration. Lissa longed to spend every spare moment in the shop. She wanted to make frequent trips to wholesalers to buy stock, but was afraid to arouse Philip's curiosity.

Hilary's committee and voluntary work proved to be the perfect alibi. If Philip believed her to be thoroughly involved with charity, the less suspicious he'd be of how she spent her time. Even so, Lissa was made constantly aware that he kept a close watch on her activities, his dark eyes often fixed upon her with disappointment and concern.

'I may wish to keep in Don Cheyney's good books, but you mustn't overdo it, my sweet. I need my wife at home.'

Lissa wheeled the library trolley around the wards of the Cottage Hospital. She attended at least two coffee mornings a week for some charity or other, and her expertise at pricing bric-a-brac for a jumble sale became legendary. And in between, she dashed down to work in the shop, or to see a supplier. The feeling that she walked a tight rope grew with each passing day.

Philip must not discover her secret until she was ready. And that couldn't happen until she had proved the business to be a success and secured independence for herself and her children.

The twins were her delight, her joy. It was as much for them that she worked so hard, and planned with such care. It was for their sake that she still occupied his bed each night.

Philip was stern and firm, but did not ill treat them. What kind of father he would be when they began to show a will of their own, however, when they in turn became rebellious adolescents, she dare not imagine. He may be all outward gloss and charm but beneath lay a determination to control and use people on a whim, with no thought for the consequences. Would there be room for them to grow in this house?

Beth and Sarah were babies still, only four years

old. Philip loved to see them dressed in their pretty frocks and shiny shoes, with ribbons in well-brushed hair. He loathed sticky fingers and grubby knees, washing soaking in a pail, toys in the living room, or even to find them not in bed when he arrived home from work. He did not see them as real children, but as pretty toys to decorate his beautiful home, and prove what a fine chap he was.

He expected the same high standards of her. 'You are learning to manage so much better,' he told Lissa, fondly patting her cheek as if she were a pretty child.

She managed by getting up at dawn. By the time Philip had showered and come downstairs to eat the breakfast she'd cooked, Lissa had cleaned through the ground floor rooms. After breakfast she played with the twins for a while, then hurried to meet Renee at the shop where they were in the process of scouring, scrubbing, cleaning and redecorating. At the end of each session she had to make sure that she left not a scrap of paint on herself.

In the afternoons she fulfilled her voluntary work obligations and later, after she got home, worn out and ready to drop, she would smile at her darling babies, freshen herself with a quick sip of tea and then take them for a walk by the lake or to play in the park. It was the best part of her day, The only time she dared relax. Then it was back to the house and the strain of continuous deceit.

But Lissa had not taken into account how exhausting subterfuge could be. And the girls were no longer babies and growing increasingly demanding.

'You bath us tonight, Mummy.'

'Make French toast for tea.'

'I want pancakes.'

'Read us another story.'

'Play jig-saws, Mummy.'

'Want a drink of water.'

Even when she had handed them over to stiff-backed Nanny Sue, Lissa must rush about giving the bedrooms a sketchy dust, and twice a week run round with the vacuum cleaner. Then there was still the evening meal to prepare, herself to make beautiful with Philip's bath run and his drink poured. Just as if she had been there all day, waiting for him to come home.

It was all too much and the strain began to tell. She forgot to eat, lost weight, got too tired to sleep, fell prone to constant colds and infections. And was sure that Philip watched her with his keen, inscrutable gaze.

Sometimes she took risks, cut corners by hiding dirty laundry in cupboards, resorted to tinned soups and sliced bread though she knew he hated both and would give her a long lecture on good housekeeping. But Lissa scented freedom and had no intention of letting anything stand in her way. This was the sixties, for God's sake, time for women to make a stand. And one day she would summon the courage to face him with her plans, she really would.

Her one relief was that he made surprisingly few demands on her sexually. Lissa decided it must be pressure of work as he often seemed preoccupied with concerns of his own. Sometimes he sat up for hours in his study, working at his desk. Such nights were bliss for she could stretch out in the wide bed and catch up on some much needed sleep, undisturbed.

But one evening she felt so ill from the tension and exhaustion that she tried one more appeal to improve her situation.

'I did wonder, Philip, about employing a cleaner? It's such a big house and I don't seem to have the same time for it, now I'm doing so much voluntary work with Hilary.'

'I do believe you have forgotten my gin and tonic.'

'Goodness, I'm sorry.' Rushing to pour it out, afraid of any little slip that would make him investigate her life too closely. 'And the twins are so much more demanding these days. I thought perhaps if I had a little more help? Not a whole battery of servants as Mrs Fraser had, but one woman would be a help.'

He looked up at her sharply. 'What do you know of Mrs Fraser?'

'I met her once. Didn't I tell you? At The Birches nursing home when I was standing in for Hilary.'

'She told you about her servants?' He sounded so startled that Lissa had to laugh.

'She told me about her darling papa and her beloved Charles. Poor old lady, mind quite gone.'

He was frowning at her again, dark eyes narrowed with displeasure. 'You do too much.' The telephone rang and he went to answer it. 'It's for you.' He sounded surprised, as if she had no right to have telephone calls.

'Who was it?' he asked when she returned, flushed and trying not to look as if she wanted to rush off and solve this latest problem which had arisen.

'Only Renee, asking how I am.'

'You're not still seeing that foolish girl?'

'Haven't seen her for ages,' Lissa lied. 'That's probably why she rang. To see how I was.'

All business calls were directed to Nab Cottage but there were times when Renee felt the need to call her at home if some emergency had cropped up. As now, with a firm having difficulties with a delivery date. Even so, Lissa decided she must speak to Renee, ask her not to take the risk again.

Dark eyes were considering her, as if trying to read the thoughts in her head. In the ensuing silence Lissa could hear her heartbeat, loud and hard rattling against her breastbone.

'Ice?' Philip asked, making her jump.

'What?'

He waved his glass at her. 'Will you fetch it or do I have to do it myself?'

She did not raise the subject of a cleaner again.

389

1964

CHAPTER 20

Life wasn't running too smoothly at Nab Cottage either. Renee's two menfolk were not hitting it off at all well and she was beginning to feel more like a referee at a cock fight than a wife and landlady.

'I can't stop here arguing with you two. I'll be late for work.'

'I'm waiting for him to tell me if it's true,' Jimmy roared, waving the newspaper in Andrew Spencer's face. 'Does the Water Board mean to flood Winster valley or not?'

The Manchester man dabbed at his mouth, buttered a second slice of bread to accompany his last slice of bacon and seemed to consider whether or not to answer the question. 'I'm not the person to ask. Most folk seem to know more about what's going on than I do, certainly the local paper thinks so.'

'Then it's just another rumour?'

'There've been so many.' He waved the bread about, almost apologetically. 'We must have more water, you can't ignore the fact. And Manchester Water Board aren't all bad. Look how they built a school for the children of the workers on Thirlmere.' He laid the bacon on the slice of bread and bit into it.

Jimmy looked stunned, his face turning dark purple. 'That was last century. What's it got to do with things as they are now?'

'I'm pointing out that the Board do try to be reasonable and considerate.'

'Like hell they do!'

Renee touched her husband's arm. 'Calm down, Jimmy lad. Don't get so worked up.'

'Worked up? Manchester Water Board is God's gift to hear this chap talk. They threaten to ruin the boating and the tourist industry, put a reservoir in one of Lakeland's loveliest little valleys, right in the middle of the National Park, and you tell me to calm *down?*'

'The engineers are very skilled. They've already built underground aqueducts from Haweswater by way of the Marsdale tunnel to the Stockdale siphon in Longsleddale and then on to Garnett Bridge. As well as the Winster reservoir, they hope to build a brand new conduit right through Longsleddale till they can carry all the Lakeland water they need, by gravity, right to the Manchester taps. A wonderful feat of engineering,' Andrew Spencer proudly announced, as if he were responsible for building it with his own hands.

'And ruin another dale in the process?'

'It's called progress. The Electricity Board have put many of their cables underground to reach the farms in those dales, haven't they? There'll be little sign of the aqueduct, once it's built, though admittedly it'll take a few years and there'll be pumping stations, that sort of thing, but all the concrete will be underground.'

'Ruining the land,' growled Jimmy. 'If you think we believe you can hide all your mess, then you must think we're daft.'

'You'd imagine, wouldn't you,' Renee said, 'that if man can fly to the moon, he could make better pumps on the tunnels you do have? To make more water come through, I mean.'

They both looked at her in surprise. 'Aye, she's got a point there.'

'I really couldn't say.'

'So is it Winster or somewhere else you're after? Good farming land. Just so industry can take hundreds of millions of gallons of water that's too good for them in the first place!'

Andrew Spencer wagged his sandwich. 'Now you are quoting rumour again.'

'Then why don't you tell us what you're really up to, and put an end to rumour?'

'Because decisions have not yet been made.' Looking more pompous than ever as he lifted the sandwich to his mouth.

Jimmy snatched it from him, leaving his mouth hanging open in mid-bite. If Jimmy hadn't been so fired up, Renee might have roared with laughter at the man's shocked expression. Wisely, she kept quiet.

'Come to my next meeting. You'll hear more then.' The water consultant closed his mouth, eyes still riveted on the sandwich.

'Happen I will,' said Jimmy. 'There are other ways. Desalination of sea water for one, the Morecambe Barrage scheme for another.'

'Ah, but are they economic? Are they viable? It's my job to consider all sides of the case.'

'And money is more important than land, and people?'

'Everything must be taken into account. I do listen to everyone's point of view, Mr Colwith, but it is only my job to suggest a suitable site. I leave arguing on policy to the politicians. I haven't put in my final report yet, but when I do, it will be when all relevant factors have been considered. We all have our own personal problems. I for one have a sick mother to consider, requiring day long care. It's human nature to want to do what's in our own interests in the end.' Then retrieving the sandwich, he filled his mouth with bacon and bread, as if afraid he might have said too much.

Lissa was surrounded by boxes, happily unpacking tiny garments and singing loudly to the strains of 'Please, Please, Please Me' on her transistor radio, when Renee arrived, breathless from running.

'I'm sorry I'm late. Ooh, what a picnic this morning!'

The months of effort were beginning to bear fruit.

They'd dusted and cleaned, tidied and repainted, disposed of the dreary mannequins and bought smaller versions for children's clothes. A new green carpet covered the floor, and there were curtained cubicles in which their young customers could try on garments. The two glass counters shone and the wall of mahogany drawers had been given a new coat of yacht varnish by Jimmy, who had been a tower of strength. Lissa said as much now. You don't know how grateful I am.'

'The feeling's mutual. I'm going to enjoy this job. Mind you, it's a wonder Jimmy had time to help, since he's so busy fighting this latest threat.'

'What threat?'

Renee leaned on the counter and folded her arms, ready for a gossip. 'That's why I'm late. They've been at it for hours this morning, our Jimmy and this water consultant. Cocky little chap. Sending my Jimmy wild he is. Tramps about the fells and dales all day, treading his muck into the house every night, and all he ever talks about is how wonderful it is that so much rain falls here. Wonderful my eye! Jimmy'll have apoplexy before he's done. They argue all the time. I'm sick of it.'

'Jimmy can hold his own corner.' Lissa smiled, chuckling as she slipped a cherry red frock onto a mannequin. It looked perfect.

'The latest rumour is that they're going to flood Winster valley. There's to be a meeting tonight. I've said I'll go with him, to hold his hand like.' She laughed. 'Want to come? We could go on to the Marina Hotel for a bite of supper afterwards. What d'you say?'

'It's silly, I know, but Philip doesn't like me going out in the evenings, except with him.'

'You are joking!'

'It's all right, I'm used to it.'

'Then you shouldn't be. Does you good to get out. Anyroad, I reckon we should have a say on what they do to the lake, don't you?'

Lissa knew Renee was right. It was important, and she should go. She couldn't remember the last time she'd been anywhere that Philip hadn't arranged for her. But then she remembered her situation and sighed. 'I'm defying Philip enough. I daren't take any more risks.'

'You still haven't told him then? About the shop?'

Lissa shook her head. 'I mean to, soon. I've been waiting for the right moment.

'You're sailing a bit close to the wind. The opening is on Saturday, after all. There'll be all hell to pay if he finds out from someone else.'

Lissa chewed on her finger nails. 'I wanted to be sure the business was going to be a success first. I could at least see if we have a good Easter. What do you think?'

She looked at her friend for reassurance, and found none.

'Judgement day is nigh.'

Renee's mind returned to her own problems, not unconnected with Philip Brandon. 'If we could just get rid of Mr Spencer we'd be on cloud nine,

Jimmy and me. He cramps our style, sitting with us every evening like a sour gooseberry. I wish he'd go jump in the lake himself.'

She sounded so vehement, that Lissa burst out laughing. 'Bit extreme. Why not simply ask him to find alternative accommodation? Tell him he's upsetting Jimmy.' As you did with Derry, she might have added, but that would have been too unkind.

Renee looked surprisingly nonplussed for someone who was rarely lost for words. 'Oh, well, he's no trouble really, bless him. I tell Jimmy he'll have to put up with it because the money comes in handy.' Snatching up a cloth she took out her frustration on the glass counter, her round bottom in skin tight black jeans wobbling alarmingly. She wished she'd never opened her silly mouth. The last thing she needed was Lissa asking awkward questions.

'Why not invite him to our opening. That might give him something different to talk about for a change. Does he have any children?'

'Oh no, he's single, lives with his mother. He wouldn't be interested. Heavens, I'm that scared.' Renee sank on to a stool, clutching a bunch of matinee jackets. And excited. Aren't you?'

'Scared rigid. I must make sure I order enough sherry. Or should we stick to wine, do you think?'

Lissa walked briskly to the office where she had a pile of paperwork that needed attention, and several telephone calls to make. She'd had the phone installed only the other day and used it for the slightest reason. She could ring Jan or Meg from the shop now and talk to her heart's content. It was really quite wonderful to have this little bit of independence at least.

Lissa gazed at him horror-struck. 'I can't. Not on Saturday.' Silently begging him to accept her word and not question her further. It was too much to hope for.

'I would have thought you'd be delighted to entertain the Cheyneys? Hilary has been very good to you of late. I thought we'd invite them to lunch.'

'I've already made plans. It will have to be next week.' Lissa couldn't believe her bad luck. It simply wasn't possible. But how to explain all of this to Philip without telling him the truth? She couldn't lose her fight now, not when she was so close to winning.

'Cancel them.'

'I can't, Philip. Really, I'm sorry.'

He started to rub the bridge of his nose, a gesture he always made when he was keeping a tight hold on his temper. He let his gaze linger over the slender lines of her youthful figure, still showing no sign of pregnancy. She was an increasing dis-appointment to him. What was this urgent matter she'd planned. Could she be meeting a lover?

She smiled sweetly at him. 'I'll ring Hilary and make other arrangements.' Ignoring his frown she went to the phone, wondering if she had the courage to tell him about the shop now. She had to tell him sometime. She'd already spent hundreds of Jeffrey Ellis's inheritance on new shop fittings, stock, wages for Renee, and a multitude of other expenses. Failure now was not an option. She daren't even consider the possibility.

All she had to do was keep Philip happy. Was that so difficult? And not appear too tired, or disagree with him too much, or he might start probing into her daily routine more closely, perhaps even regret agreeing to the voluntary work. Then she would be in real trouble. Housebound again, alibi gone. The prospect terrified her. Not that she could depend upon this ruse indefinitely. Hilary might discover the truth about the shop and blab about it to Philip. She was the greatest gossip in Carreckwater. Oh dear, Renee was right. She really ought to get the matter cleared up, but not now. Not quite yet.

The opening party was a great success. All the family came from Broombank, bringing far too much food and everyone drank to the success of the new business, congratulating Lissa on how splendid everything looked. Miss Stevens was there too, of course, wishing them all well. The shop refurbishments were generally admired and customers flooded in out of curiosity, and soon the till was ringing with welcome cash. It was all even more successful than she'd hoped.

Jan had her children with her, and Lissa wished the twins could be here too, to share her success on this special day, but knew they could never keep a secret. They would go right back and chatter excitedly to Daddy all about Mummy's party and new shop.

But she couldn't put it off for much longer, and hated herself for her own cowardice and deceit. Why hadn't she told him the other day? He'd given her the perfect opportunity. Probably because she needed to plan exactly what to say before she began.

Now if she'd been married to Derry, the thought came unbidden, things would have been so different. She wished suddenly that he could be here, to see her moment of glory.

She half glanced across at the door, wanting so much to see him, she almost thought for a moment that he stood in the open doorway. This man was tall, broad-shouldered, smartly dressed in a crisp grey suit and a very conventional silk tie. Handsome. Strong. Certainly not a Teddy Boy. But then Derry wouldn't be a boy, not now. He was walking towards her, smiling the same lopsided grin.

'Hello, Lissa.'

'Dear Lord, it can't be!'

Lissa stared up into his face in wonder. Could it really be him? So different and yet – the same – and so very beloved. She was half aware of Renee giggling somewhere in the background. Heart thumping like a hammer, she tried out his name. 'Derry?'

Then he was kissing her cheek, very properly of

course, but it felt delicious. Her heart was melting and her mind had become quite empty of all sound and sensation except the fact that he was here, holding her hands, smiling into her eyes.

'So, I was right.' The voice from the door rang out across the shop and voices instantly hushed, faces turned. 'No wonder you couldn't spare any time to spend with me today. Derry Colwith is back in town, and you can't keep your hands off him.'

Customers had quietly vanished, the door locked, and very gently Lissa began her explanation, aware as she did so of Meg ushering the rest of the family into the stock room beyond.

'This isn't how it looks. I didn't know Derry was home.' Even to say his name out loud was a delight.

'That's true,' Derry put in. 'I didn't know I was coming myself until a day or two ago when Renee invited me.'

Philip silenced him with a few clipped words. 'This is between myself and my wife.'

'Yes, but I don't want her blamed for my coming today, just to support her.'

Lissa put out a hand. 'It's all right. I wanted to tell you, Philip, about the shop – but I couldn't find the words.'

'Shop? What are you talking about?'

Lissa drew in a deep breath. 'Miss Stevens has agreed to lease it to me.'

'I beg your pardon?'

'This is our launch party, my first day of business. I would have told you before, as I said, but either you never wanted to listen or I was too afraid. Isn't that silly?' She was gabbling now, reaching for a bottle of champagne. 'Would you care for a glass?' She thought for a moment he might knock the bottle from her hands as he had once swept the pie dish from the table. Instead he look her arm in a punishing grip and thrust her towards the door.

'We agreed, that there would be no business. No career for you.'

'You did express that wish, yes,' Lissa said, in her most reasonable voice. 'But I didn't agree.'

'You didn't what?'

'There's no need for you to worry, Philip. You won't be neglected in any way. I dare say you'll never notice the difference.'

'Lot's of women work these days,' Derry tried, and was frozen with a glance.

'We'll discuss this later. The car is at the door. Get in.'

Lissa glanced anxiously behind her. 'I can't leave my guests.'

'*Get in!*'

Meg appeared, and, walking up to Philip, kissed him on the cheek, as if he were not trying to frog-march her daughter off her own shop premises.

'Philip,' she said, in her sweetest tones, 'how glad I am that you could come. Isn't she a clever girl? You must be so proud of her. I certainly am.' Meg swept a hand to indicate the displays: the rows of tiny knitted garments, pretty frocks and romper suits, neat little page boy suits with bow ties. 'She's done all this herself, you know.'

'I had some assistance,' Lissa said, rather breathless and bemused but grateful for Meg's intervention.

'Of course you did, sweetheart, but the idea was all yours.' Meg beamed up at Philip.

'She'll go far, this girl. Oh dear, she hasn't even got you any champagne. Come along, before Tam and Nick drink it all.' And taking her son-in-law's arm she led him back into the bosom of her family. 'Chicken vol-au-vent or a sausage roll?' she offered with a smile. 'Why not have both.' And Philip accepted a plate and a glass with the best grace he could manage.

The month was April, the lake water as clear as crystal. Chips of grey slate and shale shimmered beneath the surface like pale jewels. As Lissa walked along the lakeshore to Nab Cottage she watched with delight as the mute swans upended, their long necks diving deep as they sought some tasty morsel. The Lakeland air was pure and fresh, sharp with the promise of spring, and the circle of mountains seemed to lift up their faces to the smiling sun, as Lissa did. It felt good to be alive.

It had been a whole month since their launch day when Philip had discovered her secret. For Lissa, it had been the worst month of her life.

To begin with he'd hardly spoken to her for days. Then he called Hilary Cheyney and put an end to her charity work. That didn't particularly worry her but his final thrust did. He spoke to Miss Stevens and made the poor woman agree to refuse Lissa the lease.

'I'm sorry, Lissa. But I really can't become involved in marital, or legal, disputes. And Mr Brandon has all my affairs in his office. It's rather difficult. Best, I think, if you find other premises.'

'Yes, I do understand,' swallowing her bitter disappointment. 'But the season is only just beginning, all the shops are taken and we have hundreds of pounds worth of stock. Will you give me some time at least, to find an alternative?'

'What of your husband? I'm sure he meant you to close down altogether. He won't be pleased by such an arrangement.' Miss Stevens had poured tea from a pretty little porcelain teapot in her pretty little conservatory. A safe, well-ordered life, and Lissa had felt again that nudge of envy. She had neither security nor freedom.

To make matters worse she was haunted by the thought of Derry being back in town. Why did he have to come now? Of all the times to choose, he came when she was at her most vulnerable.

Lissa had not seen him since that dreadful day, nor did she wish to. Yet the knowledge that he might appear around a corner, that she might see him by the lake when she was out with her children, or hear his voice when she lifted the phone, left her jumpy and sleepless. She had lost him years ago. Now she was trapped in a loveless marriage with a husband determined to destroy every part of her life which did not include him.

A few evenings later Lissa sat on a hard chair in Carreckwater Town Hall, listening to the speaker express his concern over the latest plans for acquiring water from Lakeland, aware that yet again she was risking Philip's displeasure. Yet somehow she felt more resolved than ever to do so.

'I'll not have my wife wandering about town in the evening,' he would sternly inform her whenever she expressed an interest in going out.

On this occasion, fearing another argument, she hadn't even asked. When Renee had asked her to go to the meeting with them, Lissa had readily agreed. certain she needed to be there. She was a part of this community and had every right to know what was going on. She'd broken the chain that had kept her fastened to the kitchen sink and had no intention of putting it on again.

Jimmy was loudly agreeing with everything the speaker said. 'Hush,' Renee warned him, grasping hold of her husband's jacket as he bounced up and down, his bristly brown hair seeming to stand on end. 'Sit still, Jimmy lad, I can't hear for your noise.'

'Sorry.' He gave her an abstracted kiss and Renee rolled her eyes at Lissa. 'He gets so worked up.'

Lissa felt heady with the relief of being out of

the house, away from Philip's increasing coldness. She was determined to enjoy herself, feeling young and reckless at her daring.

'They're trying to get water on the cheap,' the speaker told them. 'So they can sell it to industry at a vast profit.'

Lissa thought this sounded like economic sense but didn't say as much as there were general murmurs of agreement all round.

'Winster is one of the finest, most beautiful valleys in Lakeland. It would be appalling if it were flooded. A national outrage.'

Lissa leaned over to whisper in Renee's ear. 'Is this threat true?'

'It looks like more than a rumour this time.'

'But Winster is beautiful, close to Windermere and in the National Park.'

'Sh!' Jimmy hissed fiercely at them both, and Lissa apologised to concentrate on what the speaker had to say.

A feeling of outrage grew inside her as the speaker described Manchester's needs and how they meant to satisfy them. She thought of the beautiful landscape which she loved: the wild life, the flowers and hedgerows and butterflies, pretty woodlands and character cottages, all to be swamped by water for the needs of faceless industry?

'We're aware that the country needs more water.' Another man was having his say now. 'But why should our finest countryside be ruined, raped, in order to get it? They talk of digging tunnels under Longsleddale. Scarring virginal land for all time. Sacrilege! They talk of damming scenically beautiful valleys as if it were of no account. Outrageous!'

Loud cries of agreement.

The speaker went on, 'The threat to this area is very real but there is also a view held by some that Winster is no more than a stalking horse. We should take care. Manchester Water Board are not fools. They will guess public reaction if they choose to put their reservoir in such a pretty spot. This may be a blind. While we're all protesting against Winster, they may come up with somewhere else, outside the National Park, which we'll gladly accept as an alternative.'

There was silence in the hall as this new fear was digested. Lissa glanced about at the troubled faces and worried with them. You couldn't trust anyone in this world. She'd learned that much herself, hadn't she?

'They may take good farmland, for instance,' the speaker pointed out. 'How would we feel about that? We all know what a precious commodity good farmland is in this area.'

The case was put for the Morecambe Barrage scheme, where water could be held in the estuary. Yet another wanted to drill bore holes and another talked at length of how new pumps could be installed at strategic points along the pipe lines to speed up and increase the flow. There were suggestions for flooding disused mines, of piping water from other areas such as the Pennines or Scotland. On one thing only was there complete agreement. It should not be the beautiful Winster valley, or any other valley in the district. Storage reservoirs were out.

Then it was the dubious privilege of the Water Board representative to face the meeting with calming words and promises to listen to every argument. A small man in a grey suit who kept pushing his spectacles up his nose.

'Is this your lodger?' Lissa whispered and Renee nodded.

'Pompous twit!'

To be fair he was listened to, if disagreed with. He explained how they needed an average of 25 million gallons extra a day from Ullswater and about 20 million from Windermere to meet future demand. This was greeted with roars of disapproval. He talked of sympathetic treatment, more meetings, even public enquiries, finally pointing out that no matter what decision they reached, it could take years before it was acted upon.

Jimmy suddenly stood up and waved a fist at him. 'Don't matter how long you take, we won't have you spoiling our dales, nor our meres, not now nor in the future. Lakeland is precious.'

'We'll bloody make sure you don't!' A voice cried from a rowdy group sitting behind.

Cries of 'hear hear', and 'you tell them, Bill', as the group grew noisier by the minute. Lissa glanced worriedly over her shoulder, troubled by the sudden shift in atmosphere.

Bill shouted, 'Take it from the lake, that's what I say. At least until they get the national grid going.'

This suggestion was met with shouts of disapproval from the boating lobby, Jimmy amongst them, arguing that if they concreted the shoreline it would make it too high and dangerous for swimmers and boaters.

The arguments grew every more raucous as the fishermen too got involved. The water consultant tried to draw the proceedings to a close, saying it had been a 'useful meeting', that nothing would be done without Ministerial approval . . .

'What about our approval?' shouted the man from behind Jimmy's chair. 'Do we have no say then?'

'You'll be given your chance at the Public Enquiry.'

'And when will that be?'

'I really couldn't say.'

'Well, you'd better bloody listen, or you can watch for me one dark night. To hell with the boats and the fish. Leave the dales alone. Use the bloody lake!'

'Sit down and shut up,' Jimmy shouted. 'Swearing does no good.'

'And who'll make me? You and whose army?' A fist came out, connected with Jimmy's jaw, and sent him flying backwards, right into the next row of chairs.

Renee jumped to her feet in terror. 'You *bastards*,' and turned on his assailant with flying fists and sharp nails.

Pandemonium broke out. Feet and fists and chairs flew everywhere. If Lissa hoped to escape she was soon disillusioned. A whole wave of people swept them forward in their rush to get out of the hall, treading underfoot those not quick enough to keep up.

'Renee!' Lissa cried, seeing the top of her friend's red head swallowed up in the crowd.

'I'm OK. See to yourself.'

'We'll have a sit-down protest,' someone yelled. 'That'll show them.'

Pinned in by a crush of bodies, Lissa couldn't have resisted if she'd wanted to. She found herself thrust down on to the pavement with the rest of the crowd, bumping her shin and elbow in the process, bringing tears to her eyes and blinding her for a moment. Then there were whistles, and more screams and shouting.

A hand gripped her collar. 'You can come with me,' said a grim voice.

CHAPTER 21

'How could you disgrace me in this way?' After an uncomfortable hour in the police station Lissa, Renee and Jimmy, along with a large group of protesters, had been bailed to appear before the magistrates the following morning where they would be bound over to keep the peace. Lissa had rung home and given the bare details to Nanny Sue. Now she was sitting in Philip's office, the green blind drawn down over the glass so that Miss Henshaw might not peer in and witness his wrath or her misery.

'I wasn't thinking of you at the time,' she very reasonably explained. 'I was thinking of the issues at hand. Besides, I'd little choice in the matter. Have you any idea of the crush I was in?'

'I can guess. What possessed you to go in the first place?'

'Violet eyes flashed fire. 'Why shouldn't I go? Where and how they get the water concerns us all. It is important.'

'You should have been at home, looking after your children. Is that asking too much?'

'I'm sorry, Philip.'

He came and stood before her, eyes condemning. 'I rang to tell you that your grandmother was ill and you weren't even there to receive the news. It's typical of you to hurt the old lady, even on the brink of death.'

Lissa gasped. 'That's not true. I don't wish her any harm. Anyway, I'm sure she isn't on the brink of anything. Rosemary Ellis is a consummate actress.'

'And you are a useless mother.'

She slapped him. Without a pause she lifted up her hand and slapped him right across the face. It was hard to tell for a moment which of them was the more startled.

'Don't ever say anything like that again.' Her voice so low pitched, filled with such fury he almost backed away. 'Rosemary Ellis has never done anything for me in my life. Never!' Tears glimmered unshed in the violet eyes.

A terrible, awesome silence. Then Philip put his arms about her and drew her close, smoothing her hair and patting her back as if she were a small child. 'Perhaps I did get a little carried away but I was upset and concerned about you. You see how you so easily get involved with the wrong sort of people.'

She wanted to protest, to say that Renee and Jimmy were not the wrong sort of people, that they weren't the ones who'd started the riot, but he wouldn't be interested.

414

'I've been too soft with you. Given you your head in too many things.'

Lissa gasped. 'Soft? When, for heaven's sake? You hate any sign of independence.'

He smiled affectionately at her. 'You don't need any, you silly girl. You are my wife.'

'I'm not a child bride, Philip. I'm a woman with a mind of my own.' Heedlessly she ploughed on. 'I can't go on like this. You must listen to me. I need my own life.'

But he wasn't listening. He was wagging a finger at her, issuing a stern reprimand. 'You should have stayed home where you belong. Haven't I said so a million times? Don't I always know what is best for you?'

His voice was so coaxing, and his smile so kind, Lissa was almost tempted to agree. It was easier. 'Perhaps,' she said.

'No perhaps about it. I shall have to exercise more discipline, not less, my dear. What would people think if they saw my wife in a protest march?'

'It was hardly that.'

He kissed her nose, such a delightful nose. He could feel his arousal starting at her increasing submission as he gently scolded her for her naughtiness, all the while busy with the buttons on her blouse.

His actions filled Lissa with alarm. How could she make any preparations to protect herself here, in his office? And if she got pregnant, how could she ever be free of him? And she must be free.

Somehow. 'Philip, please. Not here. Miss Henshaw might come in at any moment.'

'Not if I lock the door.'

She glanced about her, desperately seeking escape. There was none. How to distract him?

'Philip, there's something you should know. Something I've been meaning to tell you for a long time.'

The sound of the key turning in the lock made her jump and as he came back to her, slipping off his jacket, hanging it carefully on a coat rack as he did so, he smiled. 'What is that, my precious?'

The words were almost on her lips when the reality of her situation hit home. She couldn't tell him now, like this. She couldn't say, I've been secretly using contraception. Not while standing in his office. With the door locked. She was suddenly afraid.

Laughing softly he slid up her skirt with the palms of his hands and curled his fingers into her crotch, massaging the soft mound of flesh. Lissa gasped, stifling the sound in her throat. She pushed him away with a light laugh. Stop it, Philip! Not here in your office.'

'You are so beautiful I can't keep my hands off you. I've neglected you recently. I'm sorry, my sweet. Business worries. Grim bank managers. We seem to go through money like the proverbial water. I've had my mind on other things.' His breath was shortening, his eyes glazing over. 'It seems so long since we made love.' He kissed her throat, pushed open her blouse and slid his lips down to her nipple.

416

'But you must be kinder to your grandmother, my darling. We need Larkrigg to be truly secure.'

She pushed him away with all her strength and faced him with narrowed, incredulous eyes. 'What are you saying? Is that what you've wanted all along? Larkrigg. Is that why you married me?'

He chuckled, reaching for her again. 'You were a delightful child. How could I resist you? And I was patient, wasn't I?'

'But would you have been so keen if there hadn't been a wealthy grandmother in the background?' Her eyes opened wide now as she saw it all. 'That's why you've tried so hard to bring us together, Not for my benefit at all, but your own. Oh Philip, I trusted you. I thought you truly loved me.' She felt sick, and a terrible weariness came over her. How naïve she had been, how very foolish.

He looked confused, guilty almost. 'I do love you, my darling. What is so wrong with wanting you to have your just desserts? That family owes it to you.'

Lissa was moving away from him, disgust in her voice. 'I can't take any more of this. I'm going home, Philip.'

She unlocked the door and walked out of the office, politely declining Miss Henshaw's offer of coffee.

When she arrived home the twins were perfectly well and probably hadn't even noticed her absence. A telephone call to Broombank proved that Rosemary Ellis was indeed on her death bed and Meg agreed that it would be respectful to go and see her.

Lissa took a shower, brushed her hair, which helped dissolve her temper and made her feel better. When Philip came home he insisted that they take the twins with them and they set out on a cold April night to face the final interview with her grandmother.

The stale smell in the bedroom was so overwhelming it made Lissa feel sick. In the great bed lay a figure, white as wax and just as still. She wanted to feel compassion, to experience grief. This was her grandmother, after all. Her own mother's mother. She felt nothing.

'Have you brought them?' The voice sounded uncannily strong.

'We are all here, Rosemary,' Philip said, in a voice Lissa recognised as the one he reserved for old and valued clients. Unctuous, grasping. Like Uriah Heep, she thought, feeling a nervous spurt of laughter in her throat.

The eyes opened, regarding her with cold dispassion, and Lissa wondered why she became such a bag of nerves whenever she was confronted by this woman? She could feel Beth's small hand creeping into hers. Even Sarah was shivering, her small mouth turning down in comical self-pity.

A voice from the bed. 'Let me see them.'

There was nothing for it but to bring the children forward. Stern black eyes peered fiercely over the hump of blankets. 'Why are they whimpering? Are they stupid?'

'No, Grandmother,' Lissa said, a new firmness in her tone.

'Don't call me that. I'm not your grandmother.'

Lissa hung her head, saying nothing.'

A hand came from beneath the bedclothes, like a claw. One yellowed finger nail touched Sarah's cheek. 'That one, she's very like Katherine.' The old woman's gaze slid away to fix upon the ceiling and the hand dropped. In the silence a clock ticked and Sarah gave a half-strangled sob of fear.

'You can send them away now. They tire me.'

With relief Lissa sent the twins scampering to Nanny Sue. Straightening her spine, she faced Rosemary Ellis with resignation.

'My energy is limited,' Rosemary said. 'Please don't interrupt.'

'Very well – Mrs Ellis.' It seemed ridiculous to address her so formally.

'Katherine has expressed a wish to compensate you for her defection. Says she should have stayed and tried to keep you. I don't agree, but the young have their own ideas. Larkrigg Hall would naturally go to her in the normal course of events. I'm not going to live much longer.'

'I'm sure you'll recover and be up and about in no time,' Philip put in, smiling condescendingly.

Blackcurrant eyes turned to his. 'Don't pretend, or I might change my assessment of you. Which would be a pity since I am never wrong.' The breath rasped in her throat and Lissa grew anxious. She had no wish to be responsible for Rosemary Ellis's last breath. 'Don't tire yourself. Not on my account.'

'It's Katherine's wish, not mine you understand. Katherine's request – that Larkrigg Hall be left to you. Says she owes you that at least.'

Lissa took a step backwards, away from the high bed. 'I don't want it.'

She sensed Philip twitch as Rosemary turned astonished eyes to hers.

'Of course you want it, you silly girl. I've always known that.'

The sickly sweet smell of death seemed to clog her nostrils, the room swam before her eyes and Lissa grew light-headed, feeling as if she might faint. 'I never wanted anything of the sort. Larkrigg Hall is yours. Nothing at all to do with me.' She became aware that her voice was rising, sounding close to hysteria. How dare you accuse me of being so mercenary?'

Rosemary Ellis continued in scathing tones. 'All you have to do is agree not to pursue your claim of being Katherine's daughter.'

Lissa stared at her grandmother in total shock. 'What did you say?'

'You must give up this foolish demand to be acknowledged as an Ellis. It's not possible. Have Larkrigg Hall by all means, since Katherine seems to want that, but don't expect anything else. No money, no recognition.' She scrabbled her withered hand across the bedclothes and Lissa saw Philip put a paper into it. 'Sign,' she said, and the voice was weakening, growing tired, though rasping just as harshly.

It was Philip who took the paper from the shaking hand and brought it to her. Lissa stared down at it, bemused. He offered her a pen.

'Sign here, along the bottom,' he said, crisp and businesslike.

Lissa couldn't move. She looked from one to the other of them in disbelief.

'Don't either of you understand? I don't want your house or your money. I never wanted those things. I wanted to belong. I wanted to know that you cared about me. That Kath cared. It wasn't my fault that I was born illegitimate. Do you realise how that dreadful feeling of rejection messed me up? All those broken promises.' She paused, trying to keep a grip on herself. 'I took it out on Meg and Tam, the two people I cared most about in all the world. And you offer me your *house*, like a *bribe?*'

Philip's hand closed tightly upon her wrist. He was forcing the pen between her fingers, his voice furiously calm in her ear. 'Take the pen, Lissa. Sign. It's what your mother wants. You deserve it. She owes you that at least.'

'No!' Lissa threw the pen to the other side of the room. 'She owes me nothing.' And turning on her heel, she ran from the room.

★　★　★

421

There was snow on the roads as Philip drove furiously home, slipping and sliding on black ice. The mountains frowned at her, at their most forbidding at this time of day with darkness already closing in, though it was but late afternoon. The air was piercing cold, almost as cold as the ice forming about Lissa's heart.

'How could you?' she kept saying. 'How could you do this to me?'

The twins sat silent in the back seat, one on either side of their precious Nanny who had long since learned to give the impression of closed ears while drinking in every tidbit to relay to her dear mother whom she visited each month.

Philip changed gear, grating it loudly. 'How dare you refuse when I want only the best for us all. You have no sense of what is right, Lissa.'

'I know it isn't right for that woman to treat me with such contempt.' Or you either, she thought, not quite daring to say it.

The car skidded on a corner and the twins screamed. It must have shaken Philip too for he slowed down and seemed to draw a steadying breath, getting his temper back under control as it more usually was. 'All right, my precious ones. Daddy is sorry.' He turned to Lissa. 'You see how you make me behave? Couldn't you for once consider someone besides yourself. The girls, for instance, and me, even if you don't care about Larkrigg for yourself.'

'Why don't you care how I feel?'

'I'm not made of money. To ignore such a valuable gift would be lunacy. Fortunately I was able to put it right.'

'What? How?'

He glanced up in the driving mirror at two white faces and one pink one, avid with curiosity. 'We'll discuss this later.'

Over a dinner which Lissa could not eat, Philip explained how he had persuaded Rosemary Ellis to leave Larkrigg Hall to the twins instead.

'You may not want it but it's certainly not right to deprive the children of their heritage. Larkrigg Hall will stay in the family, after all.'

Lissa gazed at him, stunned by this new twist, furious that he had gone against her wishes. 'I hate you for this.'

He smiled. 'Hate away. It is done. In these uncertain times we may well be glad of it in the future.' I've succeeded, he thought. Now I have tied you to me for all time. He smiled at Lissa, well pleased. 'The old dear will be dead within the week.'

But she was not dead within the month. Rosemary Ellis stubbornly clung to life, determined to be as difficult in dying as she had been in living.

Lissa put on a blue kilted skirt, not too short, a lemon turtle neck sweater and a soft ginger suede jacket. She brushed her hair into a tight knot on top of her head and in her ears wore very proper pearl earrings. Quite the right outfit, she decided, to suit a staid lawyer.

423

She kissed the twins, promising to be home as usual for lunch, but instead of going to the shop, caught the bus into Kendal. She'd chosen this particular practice, hidden away down one of the yards, because it was far enough from Carreckwater not to have any involvement with Philip Brandon. She needed an independent opinion, not one influenced by that of friendship.

All through the long journey she had rehearsed what she wanted to say. But by the time Lissa was sitting in the solicitor's office, her hands clasped together in her lap, breathing in the familiar smell of dusty law books in an unfamiliar setting, every word had gone from her head.

Perhaps it was because the solicitor was younger than she had expected, and carried a slightly bored expression on his pale flat face. Surely he was too inexperienced to be of any use to her?

Lissa told her tale haltingly, with embarrassment pinking her cheeks. It did not come naturally to reveal her most intimate secrets to a stranger. He asked a few questions, made notes on a pad, then leaned back in his chair, steepled his fingers and stared at her over the tips of them.

'So there is no question of his desertion?'

'No.'

'You realise, I am sure, Mrs Brandon, that there are three grounds only for divorce. One is desertion, a long and tiring method which I prefer not to recommend. Should your husband wish to return within the three-year period, and you refuse to accept him back, then you lose your grounds.'

'He would never desert me.' Lissa swallowed and slackened her hands as she realised she'd been pressing them together so hard they were hurting her.

'The second is adultery.' The solicitor raised querying brows and Lissa shook her head,

'Not that I'm aware of.'

'Pity. He wouldn't, I suppose, do the decent thing? We could set up a hotel room, a woman?'

'He would never consent to that.' She felt unclean just thinking about it.

'Pity. He need only go through the motions.' He gave a resigned sigh. 'That leaves us with cruelty. He has not beaten you?'

'No.'

'Locked you up? Twisted an arm perhaps? Thrown anything at you?'

'No.'

'Not a single bruise to show me?'

She flushed dark red. 'None. But I have explained – about his lovemaking. If you can call it that. He's completely selfish, never waits for me and . . .'

The solicitor politely coughed. 'Were we to use inadequacy as a lover as grounds for divorce the courtrooms would be full to overflowing.' He gave an embarrassed little smirk. 'Perhaps a little discussion between the two of you might help.'

'But it's very nearly rape.'

He looked surprised by her sudden aggression and then covered it with a professional mask of sympathy. 'No such thing in marriage. Not in law.' He stared at his notepad. 'How long did you say you've been married, Mrs Brandon?'

Despair was starting to close in. 'He totally controls my life. I have no freedom, not even allowed an opinion of my own. He keeps me like a bird in a cage, watches my every move, tells me what to wear, decides when I may be allowed out, which is never alone. He almost tells me what to think. Now he means to put an end to my new business venture.'

'Curb your bolt for freedom as it were?'

'I-I suppose so, yes.'

The expression on the solicitor's face told her he was sympathetic but thought she exaggerated. His next words confirmed it. 'Few men take such good care of their wives. Even fewer like the idea of their wives working. It reflects upon their own ability as a provider.'

Lissa felt close to tears. How could she make him understand? But the prospect of a lifetime's penance for one mistake was more than she could bear. She tried again, her patience straining.

'I know he has never actually struck me, but there is violence in him, I can sense it. I feel he is barely holding his anger under control. I was very young when I married. It's proved to be a mistake and I would like out of it. Is that too much to ask?'

She lifted violet eyes, dulled by pain but still achingly beautiful, and for a moment the young solicitor very nearly, and against his better judgement, agreed to take the case. He had seen few women as lovely. He could quite easily understand any man's obsession with her. Unfortunately this husband appeared to have been particularly crass about the matter.

'I'm sorry to say that you have no grounds for divorce, Mrs Brandon. You could wait until the children are grown up but even then there is no guarantee a judge would grant you a divorce. You may still find yourself unable to break completely free.'

She couldn't believe what she was hearing. 'And if I were to take a lover?'

His head snapped up and horror registered in every muscle of his face, every line of his erect frame. 'You must *never* consider doing such a thing. Not only would you then be the guilty party and completely at your husband's mercy, but most judges would deem you to be an unfit mother. You would lose your children, Mrs Brandon, without doubt.'

CHAPTER 22

Carreckwater was a small town and it was difficult, if not impossible, to avoid Derry altogether. So when she caught a glimpse of him Lissa would turn and hurry in the opposite direction.

She'd agonised over the solicitor's advice but had known all along what her decision must be. The children must come first. They were everything to her and no risks must be taken with their happiness, bad marriage or no.

Whatever she and Derry had once shared was over. Forget him, she sternly told herself. He would go back to America and she would stay with Philip, and do her best to make what she could of her life.

Lissa was in Fairfield Park, rolling on the grass with the twins who were climbing all over her, when suddenly there he was, standing before her, and she could do nothing but sit and stare at him, her mind empty of words, of every sensation but the glory of his nearness. She felt her body come alive, as if every nerve crackled with a new awareness, every part of her reaching out to the boy she'd once known and loved. But he wasn't a boy any longer. He was a man. The Teddy Boy image had quite gone, so had the quiff and the brilliantine. The hair had grown fair now, and thicker, flopping casually over a wide brow. He was smart and assured, a new confidence emanating from him. And successful, if the cut and style of the pale grey suit were any guide.

'I rather think you've been avoiding me.'

His smile wrenched her heart for it was exactly the same, lopsided and funny, making him look rather like that mischievous young boy again. His brown eyes were as warm and merry as ever, laughing at life.

Her own must have flashed some sort of warning for she saw his expression change, grow oddly serious as their gaze held and locked.

'I really don't see any reason for us to meet, do you?' She felt oddly rumpled and grubby, brushing the grass from her skirt, all too aware of the twins' avid interest.

He picked a stalk of grass from her hair and laughed, gently teasing. 'No pony tail I see.'

The touch of his hand set her on fire. 'No.'

He looked at the children. 'Yours?'

'Yes.' She gathered them to her, as if for protection.

'They take after you. Nice kids.'

'Thanks.'

A silence grew and lengthened. Lissa got to her feet, gathered two sticky, grass-stained hands in her own. 'We must be going. Time for tea.'

'Of course.'

She started to walk away. Would he let her go like this, without saying any more?

'Lissa?' he called, and she instinctively paused, feeling her heart leap as she half turned towards him. She desperately quenched the joy soaring in her heart, determined to hide the effect he had on her.

Derry hesitated, as if not quite knowing what to say next, and she saw him draw in a quavering breath. 'I can see you're busy,' he said, and his voice was not quite steady as his eyes devoured her. 'But I'd like a moment of your time. There's something I need to say.'

She stood on the sweet green grass, her children tugging at her hands and skirt, asking for one more play on the swings, and she could find no words to answer him. How could they talk? Where? For what purpose?

She shook her head. 'There's nothing to say.' Then dipping her chin as she saw the pain come into his eyes, Lissa turned, wanting only to hurry from him.

'Why are you crying, Mummy?' Sarah asked.

'I'm not. I think I have some dust in my eye.'

'The Cobweb,' he called, as she broke into a run, trying to make a game of it as she hurried the twins along. 'Lunchtime on Friday.'

She couldn't go, of course. Nor could she deny that she wanted to, very much. How could she not? She loved him still after all these years, longed for him till her body ached with the pain of it.

When Friday came she pleaded a migraine and stayed in her room all day. How could she trust her feet not to take her to the small cafe if she let them out of the door?

Lissa knew that she must stand by her decision. She had considered every option, taken advice, and come to realise that there was to be no escape. Her duty was to stay with her husband until her children no longer needed her. Take what independence she could and be content. She must make the best of things. Hadn't everyone told her so?

But her rebellion was growing. If she didn't hold fast to her courage now, she would have no life left. 'Renee tells me trade is thriving. We're doing well. I mean to continue, Philip, for all you may force me to seek alternative premises. I mean to be a success.'

They were walking to Elterwater, through the valley where Lissa had first been kissed by Derry. Beyond, in the distance, was the Old Dungeon Ghyll where they'd enjoyed tea, pretending to be sophisticated and grown up. Lissa wasn't feeling too grown up today, more like a reckless teenager. It was exhilarating. And very possibly dangerous. 'I'm beginning to feel respect for myself again. It's a good feeling.'

He used his usual tactic of laughing at her, treating her like a foolish infant. 'Even if you had the skill

431

to run a business, which you don't since you make a mess of everything you do, you'd soon run out of money. Don't think you can ask me for a loan.'

To his fury, she only smiled. 'Jeffrey Ellis, my grandfather, invested a small sum for me as a gift when I was a child. He did love me, you see. Unreservedly, though he was kept from me in his later years. So I won't need your help, Philip.'

His face went white with cold fury. 'An inheritance! You had an inheritance from your grandfather and never told me? I do not care for secrets, Lissa. I'll have no more, do you understand? Or I may be obliged to take stronger measures, which you would care for even less.'

Lissa gazed imploringly at him, begging him to understand. 'I need something of my own. I can't become a mindless dolly bird, devoting myself to you and the children. It would only make me grow bitter and resentful.'

'It's enough for most women.'

'Is it? I'm not so sure. Has anyone ever asked them if they are happy? It'll be all right, Philip. You'll see. Neither you nor the children will suffer. I can fit everything in. You could save money by getting rid of Nanny Sue if you wish. I'll take the children to the shop with me. They'll be old enough for school soon in any case.'

'I will not have my children brought up in the back of a shop.'

Lissa sighed. 'Very well. Then don't complain about being short of money.'

'And what of Derek Colwith?'

Lissa felt the energy drain from her body and put out a hand to steady herself as they reached a stile over a dry stone wall, willing herself to be strong. 'He came with his sister Jan. I didn't even know he was back. What of it? I'm a married woman now.'

He slid his hands over her neck and shoulders, curling over her breasts and hips, down to the flatness of her stomach. Lissa willed herself not to move or reveal the revulsion she felt at his touch.

'You belong to me. Just remember that.'

How could she ever forget.

She seemed to see Derry everywhere. If she turned a corner he bumped into her. If she took the children down to the shore he would be sitting on the benches. If she took them to the swings in the park he would be leaning against the bandstand, watching her. She saw him striding down St Margaret Steps, on the path to the woods, seemingly at every turn. She even found him in the shop talking to Renee on one occasion but obstinately refused to acknowledge his presence, walking past him to her office with her face set and her chin held high.

'Sorry about that,' Renee said afterwards. 'He just popped in for old times' sake. He won't be staying long, he says.'

Won't be staying long. Lissa wished he'd never come in the first place. Oh dear God, when Derry

433

left, that would be the end. Lissa's instincts told her she would never see him again, never know the answers to the questions that haunted her. Yet how dare she allow herself to ask them? She alone knew how much she needed him. All she could do was bury that need in work.

Undeterred, she battled on. Lissa felt a real person again with a mind of her own, able to make decisions and answer queries, ring up suppliers and issue complaints or instructions with equal confidence. It really felt quite wonderful.

But each night she must return home to Philip's criticisms, an ever growing list of rules and requirements, his glowering disapproval. And his bed. Faced with this reality her strength would sometimes falter. Could she survive this task she had set herself? Could she remain with him as his wife? Even as she vowed to do so, her heart desperately sought a way to be free and yet keep her children.

She was twenty-four years old and had nothing to look forward to for the rest of her life but a bleak future with a man she could not love. Lissa realised now how much he had chipped away at her self-confidence. Her victory would lie in reclaiming a sense of purpose. Otherwise Philip would have won completely.

Lissa daringly bought herself a small Morris van so she could drive herself to wholesalers for more stock when needed. The business was beginning to do well and it gave her a wonderful new sense of freedom. It made Lissa feel capable of building a life for herself after all. She even recklessly hired a woman to come in and clean for her, although that didn't work out as Philip sacked her on the spot.

Today she was visiting Broomdale. Jan had knitted some children's jerseys in rainbow colours, and was keen to see if they were a good enough standard to sell in the shop. But first, she called in at Broombank, and there he was.

He was sitting in the wide hearth, his feet in thick woollen walking socks steaming gently before the basket grate, laughing at something Tam had said. Lissa saw him the moment she walked in and the shock of it hit her flat in the chest, quite robbing her of breath. He seemed a re-incarnation of that other Derry, the one who had fascinated her most, the one who had kissed her on their walk to the Langdales.

'Hello.' She couldn't say his name. It was astonishing really, how normal she sounded.

Derry was on his feet in an instant and Lissa saw the tell-tale flush creep up his neck. He hadn't expected her to walk in, any more than she had expected to find him here.

'Lissa. Hi. I've been staying with Jan. Doing some walking on the fells. Thought I'd call in for a chat and a cuppa.'

She wanted to say there was no need for him to explain. Jan was his sister after all. It was really none of her business if he felt he had the right to make himself at home at Broombank.

'He's a different person, is he not?' Tam said, unaware of the undercurrents. 'Not a Teddy Boy now. Grown up fine he has. A successful businessman, would you know?'

Lissa tried to force her stiff lips into a smile. 'What is it you do, Derry?' Politely enquiring, obeying the social niceties. Why stand here talking to him when she wanted to turn and run?

'I work for a management agency. We represent young people who wish to enter the music business. There are a lot of sharks out there, waiting to bite.'

'Lucky you came,' Tam butted in. 'Derry was wondering how to get back to Carreckwater. You could give him a lift, could you not?'

Panic swamped her. 'I'm surprised he doesn't have a flash American car if he's so successful.'

Derry grinned. 'I do. In the States. Nick brought me over, but his van is broken down. It's OK, I can wait for him to fix it.'

'Good,' Lissa said with a cool smile, feeling relieved.

He set down his mug, rubbed his hands on his cord trousers in a familiar gesture that showed he was as uncomfortable about this meeting as she.

Perhaps Meg saw something too for she took Lissa's arm in a comforting gesture. 'I have those jerseys ready for you in the barn, if these men will excuse us.' They walked away, Lissa struggling to concentrate on Meg's bright chatter.

436

'How's trade?'

'Excellent.'

'The shop has a good position, very central. That's essential, I suppose.'

Lissa cleared her throat. 'I may have to find alternative premises.'

Meg frowned. 'Haven't you just spent all last winter doing up the old drapery?'

'Miss Stevens has changed her mind about letting me have the lease.'

'Why?' She looked into Lissa's face. 'Don't tell me. Philip has put pressure on her.'

Lissa gave a philosophical smile. 'She has no wish to become involved in a matrimonial dispute.'

A slight pause. 'Is that what you are involved in? A matrimonial dispute?'

'No, of course not,' Lissa lied, not meeting Meg's shrewd gaze.

'Is there something you'd like to talk about? Are you all right?'

'Everything's fine. I have two lovely children, why wouldn't it be? Anyway, I'm sure I'll find something when the season is over. Assuming I decide to continue, of course.'

Meg regarded her foster daughter with quiet grey eyes. 'It all depends how badly you want something, whether or not it's worth fighting for.'

'Yes,' Lissa agreed, meeting her gaze at last. 'I suppose it does. You don't know what it means to me, Meg, to have you on my side.'

'Where else would I be? Whatever you decide to

do, Lissa, I'm right behind you. Remember that. Whatever it is.'

And they both knew she wasn't just talking about finding new premises.

A cornflower blue sky marred by streaks of grey. Dark shadows melding the mountains into greyness one moment, highlighting them into brilliant sunlight the next. The day appeared to match the confusion of her mood. Lissa simply couldn't focus on the winding lane ahead. She drew the van to a halt and yanked on the handbrake.

'Tam had no right to insist on my taking you. But you're here now, so whatever it is you want to say, get it over with quickly. I have children waiting for me at home. And a husband.'

'Why did you marry him, Lissa?'

She was filled instantly with a flush of hot temper and turned to him, violet eyes flashing with anger. 'Why did you leave, without even a proper goodbye or an explanation? Why did you promise to come home, in that pathetic little scrap of a letter, and then not keep that promise? You made a fool out of me, Derry Colwith. Don't think I'll ever forgive you for that.'

'I'm surprised it still matters so much,' he said, his voice soft, like a caress, and she realised her mistake.

'Don't kid yourself. I'm very happy, thank you very much.'

'Are you? You don't look like the picture of a

fulfilled happy woman. You look like someone who's made a bad mistake and is spending the rest of her life paying for it. Rather like me, in fact.'

She glared at him as the fury bubbling inside her slowly subsided and the crackling tension between them changed imperceptibly to another sensation, far more compelling, and far more dangerous. Dear God, how she loved him. She sensed him move towards her even before he'd put thought into action.

'Don't,' she said, holding up her hands in a defensive gesture. 'Please, Derry. Don't touch me. I can cope with anything but that.'

'OK. Can I tell you then, what happened? Will you listen without jumping down my throat?'

She turned the key, making the engine spurt into life. 'I don't want to hear.'

'Yes, you do.' He reached over and turned the engine off again. Then he got out of the van and stood, hands in pockets, staring out over the panorama of dale and fell, lifting his face to a fitful sun. Lissa was forced to follow him.

'What can I say? I was young. Obsessed with the hope of fame and fortune. Like a lot of other kids I've met since. I was sure I was the one with the special gift, the one who would take the music world by storm.' He laughed, mature honesty in it, with no hint of bitterness.

'And I came second, probably even last in your calculations?'

He gave a rueful smile. 'Like I said, we all make

439

mistakes. I'm no exception. A part of me was arrogant enough to believe I'd return in no time with money in my pocket, a record contract, and you'd be eating out of my hand.'

'I was already,' she admitted. 'I didn't want your money, only you.'

He was silent, staring up into the sky as if by watching the movement of the clouds he could make time run backwards, give them a second chance.

'I realised my mistake and came back, remember, hoping to make amends. But it was too late. You were already engaged to Philip Brandon.'

She would never forget that night. The awful sight of Derry's face had haunted her for months afterwards. Years. Lissa recognised it now as the final acknowledgement of lost hope, hastily smothered in pride. 'I think I did it out of a last, wilful cry of rebellion. And I thought I'd be safe with him, an older man who adored me. He would never reject me as you had done, as others before you had done.'

He nodded in understanding, and they stood quietly side by side, not looking at each other, not touching. The wind lifted the curls she'd left loose about her neck and slapped them against her face.

'I could tell you that it wasn't entirely my fault, that your husband had a hand in my decision to leave, but you'd only say I was making excuses.'

She half glanced at him then bit down on her lip, feeling a hard knot growing in her throat. 'Not

440

necessarily. Philip has a way of manipulating things to suit him.

'If I'd come back sooner, would you have forgiven me?' There was a plea in his voice that cut deep to the heart of her. She could almost feel the blood running from it. 'Don't – don't ask. Who knows? It's over, done with.' She turned from him, back to the van but he caught her arm, held her by him.

'It isn't. 'You know it isn't.' She could feel the heat of his fingers the length of her arm, his gaze warming her face. As their eyes met and held it was as if her soul was drawn from her body, leaving it weak and shaking with need.

'It has to be,' she managed, on half a breath. 'I'm married now, a wife and mother.'

His eyes were soft, compelling and powerful, telling her things she didn't want to know, reminding her of feelings she'd much rather not remember.

'It never will be over. Not for me. I've learned that much about myself at least.'

She must have made a small sound for he told her not to cry, even so the tears were raining down her cheeks. 'I never cry,' she sobbed. 'Never.'

'I know,' stroking the tears away with the gentle tips of his fingers. 'Crying is dangerous. It makes you weak and vulnerable.' Then his arms were around her, his mouth on hers, and he was kissing her as never before. Lissa was holding him, opening her mouth to receive his tongue, his love, as if he could give her life. He was holding her so tightly she could hardly breathe. She didn't want to breathe, not if it meant living without him. His hand was cupping her cheek, her throat, her breast.

Dear God, *what was she doing?* Dangerous emotions. Dangerous actions. She broke from him and ran to the van. Then she drove away and left him standing there, alone on the empty fells.

She could have blamed Renee for seeing him again. Acting as intermediary she'd handed Lissa a note, a knowing grin on her face.

'I won't see him,' Lissa had told her.

'Suit yourself.' Renee shrugged. 'No skin off my nose. He only wants a cup of coffee at The Cobweb, not a necking session behind the bike sheds.'

Oh, but she could no more prevent herself from seeing him again than she could stop the rain falling on the fells or the tarn freezing over in winter. Just one more time, she told herself. She owed him that. Settle the matter properly between them, without emotion this time. So despite all the promises to herself, despite the risk she ran were Philip to discover her deceit, she was going.

'Why are you sad, Mummy? Are you cross with us?'

'Of course not, my darlings. You are my world, my life, my little treasures.' Lissa, cuddling both children on her lap, warm and fragrant after their bath, kissed them each in turn and explained how they must be very good for Nanny Sue this evening.

'Where are you going, Mummy?' Beth wanted to know, pillowing her head against her mother's warm breast.

'Why can't we come?' put in Sarah, outrage on her small heart-shaped face, and Lissa laughed, kissing them both again, brushing their soft curls with a pink baby brush. Beth with hair the colour of pale chestnut leaves and eyes grown more grey than blue as the baby years had passed. Sarah's hair black as her own, the eyes as deep a blue except for flecks of pale grey which altered the light in them, almost to suit her mood. Unusual, bewitching. She smoothed their perfect limbs with a gentle hand, tucked frilled cotton nighties over dimpled knees.

'I do love you both. Do you love Mummy?'

'Yes, yes, yes.' Soft warm kisses, tight hugs, joyful giggles and laughter. With her children Lissa felt completely relaxed and happy. She must do nothing to risk that happiness, or their future, no matter what the cost to her own life. How would they ever forgive her when they grew older if they realised she had put her needs before theirs? As her own mother, Kath had done. However much Lissa might long to leave Philip, she could never risk that. Never.

'Now, my darlings, here is Nanny Sue. Will you put them to bed for me, please? I must go out to – to a meeting.' Lissa felt sure the woman would guess she was lying.

'As you wish, Madam,' said Nanny in frosty

tones. Though for all her unfriendliness with adults, Lissa could not fault the woman's care of the twins. She adored them to a point of fierce possessiveness. An emotion Lissa was familiar with in this household.

'Is Mr Brandon aware you are going out?' she asked, meaning, 'Has he given his permission?'

Lissa smiled, lifting Beth into Nanny's arms. 'He is out at a meeting himself. If he rings, I'm sure you will tell him. I promised my friends that I would go but I know the children will be quite safe with you.'

'What time shall I say you will be back?'

Lissa stifled an irritated response with a sigh, and smiled sunnily. 'You know, if you should ever lose your job here, apply for one as a prison warden. You'd be perfect. Bye, my darlings. Be good. I'll come in to kiss you good night when I get home.'

CHAPTER 23

They sat at a table in a corner of The Cobweb Coffee Bar and sipped their coffee without tasting it, without speaking, without even looking at each other. It was Lissa, in the end, who broke the silence.

'I don't know why I came,' she said, in a pitifully small voice. 'If Philip were to find out, I really don't know how he'd react. What was it you wanted, I thought we'd said all there was to be said.'

His eyes held an appeal she dare not read and could not ignore. 'I can't begin to say all I feel,' he said. 'I'm sorry if I went too far the other night. I lost control. It won't happen again.'

'I'm sorry I abandoned you on the fells. It was childish of me.' Then suddenly he was on his feet, tossing coins on the table as he'd probably learned to do in America and taking her by the arm. 'Come on, I need air. Let's get out of this place.'

Walking by the lake, the breeze in her hair, Lissa felt herself tremble at his touch. 'Someone might see us,' she said, glancing back over her shoulder.

'Meaning your husband?'

'Meaning anyone. It's a small town. People love to gossip.'

Derry dug his hands in trouser pockets, shoulders hunched. 'Leave him, Lissa. I know you don't love him. You still love me, I can tell. Come back to the States with me.'

Lissa stifled a gasp. 'I-I can't. You know I can't.'

'Bring the kids, I don't mind.'

'Philip is their father. He wouldn't let them go.'

They'd reached the dark clump of oak and beech that crowded the shoreline and Lissa halted, shaking her head in distress. 'If this is all you wanted to say then it'd better stop here. I must get back.' She half turned from him but he caught her hand, a whole aching world of emotion in his touch, and in his voice when he said her name. Then she was in his arms, willingly surrendering to his kisses, pressing her body hard against his, begging him never to let her go.'

He cradled her head against his breast, kissing her brow, stroking back the riot of ebony curls.

'I won't ask you for more than you can give. It's enough to have you here, to hold you and kiss you.' But as he stared over her head, out to the moon – silvered water, Derry knew it wouldn't always be that way.

He said as much to Lissa when they met in the same place the following week, falling into each other's arms with a hunger that could no longer be assuaged by kisses. Streaks of early-evening

446

sunlight shafted through the branches of the tall oaks, highlighting her beauty so that his stomach went weak as water inside.

For a long time they clung together, not speaking, hardly daring to breathe.

A cheeky robin hopped upon a twig and cocked his head to one side, considering them, making them both laugh while a family of moorhens, disturbed by their presence, swam away in a huff.

'Do you really still love me?' she asked, shyly, not daring to hear his answer.

He lifted her chin with one finger and grinned at her, kissing her forehead, her nose, then finding her lips. 'Shall I prove it?' he murmured.

Laughing, she shook her head. 'I have to go.'

'Not yet.' His eyes were burning with his need.

She remembered as a girl at school the biology mistress urging them to keep control of their emotions by thinking of other things. Letters to write, errands that needed running. That way they wouldn't be tempted into indiscretion. As her lips throbbed from Derry's kisses and her body burned with desire, she tried, very hard to do it now. The biology mistress, she decided, had got it all wrong.

If this was love it was wonderful, perfect. Why hadn't she trusted in it before? Derry made her feel so wanted, so loveable.

It was as if they were young lovers again, slipping back in time, trying to brush aside the years of exile. After a while she had to make him stop before she quite lost control.

'Let's sit under the trees.'

'The grass will be wet.'

If it was they didn't notice.

He pulled her into his arms again, gently kissing and caressing her. 'I won't hurt you, or go too far.' Nor did he, but there was no doubt in Lissa's mind that she wanted him to. His hands slipped beneath her blouse and the feel of them on her bare breasts made her whimper with pleasure, her heart soar with joy at this proof that she had banished one demon at least. She wasn't frigid at all. Philip was wrong. There was nothing she wouldn't agree to do for Derry. She loved him so much.

Rosemary Ellis finally succumbed one day at the end of May. It was a cold, brisk spring day for the funeral. The snows still lingered on the tops but lambs were bleating, cherry blossom and daffodils bloomed. Maytime had come belatedly to Broombank. Along the track by the little church the leaves of the whitebeam flashed with silver as they turned their undersides to the wind, and there were tiny clusters of white flowers on each stem. But the golden broom, which gave the farm its name, was waiting for any sign of frost to be gone before it deigned to bloom.

The family stood about, dressed in sober colours, Joe fidgeting in his best setting-off suit, cap pulled well down, and Sally Ann unusually smart in a black hat with a tiny veil she probably hadn't worn since the war. Nick stood alone as

Jan had stayed home with the children. Lissa wished she could do the same but braced herself against the wind, and the resolution to do the proper thing by her grandmother, whether she deserved it or not.

Philip came, of course, declaring it was his duty to pay his last respects, taking Lissa's arm as if they were the best of friends. But it was a poor, miserable affair since there was no one but themselves and Mrs Stanton, the housekeeper, to mourn.

'Poor old soul,' Tam said, and Meg rolled her eyes, giving a sad smile.

'She can keep the holy angels in their place now.'

'You'd have thought Kath would've come to her own mother's funeral, wouldn't you?' Lissa remarked, as they stood in the small churchyard, the helm wind whipping the cold into their cheeks, and bringing the predicted shower of rain.

Meg made no reply and the painful subject was pursued no further.

Derry was there too, and Lissa's heart skipped a beat the moment she saw him. Every time she saw him it was like the twist of a knife in her heart, making her think of what might have been, if only they hadn't both been so young and foolish, so quick to make decisions about the rest of their lives.

Philip resolutely ignored him, barely speaking or acknowledging his presence.

'You could at least try to be civil. He's Jan's brother, and since she is married to Nick you could almost call him family.'

'Not my family. Nor yours,' he coldly reminded her. She didn't ask again. Life was difficult enough without deliberately picking a fight with her husband.

Without even looking up she knew the instant Derry walked into a room; the hairs at the back of her neck would prickle with keen awareness as if they had a perception all their own.

Lissa could feel Philip's eyes upon her as Meg served up the meal. And despite her best efforts, Derry only had to brush past, or accidentally touch her hand for her heart to scud into rapid beats. If he needed something passing at lunch she instinctively handed it to him before he even asked for it. If he spoke, she had to bite her tongue not to finish his sentence for him. And she avoided his gaze with such studied attention she felt sure everyone in the house must guess how she felt. Including Philip.

But she could feel no guilt.

She loved Derry. Lissa knew she had done her best with her marriage but that it was a failure. She could do her duty by Philip, but never love him, if indeed she ever had.

Philip went up to Larkrigg Hall later, to issue instructions to the housekeeper who had agreed to stay on until he could find someone to replace her. Mrs Stanton meant to retire to the West Country on a small legacy left by Rosemary Ellis.

Lissa spent a relaxed hour with the twins and Jan. When Meg went off to investigate a lame ewe,

Jan took the opportunity to divulge something of her own troubles.

'Do you remember Nick once telling you about our worries with the mortgage?'

Lissa showed her surprise. 'That was ages ago, when Alice was born. He told me money was tight but that you'd catch up.'

'Well, we haven't.'

'I'm sure you will, Jan, but don't worry about it. It's not important.'

Jan hesitated, tucking her hair behind the ear. 'It's just that we've had a letter. From your husband in his official capacity as solicitor.'

Lissa grew still. 'What kind of letter?'

'It listed what we owe. Nick hit the roof. He didn't agree with the reckoning. Said we didn't owe half as much. Never seen him in such a fury.'

'There must be some mistake. I'll talk to Philip. Put it right. You can have as much time as you need.'

Lissa loved the feel of the wind in her hair. She ignored Philip's instructions these days and always let it fly free instead of screwing it up into a neat little French pleat. She loved the wind scouring her cheeks to a polished brightness, wishing she could cleanse her life as thoroughly.

She sat by the humped bridge and called to mind a picture of a laughing girl in her best frock waiting to meet her mother and grandmother for the first time. Now that grandmother was buried

451

and the dream with her. The regrets Lissa felt in this moment were not entirely selfish. Surely Rosemary Ellis had suffered more than anyone from her self-imposed bitterness? How sad that she'd denied herself the opportunity to know her own granddaughter.

Over a matter of principle and family honour, Rosemary Ellis had banished love from her life. Was that what would happen to her? Was it really for the sake of her children that she stayed with Philip, or because she wasn't quite brave enough to risk the scandal of leaving him? Could she start a new life, even without the benefit of divorce? Could she earn enough from her new business to keep them? Could she face the gossip and the snide remarks if she took Derry for a lover and lived with him unwed?

And would Derry even want her under such conditions?

If she lacked the courage to do any of these things, would she then end up as a bitter and lonely old woman, as Rosemary Ellis had been? The prospect made her shudder.

She met Philip on his way back from Larkrigg.

'Are you still thinking of moving us in there?' she asked, eyes troubled.

'That depends.'

'On what?'

'On you. Don't think I haven't seen the way you look at Derry Colwith. I won't let you go, Lissa. Not now, not ever.' He sounded so reasonable.

'What if I say I've had enough of this marriage. That I would prefer any man but you?'

He took hold of the front of her jacket and pulled her gently towards him, pushing his face close in to hers. Yet still he smiled. 'If you leave me, or take a lover, you can kiss goodbye to your beloved dale. And your precious shop.'

She tried to laugh, sound amused and incredulous, anxious to disguise the sudden spurt of fear. 'What are you talking about?'

'Let me make it quite plain that Broomdale is only safe so long as I permit it to remain so.'

'You don't have that kind of power.'

'Oh, but I do. One word from me and Winster would be forgotten. It would be Broomdale you'd be fighting to save then. All that lovely fresh water would be washing over your old home, swamping Broombank and Ashlea, your precious home.'

Lissa gasped.' Is this why you're hounding Nick about the mortgage on Ashlea? I'd rather you didn't. He'll catch up with any late payments, given time.'

'*You'd* rather?'

'Yes, *me*. Ashlea does belong to me, if you recall.'

He stared at her, then laughed. 'Soft-hearted as ever, I see, and you think you can make yourself into a businesswoman? Close your silly little shop, dear wife. I can get much more money by letting them flood the whole valley. We'd get compensation for Ashlea, and I have a buyer already lined up for Larkrigg who would dearly like to turn it

453

into an on-site hotel, high on the ridge there. Water sports are the coming thing.'

She desperately tried not to show her fear. 'You wouldn't dare!'

'Don't test me.' He smoothed down the collar of her jacket with a caressing hand, enjoying the satisfaction of seeing her face grow pale, the awful realisation of his power dawn in her beautiful eyes. But then he had always loved power. Over Felicity, over his own mother because his father had been so useless, and now over Lissa. It had to be this way. She must learn that.

Lissa tossed her head. 'You can't do it. Larkrigg belongs to the twins.'

'Rosemary left me in charge, as their guardian. If I decide it would be a good investment to sell, then I'll sell.'

Lissa couldn't care less what he did with Larkrigg Hall. Hadn't she always hated it? Broombank and Ashlea were another matter. 'How can you influence Manchester Water Board?'

'One greedy little consultant with sticky fingers and a demanding mother who will do anything for money. He thinks the project sounds feasible and is looking into it. A dam could easily be built across the head of the dale.' Philip's lips curled into a smile though it did not radiate any further as he took her arm and hooked it in to his. 'You know how I like to be in control.'

Withdrawing the arm with a grimace of repugnance, Lissa stepped back and faced him, her expression as cold and hard as his own. 'You can't control me, Philip. Not any longer. I've broken free. You might as well know I intend to create my own independence and a new future for myself.'

'And take Derry Colwith for a lover no doubt?'

'I never said so.' Lissa could feel the trap closing in upon her. It tightened her rib cage and made her breath tighten to a hard ball in her breast. She was silent for some moments then she met his assessing gaze with her own steady one. 'If I remain, as your wife, for the sake of the twins, you must promise to drop this idea.'

'Ah, promises.'

'You must, Philip. If you do not, I'll fight you every inch of the way.'

He smiled. 'And if I make this promise to leave your precious dale alone?'

She swallowed. 'Then in return – I'll stay – only on my terms. After we leave here I shall want a bedroom of my own. A separate life. Keeping up appearances, isn't that the phrase?'

He looked vaguely nonplussed by her defiance and new air of assurance, as if she'd caught him off balance for once. Then the skin about his mouth tightened and the lip curled in a snarl of distaste. 'Sounds very like an ultimatum.'

'Call it what you wish.'

'Then remember mine. Or the price might be more than you are willing to pay. Certainly more than your precious family would be prepared for.

You are exclusively mine, Lissa, and I intend to keep you that way.'

They stood on the quiet hillside and stared into each other's eyes while Lissa felt the joy of victory slip from her heart and the trap snap shut.

'Checkmate, I think?'

It was one of the bleakest of moments of her life. Something inside of her quietly died, but Lissa knew she must give Derry up. There was no help for it. Oh, but she must see him one last time, to explain this new turn of events.

As she was collecting cups at teatime she whispered desperately in his ear. 'I must see you. By the tarn, later,' without glancing up from her task.

Perhaps a madness had come over her but as darkness fell, Lissa pleaded a headache and went early to bed. Philip followed soon after, as she guessed he might, but she kept very firmly to her side of the bed as he climbed in beside her.

'Are you tired, my sweet?'

'I think I'm starting with a cold.'

She lay, not daring to move, for what seemed like hours, telling herself this was the last time she would ever share a bed with him. Tomorrow she would move all her things into the spare bedroom. Or better still, all *his* things.

Only when she was certain of Philip's deep breathing and gentle snores, did she slip from the bed. Pulling on a wrap, Lissa quietly let herself out of the house.

There was no moon but she could have found her way blindfold. The night enfolded her like soft black velvet and she moved surely up the sheep trods, through the stand of trees at Brockbarrow woods and on to the tarn beyond. Excitement beat hard and sure in her breast, and the awareness of danger was strong in her. Yet she could no more have denied herself from taking this risk than her next breath.

He was waiting for her by the glittering black and silver water and Lissa went straight into his arms.

Breathless from kissing they sat with their backs against the warm trunk of a rowan and Derry stroked her cheek, her throat, with his lips and fingers, not able to get enough of her.

'Darling Lissa, how I love you.' He kissed her again, his mouth soft and sweetly compelling. 'I always will.'

'You know that it's not enough simply to love each other, don't you? I have the twins to think of.' She explained then, carefully and in a matter-of-fact sort of voice, how she had taken advice from her doctor, a lawyer, even Miss Stevens. She looked at him with tired resignation in her lovely eyes. 'There's no help for it. If I leave Philip, they would call me an unfit mother and I could lose the children. I daren't risk that.'

Derry was silent. Only the sound of water lapping softly against stones disturbed their thoughts.

'What if I promise to be as good a father to them as he would be?'

Lissa gazed into Derry's beloved face. 'You'd

probably make a better and he'd hate you more than ever.' She didn't feel she could mention Philip's blackmail concerning the dale. Derry might react badly to the threatened loss of his sister's home and make matters worse. Besides, if she had to sacrifice Derry in any case, for her children, why trouble him with it? The problem needn't arise. 'Philip is a difficult man. He would always win. I have to make the best of things as they are. He and I have agreed terms. There's nothing more I can do.'

'Terms? What kind of terms?' Anger etched with despair was in his voice. 'A farce of a marriage, you mean? What kind of life is that? You love me, as I love you.'

'You must go back to America, Derry. Forget you ever saw me again. As I must you.'

'Come with me. We can start a new life, take on a new identity if you wish. Philip Brandon would never find us.'

'Looking over my shoulder for the rest of my life? No, I can't do that. Afraid for the twins every time they're late home from school? I must accept what cannot be altered.'

His eyes glittered in the darkness, though whether with anger or tears Lissa couldn't have said, but she felt his pain. 'I'm sorry, Derry.'

'So am I. How shall I ever live without you after this? I need you, Lissa.' His mouth came down hard upon her own and for a moment she gave herself up to the savage joy of his loving.

'Please don't,' she moaned. 'Don't ask for more than I can offer.'

They were breathless with wanting, afire with need, afraid of going too far and unable to break apart. His lips trailed over her throat and down to her breast as Lissa arched her body to let him kiss her some more, a burning ache in her stomach making her shiver with unspent emotion. Oh, how she wanted to give herself to him completely, for now and for all time. But how could she? She was married. Philip would be sure to find out and use it against her. And against her family.

She pulled away, ineffectually tidying her hair and trying not to see the dark need in his eyes. 'We'll make a wish,' she said, half laughing at the childhood memory. 'Come with me.'

Lissa took him to the edge of the tarn and, cupping her hands, filled them with water. 'Quickly! You must drink from my hands and make a wish before the water soaks away. Nick and I used to do it when we were children. Quick. Close your eyes.'

Laughing, Derry did so. 'Shall I tell you what I wished?'

'No, or it won't come true. Now my turn.'

She drank deeply from his hands and wished for happiness, pure and simple, for herself and her babies. Impossible. Hadn't she given up wishing long since?

They dried their hands on the grass and lay together, not touching now, staring up into a midnight blue sky, counting stars.

'You do intend to leave him eventually though?'

Lissa was silent for a long time, then uttered a deep sigh. 'I don't know. How can I say what the future holds? I would like to. Perhaps one day, if I could make a home and provide for my children without risk of losing them, then I would do so. But I have no grounds for divorce. None that the law will recognise. I've been into all of that. He would never hurt or leave them, or me. We are his life. He won't let me go.'

'And you won't fight him?' His voice sounded uncharacteristically harsh, and Lissa turned her face away to hide the spasm of pain it caused.

'Don't blame me too harshly, Derry. I cope as best I can but what is the point of fighting if I can never win?'

'You want me simply to pack up and go?'

'No.' She sat up, her heart breaking with the agony of it all. 'I can't bear to think of never seeing you again. But this is how it must be.'

Derry clenched his teeth. 'I couldn't bear to watch you with him, day after day. I'd kill him, I swear it.'

'I won't – sleep with him. That's all finished,' she said, wrapping her arms about Derry's neck, kissing him lingeringly on the mouth. 'I can only offer Philip duty now. That's part of the terms.'

They were silent for a long time after that, holding each other, content simply to be together and think through the reality of her decision. Then of one accord their gazes locked, saying everything that they could not.

'I won't go right away. I'll leave in a week or two,' Derry said. 'A month at most. As soon as I see that you are all right, and if we haven't thought of a solution in the meantime. Then I'll leave for America and that'll be the end.' He pulled her close, capturing the memory of this moment for all time, coming to terms with the harsh reality of a life without love.

'Oh, Derry,' and she surrendered herself one last time to his fevered kisses. But it was he who kept their emotions in check that night, he who held her in his arms until she slept, then gently woke her as a cold pink dawn streaked the sky.

Derry led her silently back to the house, steadying her when her feet slipped on the stones, both jumping with alarm when somewhere an owl hooted, then falling into a spurt of nervous laughter at their foolish fear.

Their parting kisses were painfully poignant for all they promised each other to meet one last time, like this, before he left England for good.

'I love you, Lissa.'

'And I you, Derry.'

She waited until he was quite out of sight down the lane, on his way back to Ashlea before she pushed open the kitchen door and slipped inside.

Lissa crept silently up the stairs, pulled open the creaking bedroom door with a shaking hand and slid beneath the bed clothes, certain that Philip had not missed her.

She was wrong.

'I know where you've been,' he said, his voice splintering the darkness like chips of ice. Didn't I warned you what would happen if you disobeyed me? What did he do to you?'

Lissa started to tremble. 'Nothing. We said goodbye, that's all.'

She made to get out of bed but he threw back the covers and straddled her, pinning back her arms when she would have pushed him away. 'Did you use any protection? The kind you've been using with me.'

Oh dear God, he knew.

'I've had an interesting conversation with Doc Robson.'

'He shouldn't have told you. That was confidential.'

'It was easy to persuade the silly old goat. You've made a fool out of me, Lissa, promising babies and then using a diaphragm to stop them. I don't like that. I don't like that one bit. And all this pretence of being too tired and feeling unwell. All lies. Well, you'll not cuckold me as well as deceive me. It's long past time I re-established my rights, don't you think? I'll show Derry Colwith whose wife you are.'

Then he pushed one hand flat across her mouth, laughing into her terrified eyes, while he pulled up her nightgown with the other. As he took her that night, forcing himself into her, he unleashed all the pent up frustration and ferocious anger he

462

usually kept so tightly buttoned. And when she cried out in her agony, despite his restraining hand and her efforts not to wake Meg, he told her she must be learning to show appreciation of his attentions at last.

'If this doesn't do the trick and bring babies, nothing will.'

Only when he was quite sated did he turn from her. Silent tears slid down Lissa's cheeks, dampening her pillow and running into her ear. This would be the last time, she promised herself. The very last. She fell into a troubled doze, her body bruised and her heart breaking.

When morning came Lissa found herself wide-eyed and staring, wondering if it had been the children who had cried out. But then a pain pierced her belly and she realised it had been her own cry that had awakened her. He was on top and inside of her again, grunting noisily in a sound that curdled her stomach.

When she protested, he wrapped her wrists in his pyjama cord and tied them to the bed head.

I warned you,' he told her, very quietly. 'You should have listened. Now you must learn by being punished.' Then he plunged into her, on and on, continuing to use her for his own pleasure whether she wanted him or not. As he had done even when she was asleep. It seemed, somehow, the final humiliation.

CHAPTER 24

White pointed sails bobbing on blue water beneath a sunlit blue sky. The sounds of happy laughter ringing across the lake, bounced back by the circling mountains. The hooting of the steamer taking a group of early-season trippers to a lakeside inn for lunch. Ducks quacking and squabbling over pieces of crust thrown to them by toddlers with an unsteady aim, the tramp of boots crunching on shingle. Any normal day by the lake. But not a normal day for Lissa.

She flew about her bedroom emptying drawers and cupboards, fingers fumbling with coat hangers. From the moment Philip had dropped them at the door and gone back to his office this morning, Lissa had been in a fever of activity. She had rung Renee to tell her she would not be into the shop but now, with her suitcases finally packed, she stared at them in some distress. How to get them out of the house? And there were still the twins to get ready and Nanny Sue to deal with.

Thrusting the cases back into her wardrobe she decided she would have to risk collecting them later. Perhaps she could ask Jimmy. All that mattered was that she get away.

She stood and gazed out at the happy scene, the blue and white image blurring in her tears. What a mess. Why couldn't she be happy as those people were happy? But this wasn't the moment for self-pity. She refused to be a victim any longer. The terms, so far as Lissa was concerned, had been broken. Now she must take her chances alone.

'I've decided to take the children out this morning,' she told Nanny Sue who at once frowned in disapproval.

'But it's very nearly their lunchtime.'

Lissa panicked, feeling the sweat start up between her breasts. Philip would be home for lunch. He would ring first, to check she was back from the shop. It had taken far too long to get ready but she couldn't stop now. She drew in a steadying breath. 'I'm taking them out to lunch. Miss Stevens is expecting us at twelve sharp,' she lied. 'Come along, my darlings, wash your hands and find your favourite doll or teddy to come with us. We are going to have a picnic.'

Squeals of excitement and much running about and demands to change clothes, choose another toy or take a bicycle. Lissa refused all requests, keenly aware, beneath Nanny's gimlet gaze, that time was of the essence.

'Say bye-bye to Nanny,' she called cheerily, trying not to appear in a hurry as she piled them into the old van. Where could she take them? Certainly not to Miss Stevens. It wouldn't be right to involve her in matrimonial disputes. Nab Cottage perhaps? No, Renee would not be there. Besides, that would be the first place Philip would look. The shop then. There was nothing else for it but the rooms over the shop. Stella Stevens would have to be placated about that too, in the end.

But first the promised picnic. Lissa stopped at a bakery and bought doughnuts and tiny sausage rolls, a stick of bread, a packet of cream cheese portions, and some Grasmere gingerbread. Far too much in her panic. The twins were delighted.

'Can we have Coca-Cola?' A special treat, reminding Lissa of her teenage years.

They ate the picnic by the lake. At least the twins did, Lissa's throat refused to swallow a morsel. And then they must play the twins' favourite games. Hide and Seek among the trees, The Big Ship Sails through the Alley-Alley-Oh. Going through the motions of normality when inside she was falling apart.

Derry was waiting on the doorstep of Nab Cottage when Renee arrived home to lunch. He seemed strangely silent, unlike his usual self, so she chatted on, saying how it made a nice break to have lunch at home in her otherwise busy day. They sat in the small parlour sipping tea and eating the potted beef sandwiches she had prepared, cut into triangles and spaced out neatly on a blue and white striped plate.

'Do you like the new style? You never said, when you called before.'

Derry glanced vaguely about him, trying to sound interested. 'It looks very smart.'

'I'm a girl of the sixties now,' Renee said proudly. 'With a career. But I spend my money on our home. Jimmy likes it to be comfortable.'

Gone was the brown-tiled fireplace, replaced by a neat electric fire in a teak surround. The old orange-spattered walls were now a pale cream, one of them decked out with black glass and chrome fittings on which reposed a record player, a battery of speakers, and a stack of records. Above hung a picture of a pretty Chinese girl and a photograph of Jimmy with his boat on the lake.

'I'm glad you're doing well, Renee,' Derry said and was surprised to find that he meant it. She looked different too. The orange lipstick had been replaced by palest pink against a flawless, cream-tinted skin. The red hair was puffed out on top in the new bouffant style, tucked up at the nape of her neck with a tortoiseshell comb. She looked attractive, and surprisingly smart and tidy in a neat trouser suit of pale green linen. 'Dad looks well too, happier than I've ever seen him.' He gave her a wry grin. 'I can see I was wrong about you two.'

Renee's eyes glimmered. 'Odd couple we may be, but well suited, eh?' she said dryly.

'Something like that. It all seems to have worked out right anyway.'

Renee recognised the haunting sadness in his voice. 'You haven't done so badly yourself. Got a good job in a top agency. Making loads of money by the looks of you. Swanky car back home, eh? Fancy house, I shouldn't wonder.'

Derry's eyes were bleak as they looked anywhere but into hers. 'I've done all right. I was near starvation at one time, then a guy took pity on me and gave me a job as a gofer.'

'Gofer.'

'Go for this, go for that. It's an American term.'

Renee chortled with glee. 'I like it. And the rest is history, eh?'

'I worked my way up, with hard graft and lots of boot licking. Now I'm a partner in the business. I enjoy the work, feel like I'm doing some good helping the poor over-optimistic souls to get going in the music trade on the right terms. Or gently letting down those who'll never make it.'

'So your training as a lawyer's clerk has come in handy after all?'

'I suppose it has.' He set aside a half eaten sandwich and flopped back in the chair, clenching his fists on a spurt of anger. 'But what's the good of being successful when you can't have the one thing you need most in all the world?'

'Lissa?'

'Lissa.'

They were both silent for a long moment, even the loquacious Renee lost for words. He stood up. 'I have to go. I wanted to ask you . . .'

Renee looked up at him with a smile, her eyes kind. 'Ask away, lad.'

'Look after her for me, that's all. I'll be staying at Ashlea for a week or two yet, till I'm sure she's OK. Then I'd like to spend a day or two here, with Dad, before I leave.'

'Yes to both requests. You're always welcome here, it's your second home. No more garden sheds, I promise.'

He laughed fondly at the memory but then saw that she wasn't joining in. 'It's all right,' he said, grinning. 'I bear no grudges. I probably deserved to be turfed out, behaving with typical teenage arrogance and total lack of consideration at the time.'

'No, it's not that.' Renee got up and started to tidy and smooth the blue and yellow scatter cushions on an already immaculate sofa. She spoke quickly as if to get it done with. 'I never mentioned it to your dad but I went to see Philip Brandon. I told him I wanted you out from under my feet. That Jimmy and me wanted to be on us own. It was Philip Brandon's idea to put you in the shed. He said he'd encourage you to find a place of your own.' She slanted a glance across at Derry, saw his frozen expression.

'I only wanted him to give you a raise,' she explained. 'So's you'd have enough to pay the rent. And to ask his advice on doing bed and breakfast.'

'Instead of which he made up a tale about my damaging his yacht and sacked me on the spot.'

Renee looked horrified. 'Oh, my giddy aunt! It's

469

worse than I thought. Why didn't you tell us? Did he threaten you with the police?'

'Yep.'

'So that's why you left?'

'That's why I left. That and my own arrogant ambition.'

Renee gazed at him, stricken, realising how they'd both been manipulated. 'He wanted Lissa. That's what it was all about. He'd fancied her for a long while. By heck, it's obvious now, isn't it?'

'I was all too aware of his interest. Jealous as hell I was. Only I was too wrapped up in my own ambitions, silly dreams really, to do anything about it. I stupidly thought she'd wait for me. But then it didn't work out and I couldn't come back to her a failure, could I? When I did it was too late. Philip Brandon had won.'

He sank back into his chair and Renee went to him and patted his shoulder, feeling helpless in his despair. 'What could you have done? You'd no money to fight him. Lissa chose to wed him. A mistake she now regrets and can't get out of. I've known there was summat up for ages, though it took her a while to admit to it. And it's mebbe all my fault. Oh dear God!'

'It would still have happened, Renee, with or without your complicity. And, no, I won't tell Dad you had anything to do with it, if that's what's worrying you. You don't need to blame yourself.'

Renee blinked away the prick of tears. 'That's

the nicest thing you've ever said to me. It took me ages to pacify him after your last visit.'

They both gave an embarrassed laugh at the memory of their impromptu kiss.

'You're all right, Renee, you know that?'

'Bone-head, that's me. But you don't have to worry. I'll keep an eye out for her. It'll all come to a head soon enough, you see if it don't.'

'If he treats her badly, I'll . . .'

'Don't say it. It'll do no good. Don't even think it. Now I'd best get back to work or I'll be given my cards.'

'I've done it, Renee. I've left him.'

Renee stared at Lissa in disbelief, and at the two children beside her, faces daubed with jam, innocent of their new status in life. 'Crikey, I never thought you had it in you.'

'We had a lovely picnic, Renee.'

'And Mummy says we can sleep at the shop tonight.'

'Orphans in the storm, eh?'

'There's so much I have to arrange. My luggage, for one thing. Two suitcases in my wardrobe. Do you think Jimmy would collect them for me? He'd have to go this afternoon, while Philip is in the office and Nanny is out on her walk.'

'I'll see to it.'

'Is it clean upstairs, do you think?'

'Clean enough.'

'Oh, I have so many plans, Renee. I'm going to

live up there, if Miss Stevens is agreeable. Develop the business, and be independent at last.'

Alarmed by the feverish brightness of Lissa's chatter, Renee put out a gentle hand. 'Let's get these bairns cleaned up and seen to first, shall we?'

By half-past five the shop was locked up for the day. The children had been fed and put early to bed, unprotesting for once because of the novelty of being in sleeping bags on the floor of a tiny room above the shop.

'Is this a real adventure, Mummy?'

'Yes, my darlings. A real adventure.'

'Will Daddy be coming to share it?' Beth wanted to know.

'Not tonight. Now close your eyes. You've had a busy few days. Far too much excitement.' She kissed each soft round cheek, left a small night lamp lit and crept downstairs with a sigh of relief. 'I'll count up the takings tonight, Renee. You must be worn out.'

'Not too bad. That new girl is shaping up pretty well. Been busy though. Sold three of those new quilted jackets.'

'That's good.' Lissa struggled to find the necessary enthusiasm as she clasped and unclasped her hands, unable to resist glancing at the door.

'Do you think he'll come?' Renee asked.

'I-I don't know. I hope not. I don't think I could take any more just now.'

'Did you leave a note?'

Lissa swallowed and managed a brief nod.

472

'I'll stay with you,' Renee decided.

'There's no need. I'll be fine.'

'Nevertheless I'm staying. I'll go and explain to our Jimmy, then I'll be straight back.' She grinned. 'Have you had any supper?'

Lissa shook her head.

'I'll fetch some fish and chips and a couple of beers. We'll have a party to celebrate your freedom. Why not?'

'Why not?' Lissa grinned back, trying to recapture her earlier mood of optimism.

They drank the bottled beer and ate the fish and chips, licking salt and vinegar from their fingers like giggling children. Renee insisted on staying until it was quite late before finally being persuaded to go home to Jimmy. Then Lissa climbed the stairs on weary feet, putting out the lights as she went. She was glad to be alone at last, wanting to think, work out what was best to be done, but her mind was too tired to function.

She scrubbed her face and teeth, dragged a brush through her long hair and softly kissed each sleeping twin. Then she climbed into her own improvised sleeping bag with a sigh of relief. It felt strange, and oddly exhilarating. Whatever the future brought, she would face it.

It was five past midnight when she heard the hammering on the door. Lissa struggled from her bed, rubbing the sleep from her eyes and went to the landing window.

473

Philip stood below, at the door. She pushed open the tiny window and called down, as quietly as she could so as not to wake the twins.

'What are you doing here at this time?'

'I need to talk to you. Open the door, Lissa.'

'No, Philip. I can't talk now. I won't talk now. Perhaps in the morning. Or when I feel ready.' She started to close the window when he thumped his fist against the door. The noise echoed in the empty street.

'Don't you walk away from me when I'm talking to you. You are my wife, and will obey me. Come home at once.'

'It's no good shouting, Philip, I'm not coming home.'

'I never shout.'

'No, you don't, do you? But you give plenty of orders. Unfortunately I'm not prepared to obey them any more.'

He raised two clenched fists, looking for a moment like a man ready to beat in the door if he had to. 'Where are my children? I insist on seeing my children.'

She told him, with surprising calm, that they were asleep. 'I need my sleep too. We'll talk tomorrow, Philip. There are a number of things we ought to discuss, including a divorce.' Whereupon she closed the window firmly on his silent rage.

He did not come in the morning, nor the next day, nor the day after that, and Lissa began to worry what he was up to. Her feeling of victory evaporated, almost to the extent of wishing the reckless words unsaid. She knew it would not be easy to start again from scratch, to face the gossip and snide remarks. A strange malaise came over her. She felt too ashamed even to go out. Her marriage had failed and she could not bring herself to walk down the street. She felt sure that everyone would see her shame and remark upon it. They would say that it was her fault, that she was never able to keep anyone's love, that there must be something wrong with her.

Derry called but she sent him away. 'It isn't safe. Don't come here again. My case is weak enough. If Philip were to find you I can't answer for the consequences. I must think of the children.'

Renee proved to be a tower of strength. Together they scrubbed and cleaned, tidied and decorated, turning two rooms and a small wash-room into a presentable home. The twins joined in with exuberance, not understanding anything that was going on. Renee lent Lissa a few odd pieces of furniture and carpet she'd borrowed from friends and neighbours. Then she and Jimmy carried up a table and three chairs from the stock room.

'They're not exactly polished mahogany but they'll do for now.'

'Everything's wonderful, Renee. I'm so grateful.'

'Are we going to live here?' Sarah demanded, her small heart-shaped face a mask of affronted dignity, as if she should have been consulted on the subject. 'Where will Nanny Sue sleep?'

'And Daddy?' put in Beth.

'I'll explain later,' Lissa said, wondering how these matters could ever be satisfactorily explained to a four year old. She pushed back an untidy lock of hair, thinking how dreadful she must look since she'd hardly had time to attend to herself recently. She spread out her hands and frowned at the nails, broken and chipped, the pink varnish peeling. Philip would not approve, and then her heart flooded with relief. It didn't matter what Philip thought. He didn't control her any more. She found a pair of scissors and began to cut them.

'What are you doing?' Sarah, ever curious, wanted to know.

'Cutting my nails, darling. They get in the way when I'm working. And I must work very hard in future.' She would tell them soon, she thought, when she'd finalised her plans.

And all this on top of what was proving to be a busier season than they'd ever hoped for. At least Lissa no longer had to hide herself away in the office. She could take a full and active part in the day to day running of the shop.

It was well into August before she found time to make an appointment to see her solicitor and tell him the news. He seemed less than pleased and kept plucking at his lower lip, making worried little noises. 'Such a pity that you walked out on him, Mrs Brandon. Dear, dear. So difficult.'

'I've asked Philip for a divorce and he has gone away to consider the matter.'

He had yet to acknowledge her request but Lissa was determined to think positive. He'd stormed off in the middle of that first night, but he would be forced to consider it, wouldn't he, in the end?

'Hmm,' said the young solicitor and proceeded to repeat his warning that the divorce law, as it stood at present, was not favourable to her case. 'There must be no sign of complicity between you. It was misguided to leave. Much better had it been the other way around.'

She told him what Philip had done on their last night together. The solicitor seemed remarkably unimpressed.

'As I explained before, Mrs Brandon, deficiencies in the bedchamber are hardly grounds. Many people indulge in such games. Consenting adults and all that.'

'But that's the whole point. It wasn't a game, and I didn't consent.'

'Did he hit you?'

'No.'

'Hm, so no bruises then.' He seemed disappointed. 'You are his wife, you see. Most judges would consider that complicity enough. They simply would refuse to grant a divorce on those grounds.'

'The marriage is over.' Lissa felt as if she were

battering her head against a brick wall yet knew the fault was not with the solicitor, who was only doing his job. 'He rules my life, my thinking, he suffocates me and I can't stand it any more.'

The solicitor offered his sympathies but declared himself unable to change the law. 'It is government policy not to make divorce too easy or the courts would be full of women wanting their freedom, claiming their rights.' He laughed with slight embarrassment and Lissa could only grit her teeth with vexation.

'Then what can I do?'

'Leave it with me for a while. I'll give the matter some thought, perhaps take counsel's opinion. We'll do what we can.' He spread his hands then quietly clasped them, concluding the matter. 'I'll write to your husband, sound out his feelings.'

She offered her thanks and got up to go. 'He will, of course, be entitled to access.'

'Access?'

'To the children. Perhaps every Saturday or Sunday. That is the usual method.'

Dear God, of course, access. 'I couldn't possibly allow him take them away.' How did she know that he would bring them back?

The solicitor looked surprised. 'I'm afraid you must. It is his right.'

Lissa was almost choking with fear. Couldn't the man see what Philip was like? He would take the twins simply to spite her, to use them as a pawn to control her, as he so liked to do. 'What about my rights as a mother? Can't it wait until this divorce question is settled?'

He took her elbow and led her to the door. 'Don't worry, Mrs Brandon. He's a man of honour. You surely don't imagine he would hurt them, do you?'

'No, of course not, but use them as a weapon against me.'

A smile and a pat on her hand. 'I very much doubt it. I'll be in touch. Good day.'

The bus took for ever on the journey back to Carreckwater. It crawled through every village, stopping frequently, the bus conductor chatting with everyone who got on and off as if there were all the time in the world. But there wasn't. She'd foolishly left her children behind, and though Lissa trusted Renee implicitly, how would she cope if Philip took it into his head to come for them? Lissa decided never to let them out of her sight again.

'They're in the stock room trying on hats,' Renee told her, concerned by Lissa's high state of anxiety. 'They'll come to no harm with Aunty Renee. I'd soon see that one off, should he turn up again.'

'I'm so sorry for doubting you.'

'There now, I'm almost forgetting. Jan rang, seemed in a bit of a lather. Will you ring the moment you get in? she says.'

Lissa pulled off her coat and smiled at Renee, shamefaced. 'Any tea going?'

'That's more like it. Look after the shop, Julie, and call me if you've any problems. And try not to get in a muddle with that new till.'

'Yes, Mrs Colwith,' said the young girl, trying to look important. Lissa dialled the number for Ashlea, wondering if perhaps there was some problem with Meg or Tam. Surely not, they'd seemed in the peak of health last time she'd visited.

'Hello?' Jan's voice, frail and anxious, came on the phone and Lissa's fears increased.

'We've had another letter. He's foreclosed on us, Lissa. He's evicting us, turning us out. Sally Ann is nearly having a heart attack here, and Nick has stormed off threatening blue murder.'

'Evicted? What are you talking about?'

'I'm talking about your husband turning us out on the streets. Well, on to the open fell.'

Lissa could hardly believe what she was hearing and managed, at last, to say as much.

'Why? That's what we want to know.' Jan's voice was growing hysterical. 'You promised to give us time and we've made some extra payments recently. We were catching up nicely, only he says we're further behind than we think and he won't give us any more time. Why, Lissa? What have we ever done to you?'

Lissa's heart was beating twenty to the dozen and she felt suddenly sick. It was perfectly plain how Philip's mind was working. 'You haven't done anything, Jan. I'm the one who has upset him and he's taking his revenge out on you. Only he won't

480

succeed. I won't let him. I'll fight him over this, I promise.'

'You'd better. God knows where we'll go, what we'll do, if we lose the farm. Things were just starting to improve then . . .' Tears drowned her next words and it took some time for Lissa to calm her down before she could ring off.

Lissa rang her new solicitor right away and told him to get the eviction order quashed and to take all her financial affairs away from her husband. She wondered why she hadn't thought to do that in the first place.

'Surely he can do nothing without my signature?' The solicitor agreed, and saw no reason why the matter couldn't be satisfactorily settled.

Lissa immediately rang Jan and told her the good news but when she'd rung off this time, wished with all her heart that her own affairs could be so easily settled.

Philip had very efficiently proved that he still held power over her. He'd demonstrated that he could, and would, carry out his threats. First Ashlea, next Broombank? Would he also successfully persuade Manchester Water Board to choose Broomdale as a site for their reservoir. Ruin two good farms out of revenge, and line his own pocket in the process?

Almost worse than all of that was his most dire threat of all. He would never let her go. Never.

481

CHAPTER 25

Autumn had passed and winter was approaching. There was a sharpness in the air that nipped at small fingers and toes but the twins were not short of warm woollens to keep them warm. Jan had made Sarah a red knitted coat and hat with a tasselled scarf that wound round and round her neck, and Beth a blue set, exactly the same. The twins wore them every day with pride, and to show off to their friends at the infant school they attended. Lissa was selling such items well in the shop too, while helping Jan earn a bit extra money.

The twins were learning to read and do sums, which made them feel very grown up. But it was still difficult sometimes to understand about adult things, like why a mummy and daddy lived in two different places.

Sarah had asked once or twice but got no answer that quite made sense. She missed Nanny Sue and the clean starchy smell of her apron but Beth missed Daddy most of all. Beth was Daddy's pet. Sometimes, on a Sunday, he would come and take them for a walk or to play in the park. But only for a short while. Then he would leave them with Nanny Sue and go back to his office to work. He was a very busy and important man.

The first time had been the worst. Mummy's lip had trembled like when Beth fell down and didn't want to show how it hurt. Sarah knew she hadn't wanted to let them go but Daddy had insisted. So Sarah hadn't enjoyed herself that day, thinking that Mummy might be at home, crying. She'd refused to speak afterwards, just to show she could please herself who she wished to be friends with.

But it was better now. Mummy said she knew that the twins were safe with Daddy, and would always come back, which had puzzled Sarah for a long time. How could they not be safe with Daddy?

'It will soon be all over,' he promised them. 'Then we can be together always.'

But it wasn't over. New beds had been bought for them, their bedroom walls decorated with Magic Roundabout pictures and there was no talk of going back to their house on the Parade.

Sarah didn't really mind. She quite liked living above the shop and Renee was fun. She let them play with the till sometimes and help wrap things in tissue paper for the customers.

But they both missed their big garden at home, their sand pit and swing. It seemed mean of Mummy not to let them go there more often. But she was happier these days, always laughing and singing as she worked in the shop, playing games with them. Much more fun. She would let them sit up sometimes and watch Mr Pastry on television, or eat dinner with a candle on the table as if it were a real dinner party and they were grown ups.

At other times she was too tired to be bothered and then Sarah worried. Why did she work so hard? Why was she always on the telephone or buzzing about in the van just when they needed her? It wasn't fair that both Mummy and Daddy should work so hard. But whenever Sarah complained, Mummy would only smile and tell her that she had to earn a living, didn't she, to buy them all the bread and jam and cake they liked to eat.

Perhaps it was something they had done? Did they cost a lot of money to keep? And what would happen if they grew and got too expensive to keep? Sarah worried. Perhaps if they gave up cakes for tea or saved up their pocket money to pay for the Magic Roundabout pictures? Perhaps then Mummy could afford to keep them. Or they could ask Daddy for more help.

'Is it my fault Daddy doesn't want us to live with him any more?' she ventured to ask one night. Mummy had just finished telling them the tale of the Three Little Pigs and was tucking Beth up and tickling her, so was in a jolly mood.

She looked surprised and troubled by the question. 'Darling, no, of course not. He does still want us. He does love you. It's simply that we can't be happy together. Sometimes that happens with a Mummy and a Daddy. It has nothing to do with you two. It isn't your fault, my darlings.' And she kissed them both again which made Sarah feel better.

'You love Derry, don't you?' Beth said calmly, and Lissa started. Could the child be quite so astute or was she only repeating what she had heard? Her next words confirmed her worst suspicions. 'Daddy says Derry Colwith has spoiled our lives and will be the death of us all.'

'Oh, Beth, what a dreadful thing for Daddy to say!' Lissa burst out, aghast. 'That simply isn't true. I've known Derry for a long time, since I was a young girl in fact. He's an old friend, that's all.' Two pairs of questioning eyes, one grey, one blue, regarded her with uncanny shrewdness.

'Are you going to marry him instead of Daddy?' Sarah asked, frowning and feeling that odd, uncertain feeling somewhere in her tummy.

'No, of course not,' Lissa hastily assured them and felt suddenly intensely cold, and rather sick. What had Philip been doing? Was he deliberately trying to poison the twins' minds against Derry? 'Anyway,' she laughed, 'would it be so very terrible? Derry is nice and good fun. You'd like him.'

'We like Daddy,' Beth said, pursing her small mouth.

'Of course you do, darling. And I love you both, that's all that matters, isn't it?'

Twin smiles, heads nodding, eyes wide and dark from tiredness. 'Then leave these matters to

Mummy and Daddy to worry over. Go to sleep both of you, it's very late.'

Despite her natural worries about the twins, and the inevitable confusion they suffered, Lissa was certain they would settle eventually. 'It's working fine,' she told Renee. 'Philip's accepted the separation better than I could ever have hoped for.'

Even if there never is a divorce, she thought, I'm happier here, in my private world above the shop, than in the awful pretence of marriage with him. I have my lovely girls, and the excitement of running my own business. What more could I want?

Now that she was free of Philip's critical restrictions, Lissa felt as if she had emerged from a long dark tunnel and found life shining and new at the end of it.

The one flaw, which yawned wide and dark and empty, was her longing for Derry, which never for a moment eased. He was still staying with Jimmy and Renee, seemingly reluctant to leave. Lissa took care never to mention him to Renee, nor did he ever call at the flat or ring her.

But it would have been easier to deny herself breath than not to see him. They continued to meet, infrequently, and in secret, on the quiet fells of Broomdale. Never by the lake in case Philip should see them. There they could walk together without fear of being disturbed. It was the one place Lissa felt safe. On those days, as today, she told no one of her visit, not even Meg. And she chose a time when the twins were in school.

'We really shouldn't be doing this,' she told him now, slipping her arms about his neck and laying her cheek against his chest so she could breathe in the crisp, clean scent of him. 'If Philip were to find out, I could lose everything.'

'He won't. I've missed you Lissa. It must be a whole week since I held you like this.' One hand gently cupped her breast and fire shot through her, making her gasp with pleasure and fierce need. How could she bear not to love him totally when she wanted him so much? Why did she stick so stubbornly to her worn out marriage vows? She worried that he would grow tired of her and leave, and how could she bear to lose him?

'I used to think I was frigid,' she told him, lifting her mouth to his, and blushed as she saw his eyes kindle with excitement, his arms tightening instinctively about her. For a long while they had no breath left for talking.

'Frigid my giddy aunt! Depends who's doing the asking,' and she laughed.

'I want you so much I could take you here and now upon the heather.' He slipped his hand beneath her sweater so he could smooth the silken skin of her back and then beneath her bra to caress the luscious softness of her breast. It peaked hard and wanting beneath his fingers.

Lissa never resisted his caresses, giving a soft groan and pressing her body closer, even as she protested. 'We mustn't, Derry. Don't ask. Please.' As always they would break apart, tense and troubled, to walk in silence and try not to touch each other. It was ever this way, but after a few yards their fingers would interlock, their bodies sway together again and moments later his arm would creep about her waist and she would lean her head on his shoulder with a happy sigh.

'When you go away will you forget me?' she asked, breathless with pain as she waited for his reply.

'Yes,' he teased. 'Instantly,' making her laugh. How is the divorce progressing? Will Philip ever let you go?'

Lissa turned her head away, her face tightening. 'I don't honestly know. Perhaps, when the twins are grown. For now I've given up hope. What grounds do I have? He hasn't been cruel or unfaithful or anything, and would take me back tomorrow like a shot. Everyone thinks him charming and handsome and well mannered, and that I must be mad to leave him.'

'And a bastard.'

'Derry.'

'Isn't he?'

She stared at the ground and kicked at a stone. 'Let's walk and not talk about him, you know it only upsets me.' Silence again, more strained this time.

After a time they stopped and leaned on a stile to gaze out at the mountains. Coppergill Pass, and its neighbour Dundale Knot, its bowed head wreathed in grey mist like a vicar's collar. The escarpment below the summit was pock-marked with old mine workings, grooved by shifting ice, plunging downward to the valley floor and a patchwork of green fields and grey stone walls. Sheep stood about, peacefully chewing or resting in the sweet grass, undisturbed by the two lover's quiet presence.

'I love this place,' she said.

Lissa still hadn't told Derry of Philip's threat to persuade the water consultant to choose this dale for the reservoir. She hadn't told anyone, hoping that it would never happen, though it haunted her sometimes, at night. She had hurt Meg once before, she couldn't bear to do that again. But she risked so much by continuing to see Derry. Too much.'

The water consultant was no longer living at Nab Cottage and Lissa hoped that Philip had forgotten all about his dreadful threat. He certainly seemed to have accepted the situation and was not a problem to her these days. She scarcely had time to think about him anyway, as each day seemed filled with activity. But there was still that worry at the back of her head.

'Meg and her family have worked this land for generations. Grandfather Joe, and his father before him. Meg's old friend Lanky who left Broombank to her. And she scraped and saved, working all through the war to buy it and enough sheep to get her farm going. Sally Ann too had her struggles.

How would they bear it if they lost it?' But she didn't say, 'Because of me. Because of us.'

'Why should they? It won't ever happen.'

'I hope not.' Silence for a moment. 'Philip has been surprisingly quiet lately. I don't entirely trust him. Look what he tried to do to Nick and Jan. We must be careful. A shiver ran through her and Derry felt it. It gave him the strength to tell her what he must.

He rubbed his finger on a fringe of lichen that clothed the rough wooden post with a coat of velvet. 'I've been thinking that too. I don't want you, or the children, to suffer.' He took a deep breath. 'I've decided. I leave next Monday, on the morning train from Windermere.' He didn't look at her now, though he sensed her whole body stiffen. 'See if I still have a job to go to, eh?'

Lissa did not reply. She couldn't. Her throat seemed locked fast in pain.

'Seems we must both get on with our new lives.' There was such bitterness in his voice that she tried to soothe him, in spite of the tears blocking her throat, filling her eyes.

'It's for the best.' She turned away, knowing that if she stayed another moment she would beg him never to leave, and she dared not succumb to such wanton emotion. The risks were too high.

Derry stayed by the stile, watching her lithe figure walk away, her dark cloud of hair lifting in the breeze. When she reached the standing stones by the lane she turned and shielded her eyes to gaze back at him and lift an arm in a single wave. Then she climbed into her car and drove home to her twins while Derry looked back at the mountains, no longer able to see any beauty in the scene.

The next few days Lissa walked about in a daze. She had known, of course, that their idyll couldn't last. Hadn't they accepted long since that he must leave? What then had she expected or hoped for? That Derry's departure could be delayed indefinitely? Why? For what purpose? There was no solution to her problem, no escape from her marriage. Soon Derry would be gone and she would be alone.

Lissa was at her lowest ebb when Philip called to see her that following Sunday afternoon. The shop was closed, Renee was at Nab Cottage making something delicious, no doubt, for Jimmy's lunch. And the twins were in their beds having a short afternoon nap.

'Wake them in a moment. There's something I wish to discuss with you first.'

Lissa was at once on her guard, feeling alone and vulnerable. He usually sent Nanny Sue to collect the children, as he knew she made her feel more comfortable. She supposed it was the only reason he kept the woman on, and felt oddly grateful. 'I don't want any trouble, Philip. Please don't start any.'

'Have I caused any so far?'

'N-no.' Lissa hated herself for trembling and

drew in a deep breath, steadying her nerve. She had nothing to fear from Philip any more. No longer could he bully her or demolish her with a well-chosen piece of criticism. She was free of his cutting tongue at last.

'Then let us continue to be civilised about all of this, shall we?'

'I'm sorry. Would you like coffee, a cup of tea?'

He smiled. 'I would like you to sign this paper and I will go away and leave you in peace. For ever.'

She stared at it, white and rustling in his hand. 'What is it?'

'The divorce. Exactly what you've been asking for all these weeks. To be free. I've come to the realisation that there's little point in continuing with this sham of a marriage. I dislike bitterness and rancour. Surely we can be two modern-thinking adults and accept the inevitable?'

Excitement leapt in her breast. 'Oh, Philip, do you really mean it?'

'You only have to sign.'

Caution reasserted itself as she recalled how he could so carefully control her. 'But why this sudden decision to let me go?'

'Perhaps I don't like soiled goods.'

Lissa flushed deeply. 'Derry and I never – I swear I've kept my marriage vows.'

'But not in your mind.' He held out the paper, a frown of irritation on his handsome face as she took it from him. 'I deserve a wife who gives herself whole-heartedly, not grudgingly, as you have done. I'm not made of stone, Lissa. You've hurt me.'

She looked at him properly then and saw the sadness in his eyes, the etched lines of pain about his mouth and shame flooded through her. She rested her hand for a brief moment on his arm. 'I'm sorry.' Lissa knew she'd never loved him. No wonder their marriage had failed. Now she held the key to her freedom in her hand. She only had to sign and she would get her divorce. Derry wouldn't have to leave tomorrow and they could start a new life together. Hope started up deep inside, conflicting with the strange new pity she felt for her husband. 'I realise I've been an inadequate wife. You deserve better. We simply aren't suited, Philip.'

'You think Derry Colwith will suit you better? He'll let you down, in the end, as he did before.' There was a bitterness in his voice but Lissa only shook her head, her eyes soft with love.

'Stop it, Philip. You don't know him as I do. I'm sorry that I've hurt you by leaving. But you know there's no future for us together. I must be free.'

'Then let us not prolong the agony further.' He held out the pen.

Somewhere in her head a voice spoke to her. He's a solicitor and knows the law and you know nothing. She paused. 'Perhaps I should speak to my solicitor first.'

'I've sent him a copy. Let's make this as painless as possible, shall we? You may doubt my ability as a husband but surely not as a professional man? Either you want your freedom or you don't, but my time and patience are limited, as you well know.'

Her confidence evaporated in a cloud of confusion as it always did when he spoke to her in that dismissive way. Lissa recalled how his clients always changed into their best suit before keeping an appointment with him, never questioned his word. On matters concerning his profession he was surely entirely honourable. And if she hurried she could catch Derry before he left. She signed the paper and handed him back the pen with a smile of relief.

'At least we have the twins,' she said. 'We made a good job of them.'

'Yes,' he said, folding the paper and slipping it into his briefcase. 'We have the twins. Nanny will be along to collect them as usual. Make sure they are dressed warmly. We thought a little trip to Grasmere this afternoon.'

As she unlocked the shop door to let him out he took her hand in his. 'If you change your mind I'd take you back. These papers could be torn up. I'd never let you down, Lissa. Never.'

The urge to remove her hand from his grasp was compelling but Lissa felt she couldn't do so without seeming cruel and rude. She managed a smile. 'You've no need to worry over me. I'll be fine, thanks. Let's leave it at that, shall we?'

'As you wish. Two-thirty then for the twins, on the dot.'

'Two-thirty.'

She had the twins ready in their new hooded jackets when Nanny called. Lissa kissed each in turn, making sure their mittens, hanging on a tape threaded through their knitted coat, were fitted on each small hand. 'No taking them off now,' she warned. 'It's quite cold out.' Lissa smiled at Nanny Sue. 'Watch Beth, she might be starting with a cold. Perhaps she shouldn't come with you.'

'Fresh air never did a cold any harm,' said the starchy nanny, well wrapped up in her grey overcoat, hat and warm scarf. 'Come along girls, Daddy is waiting.' And with a wave and a kiss, they left.

That Sunday afternoon Derry was saying goodbye to his sister. They'd enjoyed a substantial roast lunch and she had issued her usual list of instructions about not leaving it so long next time. Hugging her, Derry made his promises.

'I'll walk up to Broombank and say goodbye to Meg and Tam, then stay with Dad tonight and be off first thing in the morning.'

Jan looked sorrowful. 'You'll say goodbye to Lissa before you go?'

Derry drew in a quick breath and briefly shook his head. 'We've said all there is to say. Stop your bossing, sister dear. Produce lots more nephews and nieces for me.' And dodging her slap he went off, laughing. If he hadn't, he might well have cried.

Meg was far more blunt and to the point. 'I was

495

wrong about you, lad,' she said as she met him at the door and kissed his cheek. 'I'm sorry. If I hadn't interfered that day perhaps things might have been different for you two.'

Derry shook his head. 'I doubt it. Mistakes have been made, and there are complications.'

Meg stood with him in the old porch at Broombank, her grey eyes troubled. 'Lissa isn't happy about your leaving though, is she?'

Derry gave her a quizzical look. 'She's told you that her marriage is over?'

Meg gave an exasperated sigh. 'Eventually she did. She's so proud, bottles everything up. Always has. Oh, but I grieve for her, I really do. Not that I was surprised. The cracks have been showing for a while. Only this will make her feel even more unwanted and rejected.'

'She left him, not the other way about.'

'Even so, divorce represents failure, doesn't it?'

'Philip won't give her grounds, so . . .'

'So you have to go or you'll complicate matters?' A small silence fell as Meg nodded her understanding. 'We've made up our difference, Lissa and me, but I often think she'd have been so much happier if she had at least visited Kath in Canada, if only once. A girl should have the chance to get to know her own mother a little. I can see now that it might have helped, perhaps to understand who she was a bit better.'

'Would it bother you if she visited her?'

Meg shook her head. 'Not now.'

'Why did Kath make all those promises, but never came?'

Meg wrapped her arms about her body, rubbing them with work-worn hands as a chill breeze rattled around the porch. 'I don't know. Perhaps she thought it was for the best not to interfere, and she was racked with guilt. She wasn't a bad girl, you know.' Meg gave a wry smile. 'Funny, I still think of her as a girl. We were good friends once but life played a few tricks on us. All in the past now.'

Derry had meant to keep away, but he couldn't. He had to see her one more time, for all his determination not to. An hour after leaving Broombank, he called at the shop and found Lissa jubilant.

'Oh, I'm so glad you came. I've been frantically ringing everyone, trying to locate you. You won't believe what's happened.'

She was bubbling over with excitement and they sat together on the old sofa, holding hands while she told him her news. 'So you see, you don't have to go. You can stay for ever. Philip has agreed to give me my divorce. I've signed the papers.' Blushing now, dropping her gaze in a sudden rush of shyness. 'I'm free.'

He lifted her chin with a caressing hand that very faintly shook, brown eyes ablaze with love. 'And what will you do with this new freedom, do you reckon?'

Lissa felt transfixed by him, held a willing captive by his gaze. 'Have you any suggestions?'

Derry chuckled softly. 'How long will the children be out?'

She pretended to consider as she got up and drew the curtains, unbuttoning her blouse as she moved quietly back to him. 'At least three hours.'

They were both far too eager to worry about going to bed. Derry took her there and then, on the rug, with only half her clothes off. Later they bathed together and made love again, teasing and loving for the rest of the afternoon. Lissa discovered in those what it was to be truly loved by a man. Not for Derry a selfish, cruel coupling. He stroked and kissed, loved and caressed her, and they made love with joy, quenching a long held thirst.

Afterwards, they wrapped themselves together in a sheet and talked by the light of the fire.

'I've waited so long for you. Never thought this would ever happen.' Derry's arms were sheltering her nakedness beneath the sheet while he kissed her hair, her face, her eyes and ears, making her giggle with delight.

'Darling, darling Derry. Don't ever leave me. I'd die if you left me now.'

They talked of everything and nothing, as lovers do, and every touch set them on fire for more, breathless with fresh desire. And they talked of a future together.

'I'd give this all up for you,' she said. 'If your work is more important, or you could find a job here. I don't mind, the decision is yours. So long as we're together, I don't really care where we live or what we do. I shall be yours, completely.' Violet eyes shining, translucent with love. 'Mrs Derry Colwith. Doesn't that sound wonderful?'

Derry pretended to frown. 'Did I ask you to marry me? When was that? I must have missed it.'

She playfully slapped him, straddling him so she could pretend to beat him on his chest. 'OK, have it your own way. You aren't the only man in the world.'

'Vixen.' Then he rolled her over, taking her again in a paroxysm of passion that left her gasping and spent. 'What was that about other men?'

'Nothing. Nothing at all.'

Only slowly did Lissa drag herself back to the present, as if coming from a distant country, her mind drugged with love, her senses aware of nothing but the warmth of his body against hers, the sweetness of his mouth, the slick of his sweat mingling with her own.

She made tea and they forgot to drink it, still endlessly talking and planning. In the distance the church clock began to strike and they lost count of the chimes. But Lissa began to worry. 'You ought to go. Nanny Sue will be back with the twins any minute. They mustn't see you here. It would ruin everything.' She saw his quick frown. 'We must be patient and keep away from each other for a little while longer until the divorce is through. It will be worth it in the end, my darling. Then we can be together forever.'

Lissa helped him to dress which took an uncommonly long time, then hastily pulled on a skirt and blouse, desperately tidying her hair. 'I must try to look normal, as if I've spent the afternoon doing my accounts.'

'You look as if you've been happily tumbled in the hay.' He grinned. 'I'd splash some cold water on those hot little cheeks if I were you.'

Giggling and concerned, she hurried off to the bathroom as the church clock chimed six.

'Heavens, you must hurry.' She was desperate now to persuade him to leave. 'Oh, do go,' kissing him, clinging to him a moment longer as she pushed him through the door into the cold, empty street. 'Any second and they'll be here. Hurry.'

When she was finally alone Lissa flew about the small flat tidying and titivating, making it look neat and calm, as if she'd spent a quiet, lonely day instead of one that had changed her life for ever.

By seven o'clock when there was still no sign of the twins she reached for the phone. Where were they? Why didn't someone answer? Fear grew like cold molten lead in her stomach. Philip couldn't have taken them, could he? She'd done everything right, everything proper to keep them safe. *Apart from this afternoon.*

Surely Philip couldn't know that Derry had been here with her? Could he?

Oh God, what if he did? What if he had seen Derry leave? She should never have let him in, never have let him make love to her. She'd wanted him so much how could she help herself? And they'd been so thrilled by Philip's agreement to a divorce. He couldn't be so cruel, could he?

Fear overwhelmed her and Lissa felt suddenly, desperately alone. If she lost the twins her life wouldn't be worth living. Hadn't she always put them first? Why on earth had she taken such a stupid risk? Now she might have ruined everything.

For some reason it made her think of her own mother. Perhaps Kath too had tried to put her child first, and failed. Perhaps she'd wanted to keep her, and in the end couldn't. Dare she be so quick to judge others when she was capable of mistakes and selfishness herself?

The door bell rang and Lissa jumped as if she'd been stabbed. She was there in seconds, flinging open the door.

'I'm so sorry they are late, Mrs Brandon,' said Nanny Sue, looking unusually breathless and rumpled. 'The car broke down and we had to wait for the garage to come out and rescue us.'

Lissa dredged up a smile as her arms greedily gathered her children to her breast. 'That's all right, I wasn't worried.'

But as she lay in bed that night, curled up and weeping, Lissa recognised that she was still vulnerable after all. Perhaps she always would be.

CHAPTER 26

A figure stepped out of the shadows on Fossburn Street as Derry approached Nab Cottage. His skin could still feel the imprint of Lissa's touch, his mouth was still curved into a smile. He'd even started to whistle an old favourite melody, 'Young Love, First Love,' as if he were a boy again. Now he stood and stared, his whole body alert.

'Whistle away,' said the voice. 'This is your last night in Carreckwater.' Philip Brandon blocked his path, mouth twisted in malice.

'Who says so?'

Philip smiled and Derry was filled with foreboding. This man never looked happy without good reason. 'You're taking the train tomorrow. For Manchester, London, America, Timbuktu, I don't care. Just make sure you catch it.'

'I'm in no hurry to leave.'

Philip slipped his hands into his pockets, to indicate he had no need to resort to fisticuffs. Physical violence was not his style. 'I think you will be. If you've been with my wife this evening, as I suspect, you'll know she was very anxious over the fact the twins were late home.'

What game was Brandon playing? Had he deliberately brought the twins back late just to prove a point? 'I've been to the Marina Hotel as a matter of fact, for a drink.' It was true, only he'd gone there after he left Lissa.

Brandon gave a shrug of contempt. 'As you wish. I thought it prudent to demonstrate to my wife that I still hold the power. She may keep the twins only so long as I allow it. And there are rules. One of which is she is not to have anything to do with other men, particularly you.'

'That's only until the divorce is finalised,' Derry said, gritting his teeth on a fast disappearing patience.

Philip Brandon looked mildly surprised, dark brows lifted in polite enquiry. 'What divorce? I've said nothing about divorce.'

'You took a paper to her to sign. She told me.' Derry groaned as he saw Philip's smile broaden, for he'd carelessly given away the fact that he had seen, or at least spoken to Lissa today. 'She rang me,' he blustered, with little conviction. Philip only laughed.

'Then she must be confused. She often is. Haven't you noticed how very incompetent she is? Sweet but rather stupid.'

'I don't see her that way at all.'

'Then perhaps you would like to see the paper

to which she refers?' Brandon held it out and Derry found himself scanning the small print with growing horror.

'These aren't divorce papers.'

'I never said that they were. I merely acknowledged that Lissa wanted a divorce and perhaps we should be mature, modern people and end this sham of a marriage. But in my own time, if all else fails, and on my terms. Perhaps I forgot to add that small rider.'

Derry was tearing up the paper and throwing it all over the pavement. Philip laughed, a bitter, hollow sound in the empty street. 'That's only a copy, of course. I have the confession of her adultery with you, for that, as you see, is what it is, safely locked in my safe. If you want her to keep her beloved children, and you know how precious they are to her, Lissa herself being only a foster child, then you will leave Carreckwater without delay.'

Derry could feel his stomach shaking with rage. He had never felt more helpless in his life. 'And if I refuse?'

Philip shrugged. 'Then I will remove them from her care. A married woman with a lover is not considered a fit person to have care of young children.'

Derry took a half step towards him but Brandon didn't even flinch. 'I wouldn't if I were you. I am within my rights – as their father.'

'You've never been a father to them. Lissa has told me how you simply issue orders, expect them to be neat and perfect to gratify your ego. You don't even love them, not as Lissa loves them. You leave them with the nanny all the damn time.'

'Hardly unusual. Half the aristocracy was brought up that way.'

Derry was clenching his fists in fury, desperately preventing himself from smashing one in Brandon's face. 'A child needs a loving family. You're twisted and sly and yes, dammit, for all your charm you're evil and cruel.'

Brandon burst out laughing. 'How very melodramatic you sound. The point is, *I* will choose their future, not Lissa. And what I decide depends very much upon you, Colwith. When Lissa finds that you have gone, without a word, she will see that you are as unreliable as ever. As I warned her you would be. She'll be more than ready to return home.'

'*Never!*'

'As you see, I have ways of making people do exactly as I wish. I can't say it's been pleasant knowing you, but it is certainly a pleasure to say goodbye. First train in the morning, remember.'

Meg rang Lissa on Monday morning to ask her to come up to Broombank. 'I have a problem I'd like to talk over with you, it's rather urgent.'

Lissa arranged for Renee to take the twins to school and pick them up at lunchtime if she wasn't back in time. 'I'm sorry to dump them on you but there seems to be some sort of emergency at Broombank.'

She was smiling, untroubled as her mind replayed those hours with Derry. Yes, she had broken her marriage vows, and the twins being late had given her a scare. But Philip had agreed to a divorce and soon she and Derry could be together for always. Then they could lie together and love every night, without restraint or fear. Lissa's stomach clenched with excitement at the prospect. How long would the divorce take? she wondered. She could hardly wait, making a mental note to ring her solicitor and ask him.

'Don't worry,' Renee was saying. 'We can manage fine. I welcome any excuse to play with those little terrors – sorry – treasures.'

Laughing, Lissa kissed the twins and went on her way. There was a lingering tang of autumn still in the air as she drove through the wooded valleys, the bite of winter coming fast on its heel as she climbed higher. The mountains looked paler than usual against the blue sky, as if already glazed by a coating of hoar frost. Meg met her at the farm gate and Lissa saw at once that something was wrong. She looked weary, older somehow.

'You should have talked to me. I'm your mother,' Meg scolded, putting her arms about Lissa and drawing her close.

'I know, only I wanted to decide first what I was going to do. It's sorted now. Everything is going to be fine.'

They walked together over the heaf as they so loved to do and Lissa struggled to open her heart.

For such an instinctively private person it wasn't easy. She told Meg of the papers she'd signed, how she would soon be free.

'Philip has agreed then to a divorce? I'm surprised it was so easy. However, your marital problems are not the only reason I asked you to call.' Meg handed Lissa a letter. 'Take a look at that.'

They sat on the drystone wall of the old pack horse bridge while Lissa read, and as she did her heart sank. 'I never thought he would do it.'

Meg turned startled eyes upon her. 'Never thought who would do what?'

'Philip. He threatened to bribe the water consultant into choosing Broombank as a suitable site for the reservoir, if I refused to stop seeing Derry.'

A small, dreadful silence. 'And you did refuse?'

'No, but I didn't really believe he'd do it.'

Meg's grey eyes seemed to darken and grow bleak, for all her tone still rang with her indomitable spirit. 'Look at this land.' She lifted one hand in a gesture partly possessive and partly indicating despair. 'It's mine; and has been these last twenty years and more.'

'I'm aware of that, I never meant this to happen.'

'Most of this dale is good, sound land, productive enough to grow a little corn during the war. Admittedly my sheep spend most of their time high on the fells but the intake land is important to keep them in good heart at lambing times. I

507

could never leave here, Lissa. It is a part of me: the house, the land, everything.'

'Meg, I know.'

'I drained some of the wet parts,' she went on, as if Lissa had not spoken. 'It was back-breaking work. But there are still patches of bog where no bracken or good grass grows. In the spring and summer you'll find those pale mauve marsh orchids, kingcups and bog myrtle. There are the troublesome sedge rushes, yes, but even they have their uses, building up the silt, holding it together.' Her voice took on an edge of passion. 'The larks and meadow pipits love it too, as do the thrushes and merlins, the deer and the stoats, the tiny fritillary butterflies who depend on the sweet violets for their survival. We all depend on this land. And no one, *no one*, must be allowed to harm it.'

Humbled by the passion in her foster mother's voice and shamed by her own negligence in not warning her, Lissa grabbed Meg's hand and clung to it. 'Don't Meg. Please don't blame me for this. I tried. I really tried. I meant never to see Derry again but I couldn't help myself, and nor could he. I prayed it was all a meaningless threat, no more than Philip's hurt pride.'

'Yet this letter tells me Manchester Water Board are sending some geologists to inspect the land and take samples, whatever that might mean.'

'I can't believe it.' Lissa felt panic rise in her throat. 'It must be a mistake. He's agreed to a divorce. Why should he do this?'

Meg's face was grim. 'Broombank has been chosen as a possible alternative to Winster Valley, and if the samples are good, then our dale will be flooded, not Winster. My beloved home, Ashlea, and all the other farms, the land upon which we all depend, will be flooded and destroyed for ever.'

Derry did not catch the train from Windermere that Monday morning. After a sleepless night tossing and turning in a bed that felt harder with each passing hour, dawn found him walking by the lake, desperately seeking a solution. He sat on a log, head in hands as he glumly watched the swirl of mist roll over the water, swallowing up a troop of ducks waddling out for their first paddle. The tips of the far mountains seemed to be suspended in space, like fairy mountains.

Never had he felt so low in all his life. He loved Lissa and she loved him. They wanted to be together, was that so wrong? Derry refused to feel guilty about their lovemaking last evening. Hadn't her marriage been over for months, if not years? And hadn't Brandon tricked her into it in the first place? But how to get her out of it? There must be something he could do. Brandon was the slippiest customer he'd ever met.

Derry knew that given a choice between himself and her children he would lose out every time, and quite right too.

'But it's not fair to ask it of her in the first place,' he shouted, flustering the ducks.

He'd wished for Lissa, that night by the tarn when they'd drunk the wishing water together. For her to be by his side for the rest of his life. But it had been no more than a desperate, childish game. He couldn't rely on wishes, he had to find an answer.

At ten to eight he was waiting at the office door, knowing that Miss Henshaw always arrived early. She was surprised to see him but delighted to offer coffee in her inner sanctum, a minuscule kitchen little bigger than a cupboard.

'I still love my morning cup before everyone comes,' she confessed, smiling flirtatiously at him. ''Gives me a lift for the day ahead.'

'So, how're things?' Derry asked, leaning against the wooden draining board and giving the best imitation of his usual grin that he could manage.

'It's been very dull since you left, Derry. Not at all the same.'

'And Mr Brandon?'

Miss Henshaw fiddled with her glasses as they bounced against her flat bosom on their long cord, her lips pursing slightly as she picked up her cup, small finger extended. 'Much as you might expect.'

Did he detect a slight slackening of devotion in her stiff-lipped reply? Derry wondered. His mind was whirling. What exactly was he looking for? He had this idea that if he learned more about Brandon's life and professional matters, it might help. But what and how, he couldn't imagine. Miss Henshaw had seemed the obvious person to try, now he hadn't the first idea where to start. Hope slid away, and his depression must have showed in his face for Miss Henshaw leaned forward and patted his hand.

'There, there, don't look so sad. You weren't wanting your old job back, were you? I'd heard you were doing well.' She looked suddenly troubled.

'Good lord, no. I have a job, a much neglected one back in the States. I hope it's still waiting for me when I get back.' If I go back, he thought. There was no real reason why he shouldn't do the same thing here, if he wanted. He'd had to conduct some of his business by telephone since he came anyway.

She sighed with relief. 'That's all right then. It wouldn't do at all for you to come back here.' She glanced about, as if half expecting her employer to appear like a genie from behind her shoulder. 'Business is slack. Bank putting on pressure, I believe. Not that he ever tells me anything, or lets me look at the accounts but I know money is tight. He always gets slightly tetchy, you know?'

'I remember,' Derry grinned, glad that he was no longer under Philip Brandon's edict. 'It's an ill wind, as they say. Did me a favour sacking me, as it's turned out.'

She set down her cup. 'Well, I can't sit about here gossiping all day. I must get on. I've a funeral to attend later this morning.'

'Oh, I'm sorry. Anyone close?'

'A client.'

511

Derry lifted one brow, almost his old cheeky self. 'I thought Brandon usually did those, enjoying the kudos and the funeral teas. Not like him to let you out of the office. How will he manage without you? Even for an hour.'

Miss Henshaw clattered the cups as she washed them up, handing them to Derry to dry. 'I insisted, as a matter of fact, though it really shouldn't be my place,' she said, tight-lipped. 'Mr Brandon had declined.'

Derry's eyes narrowed with speculation. There was something not quite right here. Brandon never missed the funeral of a valued client. It was part of the deal. He read the hatched, matched and dispatched columns every day in the local paper to check if an esteemed client would be requiring his probate services. And he always liked to be seen to be doing the right thing. 'Anyone I know?' he asked.

Miss Henshaw set the cups and saucers back in the tiny cupboard and slammed the door with a firm click. 'A dear old lady. Elvira Fraser. Utterly senile by the end and not a penny to her name, but it wouldn't have hurt him to go anyway. I don't understand him these days, I really don't.'

'Elvira Fraser? I seem to recall that name.'

'Lived on the Parade. Had a falling out with her son-in-law and came to us for cherishing and support.' Miss Henshaw half glanced about her again, then leaned forward and whispered in Derry's ear.

'Philip bought her house, after she'd had a stroke and ended up in The Birches nursing home.'

'I see,' Derry said, not quite seeing at all but feeling a quickening of interest. 'I remember her now. I once took some papers for her to sign, didn't I?'

Some papers to sign. It was like an echo in his head. Lissa had signed some papers. So had Elvira Fraser. But then Philip Brandon dealt with forms and papers every day, he was a solicitor for God's sake, so where was the significance in that? The significance was that Lissa had not signed what she'd thought. Not divorce papers at all, but a confession to adultery. He still had to break that awful news to her.

Had Elvira Fraser signed what she expected?

Miss Henshaw was still talking and he hadn't heard a word. 'I do remember her. Quite a sparky old thing. Reminded me of my gran. Where is this funeral?'

'Oh, how lovely of you to come. I was so disappointed in Philip.' She told him the time and place, then, on hearing a sound from the inner office, shooed him away. 'Go quickly. He's arrived.'

Giving a wicked wink, Derry wrapped his arms about Miss Henshaw's birdlike figure and kissed her soundly on her flushed cheek.

'Bless you, Vera, I knew I could depend on you.' Then he was gone, leaving the back door swinging open as he'd always used to.

'Oh dear,' she mourned. 'Nothing has been at all the same without him.'

⋆　　⋆　　⋆

513

The lady at The Birches remembered Elvira well. 'Though she hasn't lived here for quite some time. Ran out of funds, poor thing, and had to move into council care. A not uncommon occurrence, I'm afraid.'

'But how did she lose her money? I always thought Mrs Fraser had substantial funds. That house must have been worth quite a bit for one thing, and then she had shares, money in the bank and so on.'

The matron shook her head. 'Property is often mortgaged and they've usually been living above their means for years, poor dears. Still living in the style they were used to back in the good old days of Empire and servants. Edwardian affluence, a world gone by. I know nothing about her investments, but prices rise and income shrinks.' She gave a resigned shrug, her mind already on the next task. 'It's a changing world.'

Not if it's invested properly, Derry mused to himself as he bade her goodbye and took his leave. 'Thanks anyway. I'll try the council home.'

Whatever it was he wanted from them, and he wasn't entirely sure himself, they could tell him nothing more. Yes, they said, Elvira Fraser had lived with them. Old, confused, still expecting her young husband to call and collect her. Now she was dead. End of story.

But Derry felt certain this wasn't the end of the story. There was more to this than he'd yet discovered. He'd go to the funeral. Just in case. Then he would go and see Lissa.

Lissa rang Renee to say she would not be home as early as she'd hoped, and would Renee collect the twins from school at the end of the afternoon session as well as the morning, and look after them till she got there?

'It could be early evening. I can't explain on the phone but I wouldn't ask if it wasn't important.'

'No problem. They can have lunch at the shop here with me. And Jimmy'll love having them home for tea,' Renee said.

'Thanks.'

Lissa spent the next several hours hanging around waiting rooms and chatting people up who might help them in their fight. Meg talked with the local newspaper to enlist their support, but Lissa insisted on doing most of the legwork. She felt it was her fault that they were in this mess, so it was really up to her to get her out of it.

She gained five precious minutes to speak with a National Park authority spokesman, who was very sympathetic but admitted they could do little since Broombank was not quite in the National Park and many people would be agreeable to the pressure coming off Winster.

The Friends of the Lakes took a similar line but offered their support, so long as it didn't prejudice their own efforts.

Lissa was worn out by the time she returned to

Broombank, but her frustration and lack of success made her all the more determined. 'I called at Lord Carndale's place but he wouldn't see me. I'll try again later. He is a neighbour after all, and may be able to put the right word in the right ear.'

'I'll come with you,' Tam offered. 'I worked for the old boy once. He's fair and I'm sure he'll do all he can, but a bit deaf and doesn't readily take to strangers these days. He has a son though, who may be willing to help. Let's hope so.'

'Great, then we must have a word with the mayor and the town council and work our way through the District and up to County.'

'Why stop there?' Tam grinned. 'How about Westminster and the Lords?'

Lissa stiffened her spine, jutting her chin almost as Meg did. 'I'd willingly try.'

'You've got a lot more spunk than you used to have,' Tam said, admiringly. 'It's good to see it, lass.'

'I've had to learn how to fight and stand up for myself. Perhaps it's being a mother,' and she caught Meg's smile and laughed. Meg suggested they also go and talk to the National Farmers' Union representative, and so it went on as they worked out their plan of campaign. Time flew by without her realising.

The funeral took place at the local parish church. A small knot of people whom Derry did not know gathered about the open grave. Miss Henshaw stood by his side and next to her was Miss Stevens, who had been an old friend of Elvira Fraser's. Derry felt as if he were an intruder, but then remembered the old lady's essential dignity, her kindness to him when he, young and green, had no answers to her many questions. How sad that she should lose the ability even to think of the right questions to ask in the end, let alone understand the answers. Anyone could take advantage of such a situation.

A young man approached and thanked Miss Henshaw for coming. 'Glad to, I liked her enormously.' They exchanged small talk about the weather being fine for once, though the skies were darkening, and how he appreciated the fact that a representative from The Birches had also attended.

'She did at least find a modicum of happiness there for a while. My grandmother once had the reputation of being a tartar. Made my late father's life a misery, I'm afraid. He never quite came up to scratch in her opinion.' The young man, named David, smiled. 'But she was simply sad in the end.'

'Sad that she lost her money, despite careful investments,' Derry put in.

The young man glanced sharply at him and Miss Henshaw hastily introduced him.

'Mr Colwith used to be a clerk in Mr Brandon's office many years ago. He's quite important in a music agency business now but he still remembers visiting your grandmother, taking papers for her to sign.'

517

'Ah.' The young man nodded then glanced about him. 'Mr Brandon didn't find time to come himself then?'

Miss Henshaw flushed. 'He's very busy, I'm afraid.'

An awkward pause then someone came and spoke to him and he started to move away. 'You'll come to the Marina Hotel for a spot of lunch, both of you? You're very welcome.'

'Can I give you a lift?' Derry quickly put in.

The young man looked surprised, almost as if he'd not expected them to accept. He was about to refuse the offer when he met Derry's gaze and changed his mind. 'That would be good. Thanks.'

It was raining by the time Renee darted between the traffic at Benthwaite Cross and on up the hill to Hazelwood Crescent where the small infant school was situated. The twins loved it and of course adored their teacher.

Not like when I was at school, Renee thought, recalling being made to stand in a corner on more than one occasion.

She glanced at her watch. Almost ten past twelve. She was late after all, but Miss Swift, their teacher, was very understanding and any child not collected on time was kept with her. Lissa had told her this, so Renee wasn't worried that the twins would wander. It was considered almost a treat to help teacher clear away and make ready for the afternoon lessons.

They'd eat their sandwiches by the lake, she thought. Sneak a half hour off work until it was time to take them back. Lissa wouldn't mind. Nor would the ducks. The twins liked to feed them, and she could do with a bit of fresh air.

Renee turned the corner into Hazelwood Crescent and hurried through the main swing doors of the small school, quite out of breath from running. Miss Swift was in the classroom, painting clowns on the windows in poster paint.

'Hello, Renee. I didn't expect to see you today. Is Mrs Brandon feeling any better? I heard she was unwell.'

'Unwell? She's fine, only she got held up at Broombank so I'm deputy today.' She glanced about the classroom. 'Are they hiding? Come out, you two terrors.'

'Mrs Swift frowned. 'They aren't here.'

'What do you mean, they aren't here?' A terrible dawning fear.

The infant teacher smiled reassuringly. 'No need to panic. They're quite safe. Mr Brandon collected them, not twenty minutes since. They'll be home by now I should think. Quite safe, you see.'

Renee went straight to number 22, The Parade, and hammered on the door. Her guilt at being too late to prevent Brandon collecting the twins was almost overwhelming. Lissa would never forgive her.

It was opened at once, as if he'd been expecting her, or Lissa.

'Where are they?' Renee demanded, in a voice

like thunder. Dark brows rose in mild surprise. 'I'm afraid I don't quite understand.'

'Don't play the innocent with me.' Renee brushed past him, marching down the long passage and straight in to the kitchen. 'You aren't supposed to collect them.'

'Nor are you.'

'Lissa asked me, as a favour, since she was a bit tied up at Broombank.'

Philip smiled, as if at some private joke. 'Seems she's more and more tied up these days. She should put the children first for once.'

Renee opened her mouth to dispute this but thought the better of it. You couldn't win an argument with a lawyer, particularly this one. Hadn't she tried in the past? 'Well, where are they?'

'Nanny has taken them for a dental check up, if it is any concern of yours. They are my children and you may remind Lissa that, as yet, no court has given her custody.'

'Or you access,' Renee hit back but inside felt a flutter of nervousness. Dental check my eye, she thought, worrying more than ever.

'Which can easily be rectified.' He took Renee's elbow in a firm grip and led her to the door, Renee protesting all the while as she struggled to free herself. 'You can tell her that I wouldn't have been forced to take the action I have if she'd left Derry Colwith alone. If children will play with fire they'll get their fingers burnt. Tell her that.'

'What the hell are you talking about?'

'I think you know well enough.'

Renee was beside herself with fury. 'I know I shouldn't have tried to put her off our Derry in the first place. I shouldn't have told you that she thought herself a bit too grand for him. I was wrong, and look what a mess I've made of everything by interfering.'

This seemed to amuse him and he laughed all the more. 'Don't blame yourself. Nothing happens in my life that hasn't been carefully planned out beforehand.'

'No, I can believe it. And you can take your hands off me or I'll set my Jimmy on you.' Renee wrenched her elbow free and stood facing him, blue eyes blazing, red hair standing out like flames about her head. Philip Brandon, however, didn't seem at all put out by this threat, his handsome face as mildly composed as ever. Then almost as suddenly the smile died and he was advancing on her, forcing Renee to retreat backwards up the passage.

'Tell Lissa that she may come and see the children at any time. That they are safely at home, where they belong, and where *she* belongs. The solution lies in her hands. Tell her that.'

Renee was astounded, gave a false little laugh, determined not to let him see how her heart was pounding. 'You expect Lissa to come back?'

'Oh, she'll be back all right, once she realises what is best for her, and for the twins. Once Lissa realises she could lose them, and her precious Broombank, if she doesn't. She's confessed to

521

adultery in her futile efforts to gain a divorce, and compounded her sin by permitting your precious stepson to visit her yesterday afternoon while sending the children off with nanny.'

Renee gasped. 'Were you spying on her?'

'It was quite by chance that I saw him, but the courts will take a very dim view of such loose behaviour. She's unfit to be given custody of the children. Whereas I have done nothing wrong. Nothing at all. Tell Lissa I will forgive her all her indiscretions and she may return at any time.'

'You dirty, blackmailing bastard. You'll get no help from me. You can deliver your own damned messages.' Renee was stopped by one finger pressed against her lips, silencing her most effectively.

'I dislike people who disagree with me,' he said, so pleasantly they might have been discussing the weather, except for the feverish glitter in his dark eyes.

My God, he's up the pole, Renee thought. Stark, raving mad.

'I won't have it. Not from Felicity, not from Lissa, and certainly not from you. Do you understand?'

The finger slid from her lips and trailed down her throat, tracing a path to the cleft between her full breasts. 'Ere, gerroff,' Renee choked, knocking his hand away. No wonder Lissa had left him. He was creepy. 'I'm taking them nippers back with me. Soon as I can lay my hands on them,' she said, with more bravado than she felt. He had beaten her, as he did them all, in the end.

CHAPTER 27

Derry was waiting at the door when Lissa got home that evening. She wanted to fling her arms about his neck and kiss him but he led her into the little living room and turned her to him, his face serious.

'You must listen carefully.' He made her sit down and fold her hands on her lap instead of about his neck and concentrate on what he had to say. 'Philip cheated Elvira Fraser of most, if not all, of her money. I believe he took it, bit by bit, from her accounts, assuring her that he was investing it safely when all the time he was feeding it into accounts of his own.'

Lissa stared at him, bemused. 'What are you saying? What is all this?'

'I even remember acting as errand boy for him, only I was too young and green to understand what he was up to. And who is there to check on him, a solicitor in sole practice?' He explained about attending Elvira Fraser's funeral, and of his visits to The Birches and the council home.

'I spoke to her grandson, David, and he's going to do some investigating.'

Lissa said, 'Elvira Fraser? I met her once. She was old, and sick. We bought her house, which is all very sad, but how does that affect me, or Philip?'

'I'm not sure she was even aware at the time that she was selling it. Philip had her sign so many papers, her mind was probably spinning. And she was old, vulnerable, and at odds with her family. A perfect candidate for an unscrupulous solicitor. Perhaps there were other clients, equally vulnerable.'

Lissa stared at Derry as if she had never seen him before. 'Are you saying that Philip is a fraud?'

He put out his hands, stroked her arms, urging her to remain calm. 'I have more news for you, Lissa. And it isn't good.'

He hunkered down beside her, gathered her hands warmly into his own, and her smile, so full of trust and love, almost made him change his mind. But no, she must be told, and he was the only one to do it.

He revealed what Philip had told him, that she'd signed a confession of adultery, and not the divorce papers at all. Lissa sat in stunned silence, her confidence crumbling before his eyes.

'I signed a confession?' Her voice barely had the strength to reach her lips. 'It wasn't the divorce papers?'

Derry shook his head, stroking her hands, wishing he could do anything to take this pain from her. 'Philip intends to use it to blackmail you to return to him.'

Lissa started, as if he had slapped her. 'Return? Never. What if I have admitted to adultery?' she went on, in a wild moment of bravery. 'What of it? I've seen today how he means to wreck the lives of a dozen families in my dale and I've spent all day fighting him. I shall spend my life fighting him if I have to.' Tears were shining in her eyes, spilling over on to pale cheeks. 'He thinks he can ruin Broombank, destroy my family's home and my independence. Well, he can't. We won't let them flood the valley, we won't.'

Her voice was rising, growing close to hysteria and Derry put his mouth to her cheek, hushing and soothing her. 'Tell me slowly what else has happened.'

Lissa gulped and swallowed her tears and explained about Meg's letter from the Water Board, and of Philip's involvement. 'I won't let them do it, I won't. I thought it was simply an empty threat. I never imagined he had the power, not really.'

'I'm sure you didn't, my darling. But then it isn't really power. He simply cheats.'

'Oh, Derry, it's the same thing in the end.' Her mind was in turmoil, her heart plummeting in despair.

'Let's go and see this water consultant. Is he back at Nab Cottage?'

She was at once on her feet. 'I'm not sure, but I have to collect the twins from Renee in any case.

I shall tackle him on the subject at the same time. Philip won't beat us, Derry. We won't let him.'

'No,' he agreed, holding her close and not letting her see the concern on his face. 'We won't let him beat us.'

The water consultant was not at Nab Cottage but Renee was, sitting in her chair by the new teak effect electric fire, her face a white mask of anguish. Even her lips were white, with not a trace of lipstick.

'Oh, Lissa, what can I say? I was barely ten minutes late. Ten minutes! I was so busy doing the orders that I forgot the time. But I knew the teacher would keep them safe, only I never expected Philip Brandon to beat me to it. I went round, right away.' She was gabbling now, trying to assuage her pain and the terrible shame of failure.

'What are you saying? What happened? Where are they?' Lissa was distraught but desperately struggling to keep a hold on her fast disappearing control.

Renee struggled to speak through the lump in her throat. 'Dental check-up, he said. With Nanny. But he's taken them back home and intends them to stay.'

'Oh, dear God!' Lissa's cry of anguish cut Renee's heart in two.

'Don't,' she gasped, reaching out to grasp her friend, voice and heart broken. 'I'll get them back for you, Lissa, I promise.'

'Did he hurt you?' Jimmy wanted to know, bouncing to his feet. 'I'll kill him if he did.'

'No,' Renee lied, instinctively touching her throat. 'Why would he hurt me?' She'd thought for a minute that he might snuff her out with his finger and thumb, like a candle.

Derry put his hand on Renee's shoulder, trying to console her. 'It wasn't your fault, Renee. Don't torment yourself, but you'd best tell it all. What exactly did he say?'

When Renee had finished, the tears were raining down and washing mascara in black streaks down her death pale face. Nobody could find any words of consolation or hope. He had won. It was as simple as that.

Lissa turned on Derry like a lash. 'It's all your fault,' she screamed. 'If you'd gone back to America, like I asked you to long since, as Philip asked you to, this would never have happened. You've lost me my children. I'll never forgive you for that. *Never!*'

Derry stood like a man felled. Then, very quietly, he nodded. 'You're right. It is my fault. It's been my fault all along, just because I love you.'

'Lissa, love.' Renee rushed to her but Lissa shook her off, tears of anger and pain and grieving running in scalding rivers down her ash pale cheeks. When she spoke again her voice was calm, but hard as iron.

'I'm sorry Derry, but you'd best go. Philip has won. If I'm to keep my children I must return to him. Just as he always planned.'

'What about us?'

'We're finished. It's over.'

Lissa went back to the house on the Parade the very next day, if on very different terms. She insisted on her own room, that they be man and wife in name only.

'I will not share your bed. And you don't ever touch me.' Violet eyes held a new resolution that even her husband could not ignore. 'Nanny Sue must go. The children have no need of a nanny now they are at school. The rest of the time they can spend with me, either at home or at the shop. And before you say it, no, I will not be giving up my business. I shall employ a cleaner, or whatever help I need so that your life is not disturbed, but my work will continue.

'I'll host your dinner parties and otherwise be a wife to you until the children are grown. Nothing more. Is that clear? Those are my terms for returning, take them or leave them.'

Philip smiled at her, lounging against the door frame of the room she had selected as her own, watching her unpack the few belongings she had taken with her. He'd celebrated her return with half a bottle of scotch and felt particularly mellow. 'I accept them. This is where you belong, Lissa, with me to care for you.'

'I need no one to care for me, thank you very much,' she said, tone sharp as spears of ice. 'In future I'll look after my own affairs.' She glanced at him then, trying to ignore the triumph in his eyes. 'Is it true that you took that old woman's money?'

'What tale is this you've been listening to?' His face was instantly inscrutable and all Lissa's doubts returned. Could he really be capable of professional malpractice?

'It has been suggested to me, by a friend, that Elvira Fraser's grandson is not happy about the way her affairs were conducted. Is that true?'

Philip stretched his eyes wide in a shocked innocence so genuine, Lissa found it hard not to believe in him. 'I can guess who that friend is, and it seems to me it's in his interests to malign my good name, since he is sleeping with my wife.'

Lissa jerked, the spiteful words hitting home. 'Is it true?'

'You must believe what you wish to believe. Elvira Fraser was an old and valued client. Were she still with us today she would, I am sure, vouch for me.'

Lissa struggled to recall some of the old woman's words on the day she had met her in the home, but they were so jumbled as to be incomprehensible. She slammed shut the wardrobe door and tilted her chin high.

'I want you to realise, Philip, that you won't win over Broombank. Nor will I permit you to sell

Larkrigg. If it belongs to the twins, then it must be kept for them. I'll fight you on those issues till my last breath. Do you understand.'

'Yes,' he said mildly. 'I understand perfectly.'

It was Renee who gently broke the news to her that Derry had finally gone. 'He caught the train to London this morning. Said he had some business to do there before going back to the States.'

'I really don't want to hear,' Lissa said, heart breaking.

It made the hurt worse to think that her last words to him had been harsh and cruel, but then perhaps it was for the best. It might help her to keep the reality of her situation in mind and forget about romance and the love. Look where her quest for love had led her? None from her real mother, none from her husband, and that which she had found with Derry had constantly been denied her.

She must think of her children now. If Philip had won the battle of their marriage and broken her heart in the process there was other work left for her to do. A shop to run for one thing. Broomdale for another. She was determined not to see that valley flooded.

The business suffered from neglect in the weeks following as Lissa returned with renewed vigour to the campaign against the water board, though with more sense of desperation than design. It was hard to know how best to fight it since all the arguments had already been made by every association in Lakeland and beyond. Lissa spoke to all of the local councillors and succeeded in enlisting the support of many. She visited every house in the area with leaflets she'd had printed, gave endless interviews to the press and held meetings in the old school hall. Time after time she hounded the National Parks Committee, the Planning Board and every other body she could think of, to give her their support. They were always sympathetic but continued to put their main resources into saving Winster. Reasonable as this was, it left Lissa feeling isolated.

She even tackled Andrew Spencer, the water consultant, and though he admitted to accepting Philip's bribe, he insisted it was out of his hands now.

'They'll send in the geologists and the engineers and that'll be that. Then the Board will make the decision, not me.'

'The National Farmers' Union is right behind us,' Meg told him. 'And both the District and County Councils. They want water extraction from the lakes rather than a reservoir. With suitable conditions attached, of course.'

'But how to win our case?' Lissa groaned. 'We need evidence, some good reason to put forward for them not using Broomdale.'

'You mean beyond the fact that it'll destroy top grade farming land and wild life habitats?' said Meg dryly.

Lissa acknowledged these words with a sad

shake of her head. 'Having right on your side is never enough though, is it?' It hadn't been enough to win her freedom from Philip. And in their cold, sterile life together Lissa despaired of ever knowing the joy of love again.

It was apparently, perfectly legal for him virtually to rape her within the sanctity of marriage, just as the Water Board was permitted to rape their land.

'You look done in,' Meg told her softly. 'You need to get more sleep.'

'Of course I need more sleep,' Lissa snapped, then apologised when she saw Meg's face. 'Sorry. Not your fault. But what can we do? Everyone is sympathetic, or supportive but more concerned over the possible loss of Winster. Jimmy and the other boatmen are worried that the extraction of water from the lake will lower the water level too much, ruin the shoreline and prove a hazard to the tourist industry. Others are concerned about the rivers, or tunnels under Longsleddale. How can we all win? It isn't possible.'

And how could she find the strength to continue with her fight? She was tired of fighting. Her own future looked bleak whatever happened, and all her energy was used up.

Lissa sat by the big hearth at Broombank, despair and failure eating into her soul. In this mood she almost believed Philip's judgement of her to be correct. She was incompetent. A useless mother, wife, and even daughter to Meg. She could feel the tears standing proud in her eyes but refused to shed them. The time for crying was done.

'Thee'll get no work done by laiking theer,' said Joe, coming in on an icy blast of wind and settling himself with his pipe in the opposite corner.

Meg gave a hollow laugh. 'It's good to see you're so busy, Father.'

'A chap can take a spell to put up his feet I dare swear, when he's visiting his family.' He adjusted his cap upon his head, without removing it, and looked from his daughter to his granddaughter as he sucked on his pipe and waited for his pint pot of tea to be brought to him. 'Well, you two's a cheerful pair, I must say. Lost a shilling and found an 'appeny, have thee?'

'Don't start, Father,' Meg warned.

'Is it this water business?'

'Yes, it is.'

'Don't say they've got you licked?'

Lissa sank back in her chair and tried to smile. 'Yes, Grandad, I think they have. But then, when do I ever win?'

'I don't know what you're both worrying over. It'll never happen.'

Lissa sighed, unable to summon the energy to bring one old man into the present. 'It's looking as thought it will.'

'Over my dead body. Anyroad, it'll cost too much. Don't carry water well, don't limestone.' His tone was scornful. 'This dale ain't like

Thirlmere, or Mardale, with half a lake in it already. And the dam'll have to be twice as wide. Bankrupt the Water Board, it would. Won't be done in my lifetime, that's for sure. Never find the money.'

Lissa leaned forward in her chair, staring at the old man. 'What did you say?'

Joe was always happy to repeat himself when he had an attentive audience, so he said it all over again, at leisure. But Lissa was on her feet before he'd finished.

'I have to go.' Then she was running out of the house, getting in the van and driving with the wind in her tail all the way back to Carreckwater.

At Nab Cottage the water consultant had just sunk his knife into a steak and kidney pudding, his favourite repast, when Lissa burst in without even a knock.

'When are the geologists coming?' she demanded. Jimmy, Renee, and Andrew Spencer stared at her, mouths agape as if she had dropped through the roof.

'Er . . . it's on their rota of visits,' said the Manchester man in pompous tones. 'I can't say exactly when. Why?' He lifted a forkful of succulent steak and steaming pastry to his mouth but Lissa stopped him.

'You know that any dam they build will have to be wider than Mardale's, and more expensive?'

'We've taken that into account,' he informed her

loftily, irritated by the way she was holding on to his wrist while the tantalising drift of steam from the rich meat and gravy tickled his nostrils. 'The reservoir would also be twice the size and therefore more profitable.'

'Have you taken into account the quality of the stone?'

'That is for the geologists to investigate but I see no problem.' Again he attempted to lift his fork but Lissa was having none of it. She held fast.

'There's a limestone pavement runs right under the dale, did you know that? Full of cracks and crevices, nooks and crannies that would never hold water in a million years. Never has so far, apart from one boggy bit that we leave to nature. Have you taken that into account, Mr Water Consultant?'

He looked stunned and tried, ineffectually, to disguise his concern.

Lissa shook his arm. 'Well, have you?'

The portion of steak pudding fell from his fork to the floor and he grieved for it. 'Broomdale is gritstone and granite, like Shap Fell,' he insisted.

'Some of it is, yes, but my grandfather has lived in that dale all his life and if he says there's limestone, then there is.' She offered up this information with triumph in her voice, a toss of silken curls and a wide smile. 'Wouldn't that make a big difference to your Board's plans?'

'The limestone could be sealed.'

'At what cost?'

Too high, said the expression on his pale face and he set down his fork with a trembling hand. Much as he'd enjoyed these visits to the Lake District, and there was no doubt that he had benefited financially, as had his dear mother who now had her own personal attendant to save him the bother of fetching and carrying for her, nothing at all had gone right. Manchester Water Board had grown irritated with his frequent alterations of plan and gone so far as to appoint other consultants to check out the area. Nor had they expected such opposition, so well planned and orchestrated. It was developing rapidly into a nationwide campaign being talked about on radio and TV. Barristers, members of parliament, poets and every man and woman in the street deemed themselves fit to express an opinion on the subject. It was really most disconcerting.

Lissa could see that she had won. It was written plain in his eyes.

And so it proved. By Christmas, Meg had word that the Water Board would not be pursuing their decision to create a holding reservoir in Broomdale. The land had proved unsuitable for their purpose. The family were jubilant.

'Bless you, Grandfather,' Lissa cheered, hugging the old man.

'Nice to know we old 'uns still have some use,' said Joe, pink-cheeked and smiling for once.

Victory was sweet. Lissa's achievement turned her into a local heroine, at least for a time. Even

Grandfather Joe was quoted in every paper, and there was a picture of him standing on Broombank land, the neb of his cap set straight on his round head, looking as proud as if he'd saved it single-handed.

Their success seemed to add further fuel to the ongoing contest with the Water Board but everyone knew that it was only a matter of time now before they admitted defeat over the question of another reservoir. The debate would continue, the battle rage on for a while yet, and a major public enquiry was planned, but the people of Lakeland had the bit between their teeth and did not intend to lose. The land was too precious, the loss to the nation would be too great.

CHAPTER 28

Victory over Broombank also meant that Philip lost his prospective purchaser for Larkrigg Hall. All the fight seemed to go out of him after that. He spent more time locked in his study with a bottle of whisky at his side. Correspondence came regularly from the bank manager, and frequent telephone calls were taken behind closed doors.

Lissa found herself consoling him, almost forcing him out of his study to eat or go out, but he showed little interest in attending either the Golf or the Yacht Club. Each evening he downed several gin and tonics, barely picked at his food and then started on the whisky. It was Lissa who made the decisions now.

'Larkrigg must either remain empty until the twins are old enough to decide for themselves, or we could perhaps find a tenant. In the meantime I'll have the water turned off and see the windows are properly boarded up.'

'We should still sell it. It could save us. Do you realise we could lose our home?' His eyes were bleary with drink and worry. 'I owe the bank more than I can repay and as a solicitor I'm not permitted to go bankrupt. I'd be struck off.'

This news jolted Lissa but she knew better than to show it. 'Then let them have it. It's only a house. We could live in the flat over the shop.'

She might very well have suggested they camp in a cave, so horrified was his response. 'Never. I refuse to live in a flat. I have my status to keep up.'

'Perhaps if you'd been satisfied with less status we wouldn't be in this mess. What has happened to all your money? Why are we in such dire straits?'

'Nannies, cars, houses, entertaining. And that damned Manchester man, greedy little tyke!'

Lissa wanted to say that the source of the greed was closer to home but managed to hold her tongue. A small frown creased her brow. 'You did pay Elvira Fraser a proper sum for the house, didn't you, Philip?'

He made a sound of disgust and reached for the whisky bottle again. 'Questions, questions, questions. Do you never stop?' Watching him, Lissa thought that if he really had got the house cheap or, if Derry was right and perhaps paid nothing at all, then to lose it to the bank would be fitting retribution for Elvira's penniless death. But not for the world would she say as much.

With Broomdale safe and her little shop continuing to thrive, Lissa wished she could solve her personal problems as easily. She'd created as good a life for herself as she could but Philip still had no intention of letting her go. He had merely lengthened, not cut, the chain.

She once spent an afternoon, when she knew that Philip was safely out of town, going through the desk in his private study at home. She wasn't sure what she searched for but found nothing of interest, nothing that she understood. There was probably nothing to find.

'Why don't you search his office?' Renee suggested when Lissa confessed to this piece of snooping.

Their friendship had been bruised by Renee's failing to collect the twins that day, but Lissa had forgiven her. Renee loved the twins to bits, and how could she have known Philip would use blackmail in that way? The fault was as much her own. She shouldn't have been so trusting as to sign a piece of paper unread, should have realised it might not be what it seemed. But then it was easy to be wise after the event. He had tricked them all.

Now there would be no divorce. Derry was gone, and she was back where Philip wanted. His good little wife.

'I did hope he might take a mistress,' Lissa told Renee, with a wry smile. 'But he's taken to drink instead.'

'That's men all over. Never do what you want them to.' And they both had to laugh.

Sarah came skipping into the shop, plump cheeks glowing. 'It's snowing again, Mummy. Can we go skating on the lake?'

'No, darling.'

'Please.'

'There isn't enough ice on the lake. It would break. Absolutely not.'

Beth came in and added her own pleas to her sister's, tugging at Lissa's hands, one on each side.

'At least you have these two to keep you going.'

'Yes,' Lissa agreed, eyes shining with love and laughter. 'Thank goodness. I'll take you to play snowballs. Will that do?'

She wrapped them up warmly and off they went, hand in hand along Carndale Road, through St Margaret's Churchyard, past the Marina Hotel and down to the benches by the shore. She never thought of those youthful summers now. It was too dangerous, and much too painful.

'Let's build a snowman,' Beth shouted, grey eyes bright.

They were searching for bits of stick to mark his nose and eyes when Renee came hurrying up, holding her side and panting for breath. 'It's Miss Henshaw. She says you are to come at once to the office.'

'What is it?'

'I don't know. Go on, I'll look after these two.'

Lissa turned and ran back up the church steps and across the busy crossroads of Benthwaite Cross. She did not stop even to think, or hope, what this summons might be about. Miss Henshaw was waiting for her at the door, a rather shabby but flustered woman in a navy suit with her glasses dangling on a chain about her neck.

'We have visitors,' she said, half under her breath as she pulled Lissa in to the little kitchen and closed the door. Lissa's heart leapt, robbing her of the ability to speak for a whole half minute.

'Who? Who is it?'

Miss Henshaw was wearing her professional expression, though there was some other emotion behind it too. Disbelief, uncertainty, fear? 'Two accountants, sent by the Law Society. They're going through all of Mr Brandon's papers. Taking the place apart they are. They arrived just after lunch and Mr Brandon, well . . .' Miss Henshaw paused, drawing in a shaky breath. 'I can't say where he is now. He lost his temper when he saw them, blew up he did. Never, in all my life, have I seen him lose his temper, but he did today. A shocking rage he was in, throwing books everywhere. Now he's taken himself off, I don't know where. In a huff I shouldn't wonder. He's not a happy man. Not at all.'

Lissa felt numb. Whatever was going on? 'Why are they here? Who brought them in?'

'Elvira Fraser's grandson. He not satisfied about what happened to all her money.'

'Is he the one Derry talked to at the funeral?'

'Derry?' Miss Henshaw nodded, fingers twitching on her chain. 'I suppose he did, yes, now I come to think of it. The grandson claims to have found letters in his late father's desk proving that Mr

Brandon had made himself entirely responsible for the investment of Mrs Fraser's funds. He wants to know where every penny has gone and has put in an official complaint to the Law Society. I must say, Mrs Brandon, that it doesn't look good.'

'No,' Lissa agreed. 'It doesn't.' Then why was her heart beating almost with delight? As if her wishes were at last about to come true?

Moments later her mood changed as Jimmy burst through the door, bristly hair standing even more on end than usual.

'He's done it again,' Jimmy cried. 'Came up whilst me and Renee were helping the twins finish the snowman and just took them off. Only this time she's gone with him, says she's not letting them whippersnappers out of her sight.'

Lissa felt herself grow quite cold, yet her voice was oddly quiet. 'Where has he taken them, Jimmy?'

'Don't you fear, Lissa, he seems very calm and them two is happy as gnats. He's taken them up to Larkrigg.'

'Oh dear God.'

The trees by the tarn were feathered with snow, hanging as heavy as lace over the white-encrusted surface. A dry, freezing cold bit through Lissa's thick woollens and her breath froze into puffballs of ice on her cheeks. She struggled through the thick snow, frustrated by its cloying softness in her anxiety to reach the colourful figures out on the ice. Renee crouched beneath the rowans, shivering and making tiny keening sounds in her throat.

Lissa pressed a hand to her shoulder. 'Don't fret, Renee. I'll soon have them home and safe. Where is he?'

'He wouldn't listen,' she mourned. 'Oh, hecky thump.' Renee slid her eyes round to where Brockbarrow wood stood, black and forbidding against the stark white of the snow. 'He's over there, brooding.'

'Beth! Sarah!' Lissa called, waving to her excited children.

'We're skating, Mummy. Watch.'

The twins, both dressed in their red and blue hooded jackets and thick trousers, ice skates clamped to their small boots, slid about in the middle of the ice, wobbling madly. Lissa's heart-beat quickened, but she smiled reassuringly at them. 'I must speak to Daddy, then I'll watch you skate. Take care now. Come away from the middle. Keep to the edges where the ice is thicker.'

'Yes, Mummy,' they said, in sing-song, happy voices.

Lissa found him at the opposite edge of the small copse, seated on a rock above Whinstone force. Below him shafts of water split and cascaded over jagged stones, the brilliant spray crisp as diamonds in the sharp air.

'Hello, Philip.' The gushing sound of the water hammered in her head. It made her feel giddy. The falls here, high on the fells, made Skelwith force look like a trickle. 'Can we sit somewhere else, please?'

He did not respond. He sat unmoving for so long that she touched his arm, in case he hadn't heard. When he turned towards her his face was empty, bleak as the landscape. 'Hello Philip,' she said again, trying to put some warmth into her voice. 'I thought I might find you here.'

'Why have you followed me?' His voice was bitter yet rich with self-pity. 'Why aren't you working, as you always seem to be these days.'

'I was concerned about you.' Lissa propped herself on a rock beside him. It felt dangerously slippy with spray from the water. 'Miss Henshaw told me about the Law Society's visit. Why did you do it, Philip?'

'It was necessary.' The eyes he turned to hers were vague, as if they looked into some other place.

'Did you really embezzle Mrs Fraser's money?' When he chuckled she could only stare at him, appalled. 'Why? Why couldn't you earn your money honestly, as other people do?'

'I am not other people. I deserve more. My mother always told me I was special, and I am. We were quite poor then,' he said, as if it were some sort of crime. 'My father was useless, an ineffectual idiot besotted with books and fishing and points of law. He let my mother down, showed her up before everyone by being totally lacking in ambition. Once I had control of my own life, I

545

vowed never to let that happen to me, or any wife of mine.'

'But to cheat an old woman is despicable.'

He glared at her, eyes burning with unexpressed fury. 'People like her have too much money, why shouldn't I have some of it?'

'You mean there were others?'

'Her family never visited her so why should they inherit what they don't deserve?'

'Even so . . .'

'You don't understand,' he snapped, grasping her arm and wrenching her suddenly towards him. 'You *never* understand anything, do you?' The gushing drops of water spun before her eyes and Lissa instinctively shrank away, her finger nails scrabbling for purchase on the slippery rock beneath her. Surely he wouldn't toss her down the waterfall? The dark anger in his charcoal eyes told her he was capable of anything in his present mood.

'Philip, please be calm. Why don't we go home? It's cold and the twins will be wanting their tea.'

'I never had this trouble with Felicity.'

The sudden reference to his former fiancée took Lissa by surprise. 'I beg your pardon? What has Felicity to do with all of this?'

'She did as she was told. You never would, not once. Felicity was humble and sweet and obedient.'

Out on the ice came a loud squeal and Lissa jerked her attention back to her children. She could just make out Sarah pulling Beth about by her coat tails as if she were a sled and they were both squealing with delight. Then she was brought sharply back to her predicament by the sting of icy water upon her face. One wrong move and both of them would plunge thirty feet into the abyss, beautiful in spring and summer, lethal in winter, as now.

'You aren't well,' Lissa gently reasoned. 'It must have been a shock seeing the Law Society move in. But we can face it.' She swallowed. 'Together.'

It would be the end of his career and they both knew it. His laughter rang out, bouncing back off black rocks and Lissa shuddered, fear crawling up her spine.

'Felicity was considered delicate,' Philip said, conversationally. 'She was an only daughter. Spoiled, of course.' He smiled at the memory. 'Her father knew I wanted to marry her but did everything he could to stop us. He didn't consider me quite suitable.' Philip patted his pocket. 'Not enough in here to match his own fortune.'

Lissa struggled to take in what he was saying, hoping that if she kept him talking she could gradually ease him back from the brink of the gorge. 'Did Felicity want to marry you?'

'Of course, but in the end she wouldn't because of Daddy. He'd convinced her she was too delicate for marriage.' His lips curled at the corner into a parody of a smile. 'Even got a doctor to agree, would you believe? Utter nonsense. It didn't matter to me if she was. I loved her and would have looked after her.'

'Oh, Philip.' Lissa felt her blood start to freeze, and, as she shifted a foot to more solid ground, accidentally loosed a stone which fell and bounced from rock to rock till it disappeared, swallowed up by frothing foam. 'So what happened?' She really didn't want to know. All Lissa wanted was to get off this icy rock and take her children home to a warm fireside.

'My darling Felicity simply could not disobey her beloved father and that, she said, was the end of it. I took my revenge, of course. I had every right to do so. They ruined my life. Instead of being a member of a well-respected family with a rich and beautiful wife, I was to be deserted, jilted, cast aside. I couldn't let that happen. Not when I'd worked so hard.'

Lissa scarcely dared breathe.

'I did explain to her how it had to be,' he said, sounding perfectly reasonable as he turned to Lissa. 'I suggested it would be far less painful than living a lonely life without love, under the thumb of her father. She agreed, in the end. Always compliant, my sweet Felicity. It was all so very simple, and everyone was most sympathetic. How tragic, they said, to lose a fiancée by drowning, mere days before the wedding. For one so young to take her own life in such a way was so very sad.'

Oh, dear Lord, what was he saying? Lissa found she was shaking uncontrollably, her eyes flickering from the hard planes of his face to the gushing water below.

548

'What future did she have, without me?'

She gazed at him in horror. 'But why, Philip? Why? You gained nothing from her death, nothing at all.'

He looked puzzled. 'Of course I did. I kept my good name, the respect and status that was due to me. And I gained my revenge. Her father deserved to suffer as I had.'

Lissa could find nothing else to say. Her silence was overwhelmed by the roar of the water, muted only slightly by the icicles forming at its edges. She had no wish to repeat Felicity's mistake. The poor girl must have lost all will to resist, but she'd fought for her freedom and gained it. She was her own person now and must cling on to that with all her strength. She looked down at his fingers, curled possessively about her arm. 'Let go, Philip.' Cold panic threatened but Lissa knew it was vital to remain calm, to stay in control. 'We have to take the twins home for their tea. We mustn't have them catching a chill now, must we?'

He was shaking his head. 'There's nothing left for me, Lissa. Nothing left for either of us. If I can't have you, nobody will. I explained all of that to Felicity. I can't let it happen again.'

It happened so quickly there was nothing she could have done to prevent it. One moment she was desperately clinging to the rock, the spray of iced water stinging her eyes and nose as she battled to free her arm from his menacing grip, the next a cry rang out. Renee's voice calling her name. A great cracking sound ripped through the air like a gun shot, only half swallowed up by the screams of her children.

Somehow she'd torn herself free of his hold. She was running, slipping and sliding, hampered by the thick snow, breath a hard ball in her frozen breast as instinctively she leapt forward, out on to the ice. It was quite the wrong thing to do. Then Philip was there beside her, taller and faster, halfway across before Lissa thought better of it.

'No,' she cried. 'That's not the way. A tree branch. We need a branch. *Renee!*'

The ice was breaking up even as they frantically searched, her children huddled precariously together on one small ice floe, arms about each other, in danger of slipping into the water at any moment.

Then Renee was thrusting a long branch out on to the ice. 'I'll hold it, go on.'

Sarah and Beth, too stunned to cry or move, clung to their small island of ice.

'Come to Mummy, my darlings. Be brave. You can do it.' Lissa was lying on her stomach on the ice, urging them, filling them with her energy and confidence till first Beth and then Sarah finally found the courage to let go of their island and slide across the yawning gap of black water to grasp her hand and the long branch that Renee held so firmly. Then they were in her arms and they were all crying and sobbing together. Her wishes had been answered and her lovely children were safe.

Philip's body was not found until the thaw came. Then he was buried with due ceremony in the small churchyard at Carreckwater. The Law Society found all manner of problems in his practice. Any number of bank accounts in various names had once held money which should rightly have belonged to Elvira and several other clients. Philip's mistake with Mrs Fraser was to imagine that she would stay at odds with her family. Her grandson, David, had proved him wrong, often visiting his grandmother in the home. He could at least be satisfied that justice, of a sort, had been done. Even sad Felicity's fate had been given restitution. Philip had died in much the same way.

The house on the Parade was taken by the bank, in lieu of debts, and Lissa moved back into the rooms above the shop with her twins.

Not that this troubled her. Lissa felt she had been given a new life, a new beginning. And if there was sadness in her still, no one would have guessed. Or so she imagined.

She was visiting Broombank, at Renee's suggestion, celebrating the passing of winter. 'Jan's pregnant again, did you know?' Meg told her.

'Oh, that's lovely. When is the baby due? I must go and see her.'

'She's down by Allenbeck, having a picnic with Nick and the children. I said I'd send you down as soon as you arrived. You can leave the twins with me. We'll play Shipwrecks and Pirates in the barn.'

Loud whoops of excitement from Beth and Sarah, and so, laughing, Lissa left them to play, not unwilling to enjoy a half hour of peace. There seemed little enough of that these days. The walk would do her good, and she looked forward to congratulating Jan on her news

Spring was well advanced and the broom a blaze of gold as she followed the sheep trods over the fells. Lissa saw a two hares boxing and crept by on tiptoe so as not to disturb them. Overhead a lark soared, singing its joyous song, and as she reached the little pack horse bridge her mind turned back to her girlhood days. She couldn't help but smile. Nick would tease her again, as he always did, about falling in. No doubt Robbie and little Alice were giving him heart failure in this respect now. Lissa sincerely hoped that the twins would never fall into anything. If they had gone in the water and slid beneath the ice, that would have been the end. But her wishing water had kept them safe, hadn't it? Only Philip had been lost.

'Nick? Jan?'

She mustn't let herself think of that day. Lissa had suffered nightmares for weeks afterwards remembering the accident, what Philip had told her, and how her own life had seemed to be in danger. Perhaps, in time, she might find it in her heart to forgive him, and forget.

She saw his legs first. Sensible boots with green woollen socks tucked over cord trousers. She'd know those legs anywhere for all they were no longer in crepe soles and tight blue jeans. He was sitting with his back against the drystone wall of the bridge and Lissa leaned over to look down upon him, at his fair hair falling across his brow, at shoulders broad and strong in a chunky sweater.

'This is a long way from the States,' she said, a lightness to her tone which belied the heavy thump of her heart.

'I missed my lift again,' he said, without even glancing up. 'You can't rely on anyone these days.'

Lissa came down from the bridge, hardly able to drag her eyes from his beloved face. 'Where are Jan and Nick? I was told I'd find them here.'

'That's Renee and Meg for you. Conspirators now.' Derry grinned and Lissa's lips curled into an answering smile.

A rush of shyness made her feel suddenly awkward though her whole body was tingling as if it had been set alight like a fire cracker. Lissa ached to touch him, to make sure that he was real. But her mind rushed ahead. What if he hadn't forgiven her for shouting at him and blaming him for everything on that last day together. Should she apologise? How?

Then he got up and came towards her, still the same swaggering, arrogant walk, oh, and how she loved it. 'You and I have some unfinished business.'

'I'm so sorry,' she blurted out, interrupting him. 'I shouldn't have blamed you because of what Philip did. I was upset, that's all. I didn't really mean it. Can you ever forgive me?' She did not doubt that he would but when she moved towards him he held up a hand to stay her, looking very stern.

'You must learn, Lissa, not to make hasty assumptions about people. Things in life don't always happen exactly as one would wish.'

She smiled, knowing how he loved to tease her. 'I realise that now. If I'd had the patience to wait for you when you first left town, none of this would have happened.'

'Sometimes you can't have what you want right away. You have to wait a little longer.'

She reached for him then, her whole body refusing to be denied for another second. 'I do understand, really I do. I'm free now, Derry. Did Meg tell you?' Why didn't he come to her? Why didn't he take her in his arms and kiss her, as she so longed for him to do? What was holding him back?

But instead of taking her in his arms Derry did a little side-step. There was a rustling from the bushes beside the bridge and another figure emerged. A woman's. She was tall and beautiful with brown hair that swung in a page boy bob about her face, as smooth as a thrush's wing.

'Hello, Lissa.' She moved towards her with a graceful, swaying movement and even before Lissa looked into her eyes the prickling in her spine told her who this woman was.

'Kath?'

A rueful smile. 'I've missed your birthday again, haven't I? Sorry. Rather too many in fact. I dare say I've a lot of explaining to do, huh?'

Lissa remained silent. For the life of her she could think of nothing to say.

'Better late than never though?' Kath smiled and her hazel eyes held an appeal. Listen to me, they said. Give me a chance. Then laughing softly, as if embarrassed by Lissa's steady gaze, she glanced at Derry. 'I'm not surprised you're so anxious to kiss this young fella. And I think he's ready enough to oblige. What if I were to walk on ahead, then you two could set that little matter to rights? I owe him a favour. Maybe then we can talk, and you'll let me give my excuses in person so we can catch up?'

Lissa stared at Kath, bemused, struggling to put her thoughts into order. 'All right,' she managed.

'Good.'

Lissa watched as Kath turned and started to walk up the hill to Broombank. Then she ran after her and put a hand on her arm. 'Meg is up there.'

'I know.'

'Meg is my mother. I want you to understand that. And Tam is my father. They are my family now.'

'I do understand, honey. But you and I could at least be friends. Now I've plucked up the courage to come. How about it?' She looked oddly uncertain, as if she half expected Lissa to tell her she wasn't wanted, that it was far too late.

Lissa's smile lit her face. 'I'd like that,' she said. 'Very much.'

When Kath had gone, Lissa turned to Derry and held out both hands to him. 'This is your doing, isn't it?'

'By way of a peace offering.' He gave his lop-sided grin. 'And to make up for past mistakes.'

'Thanks,' she said, violet eyes shimmering with tears and happiness. 'Now I seem to have two mothers, and more love than a woman deserves.'

Derry took her in his arms at last, his mouth seeking hers. 'So long as you're content with only one husband, I can live with that.'